THE
RED WOLF'S
PRIZE

REGAN WALKER

ISBN-13: 978-06-15978-14-7

HE WOULD NOT BE DENIED HIS PRIZE

The door opened with no warning knock.

Serena gasped and pulled the cloth over her breasts and belly, keenly aware her legs were bare for anyone to see.

The Red Wolf stepped into the chamber, his piercing gray gaze sliding over her body and coming to rest where her breasts strained against the thin cloth. She could feel the heat of her blush as she looked to see the drying cloth clinging to her wet skin.

Without saying a word, he turned to the side and took off his belt. Then, with a grunt, he pulled his mail over his head and struggled out of his tunic. She would have offered to help had she not been so scantily clad. Had she not been so shy of his disrobing before her.

When his tunic slid to the floor, she nervously asked, "What do you intend, my lord?"

"I should think that was obvious, my lady. I am claiming my bride."

"Now?" She gripped the drying cloth more tightly to her still damp body. The long strands of her hair, wet from the bath, clung to her skin. No man had ever seen her in such a state.

"Yes, now." His eyes considered her carefully, and he shook his head. "God knows I've left it overlong."

While still staring at her, he shed his spurs and boots and doffed his linen shirt, leaving his chest bare and his lower body clad in only hosen and braies. He was a beautiful man with his bronze skin and muscled chest. Her eyes were drawn to the white cloth circling his upper arm.

"Your wound," she said, as she focused on the white bandage around his upper arm. The wound from the arrow he took for Jamie. How could she not love such a man?

"Aye." He glanced down at the bandage. "My token from the siege at Exeter."

"Does it pain you?"

His gray eyes narrowed intently. "If you are asking if it will impair my performance in our bed, nay."

www.ReganWalkerAuthor.com

Scotland

Britain
1068

NORTHUMBRIA

Talisand ·

· York

England

· Adlington

MERCIA

Wales

London
·

WESSEX

Exeter

CHARACTERS OF NOTE
(BOTH REAL AND FICTIONAL)

Sir Renaud de Pierrepont (the "Red Wolf")
Lady Serena of Talisand

With the Red Wolf:

Sir Geoffroi de Tournai
Sir Maurin de Caen
Sir Alain de Roux
Sir Niel le Brun
Mathieu, the squire
Maugris, the wise one

Sir Hugue, the mercenary knight

At Talisand:

Cassandra, handmaiden to Serena
Maggie, cook and housekeeper, mother of Cassandra and wife of Angus, the smith
Theodric, captain of the old thegn's guard
Leppe and Alec, guards
Hunstan, steward
Jamie, the orphan
Aethel, herb woman
Eawyn, widow of Ulrich
Rhodri, Welsh bard and teacher of the bow
Eric, serving lad then stable boy
Ingrith and Annis, weavers
Hulda, Godfrith and young Edith, potters

Others:

William I, the Conqueror and Duke of Normandy
Morcar, former Earl of Northumbria, and his brother Edwin, Earl of Mercia
Fugol, merchant spy for Morcar
Steinar, brother to Lady Serena

PROLOGUE

County of Maine, south of Normandy 1063

"Wolves!" Renaud de Pierrepont's voice was a low hiss as the howl of a wolf pierced the thin night air, setting every nerve on end. The heat of the battle lust from the assault at Mayenne had worn off long ago. The wind blowing in gusts off the snow caused his sweat to grow cold.

Clutching his mantle tightly around him, Renaud glanced at Geoffroi de Tournai, riding beside him. The knight's eyes were focused on the dark woods as if trying to penetrate their depths.

"The beast is close," whispered Geoff.

Renaud's horse tossed its head, sidestepping away from the rock outcropping in front of the trees. Reining him in, Renaud took off his glove and reached out to stroke Belasco's sleek gray coat.

The predator howled again.

"Do I imagine it, Geoff, or are there more in the woods these last days?"

"'Tis the lack of game, Ren. The wolves suffer along with our men. No knight can fight without meat to sustain him."

"Cheer up, my hungry friend," encouraged Renaud. "The campaign for Maine is over. Duke William has his victory. We will soon return north to his table in Rouen where food and wine are plentiful."

Geoff grinned. "And you can claim a share in the duke's victory since 'twas you who provided the strategy that gave him his victory."

"It was only a thought I had that appealed to him. *He* is the master of strategy."

"'Twas more than that, Ren, and well he knows it. William values your advice as few others. 'Tis a fact he is a worthy master. Make no

1

mistake, you will have your reward."

"I am but William's man, Geoff. Mayhap one day that will—"

Without warning the wolf leaped from the rocks and sank its claws into his hauberk, cutting off his words. Yellow eyes flashed as the beast bared its teeth and reached toward the pulsing vein that held his life's blood. Gripping the fur of the wolf's shoulders, he strained to hold the beast at bay.

The panicked horses screamed. His stallion reared, toppling man and beast to the snow-covered ground. Renaud hit the frozen earth with a heavy thud, his breath leaving him with the force of a fist in his gut. Gasping for air, he struggled to hold the beast's snapping jaws away from his neck.

Geoff quickly dismounted and drew his sword but it was a fruitless effort.

Renaud and the beast rolled across the frozen ground, locked in a battle to the death, leaving Geoff no clear target.

Renaud grunted as his bare hand slipped on the wolf's throat. The beast jerked its head around and sank its teeth into the flesh of Renaud's wrist. He shouted his anger as pain burned through his arm and blood trickled over his hand.

For a scant moment, the wolf released its hold on his wrist allowing Renaud to grip the wolf's neck below the snapping, snarling jaws.

Geoff circled the battling pair, looking for any opening to offer assistance.

Razor sharp claws raked Renaud's hauberk as the beast sought to tear the flesh beneath.

Rolling on top of the wolf, Renaud delivered a crushing knee kick to its body. But the wolf's desperate fight continued.

Drawing upon his remaining strength, Renaud straddled the thrashing animal. With an anguished battle cry, he jerked the beast's head to the side and twisted the corded muscles of its neck.

The wolf's neck gave with a crack. Its body went limp.

The battle was over.

Renaud gasped in the frigid air, his frosted breath escaping his lips in a rush, as relief flowed through him. His throat burned and his lungs heaved as he looked down upon the dead wolf still clutched in his hands. The smell of blood, like iron and earth, rose to his nostrils.

"*Mon Dieu!*" He thrust the carcass away.

Geoff sheathed his sword and rushed to Renaud, kneeling at his side. "Here," he said, handing him a cloth, "wrap this around your wrist 'til we can see to it properly. We had best be away. The scent of blood will draw more."

Still breathing heavily, Renaud wrapped the cloth tightly around his damaged wrist and rose, brushing snow off his mantle with his uninjured hand. He whistled and his stallion turned toward him from where he pawed at the ground a short distance away. It seemed the animal was as eager as his master to leave the dark threatening woods.

Renaud strode toward his approaching horse with Geoff close on his heels. The woods had gone quiet, the jingling of their spurs on the ice-crusted snow the only sound.

He paused as a thought came unbidden. Turning, he looked past Geoff to the dead animal lying in the snow. The full moon's light reflected off the white-blanketed earth revealing the copper tinge of the beast's fur. An unusual red wolf.

"What is it?" Geoff asked.

"Bring the wolf. I may have a use for its pelt. Mayhap 'twill serve as a worthy reminder to any who cross me in the future. Their fate will be the same."

4

The wolf will hunt for the jewel hidden among the stones, and if he finds it, his cubs will advise kings for generations.

—Maugris' vision during the crossing to England, September 1066

CHAPTER 1

The North of England, spring 1068

Serena contemplated her reflection in the small silvered glass.

Soon I will be another woman. Soon I will have another life.

While she could not change her violet eyes or her curves of a woman full grown, her flaxen hair was another matter. Undoing her long plait, she let the loose waves fall below her waist to shimmer in the early morning sunlight streaming into her bedchamber through the open shutters.

With a sigh, she lifted her hand to touch the gilded frame of the silvered glass. She could still hear her father's voice when he told her he had bought the extravagant gift from a Spanish merchant who claimed the Moors had made it. No one at Talisand had ever seen such a magnificent wonder before he brought it home to the manor. Tears came to her eyes as she remembered the look on his face, the warm smile reflecting his love.

Her father had been her protector and teacher, a man of great wisdom and a thegn dearly loved by his people. Deprived of his guiding presence, and with her brother in Scotland, Serena was all too aware she alone of her family was left at Talisand. Fear crept over her like a winter chill as she remembered the messenger who had come with a writ from the Bastard King.

She was to become the bride of the new Norman lord of Talisand.

Nay, I will not!

But how could she deny so fearsome a warrior as the knight they called the Red Wolf?

Serena's brow puckered in consternation. And what would become of the other women at Talisand? Would not the Norman conquerors claim them as spoils? Peasants fleeing the advancing horde the year before had spoken of the knights' villainy. Women were merely vessels to satisfy their lust.

Anger flared in her eyes staring back from the silvered glass. She would not have it! The young women of Talisand would not fall victim to the rampaging knights if she could help it.

But what choices were left? Some English women had taken the veil, but she was not suited to the cloistered life and that would not be a choice for the maidens at Talisand. But mayhap she could save the most vulnerable.

The door opened and Cassie, her handmaiden, entered with her mother, Maggie.

"'Tis ready, m'lady," said Maggie, handing Serena a leather flask. "I have made ye the dye from walnuts."

Serena accepted the flask and poured the dark liquid into a bowl.

"'Tis a shame to dye such beautiful hair," remarked Maggie.

"She must, Mother, if she is to look the part of a servant," Cassie insisted. "'Tis nay just her speech and her clothes that make her stand out. 'Tis her hair that tells all who she is—like a pale flame on a dark night."

Maggie nodded, resigned. "Then oil yer hands and the skin around yer face, m'lady, before ye apply the dye. It will make yer hair brown like mine, but ye will have to add more as yer hair grows. And remember to keep yer hood up should it rain for water can make the dye run."

"I will, Maggie, and thank you," said Serena as she spread the oil on her face and hands.

Cassie oiled her own hands and began to work the dye into Serena's hair. "I know the messenger said ye were to be the new lord's wife, but it might be well ye are leaving. The tales of the Normans' brutality are frightening. Ye must be safe."

"To be sure," echoed Maggie, "the Norman who comes isna a man yer father would have chosen for ye. Mayhap it will be easier for us to accept his yoke, knowing ye and yer brother are beyond his grasp and safe in me own homeland."

"I could not bear to take a Norman as husband," Serena said with firm conviction. Cassie poured the last of the dye onto Serena's head and she let the dark liquid drip from the wet strands into the bowl. She was glad she would not have to color her brows. Like her lashes, they were already dark. "It is not enough the Bastard from Normandy has taken my father and my country. Now he would give my family's lands to one of his knights."

"If the traveling cottars' words be true," offered Cassie, "the one who now claims Talisand is one who fought with the Bastard at Hastings. He might even be the knight who slayed yer father, the thegn!"

"Yea, 'tis a hard time that has come upon the land," said Maggie, regret showing in her eyes, the same vivid green as her daughter's. Then shooting a glance at Cassie, she added, "When I think of the men the Norman lord brings with him, I fear for me own daughter as well."

"I want to go with Lady Serena," the flame haired Cassie blurted out while she squeezed the excess dye from Serena's hair. "She will be saving me and the others from certain rape."

Maggie smiled sadly. "Aye, but will ye be safe?" She handed the drying cloth to her daughter. "'Tis a long road ye travel. I worry for ye both. The woods are full of thieves."

"Nay, Maggie," insisted Serena. "The woods are full of fleeing Saxons."

Cassie wrapped the drying cloth around Serena's head. "Would it not be better for us to flee than to stay and fall prey to the Bastard's men? Have we not heard the tales of their terrible deeds as they ravaged Wessex?"

Maggie nodded, her countenance fallen. "Aye, I have heard of the killing and the burnings. They even robbed churches. 'Tis a gift from God we have escaped such, and only because Talisand lies so far north. I pray the new Norman lord will not harm the villagers. They will now be his villeins, caring for fields that are his."

"I will worry for you," said Serena fighting the urge to stay even as she knew she must go.

"Ye must not worry about me and Angus," said the cook. "The Red Wolf will need me to feed his men and Angus to keep his horses shod."

Cassie nodded to her mother. "Aye, ye both will be needed."

"At least the young women I take with me will not be here to face the Red Wolf and his men," encouraged Serena. "We will search for my brother and accept the sanctuary offered by Scotland's king." Serena finished blotting the moisture from her dyed hair and unwrapped the drying cloth. "I wish I could take all of the women, but not all want to go. Like you, Maggie, some have husbands."

"Do ye know where yer brother, the young master is, m'lady?" asked Maggie.

"Steinar's last message said he was at King Malcolm's court in Dunfermline, north of Edinburgh, where many Englishman gather, hoping for an opportunity to return to fight for Edgar Ætheling, the true heir to the throne."

Maggie sighed. "At least ye and the young women will have protectors traveling with ye. And I will pray ye stay safe."

"We welcome your prayers," said Serena. Looking into the faces of the two women who were so dear to her, she added, "I am glad for all you have done for me. Your friendship has meant more than your service. And your company, Cassie, will be most welcome." She thought of those women who would travel with them, and the face of another rose in her mind. "Do you think Aethel would want to go with us? Her knowledge of herbs would be welcome."

"Aethel? Nay lass." Maggie gave Serena a wry look. "That one would lift her skirts for any Norman who would have her. She'll nay be running from them."

"I suppose you speak the truth," Serena admitted. "Since she went to my father's bed, she has not been the same."

"Or ye just didna see what she really was all along," chided Maggie.

The words saddened Serena. It was true that after being rejected by Theodric, the captain of Talisand's guard, Aethel had changed. The dark-haired beauty attracted many men, including Serena's father, the lonely thegn, but Aethel did not seem to be happy even with him.

"That leaves only Cassie and me and the three other women," said Serena. "Leppe and Alec will go with us, disguised as village cottars. Of the Talisand fighting men that still remain after the slaughter at Hastings, they are among the best and will be faithful to protect us." Wanting to assure Maggie they would have protection, she added, "Theodric and the other guards will stay to defend Talisand, if need be. I have asked steward Hunstan to visit the other manors to warn them of the Normans' coming."

"How soon do they arrive?" Maggie asked, glancing anxiously in the direction of the main gate.

"I know not the day," said Serena, "but I expect it will be soon, so we must be away this hour. I fear I have waited too long as it is."

Maggie nodded and looked at her daughter. "Send word as soon as ye're able."

Cassie's eyes filled with tears as she embraced her mother. "I will."

Blinking back her own tears, Serena sought to keep her voice steady. "Do not worry for us, Maggie. I have my bow and my seax. We will be well. And we will see you again, for I intend to return with Steinar to chase the Normans from Talisand."

Serena glanced once again at her reflection. Her hair now bore the color of the brown stain and was nearly dry. She felt changed inside as well as out.

"Ye look so different!" exclaimed Cassie as she formed the newly dyed tresses into a long plait.

"Aye, she does," said Maggie. "But the color does not hide her beauty. Mayhap a plain tunic will help." Maggie handed Serena a dark green tunic, and she slipped it over her shift.

As the folds of the rough wool settled around her, she felt her new life settle around her as well. The servant's garment was a stark contrast to the soft wool of the fine gowns she had worn as the Lady of Talisand. She looked down at her ankles that showed beneath the hem. The borrowed tunic did not fit well, either.

Seeing her shrug, Maggie said, "It will do 'til ye reach Scotland."

Serena sat on the chest at the end of her bed and pulled on the woolen hose and soft leather half boots the female servants wore. Cassie handed her a leather belt, which Serena wrapped around her waist. She secured to it her seax, the single edged blade her brother had given her last Christmastide. Grasping the polished wooden handle, she silently vowed to use it if threatened.

"Let me help ye with yer cloak," Cassie said, draping the dark wool mantle around Serena's shoulders and fastening it with a plain metal brooch. "'Twill serve to keep ye warm against the night air." Smiling, Cassie took a step back and examined Serena's disguise. "Ye make a convincing servant, m'lady, dressed as ye are. Except ye're too fine of feature. So remember to keep yer head bowed and yer eyes down should we encounter any men. And since yer speech is a wee bit proper, say nothing, lest they wonder if ye are truly one of us."

"I will try and do as you say, Cassie. In time, I might be able to disguise my speech as well." She would do whatever she must to escape the plans the Normans had for her. "You will have to be my guide in this new life."

"It is time," Maggie said, turning toward the door. "I will have a word with Leppe and Alec afore ye go, though I know those two will protect ye with their lives."

* * *

An hour later, Serena left the manor to begin the journey north. Seven walked along in silence: Serena and Cassie, three other women and the two men. The morning mist still clung to the wild grasses under Serena's feet, dampening her leather boots. She was glad her borrowed tunic was as short as it was, else her hem would also be wet.

When they reached the edge of the woods, Serena paused and looked back. The sun cast its rays on Talisand, making the manor, hall and thatch and wattle cottages appear to glow. To Serena, it was like something out of a dream, like a village descended from heaven. The place of her home and her heart and the memories of all she held dear.

Tears brimmed in her eyes and escaped down her cheeks. Would she ever see her beloved Talisand again?

Garbed in a belted tunic and short brown cloak a shade darker than his long hair and beard, Leppe gently touched her arm. "My lady, we must hurry."

She nodded and let him lead her away. Away from her past and the dreams she had once for her future. Soon the fierce knight called the Red Wolf would descend like a devastating storm to claim his spoils. Nothing she could do would prevent it. Concern for her people weighed heavy on Serena's shoulders. The Red Wolf's reputation was that of an undefeated warrior, as vicious in battle as the animal whose fur he wore.

She prayed he would not harm the people he would need to work the land.

CHAPTER 2

It was late afternoon when Renaud and his knights crested the last hill, and he raised his hand halting the column of men. Reining in his horse, he looked west and paused to consider the sight before him.

The sun was still shining for the days had grown longer with spring. Renaud gazed over the wide valley, green from the rain. Colorful wild flowers and clusters of birch trees dotted the sloping land where white, wooly ewes and their lambs grazed. Ahead in the distance he could see a large manor house next to what appeared to be a great hall, all surrounded by a palisade of wooden poles sharpened to a point. Behind the manor ran the River Lune, the name he recalled when he was first told of Talisand. A village lay to the north, the cottages with their thatched roofs appearing golden in the afternoon sun. From where he sat astride Belasco, dense woods to the north of the village extended as far as the eye could see.

It was more than he had expected, the peace so real it was tangible, and a world away from the harsh sounds of London and the destruction in the south. He could still see the faces of the Saxon dead in the battles he had fought. As much as he wanted to forget, even in this peaceful place, they haunted him. With a deep sigh, he focused on the river. The wide blue riband of water flowed behind the *demesne*, acting like a moat to protect the manor and its outbuildings.

Idly stroking the pelt of the wolf that lay over his hauberk, a fierce pride rose in his chest as he realized these were now his lands by William's decree.

"There lies the prize William has given me. There lies Talisand."

"Yea, you have done well, Ren," agreed Geoff, "and now you are an earl besides."

Renaud smiled at his friend then turned to his other side to see the pale blue eyes of Maugris.

The wise one stared back from where he sat astride his palfrey, his silver hair blowing across his wrinkled forehead. He nodded. "Yea, my lord, *there* you will find your prize."

"Glad I am, Ren, that we will arrive in ample time for the evening repast," Geoff said as he shifted in his saddle.

It had been a long day, one of many with meager rations, and Renaud knew his men were eager to arrive at their destination. "I see you are ever mindful of your next meal, Geoff. For you, Talisand is merely another place to dine." He laughed aloud.

Geoff grinned sheepishly.

"Oh, and it might be best not to call me by your pet name, at least not in the presence of the new vassals, or they will think the stories of the Red Wolf are mere legend and will disregard my commands."

"As you will, *my lord*," Geoff acknowledged, emphasizing the manner of address that was new.

The wind rose and Renaud heard his banner flapping behind him. A grunt from Sir Alain de Roux, the knight who bore his standard, caused Renaud to turn in his saddle. The wind had rendered the scarlet wolf on the midnight blue field a snarling beast. The burly knight struggled to gain control of the waving banner.

Renaud chuckled. "Sir Alain, will you wrestle that wolf 'til gloaming?"

The knight, whose size and coloring always reminded Renaud of a large brown bear, just smiled. A man of few words, Sir Alain was steady and reliable, trusted to watch the Red Wolf's back.

With one last tug at the cloth, the knight reined in the standard.

Renaud looked beyond the huge knight to the rest of the company. Some men were new. The lands of Talisand were rumored to be rich. For that reason, as well as his success in battle, many had been eager to accompany him when he had left London. Behind his squire, Mathieu, and his five knights, rode the men-at-arms and retainers, along with the craftsmen they'd brought with them to begin work on the castle William expected to be finished before summer's end.

Carts carried the tents and supplies they had brought with them, including casks of wine. Spotting Sir Hugue, Renaud was reminded of the few mercenaries who had joined them. He would have to keep a close watch on the men he knew less well. They, too, had come seeking a place in William's England and in the den of his wolf.

"*Bon.*" Renaud faced forward and raised his hand. "*Pour Talisand!*"

At the clenching of his knees, Renaud's stallion moved forward. The column followed, moving *en masse*.

Renaud's mind filled with the faces of the jealous barons and knights at William's court who had whispered the Red Wolf was the king's pet, a knight so favored his requests were never denied. In their jealousy, they had failed to see the reason for the king's favor. Renaud never acted without first consulting William in private. Then, too, he knew well the mind of his sire.

There was only one thing that could have moved Renaud from William's side—his dream of having his own lands. As a younger son of a Norman nobleman, Renaud had known he would have to fight for any lands he would claim as his own. And fight he had, both in Normandy and England, for there had been rebellions in the south after Hastings.

Aware that Renaud's devotion ran deep, but also knowing of his knight's dream, William had finally sent Renaud away with orders to take and hold Talisand, to raise a castle that would be a guard against the king's enemies to the north and a symbol to the English of his domination.

William's last words came to his mind. "Take as your wife the heiress of Talisand and raise up sons to serve my heirs."

"What have you heard of the Lady Serena?" Renaud asked Geoff as they drew nearer to the manor, and the bleating sheep scattered before their powerful horses.

Geoff seemed to ponder the question. "When you were granted Talisand, I heard the men at court whispering the Red Wolf had done well, that the lady is rumored to be fair of face with hair as pale as the moon. Though at seventeen summers, she will be older than most girls at her marriage. Earl Morcar, who went with William to Normandy last year, spoke of her as if describing a vision."

"It would matter naught to me if the lady's face was as plain as the side of a stable," Renaud replied. "William has commanded she be my wife and so she shall be. Have you heard aught else?"

"Nay, though I assume as the daughter of a thegn, she can manage a household."

"It is good we tarried so long in London," said Renaud thoughtfully. "Like the king, we have learned some of the barbarous English tongue. The serfs will not be familiar with our Norman French. This far north, I would not expect any of them to speak the language of William's court."

"She is supposed to be quite good with a bow," Maugris interjected under his breath, just loud enough for Renaud to hear. "'Tis unusual."

Renaud raised a brow at the old one's words. "And how would you know that, wise one?"

A small smile twitched at the corner of Maugris' mouth. "I have ways of knowing many things, my lord."

Renaud smiled. "Yea, you do, and your counsel is always welcome. Mayhap you can help me understand these people, Maugris. I expect they will be hostile to the idea of a Norman overlord, though I have little patience to give them. Still, we must find a way to make them work for us."

"That is one reason I have come, my lord. Your older brothers have your father's counsel, and you will have mine. As I once served your father, now I serve you. I do not expect to return to Normandy. My fate lies with the Red Wolf and his cubs."

"I am glad of it, Maugris. I would miss your old face were you to have stayed behind at my father's *donjon*, though I am glad your countenance is no longer green as it was on the crossing."

"I do not favor the sea, my lord, or boats upon it, as you know." The old man's face bore a grin telling Renaud that the unpleasant voyage and his *mal de mer* were now consigned to memory.

Having crossed the large swath of pasture, they arrived at the palisade. Renaud was unsurprised to see a crowd of villagers lined up on either side of the open gate, curious to get a look at their new lord. The faces of the young children, particularly the boys, were agog at the knights, enthralled with the hauberks they wore, the lances they carried and the powerful horses they rode. But the faces of the men, as Renaud had expected, wore scowls and hostile grimaces. Obviously the stories of the Normans, and the tale of the one called the Red Wolf, had traveled far.

Renaud and his men passed through the open gate and dismounted in the yard in front of the manor. Mathieu gathered Belasco's reins while still leading the powerful black destrier Renaud reserved for battle, and led the two horses toward the stable.

"See if you can find the one responsible for the running of the manor," Renaud said to Geoff. "Surely they must have a seneschal. I know you will naturally want to determine when we might have a meal." Glancing down at the mud that had spattered his leggings, he added, "I'd like to bathe before I meet the Lady Serena."

"Yea, my lord," Geoff said respectfully in the English tongue, darting a glance at the watching villagers as he walked toward the door of the manor.

Renaud waited for his men to draw near. When he spoke, it was in Norman French. "Sir Maurin, you speak some of the English tongue. Round up the thegn's men and see they swear fealty to me. Any who do not must leave." To the rest he said, "The usual rules apply concerning the women. Take care lest you consume too much of their ale in these first days. Though we are expected, I cannot predict our reception. Many will yet be unhappy a Norman lord has replaced their thegn. It would be best if you could learn to speak their language. Do not flaunt the power we have over them lest they hate us all the more. In time, they will accept their fate or rue the day."

Maugris whispered in his ear a reminder that the men would be concerned with their comforts. Raising his head, Renaud said, "I've sent Sir Geoffroi to see about a meal and lodging for the night, but there may not be room enough for all of you to set your pallets in the hall. Sir Geoffroi and I will lodge within the manor. The remainder will sleep in the hall or in tents until the castle is finished. Knights have first choice."

The men nodded, their faces telling Renaud they were pleased. The road had been long and the weather not always fair. Spring had brought heavy rains and they were often soaked to the skin while traveling north. Hard biscuits and dried meat were their only fare when their pace did not allow them to hunt. Now his men would have hot food to warm their bellies and more than soggy ground to lie upon. He prayed Talisand possessed a decent cook.

Leaving his men to their duties, and with Maugris following, Renaud headed toward the manor's entrance. Many eyes followed him. Whispers from the young lads told him his fierce reputation in battle had preceded his coming. At the door of the manor, he paused and turned. This time he spoke in English as he addressed the villagers.

"I am Sir Renaud de Pierrepont, now Earl of Talisand by King William's decree. I come in peace. If you show me the same, we will do well."

The English remained silent, their stern faces disclosing little. Were they surprised to find he knew some of their language? Whether they yet accepted their fate was not clear, but it mattered little. They were now his serfs and had no choice but to follow his orders.

Inside the manor, Renaud allowed his eyes to adjust to the light from the small windows, their shutters open, as he surveyed the interior. What he saw surprised him. Colorful tapestries depicting animals and plants draped the whitewashed walls. In between them were iron sconces that would hold torches at eventide. The furnishings were elaborate even for a thegn's dwelling, making Renaud think the old lord must have traveled or traded well. Many of the objects he saw were from distant lands, the kind of things he had seen in Rouen and his home in Saint Sauveur.

In the entry a brazier radiated heat, sending a thin column of smoke wafting up to a hole in the roof. A small woven rush mat lay in the center of the space and there was a bench placed to one side. In front of him, on the left, stairs ascended to the floor above where an open corridor with a half railing ran in front of several doors.

To the right of the stairs under the upper story was an entrance to another corridor. From the savory smells coming from that direction, he judged it to lead to the kitchen.

On his right, a wide opening in the wall led to the large timbered hall he had seen from afar, the two buildings having been joined. Peering through the opening, he saw two long trestle tables set upon the floor that was covered with what appeared to be clean rushes. The benches, he was pleased to discover, would seat all his men. A raised dais, the place the thegn would have taken his meals, was set at a right angle to the tables. In the middle of the hall was a stone hearth.

All he observed was clean and neat. It cheered him to think that Talisand was well kept by the lady of the manor, soon to be his bride. Mayhap it was not a bad thing if she were fair of face, as Geoff had said. If he had to look upon her each day, he would prefer a pretty woman to a plain one.

Just then, Geoff came through the doorway that Renaud had assumed led to the kitchen, approaching with a worried look. "Something's amiss, my lord."

Renaud scowled. "What is it?"

"When I asked for ale and food for the men, the few servants I saw rushed about with little aid. When I inquired further as to where the serving wenches were, the servants averted their gazes. I fear some of the women are in hiding or have fled, no doubt in fear of our arrival."

"It would not be unusual given the actions of William's army," said Renaud. "Send out a detail to search the surrounding area. If they are not found in the village, tell the men to search the woods to the north."

Geoff hurried toward the manor's front door, but before he reached it Renaud asked, "Is there a seneschal?"

Geoff turned. "Aye. A steward named Hunstan, but he has gone to the three smaller manors to tell them of our anticipated arrival." At Renaud's raised brow, Geoff smiled. "Those manors are a part of Talisand, now yours as well. The housekeeper said the man would return in a day or two. There is also a captain of the old lord's guard, named Theodric. He lives in one of the manors. I have not yet found him. He might be assisting the men."

With a flick of his wrist, Renaud dismissed the knight. *More manors?*

"Talisand is rich, indeed," said Maugris standing at his side.

From the hallway that led to the kitchen, a woman of middle years hurried toward them. She was plump and her manner pleasant. Her rosy cheeks and green eyes, the color of spring grass, rendered her a robust sight. But as he looked more closely, her brown hair, laced with gray, was in disarray and her expression anxious.

She curtsied before him. "I be Maggie, m'lord. Cook and housekeeper. Me husband, Angus, is the smith. The lads are bringing ale and soon ye and yer knights will have a hot meal. I imagine ye're hungry. Do ye have many with ye?"

"A half dozen knights and a score of men-at-arms and other retainers and squires. Your servants seem small in number, Goodwife Maggie." Then with raised brows, he said curtly, "Are you missing some?"

A troubled expression came over the woman's face. She looked down for a moment before she spoke. "Some of our lasses feared for their virtue, m'lord. They have left to follow Lady Serena."

Renaud's gaze narrowed, furrowing his brow, shocked at what he had heard. He attempted to hide the anger welling within him, but his jaw involuntarily clenched. "The Lady Serena is gone?" His voice was as cold as his heart at the realization she had run.

"I am verra sorry, m'lord."

"Where is she?" he demanded.

The woman twisted her hands at her waist. "In truth, I do not know, m'lord though her destination was Scotland."

Seething, Renaud felt a muscle in his jaw clench. So the English maiden had fled rather than be wed to a Norman knight? She would not get away with such an insult! He would send a man after her, even to Scotland if need be. William's decree had begun the marriage; consummation would establish it. And he meant to consummate it and soon.

He was still pondering whom he should send after his errant bride when Maugris introduced himself to the housekeeper. "I am Maugris, Maggie."

Taking in Renaud's scowl, Maugris said in a calm voice, "Perchance in time Lady Serena will be found, my lord."

Renaud stroked the pelt of the wolf in an effort to calm himself and let out a breath. Maugris's message was clear. He should wait. It was only his respect for the old man that stayed his anger from turning into action.

"I truly hope so," he said to Maugris. "It would displease the king to find the woman he gave me is now in Scotland." Then to the housekeeper, "And it pleases me not at all."

For a moment an uncomfortable silence hung in the air, interrupted by the housekeeper's anxious question. "May I show ye to the lord's bedchamber?" It was clear to Renaud she was eager to leave behind the subject of her missing lady.

Geoff stepped through the front door and joined them, acknowledging

Maggie with a smile.

"It seems Lady Serena has chosen to flee," Renaud informed Geoff.

"With the other women?" Geoff asked incredulous.

"I know not, but I will soon have the truth of it. Come, let us see the chambers above. I will deal with my rebellious bride later." Renaud and Geoff followed Maggie up the stairs. Maugris chose to remain below, seeming to take all in with his knowing blue eyes.

Though still angry that the lady had fled, Renaud turned his attention to his new manor. As she ascended the stairs, the housekeeper told him there were three chambers above. The lord's chamber was the first she directed them to at the far end of the corridor.

"'Tis the largest o'course," said Maggie, "nearly twice the size of the others."

The bedchamber they entered contained a poster bed with dark green curtains and furs strewn on the cover, extravagant even for a wealthy thegn. The bed cushion looked well stuffed and comfortable. His gaze lingered on the soft coverings in anticipation of his rest that night. He had not slept in a bed since he had left London.

Several chests lined the wall on the other side of the bed beneath a small window. Directly in front of him was a trestle table and bench seat, which would provide him a place to work. Behind the table, on the wall, were wooden shelves that contained scrolls and other writings. The old lord had been a man of letters, it seemed.

Renaud walked to the window above the shelf, his boots crushing dried rushes underfoot releasing a pleasant scent of herbs. He opened the shutters, allowing light to spill forth so he could examine the writings.

"Was the old lord educated?"

"Aye, m'lord," said the housekeeper as she lit rush lights near the bed, the slender torches adding light to the chamber. And then with a note of pride, she added, "The children as well."

"Most unusual...." He fingered some of the writings and was surprised to see a collection of poems in Norman French. As he looked around, he saw no feminine touches to indicate a lady of the manor.

"Does the old thegn's wife still live, Maggie?"

"Nay, m'lord. She died giving birth to Lady Serena. The lord never took another to wife." The housekeeper looked toward the door as if wanting to move beyond the pain the memory obviously brought her. "The other two bedchambers can serve for yer men if ye desire, m'lord," she said.

"Whose bedchambers are they?" Geoff asked.

"They belonged to Lady Serena and her brother Steinar. Neither is here now, o'course."

Renaud exchanged a look with Geoff. The reminder of his missing bride brought his frown back.

They left the bedchamber and walked the length of the narrow corridor open to partial view from the entry below.

Each of the two other chambers was also decorated with tapestries. Like the master's bed, they were draped in curtains and had bed cushions that, although smaller in size, invited the weary to rest. From the softer colors and the gowns in the wardrobe chest, Renaud assumed the chamber closest to the lord's had belonged to a woman.

Lady Serena's chamber.

Renaud caught the faint scent of flowers and wondered how long she had been gone.

As he turned to leave, his attention was drawn to a flash of light from a silvered glass. "Only in Rouen have I seen one so fine."

"'Twas a gift to Lady Serena from her father," offered the housekeeper, her voice reflecting a sadness he did not understand.

Surrounded by the lady's things, Renaud was suddenly curious. "Did the old thegn pledge his daughter to anyone?" Other questions he did not voice. Had she traveled north with a young man? Was she promised to one of her own?

"Nay, m'lord, though there were many who asked for her hand." The housekeeper shook her head. "There was talk of a betrothal to Earl Morcar, brother to Earl Edwin of Mercia, but the old thegn delayed. I think he dinna want to lose her to a husband, even if he be an earl." Mayhap the housekeeper realized that Renaud was now an earl, for her cheeks suddenly reddened, and she hastily added, "We lost the old lord at Hastings. Had he returned, he would have arranged a marriage to some worthy lord, 'tis certain."

Some worthy English lord, she means.

Renaud touched the fine surface of the glass, not sure why he was pleased that Lady Serena had not been betrothed to another. It mattered little. She would be his wife. He had only to find her.

"Geoff, take the bedchamber farthest from mine, the one that belonged to the son. I would hold Lady Serena's chamber unoccupied for now."

"Yea, my lord. I am content just to have a bed." Geoff smiled broadly at the housekeeper and she returned his smile.

"I will see to yer bath, m'lord," said the housekeeper. "We've a serving lad, Eric, who will assist ye since we are a bit short on lasses." Not waiting for a response, she dipped her head and shuffled out the door.

Renaud faced his friend. "Our squires can sleep on pallets in our rooms for now. I imagine Maugris will prefer to be out among the stars as is his wont, at least until winter. By then the castle will be completed and there will be room for all."

"Aye, Ren. I'll see about the men. And our supper."

Left alone, Renaud lingered for a moment in Lady Serena's chamber trying to conjure an image of the woman. Trying to understand what had driven her from her home. He knew some of the English women had taken the veil rather than be forced to marry Normans. *Would she?* William would not break such a vow to the Church, no matter he had given the woman to his knight.

Renaud wandered back to his bedchamber, content with his new *demesne* and the future it portended. The decorative tapestries on the walls and the rich fabrics on the bed reminded him of the old thegn's wealth. There was even a rush mat on the floor painted with geometric designs in brilliant shades of red, gold and green.

He smiled, gratified the day had arrived when he could set aside his sword, at least for the moment, and claim his place in William's kingdom. In the back of Renaud's mind was the nagging concern that the English might never accept their Norman king or his overlords, but Renaud did not dwell on it. The peasants, now serfs, had little choice, and William was not one to be thwarted. But Renaud wanted more. He longed for peace and an end to war.

An hour later, after having bathed and changed, he left his chamber and descended the stairs, his thoughts returning to the servant girls who had fled. He understood why they had done so. His own sister, Aveline, had been thought a servant the day she was working in her garden, digging in the dirt in a plain brown gown, when an errant knight had come upon her and, thinking to have his pleasure, took her by force. Hearing her screams, Renaud had come running and killed the rutting knight, but he could not restore to the beautiful Aveline what had been so brutally taken.

After what happened to his sister, he could well comprehend the fears of the servant girls at Talisand. It was the worst part of a war that was fought not on a battlefield so much as in the towns of the conquered. Though sometimes necessary, the destruction of innocent lives always sickened him. He knew the taking of spoils included rape, though William frowned upon it, and Renaud would not allow it to be counted among his men.

He could only hope the women would return.

CHAPTER 3

The fire in the hall's hearth burned slowly as the smoke ascended to the opening in the roof, drawing Renaud's attention to the carved timbers above him. Soot had darkened the wooden members, but he could still see the rich ornamentation and the intricate patterns and scrollwork he had observed in other English dwellings, particularly in the churches.

He had left his hauberk, spurs and the wolf's pelt in his chamber and now sat at the table on the dais enjoying the evening meal. Torches set into the wall cast a warm glow about the long timbered room, and candles set upon the tables flickered as servants with expressionless faces laid trenchers of food before him and his men. Gazing about the room, he paid scant attention to the low male voices and hearty laughter coming from his men. A few dogs lurked in the shadows among the rushes, eager for a scrap.

Renaud took it all in and marveled that this now was his as well as the lands that were a part of his earldom. He ate with relish the venison, fish and roasted vegetables the cook had prepared. His prayer had been granted. Maggie was a fine cook. Taking up his goblet of French wine, Renaud leaned back in the lord's chair, well satisfied. The wine and a full stomach lulled him into a mollified state after his anger of the afternoon.

A dark-haired woman ambled toward the dais carrying a pitcher of wine. As she refilled his goblet, she leaned over the table, allowing her long dark hair and breasts to fall into his view. His eyes gazed upward to see her smiling. He did not fail to note the invitation in her dark eyes.

"My name's Aethel, m'lord." The seductress slowly grinned. "Is there aught else ye would require of me this night?"

"Nay. That will be all."

21

As she sauntered away, hips swaying, Geoff leaned close to whisper. "It seems not all at Talisand resent Normans, Ren. If you want her, I wager she's yours. Best to take her afore Sir Alain does. See there, he stands in the corner with his arms crossed watching her with possessive interest."

Renaud followed Geoff's gaze to see his standard bearer watching the wench. "Nay, I want her not. She reminds me of the serving women in Rouen, comely but available to any of William's knights." He took a long draw on his wine. "Let Alain have her if he will. Mayhap he will make an honest woman of her."

"Yet she seems to favor you."

Renaud shrugged. "Or, she favors the title I now carry."

"I see you have not changed," teased his friend, "still the warrior priest."

"Ah… That description bandied about London. I'd forgotten," he said thoughtfully. "Why? Because I protect the women?"

"Yea, that and because you wear honor like a cloak and expect the same of your men. You would seek to gain a measure of trust with the vanquished when other knights care nothing for such sensibilities."

"You know me well, my friend."

"Ah, but there is more to the tale. In London, William's courtiers wondered at the rules you adhere to and the discipline you insist your knights follow. Some consider the justice you mete out for breaking the rules harsh—the lashings and, in some cases, death by the sword. It has earned you the reputation the Red Wolf has today."

"The rules are necessary," Renaud said dismissively. "I'd not change them. To fight battles without discipline is to set out to lose."

"And then there are the many women you have denied your bed," Geoff said with a wink. "I believe that is what accounted for the label 'priest'."

Renaud could not resist a small laugh. "I am not celibate, as you know. Merely particular—and too consumed with William's many tasks to spend my evenings wenching."

"Well, many who serve William do."

Renaud shrugged, tired of the subject. Sated from the evening meal, he rested his palm on his stomach. "That food was most welcome after the meager fare we have had these last weeks. Still, I am glad we brought those casks of wine. I much prefer it to the English ale and to the wine they make in England."

"Aye, 'twas a veritable feast," said Geoff, filling his mouth with a choice bit of venison and following it with a swallow of wine.

At the sound of the door to the yard opening, Renaud turned. A knight wearing a hauberk came toward him at a brisk pace, his spurs making a slight jingle as they hit the floor. Renaud recognized Niel le Brun, the knight Geoff had sent with Sir Maurin to find the missing servant girls. Once Renaud's squire, the young knight had earned his spurs with the jagged scar on his left jaw he had gained at Hastings.

"My lord," said the knight, pausing for Renaud to acknowledge him. "We found five women and two men several hours' ride north. They were traveling on foot. When I assured them no harm would come to the women if they returned, the men admitted they were from Talisand. The weapons they carried are now in the armory: several bows, some carried by the women, a seax, and the scramaseax knives the men carried."

"Where are the women now?"

"Sir Maurin has taken them to the manor's entry where he stands guard. I thought you would want to speak to them."

Renaud pushed back his chair and rose. "Yea, I will see them."

Geoff stood, casting a regretful glance at his trencher and the still uneaten venison.

"Your food will keep, Geoff. Let us see what the woods have returned to us." Renaud was anxious to get a look at the women. He hoped Lady Serena was among them.

Curiosity compelled him forward, and with Geoff at his side, his long strides soon covered the distance to the wide doorway leading from the hall to the manor.

Crossing the threshold, he saw a small group of women gathered around the brazier. Two bearded men stood in front of them, their stance that of protectors, no matter they had been relieved of their weapons. They wore the shorter tunics of the English and both had shoulder length hair, one brown and the other fair with a golden mustache. Among the women, he glimpsed a redhead and several with hair in various shades of brown. Not a flaxen one among them.

Disappointed, and angrier than ever that his bride had escaped, his eyes narrowed on the women. "I am Sir Renaud de Pierrepont, now Earl of Talisand by King William's decree. I understand why you fled but you need have no fear for your virtue. Any who ride with me know my command in this matter. Return to your work; you will be safe for I protect what is mine."

His task done, Renaud turned and confidently strode back to the hall, dismissing Sir Maurin with a flick of his wrist.

* * *

A great wave of weariness swept over Serena as the two Normans turned their backs and, with long strides, returned to the hall. She had walked for most of the day and then been forced to ride in the lap of the knight who brought her back to the manor. Night had descended and the spring air grew chilled. Yet she knew the weary feeling was due to more than the long journey or the cold. She was anxious and angry with herself.

They should have left days earlier.

Serena had watched the two Normans approach from where she stood behind the other women. Leppe had placed her there in an attempt to protect her from the probing eyes of the new Norman lord. The moment she had set eyes on the knights, she knew which of the two was the Red Wolf. He came through the door wearing a fierce scowl as his eyes roved over the women like a beast seeking one to devour. She had known he was looking for her and had dropped her gaze to her stare at her feet.

But when he began to speak, she could not resist raising her head to look at him. He was different from Sir Maurin, the knight with the weathered face who had carried her back to the manor and spoke to her in stilted English. This one, who claimed to be the Earl of Talisand, was used to giving orders, his air of command proclaiming it so in English any would understand.

He had glowered at them, his piercing gray eyes like a threatening storm. Power like soundless thunder emanated from his lean muscular body as he stared at the small group huddled in front of the brazier.

Unlike Englishmen, his face was devoid of any beard and his dark reddish brown hair fell in waves only to his nape. He stood erect as if surveying a battlefield but he wore no knight's mail, only a dark green tunic and a leather belt studded with silver. His legs spread apart and his hands fisted on his hips, he stood like a Viking on the deck of his ship. She supposed that he was. The Norsemen who invaded Normandy had left their mark well enough. And now one of their descendants had invaded Talisand.

She was glad she had not willingly accepted her fate of belonging to him for he had the undeniable look of one who tolerated no weakness and no dissent. A warrior who demanded his due. It gave her a secret joy to know she defied him and the Bastard King. Yet despite that, she was intrigued. He was undeniably handsome in a raw sort of way, and now he was the master of all that was hers. She was more determined than ever to despise him.

The knight who had stood next to the Red Wolf was unlike his lord, so fair as to appear nearly Saxon, save for the shorter hair and the lack of a beard. He was not so tall, either, and carried more weight. The lines around his mouth and eyes suggested he laughed often.

She remembered well the Red Wolf's words. They had been few, as if he carefully doled them out, telling the women they need not fear ravishment, that he protected what was his. She wondered if his words were truth. If the messengers had been correct, the Normans had raped, burned and pillaged half of England. It vexed her that this Norman knight considered the men and women of Talisand his, no matter it was now true. Once free, now they were reduced to mere possessions. She hoped it would not always be so.

She turned from the entry and, with the other women, headed to the kitchen. Worry dogged her as she thought about the fate of her people. She decided to stay, at least for a while, to see how the Norman lord would treat them. But how long could she maintain her disguise as a servant when all those at Talisand knew her to be their lady? They would risk all to conceal her, but could she ask such a thing of them?

* * *

"Faith!" Serena shouted as the heavy kettle slipped from her hands and crashed to the floor with a loud clang, splashing hot liquid onto her tunic. Exasperated, she wiped her hands on her apron, and bent to clean up the remains of the broth. "Oh, Maggie, it seems I have little talent for kitchen duties."

Serena's insides churned in frustration. She had been working in the kitchen and serving at the tables in the guise of Sarah for a week, diligently trying to blend in as one of the servants. But untrained for the work, she had little patience for mixing, lifting and serving. Her talents lay in the managing of the household and in other pursuits not so typical of a thegn's daughter.

"Ye're trying, m'lady," said Maggie. "'Tis all that matters, truly. Most of the lasses assigned to the kitchen have been raised to the work like me own daughter. Mayhap yer father shouldna have indulged ye by allowing ye to hunt. Yet ye do sing like an angel and that always pleases a man."

Serena looked up at Maggie from where she had stooped to clean up the mess. She would have rolled her eyes had she not seen the smile on the older woman's face. But she must correct the manner in which the cook had addressed her. "Just call me Sarah, Maggie."

The housekeeper reached down and helped her to rise. "Dinna worry about the broth, Sarah. Leave it be. I can make more."

Cassie left the bread she had been preparing for the noon meal and came to kneel beside the spilled broth. "I will do this."

"Cassie, you are ever kind, but you know as a servant, I must do my share of the work."

The sound of skipping feet drew Serena's attention to the small boy with blond hair who had entered the back door left open on warm days for access to the herb garden.

"'Tis young Jamie!" exclaimed Cassie.

"Ser...Sarah!" The boy ran to Serena and wrapped his arms around her tunic, joy lighting up his young face. "Sarah, see what I have brought ye?" He pulled a bow from his shoulder where it rested with a quiver of arrows and proudly thrust it upon her. "Yer bow."

"Jamie, you prince!" she said, taking it. "Where did you find it?"

"When the knights brought ye back, they put it in the armory. I recognized it from the Welsh symbols Rhodri carved in it when he made it for ye. I knew ye'd want it."

Serena smiled and kissed the top of his curly, sun bleached head. "Now I have only to recover my seax."

"I will look for that, too," said the boy eagerly.

Maggie gazed in Serena's direction, her eyes fixing on the bow. "Now there is something ye're good at. And since the knights have been concerned with their swordplay and building onto the stable, they have yet to hunt to add to our stores of meat. Can ye do that for me on the morrow? I need rabbits for stew."

"I would be happy to hunt, Maggie. I am better at that than making broth."

"Yea, 'tis true, ye are." Looking down at Jamie and then at Serena, she said, "Go on then, take the lad for a walk to the stable. He loves to see the knights' horses and some air will do ye both good. I'll make the broth. If ye want, ye can return in a wee bit to serve the midday meal."

"You are a generous woman, Maggie, to be so kind to one of the servants." She gave the housekeeper a wink. "I welcome some time with Jamie."

"Give me the bow," Maggie said, reaching for it. "I will see yer weapon well hidden here in the kitchen." She took the bow and quiver of arrows, covered them with a drying cloth and set them behind the wooden cabinet in the far corner of the room.

Serena took off her apron and wrapped her arm around Jamie's shoulders. "So, Jamie, shall we take a walk to see the horses?"

"Yea. I would like that! The knights' warhorses are fierce, Sarah. Even the squires can hardly control them, but there are others they ride that are not so wild. I've made friends with some of those." He took her hand and pulled her toward the door. A smile broke out on his face, which added to the ruddy glow on his cheeks, making him look like a cherub who had spent the morn in a field of wheat. Serena did not like to think about Jamie near the Normans' fearsome destriers, warhorses trained to kick and bite, as much weapons as the knights' lances and swords.

Passing through the herb garden, Serena noticed Aethel digging among the new plants. "Good morning Aethel. You seem to be working hard."

The woman sat back on her heels and brushed a lock of dark hair from her eyes as she gave Serena's clothing a long perusal. "The new herbs will be needed for healing as well as for savory dishes. It is just my usual work...*Sarah*."

Ignoring the look Aethel gave her, Serena said, "I admire your knowledge, Aethel." The compliment was sincere. Though Serena had often acted the healer, she had counted upon Aethel's knowledge to tell her which herbs to use.

Aethel smiled briefly and bent her head to her task.

"How are you getting along since the Normans have come?" Serena asked her.

"Well enough," Aethel said without looking up.

"It is not easy for any of us," Sarah remarked absently. Jamie impatiently tugged on her hand. Giving into his urging, she wished Aethel a good morn and continued on the path leading to the yard and to the stable set just inside the palisade.

New grass grew at the edge of the palisade and wild flowers had sprung up in clusters around the manor, causing Serena to marvel at the beauty of the place she called home. Despite the Normans' coming, there was a sameness to Talisand she found comforting. Workers mended the palisade, carts creaked as they rolled by and brown chickens pecked at the dirt. The only differences were the sounds of clanking metal as the knights engaged in swordplay outside the palisade, and the dull thud of hammers pounding in the work they'd begun on a new stable.

"I have missed you, lad," she said to Jamie as they walked along side by side. "Where have you been keeping yourself?"

"I have been watching the knights! Each morning, they practice with their swords and talk of the Red Wolf's plans for Talisand. They say we will have a grand castle set upon a great mound of dirt." Jamie babbled on excitedly as they covered the ground to the stable, the sun warming Serena as they walked. "The men have even let me hold their swords!" A look of guilt suddenly came over his face and he dropped his gaze. "I know they are Normans, Sarah, and I should not like them."

"'Tis all right, Jamie. I can see they have bewitched you. Besides, 'tis best you do not anger them by telling them what we think of Normans." She feared for the boy if he did.

They walked to the stable's entrance, his small hand in hers. His face glowed as he told her of the knights. She could see the boy considered the presence of the warriors an adventure. She hoped they presented no threat to the child. His life had certainly become more exciting with their arrival. While she hated the invaders of her country who had taken her beloved family and her lands, Jamie, orphaned as a small boy, had no mother or father to see to his training. Now that he was growing into manhood, the Norman knights with their swords and horses would be tempting. While she acted the part of his older sister, assuring his needs were met, she knew he longed to be a part of the world of men.

* * *

Standing on the roof walk of the manor house, Geoff at his side, Renaud raised his hand to shield his eyes from the blinding sun as he gazed into the distance, surveying the land around the manor. He had yet to select the site for the castle though he had identified a location that would serve.

"That reminds me, Ren," Geoff said, the knight's gaze fixed on the yard below.

Roused from his thoughts, Renaud faced his friend. "Yea?"

"See the girl walking with the lad, just there?"

Renaud's gaze followed Geoff's finger pointing to a girl with a long brown plait walking toward the stable with a boy of about ten or eleven years. "I see."

"She was one of the servant girls brought back that first eve. I think she may become a problem with the men."

Renaud frowned. He did not need another problem just now, particularly not with his men who were just settling in. "Why would she be a problem?"

"Watch her at the midday meal instead of eating in your chamber as you have been doing these last few days and see for yourself. The men are taken with the wench. They compete to try and win her affection while she serves. I am worried it will lead to fights among them."

"Does she tease them?" The face of the dark-haired temptress who served in the evening flashed in his mind.

"Nay. She does not even look at them. But she is very comely and Sir Maurin, who carried her back when they retrieved the servant girls, seems to have a fondness for the wench. The younger men have no intention of deferring to the knight where she is concerned. Instead, they compete to win the girl's favors. She encourages none. Mayhap she is even hostile to their smiles. From the looks she gives us, I think she has no kind feelings for Normans."

Renaud was not about to let his men fight over a wench. There was much for them to do to remain ready to serve William should they be called to battle. And they must soon hunt to provide meat. "See that she is taken off serving duty. Send her above stairs to work as a maid. I would see her there this afternoon so I may judge for myself."

"That I will gladly do," said Geoff giving Renaud a look that said he was pleased his lord had relieved him of an unwanted problem.

CHAPTER 4

Renaud lingered at the high table in the hall until he glimpsed the servant girl with the brown plait carry a pile of linen through the entry heading toward the stairs to the bedchambers. Slowly rising, he nodded to Geoff and followed after her.

Quietly, he stepped through the open door of his chamber. The girl had her back to him as she freshened the bed, the stack of clean linen resting on a nearby chest. He did not acknowledge her but went directly to the trestle table, poured a goblet of wine and sat, pretending to examine a drawing of the lands surrounding the manor.

She turned. "I can come back later, my lord." She spoke meekly, barely looking at him as she hurriedly finished with the bed and began a hasty retreat to the door.

He replied in the English tongue, as he did to all save his men. "Nay, you may stay. Your work will not disturb me."

Out of the corner of his eye, he saw her back stiffen. Slowly, she retraced her steps and resumed her work. Her movements were rushed as if she were trying to complete her assigned tasks in haste. Was she nervous at being alone with him? Even with that, Renaud thought her movements graceful as she walked to the shelves near where he sat. She held her head high, unusual for a servant in the presence of her lord. Though her long plait was the dull color of country earth, her profile was refined and her features delicate. He rose and silently moved to stand behind her where she dusted a carved box.

She must have sensed his approach.

"My lord?" she said, turning to face him.

Blue-violet eyes held his gaze only a moment before looking down at the floor. Set in her ivory face they reminded him of violets in the snow.

31

So mesmerized was he that, for a moment, he forgot his question.

"Your name is Sarah?"

Keeping her eyes focused on the floor, she said, "Yea, my lord."

"How long have you been at Talisand?"

"All my life, my lord." Her voice was soft, a low purr, and with her words a flowery scent drifted to his nose. He was captivated and wanted to touch her. How long had it been since he'd had a woman? And this one was causing his manhood to stir.

Turning back to the shelf, she resumed dusting the carved box, as if to put an end to the conversation. His gaze shifted to her hand as she set down the box. Delicate fingers and ivory skin. It was not the hand of a kitchen wench.

"Let me see your hand." She started at his request, and though he could see she wanted to resist, she did not fight him when he reached for her hand and brought it close to his body turning her palm upward.

It told him much.

"These blisters are new. You have not always worked in the kitchens nor done the wet work of the laundry, have you?"

She shook her head in silent agreement.

"What were your tasks before I came to Talisand?"

Looking down at her feet, she said, "I was with the Lady Serena, my lord."

"Ah, a lady's handmaiden then." So that is where the girl learned to speak so well, for her speech was not that of an ordinary servant nor her manner that of a scullery maid.

He waited for her to say more but when she did not, he said, "Tell me about her."

She looked up. "What would you know, my lord?" Blue violet eyes held his. He could get lost in those eyes.

"How does she look?"

"She is tall and her hair is the color of summer wheat, my lord."

"And her character?"

Turning her gaze again to the floor, she hesitated before speaking. "She loves her people and her family, my lord. She is very loyal. Had she been a man, she would have fought with her father at Hastings. Most of all, she loves Talisand and would die for its people."

Her voice, nearly breaking at the end, told him her words were spoken with deep emotion. She was close to the Lady of Talisand and to the old thegn.

"I'm told her brother took the lord's place for a time," he said, hoping she would continue to talk.

She raised her eyes to his. "Yea, Steinar did lead Talisand for a time, but then he was drawn away by other battles." When she spoke the young man's name, a tender look came into her eyes. Did she love the old lord's son? Mayhap she was his leman. The possibility was not to his liking.

Still holding her hand, he looked down at her palm seeing other signs. "These are the calluses of an archer. How is it a lady's handmaiden comes to use a bow?"

The girl's eyes shifted to her hand where Renaud had begun moving his thumb across her palm in slow sensual circles. He was not unaffected and, he suspected, neither was she.

"Rhodri taught me, my…my lord." She spoke in a halting whisper, confirming his touch was disrupting her thoughts. Then she added hastily, "I was not the only one. It was the old lord's desire that Rhodri should teach all at Talisand who cared to learn."

Renaud remembered that when the young servant women had been returned to the *demesne*, Sir Niel had taken several bows from them.

He stopped stroking her palm. She tried to pull back her hand but he had no intention of releasing her. "Who is this Rhodri?"

"He is a Welsh bard, my lord, who is also skilled with a bow. The thegn met him on his travels and invited him here. He lived among us for several years."

"Where is the Welshman now?"

"I know not, my lord. Peradventure he is in Wales, though his music and his skill with a bow are much in demand. He may yet be in England."

"A bard and a bowman…an unusual combination." Renaud frowned in concentration as he considered the idea.

"Not for a Welshman," she said, matter-of-factly.

Renaud smiled, amused. She was so serious, so insistent, this servant who acted like no servant he'd ever known. "Aye, mayhap you are right. Many Welshmen would have both talents."

He let go of her hand, but remained close. He knew now what had attracted his men for he, too, was falling under her spell. She was beautiful and well-spoken and something about her enticed him. If she had been the leman of this brother of Lady Serena's or the bard Rhodri, it was possible she was not a maiden and would accept an invitation to come to his bed. If Lady Serena lingered in Scotland, he might have no woman for some time.

He brushed his knuckles along her jaw from her ear to her chin and then down her neck, feeling her skin like warm silk. She shivered and looked away.

His mind conjured a picture of the feminine creature naked in his bed.

His heart beat rapidly and his loins grew heavy. Wild images began filling his head.

He imagined taking the beautiful serving girl in his arms and kissing her softly, deeply, hearing her purring with delight. In his mind he lifted her in his arms and carried her to the fur covered bed. Throwing her gently to the bed cushion, he covered her beckoning body with his own, pressing firmly into her softness as he kissed her again, letting his kisses rain over her face and down her neck, following a trail to the swell of her breasts. His excitement was growing, his hardening manhood the proof.

"My lord," Sarah whispered. "My lord, is something wrong?" This time the question was louder than before, bringing him back to the present. He blinked.

The girl looked as if she was preparing to flee. It had been too long since he'd had a woman. His heart pumping, he controlled his breath and shook himself out of his fantasy.

"Sarah, would you come willingly to my bed?"

Angry violet eyes glared at him. "Nay! I may be seventeen summers but I am a maiden still!"

So, the kitten has claws. Her fierce reaction suggested she spoke the truth, or was it only that she hated Normans enough to lie and lie well?

"You have said no woman would be forced by you or your men," she reminded him.

He slid a finger along her jaw and saw her shiver. "You could come to me of your own accord, Sarah. I desire you." It occurred to him then that if she were a maiden still, mayhap he should help her find a worthy husband among his men, but he found no joy in such a thought. No, he wanted this one in no other bed but his own.

She glared at him. "Are you not promised to Lady Serena?"

He stepped back at her challenging words, forcing his ardor to cool. "Yea, she has been given to me by William's decree, and I will take her to wife because I must. It is my duty. But she is not here. Even if she were, you could be my leman." He knew he would never have a desire like this for the woman William had ordered him to marry. And he did not want to let the comely servant go.

"Nay! I would never come willingly to a Norman's bed. And I will be no man's whore."

Her words hit him like a hard slap. He was surprised a servant would be so adamant to refuse her lord, now an earl, even if he were a Norman. But he would not press the matter. He could be patient, at least for a while. With the challenge of wooing Sarah to his bed, he might not mind the absence of Lady Serena.

Stepping away from her, he flicked his fingers toward the door. "Go then. Your work is done here for today."

* * *

Serena looked up at the clouds gathering above her. Hunting the next day not far from the village, she was hurrying to take enough rabbits to satisfy Maggie before the deluge began. She'd taken four when a woman's scream broke the quiet of the woods. Dropping her catch, she ran toward the sound. As she neared the small clearing just ahead, she heard a familiar voice.

"Nay! Let go of me! Do not do this!" the woman pleaded.

"Come wench! Give me what I want and I will gladly release you." The man's voice was deep, husky and harsh.

Serena stepped into the clearing just as she heard the sound of ripping cloth. She had known who the woman was. Eawyn was her friend. And she knew the knight from the hall when she had first served the Normans their evening meal. His leering glances had made her uneasy.

With one hand, the swarthy dark-haired knight held the woman in his grasp while wrenching down her tunic and shift, tearing the cloth still further. Eawyn struggled to pull away while clutching at the torn fabric with her free hand, trying in vain to cover her naked breasts.

He reached out to touch one of the pink-tipped mounds of pale flesh, and Eawyn let out a pathetic wail.

With lightning speed, Serena moved her bow into place nocking an arrow and pulling it back, ready to fire.

The knight threw Eawyn roughly to the ground, falling heavily atop her. With her hands pinned beneath his weight, there was nothing Eawyn could do to fight off the inevitable.

"Release her!" Serena shouted.

The knight did not stop but mercilessly squeezed one of Eawyn's breasts, while violently sucking the other into his mouth. Eawyn writhed beneath the Norman, struggling to free herself while he shoved his other hand between her legs, pulling up her tunic.

"Stop, I say!"

The knight turned to see Serena's poised bow. Rolling off Eawyn, he rose from the ground, dragging the terrified woman with him, still holding her in his punishing grip. "Ah, another young beauty...and this one with a toy in hand. Come join us wench and we shall have good sport. There is more than enough of me for the both of you."

With cold determination Serena looked into the dark eyes of the beefy knight, who unlike his fellow Normans, wore a mustache and short beard and was all the more menacing for them.

35

"I will not miss my mark, Norman. Let her go *now*, or I'll dispatch you to hell where you surely belong." She would not hesitate to kill this man who would defile one of Talisand's women. The vengeance she craved ran strong and deep. Not just for Eawyn, but for her father, Talisand and all of England.

Still holding the struggling Eawyn, the knight laughed.

Serena would give him one last chance. She aimed for the arm that held her friend. Letting the arrow fly, its metal tip sank deep into the fleshy part of his arm, sending a warning the knight could not ignore.

With an oath, he let go of Eawyn. "What have you done, wench?" He looked at his arm dripping blood. "For this you will pay!"

"I think not," Serena said. "Now, move away from her." Serena quickly nocked another arrow. This one she would aim at his heart.

"Nay, I shall have my feast here in the woods," he said defiantly, his dark eyes crazed as he gripped Eawyn with the hand of his uninjured arm. "And then I shall have you before I kill you!"

"Say your prayers, Norman, for hell awaits you!" About to let her arrow fly, Serena heard heavy footfalls behind her, snapping twigs.

"What goes here, Sir Hugue?" The blond knight who was companion to the Red Wolf stomped into the clearing and stood next to Serena. In a gentle voice he said, "It was good your aim went amiss, Sarah. You do not want the death of a knight laid upon you. Put down your bow. I will handle this."

Serena slowly lowered her bow but did not take the arrow from its place, nor her eyes from the one called Sir Hugue. Inside she still seethed.

At the blond knight's words, the knight who held Eawyn released her and stepped back, lowering his head as if a humble suppliant. To Serena, his submission appeared feigned. His arm where the arrow pierced it dripped blood but he seemed not to notice. "Naught but a bit of sport, Sir Geoffroi. And for it, I took an arrow in my arm from the wench."

Eawyn ran to Serena who dropped one of her hands from her bow to wrap an arm around the distraught woman who was desperately trying to cover herself.

Serena whispered in her ear, "Do not reveal my identity."

Eawyn's dark tresses had come loose from her plait to fall in strings around her face and her blue eyes were full of tears, but she nodded even as she continued to sob.

"The maid does not look willing to me, Sir Hugue." Sir Geoffroi's voice brooked no excuse. "What were you thinking? Do you not know the Red Wolf's rules concerning the women?"

"Aye, I know his rules," Sir Hugue scoffed. "We are not to take a lady unwilling. But surely that does not include the servants!"

The knight named Sir Geoffroi narrowed his eyes at the other man's words. "It does and you know it."

Serena was aware that most knights only respected the virtue of women of their own rank, but she had heard the words of the Red Wolf. He held his men to a higher standard. Though she had doubted the truth of it at the time, now she believed.

Before Sir Hugue could answer, Serena spoke, her voice livid with disdain. "Even if that could excuse him, which it does not, Eawyn is no servant. She is the lady of the west manor and widow of Ulrich, one of the old thegn's most trusted men. Though she is now on foot, she would have ridden here on a horse. Her black palfrey cannot be far. This Norman should die for the offense he has shown this gentle woman." She let go of Eawyn and raised her bow, again aiming at the knight's chest, sincere in her desire to see the miscreant dead.

Sir Geoffroi's hand on her arm stayed her pull on the arrow. "Put down the bow, Sarah. I will protect Eawyn." The blond knight took off his mantle and draped it around the sobbing woman's shoulders, covering her nakedness. Glaring at the knight before him, he ordered, "Come with me, Sir Hugue."

Reluctantly, Serena lowered her bow. The knight called Sir Hugue uttered a disgruntled noise and followed Sir Geoffroi. The blond knight rested his hand protectively on Eawyn's shoulders, and with gentleness guided her in the direction of the manor.

Her heart still racing from the encounter, Serena went in search of her rabbits and Eawyn's horse. She hoped Sir Geoffroi would report to his lord what had happened. The Red Wolf would see the knight who had harmed Eawyn was punished.

Or Serena would see to it herself.

CHAPTER 5

"I tell you, Ren, the servant girl Sarah would have killed the mercenary, no matter how many arrows it took her to see the task done. She had already managed to strike him in the arm. You should have heard her when she told him he would soon be in hell. Had I not been riding by and heard the widow's screams I am certain the mercenary would now be lying cold and dead among the trees with arrows sticking out of his various parts."

Looking up from the castle plans spread over the table in his chamber, Renaud watched Geoff pace the room. It was clear this servant girl had gained the respect of his most senior knight. He sat back. "Why was Sarah in the woods?" She should not have been alone. Anything could have happened to her. The mercenary might have found her instead of the other woman.

"She was hunting rabbits for the cook. Apparently she recovered her bow from among those we had stored in the armory. I suppose that was a good thing."

"The girl hunts?" Renaud raised a brow. He knew she had been trained by the bard to handle a bow, but he had thought it was only for sport.

"Maggie says she does, though I had not really thought much about it 'til now. 'Tis most unusual for a serving wench."

"Yea, but she was one of the servants Sir Maurin recovered that first night. Sarah told me a Welshman the old lord invited here taught many to use the bow, including her. I had not realized she hunted as well."

"I've not seen servants taught archery," Geoff said, drawing his brows together. "The thegn must have been an unusual man."

"We know he was. But why was the widow in the woods alone?"

"She came to let you know she has remained in the west manor she occupied with her husband. From what she told me, Sir Hugue dragged her from her horse."

The thought of any woman being dragged from a horse and made to suffer the lust of one of his knights sent Renaud into a rage. "Damn the mercenary! He knows the rules."

"Eawyn told me her husband was killed with the English who fought the Norwegian, Harald Hardrada, at Stamford Bridge."

"Does she also bear hatred for Normans?" He would not be surprised given what she'd experienced. Even if the widow's husband had not been slain by a Norman, Renaud was keenly aware the English blamed them for all that had happened since Hastings, and now she had been nearly raped by one of his own.

"From what I can tell, Eawyn is a gentle lady and, unlike the servant girl Sarah, not given to strident disdain for her new masters."

"Sir Hugue has not long been with us, has he?" Renaud wondered what punishment would satisfy the lady and his own need for justice.

"Yea, not long. I do not trust him, Ren. He knew your rules—they all do. He simply chose to ignore them."

"Where is he now?"

"In the hall with Sir Maurin and some of the men. His wound has been tended."

"I take no joy in losing a man, even a mercenary, and a hundred stripes on the back of a fool availith little. But he must serve as an example to those who would question my orders, especially when it comes to the honor of Talisand's women. 'Twas my honor he besmirched as well as hers, since I assured the women they would be safe."

"Your knights know why you feel as you do. They do not question your rules and, at the risk of the Red Wolf's ire, none would challenge them. But there are not enough whores at Talisand to satisfy their lust. That is why they work so hard to win the affections of the young women in the village. Many hope to marry and settle here."

That his men wanted to stay at Talisand pleased him. "I shall discipline the mercenary." Renaud set aside his drawings and rose. "Come, let us see to this unpleasant task."

* * *

Serena looked up as the murmurings of the Normans came to a sudden halt when the Red Wolf strode through the doorway leading from the manor into the hall. His face bore a thunderous expression, and his hands were curled into fists at his side. She could feel the anger flowing from him, and stepped back, curious to see what he would do to one of his own who had disobeyed his command. Despite her intention to hate the new lord of Talisand, she was glad for his anger, his confident manner and the deferential nods from his men. They would not question his discipline.

The hall was crowded with knights and a few of the strong men of Talisand, including Leppe, Alec and Theodric, the blond giant who had been her father's captain. She was glad he had stayed, though she knew it was difficult for him to serve a Norman. But he had a family to think of.

Serena had asked Sir Geoffroi if she and Eawyn could be present. Reluctant at first to grant her request, Serena had pleaded with him, saying Eawyn had a right to know what would happen to the knight who tried to violate her. Sir Geoffroi had relented.

The Red Wolf stepped briskly to where Sir Hugue stood, guarded by Sir Maurin, who had carried Serena back to the manor that first night.

"Sir Hugue," began the Red Wolf, "you have violated a standard to which I hold all of my men. If Sir Geoffroi had not discovered your attack on the young widow, had you succeeded, the penalty would have been death."

Sir Hugue paled in the face of his lord's wrath.

"William himself has decreed such before," stated the Red Wolf. "Still, while you will not forfeit your life for what fell short of your vile intent, you will be punished. Twenty lashes and you will leave Talisand, never to return. I refuse to count among my knights a man without honor."

Sir Hugue's eyes flamed in rebellion but he held his tongue. In the faces of the Norman knights, Serena saw acceptance of their leader's judgment, even respect. She was confident there would be no second chance for this defiler of women. And with that knowledge came another revelation. For the second time, Serena wondered at the powerful knight to whom she had been given by the Norman king. The Red Wolf's uncompromising character had stirred a feeling inside her that she did not comprehend. Mayhap it was the same respect displayed by his men. Mayhap it was more. Those same tingling feelings she'd experienced when he stroked her palm returned. Against her will, she was drawn to the uncompromising knight. Yet at the same time, she wondered what punishment he would mete out for her, who had deceived him and denied him the wife he was due.

Sir Maurin took Sir Hugue by the arm and, with another knight, led him toward the door to the yard where presumably the punishment would be carried out.

The Red Wolf turned to Eawyn, his eyes first pausing on Serena. "Eawyn, I am sorry for what has happened. I know you came but to speak with me. I welcome you."

Eawyn had calmed, but her cheeks were still flushed and stained with tears. Serena had taken her to the chamber above stairs and given her one of the Lady Serena's gowns to replace the one that was ruined, explaining to the others that Lady Serena would have done no less. Sir Geoffroi stood on Eawyn's other side lending the young woman his strength as she leaned close to him.

"Thank you, my lord," Eawyn said to the Red Wolf. "I did but want to tell you I was living in the west manor should you have need of it for your knights."

"You can stay there for the present, Eawyn, but I will have one of my men escort you back. Do you dwell there alone?"

"Nay, my lord. I have a female servant who works at the manor, a stable boy and men who dwell nearby and tend the fields and see to the stock. The men have all sworn fealty to you. I know I should not have come to Talisand alone, but I had done so before, and I did not want to take the men from their work as they plant the new wheat."

He nodded and turned to Sir Geoffroi. "See that one of the men escorts the lady back to the west manor."

"Would it be acceptable, my lord, if I undertook the task?" asked the blond knight.

Serena did not miss the tenderness in Sir Geoffroi's eyes as he glanced at Eawyn. She remembered his kindness to her friend in the clearing.

The Red Wolf gave his knight a curious glance before nodding. "As you wish, Sir Geoffroi."

* * *

Tired, Renaud climbed the stairs to his chamber, every muscle in his body tense from the trials of the day. The duties of being lord of Talisand were ones he readily accepted, even looked forward to, but they did not allow him the single focus that warfare did. It was a different kind of fatigue, not so much bone weary as mind weary, and it left its mark.

When he reached his chamber, the door was ajar. Thinking it might be his young squire's doing, he pushed it open and surveyed the room, looking for Mathieu's brown head of hair. The usually dark chamber was aglow with light from candles set on each of the tables and rush lights near the bed. Renaud was instantly wary. It was not Mathieu's habit to spend the candles so freely.

His eyes were drawn to the bed cover, which had been turned down. Resting upon it was a woman, the same dark-eyed wench who served him wine at the evening meal.

"What are you doing here?" he asked. As he said the words, he realized the question was unnecessary. The woman was in his bed, her dark hair splayed over the pillow and her breasts barely covered by the thin undertunic she wore. Her intent was easily discerned.

"I thought ye might want some company m'lord."

"Where is Mathieu?"

"I sent him away, thinking ye might prefer to be private."

She rose up and sat back on her heels, the effect being to push her breasts out in blatant offering.

The woman was attractive and clearly had seduction in mind. But she held no appeal. Mayhap it was her dark eyes. There was only one woman at Talisand he wanted in his bed and her eyes were the color of violets.

"I appreciate your offer, Aethel…is it? But not tonight."

"Yea, m'lord, I be Aethel." She climbed off the bed, and came to stand in front of him, reaching her palm to his chest. "Ye're a fine man, m'lord. I would be proud to warm yer bed. Are ye certain ye'll not be wanting me this night?"

Her scent of heavy spices wrapped around him like a cape as she sensually slid her palm up his chest to his neck. He stopped her progress, pulling her arm from his body. "Quite certain."

A knock sounded on the door. Renaud was relieved, hoping his squire had returned. After the day he'd had, he had no desire to deal with the schemes of this woman. But when he opened the door, Sarah stood before him.

Merde!

Sarah's gaze shifted from his face to where Aethel stood to the side. Renaud clamped his teeth on another oath.

Averting her gaze, Sarah said, "Forgive me, my lord. I was told Mathieu had need of me."

Before he could ask her to stay, she hurried away, her cheeks flaming in what he assumed was embarrassment at the scene she had witnessed.

A feeling of regret washed over him. He sighed and turned to the scantily clad woman "Out!"

Disappointment and anger flashed in Aethel's dark eyes as she grabbed the robe she had draped over a chest and stomped toward the door.

Reaching for the handle, she looked back over her shoulder. "She will nay have ye, m'lord."

"Of whom do you speak?"

"Sarah, m'lord. She hates all Normans."

"Aethel?"

"Yea, m'lord?"

"Never come to my chamber again."

Without another word, the woman departed, briskly closing the door behind her.

Renaud poured himself a goblet of wine, took a large swallow and slumped onto the edge of his bed. What was it about women that produced such different reactions? Aethel, who came willingly, though uninvited, to his bed, and Sarah, who he was certain would deny him even a kiss? It might be because Sarah was still a maiden, but he knew it was more. Sarah was a proud *English* maiden who had no love for his kind. He was certain Aethel would not care about a man's origins if he pleased her in bed. But to Sarah, the Red Wolf was the Norman who, along with his liege, had conquered her people.

So, why was he so attracted to her? It was not her dull brown hair, or her attitude, though it might be her violet eyes and her lithe form. What man would fail to be attracted to her lush curves? Even her servant's attire did not hide them. But there was something more—something in the way she held herself, the way she looked him in the eye as if they were equals, and her courage in facing down the mercenary. She was like no woman he knew. After the women of William's court, the novelty of a woman like Sarah, even though a servant, was refreshing.

* * *

"I believe I am in love," said Geoff as he took his place next to Renaud at the dais the next day, a blissful smile on his face.

Renaud considered his friend. He had a dazed look about him like he was waking from a dream. "And what, or should I say, *who* has brought about this revelation?"

"Eawyn insisted I stay for a meal and the food she prepared was better than that at Rouen. It did not lack for being served by such a lovely woman either…hair the color of a raven's wing and eyes like a summer sky. She invited me to stay the night." Renaud could not hide his surprise. Seeing it, Geoff added, "In an alcove reserved for guests, of course. Yea, I think it must be love."

"I see. Well, if you can shake yourself from the dream, Geoff, I want you to plan an archery contest for the morrow. I would see my archers compete with those trained by the Welshman, including any of Talisand's women who would want to participate." He had not forgotten that Sarah used a bow.

"The men would like that, Ren. It will give them a chance to demonstrate their prowess as archers and interact with the younger women. Will you compete?"

"I am not an archer."

"Yea, but neither is Sir Maurin, and the two of you could best any of them."

"I suppose I could use the practice. But I plan to watch, too. I am interested to see how the shorter bows the Welshman fashioned for the women fare against the longer ones. It will also allow us to judge how many of the Englishmen can be considered candidates to join my archers."

"'Tis a grand idea, Ren. It will be a welcome diversion and may serve to provide some entertainment for the people."

* * *

The next day, Serena stood with Cassie at the gate watching as the Red Wolf's men posted three targets outside the palisade and marked out a line with flags, indicating the place from which the archers would shoot. Normally such a sight would cause her to feel great excitement, but instead she was wary. The Red Wolf had invited all at Talisand to participate, giving notice there would be rewards for those scoring the highest points. *What was his purpose?*

"Will ye join in the contest?" Cassie asked, holding her hand over her eyes to shelter her gaze from the midday sun. "Ye could best any of the Red Wolf's men. Ye know ye could. Ye are even better than Leppe and he is the best."

"Lady Serena may shoot well, but she is not here, Cassie. Remember? I will encourage Leppe to compete, but I am thinking Sarah is only a fair shot. After all, Sir Geoffroi thought I missed my target when I sent that arrow into the mercenary's arm. No, the servant Sarah will pose no threat to the Red Wolf's men or their display of skill. Yea, I will participate."

A grin spread across Cassie's face, a younger version of her mother's with the same green eyes save they were framed by her father's red hair. "Ye're a devious one, Sarah."

"Mayhap I am," Serena said with a faint smile. "But in this case I must act consistent with my disguise, else I be discovered."

Cassie told Serena that a score and one had entered their names in the archery tournament: fifteen of the Red Wolf's men, including the Norman lord himself, and six from Talisand: Leppe, Theodric, Alec and three women. Rhodri had taught many more but, regrettably, only the six had the skills necessary to compete.

As the match began, Serena felt a slight wind stirring wisps of her hair, but it was naught a skilled archer would fail to consider.

The first round included Cassie, Theodric, and Sir Maurin, who Cassie had bragged was a skilled archer.

Theodric went first, his shot hitting at the edge of the red center. Serena smiled, pleased to see him do well. Cassie went next. Her arrow, though close, fell short of the target's center. Serena thought her handmaiden's anxious looks at Sir Maurin might have thrown off her aim. Finally, Sir Maurin stepped to the line, his weathered face void of emotion as he studied the wind moving in the trees. Then, with a confident look, he let his arrow fly, the shot piercing the red center. Many "Ahs" were heard from the crowd, but the people of Talisand who crowded around did not smile as they had for Theodric.

The next round matched Alec and a woman from Talisand against the Red Wolf. Serena's eyes fixed on the proud Norman knight as he sauntered to the line. Pulling back on the arrow as if 'twere nothing, he sent the shaft soaring. It hit dead center with a loud thwack. The crowd let out a sigh. Unfortunately, the Talisand archers, who followed the Red Wolf, were unable to sink their arrows into the center of the target.

Other rounds followed. In his round, Leppe's arrow found dead center, and Serena silently cheered. He had always been the best of Talisand's archers taught by Rhodri, save possibly for herself, but she had practiced much.

The Norman archers who followed did well, some consistently hitting the target.

When it came time for her to shoot, Serena stepped to the line. She nocked the arrow and focused her eyes on the target, her stance sure. The crowd grew quiet as the villagers waited to see what their lady would do. She worried over their reaction and what it might reveal. She had not taken into account their anticipation.

Serena stood, legs apart, and pulled back the arrow, changing her line of sight at the last minute to focus on the edge of the target, not its center. When she let the arrow fly, a whooshing sound filled the silence. The thwack of the arrow as it hit the wide edge of the target echoed through the air. The stunned crowd looked on.

A clear miss.

She stepped back into the crowd, smiling to herself—until she saw Maugris nearby, his blue eyes staring intently at her.

Wiping the smile from her face, she scurried away. The old Norman's gaze haunted her. It was as if he could see right through her. Dismissing her worries, she hurried to find Cassie so they could watch the last rounds together when the best archers of the day faced off.

Two more rounds eliminated all but four: Leppe, Sir Maurin, the Red Wolf and another of the Norman archers. Each took a shot at the target. Each hit the center.

"Move the target back twenty paces!" shouted Sir Geoffroi from the sidelines.

The target was moved back and each man took up his stance. The shots that followed were fired in rapid succession. The small wind picked up to rustle the leaves of the trees nearby. Serena was disappointed to see Leppe's arrow hit off center this time, but was mollified when the Norman archer's shot also fell short of the center circle. Only the Red Wolf and Sir Maurin remained. Their shots again hit the center of the target. This time, even the faces of the villagers bore smiles.

Upon the order of the Red Wolf, the target was moved back another twenty paces. The tension grew palpable as all eyes fixed on the two men standing next to each other, their eyes focused on the distant target.

Cassie bit her lower lip and her hand gripped Serena's forearm. "'Tis exciting, no?" whispered her handmaiden.

"Yea, it is. I only wish Leppe was still in the competition. I'd like to see him beat the Normans."

Sir Maurin shot first. With a whoosh, his arrow flew to hit the center. The crowd sighed in unison, "Ah…."

"See if you can split the shaft," urged Sir Geoffroi from behind the Red Wolf loud enough for Serena to hear.

The Norman lord took a deep breath. For a long moment he watched the leaves of the trees, moved by the rising wind. Then, he narrowed his eyes on the target like a beast focusing on its prey. "Aye, I shall."

With a whoosh, his arrow flew and a cracking sound echoed through the open meadow as the Red Wolf's arrowhead split the shaft of Sir Maurin's arrow. The crowd gasped.

With a small smile, the Red Wolf turned to Sir Maurin. "Would you try again?"

"Nay, my lord." Sir Maurin bowed in grand gesture. "I concede and congratulate you."

* * *

Renaud walked toward the place where he was to give out the prizes, his pace slower than usual as he pondered the servant girl Sarah. She had been quick to hurry away from the shooting line when her arrow failed to achieve the target's center. But something about the whole scene bothered him.

As if reading his thoughts, Geoff leaned in to whisper. "Ren, why do I have the feeling Sarah is better with the bow than her performance today would suggest?"

Renaud remembered the faces of the crowd gathered to watch the match. "Mayhap it is because the English held their breath as she stepped to the line, as if they expected something unusual."

Geoff's brow wrinkled in confusion. "What is your meaning?"

Renaud paused in his stride and looked at the blond knight. "When she first began to shoot, they held their breath. I think they expected a show. With her shot, their faces bore stunned disappointment. You had only to look at them."

Geoff turned toward the mingling crowd of villagers, servants and children who had come to witness the competition. "Ah...I remember now. They walked away with downcast eyes. But Ren, though I did not doubt her intent to kill Sir Hugue, even rising to defend another woman's honor, she missed, hitting only his arm."

"You may be right. Still, it is curious. Mayhap she refused to do her best in front of her Norman conquerors." Renaud rubbed his chin in contemplation. He was certain the girl could do better than she had. And if that were so, why had she held back?

They resumed their stride toward the place where the prizes were to be given.

Geoff wondered aloud. "If the girl has a talent with the bow, why would she hide it when there was a chance to make us Normans look the fools? She has no fondness for us."

"Why indeed? I know not, but I intend to find out. This will not be the last shooting match at Talisand."

Just then, a lad with golden hair streaked across Renaud's path. He called out to the boy. "Say there, lad, come here."

The boy looked up at the two knights, his smile telling Renaud he was eager to please. "Yea, sir?"

"What is your name, boy?"

"I am called Jamie."

"Jamie, can you tell me, of those the Welshman trained to the bow, who is the best?"

"Oh, that would be Lady Serena, sir. Rhodri said her arm is so fast 'tis as if the bow is part of her, as if they are one. She is both fast and sure. Serena never misses." Pride gleamed in the young boy's eyes as he spoke of his lady.

Renaud frowned. The lad's mention of Lady Serena only reminded Renaud the woman who was to be his bride had defied William's order, a lady of many talents it seems, including escape. He remembered Maugris had also said Lady Serena was good with a bow.

One of the mercenaries Renaud had dispatched was already winding his way through Scotland in search of the lady, a man who spoke both English and Gaelic. Yet it would be some time before he could expect a message.

He thanked the boy and watched him walk away, relieved there were some among his new villeins who did not hate Normans. He and Geoff approached the table set with the awards to be given, and Renaud shoved thoughts of Lady Serena to the recesses of his mind. "How many of the Englishmen could stand with our archers?" he asked Geoff.

"Based on today's performance, I would venture at least two, and possibly with more time and training, the other one who competed."

"See that those you consider candidates are invited to train with my archers. When William next calls upon us, we shall take the proficient ones with us. Now I must see to the prizes. I will pass my own to Sir Maurin."

CHAPTER 6

The rider approached the gate as Serena watched from the roof walk. She had gone to the roof that morning to think, as she often did when the knights engaged in their swordplay outside the palisade, and had spotted the familiar head of dark curls, the Welsh pony and the small harp and bow dangling from the saddle. Her heart leapt in her chest.

Rhodri!

Lifting her tunic, she ran down the stairs leading from the roof to a small landing on the outside of the manor and then down another set of stairs to the ground. She raced across the yard and out the gate guarded by the Red Wolf's men.

When she reached the rider on the pony, she whispered, "Rhodri, I will see you through the gate. Say nothing until you hear me out."

"What are you up to, my lady? And why are you dressed in such manner and your hair that awful color?"

"Shssh!" she hissed, as she led his horse forward. To the Norman guard she smiled sweetly and said, "Sir, 'tis an old friend of Talisand, a bard to entertain us."

The guard's harsh eyes examined the Welshman, pausing on the harp. He nodded and waved them on. By now the Red Wolf's men knew her, unaware her recent pleasantries were only an act.

Serena walked alongside Rhodri's horse leading him to the far side of the yard where they could talk without being overheard.

He reined in his pony, and she looked up at him. "I am in disguise, Rhodri, as you can plainly see. The Normans have come to Talisand at the Bastard's command, and I am hiding among them. Do not give me away. I am the servant Sarah."

"Fine," he said casting his gaze over the yard at the Normans who had

51

not been there before and then back to Serena. "But welcome me. I have traveled far to come to Talisand and I have missed you sorely, Ser...Sarah." He dropped from the saddle to stand next to her, looking directly into her eyes for they were the same height. She gave him a warm embrace. He grinned and his dark curls tossed about his handsome face. A well-trimmed mustache and clipped beard only made him more attractive. "I have heard your father was slain at Hastings. I am sorry."

Serena's eyes filled with tears and her arms dropped to her side. "Aye, Rhodri, the old thegn you loved was slain at Senlac Hill with King Harold. Steinar has fled from yet another encounter with the Normans to find refuge with some of his men in Scotland. I intended to join him but I left too late. Alas, the Normans found us as we traveled north and brought us back. That is why I am here now."

"They do not know who you are?"

"Nay."

"Steinar will be worried you are not safely in Scotland."

"I had planned to follow after him," she added hopefully.

"Then why do you remain?"

"I have stayed to be certain the people of Talisand are being treated well." Even as she said it, Serena wondered if there was not another reason. She was curious about the Red Wolf.

"Have any of the Normans touched you?" he asked with a look of concern.

"Nay, thank God. They leave the women alone by the command of their lord, the one they call the Red Wolf."

"Ah, I have heard of the knight who wears the wolf's pelt. He is a favorite of their king. So...the Red Wolf is *here*? That I must see."

"He has been given Talisand, Rhodri."

The bard frowned. "Steinar will not be pleased to hear of it."

He spoke the truth but Serena could not linger on the loss of their lands when what she wanted was to gain them back. Taking his arm, she said, "Come, I will see your horse is tended and then I will see you fed." A sudden happiness rose within her at having Rhodri back at Talisand. For the first time in a long while there was a smile on her face. "It is so good to have you with us again!"

* * *

Renaud looked up as Sarah entered his room, a stack of fresh linens in her arms and a smile on her face. He had not seen her smile before and wondered at the source of her mirth. He had been going over the final changes to the plans for the new stable and, though he would have denied it had Geoff asked, he was waiting for her.

"Good day to you, Sarah."

She started, clearly surprised to see him. Mayhap she had thought to sneak into his chamber while he was gone. He often sparred with his knights at this hour. "My lord, shall I return at a later time?" She turned toward the door.

"No!" Then in a softer voice lest he betray his interest, he added, "I would have you stay. Will you join me in some wine?" He poured the red liquid into a goblet and extended it toward her.

The girl's eyes immediately focused on the floor. "Nay, my lord, but thank you. It would nay be proper."

He considered making it an order but relented. She was always polite, this one. Too polite for one who clearly disliked Normans. He had allowed her to be distant for the last few days. Now it was time to court the kitten, to see if she would keep her claws sheathed as the warrior advanced.

She carried the linens to the bed and began to take off the old bedding. Her movements were innocently seductive, her shape barely hidden in the loose tunic that did not even cover her ankles. He rose and walked to stand behind her, trailing a finger down the soft skin of her nape under her plait. She quavered. His groin swelled in anticipation.

"Did you enjoy the archery contest, Sarah?"

Slowly she turned to face him. He stepped closer. He knew she would back away if she could, but the bed was behind her leaving her nowhere to go, which had been his intention.

She looked up at him. "I did, my lord."

He wrapped his hands around her upper arms and brought her closer still. Her full lips opened as if in protest, and he saw alarm in her eyes. "Sarah, why did I have the feeling it was not your best performance?"

She tried to wriggle out of his grip. "My lord, I ask you to unhand me."

"Not just yet. Answer me." His grip was firm but he was careful not to hurt her. He began to run his hands up and down her arms from shoulder to elbow in a slow sensuous movement. He could feel her body relax despite what he assumed was her intention to remain rigid as he gazed into her eyes. They had changed to the purple of the night sky.

"I do not always hit the target, my lord. But I do enjoy the sport," she replied breathlessly.

"And you shall have your reward." He pulled her into his chest and his lips quickly descended to hers. Her mouth was soft and as sweet as he'd expected. He was careful to make the kiss tender so as not to frighten her. He could afford time for a slow seduction. But he had not considered that her lips would be so inviting or so warm. It nearly undid him. "Ah…Sarah," he breathed into her luscious mouth and then let his tongue slide over her full bottom lip. "Your taste is sweet nectar to this starving man."

When she opened her mouth to speak, he slid his tongue inside, using all his self-control not to plunder but to slowly kiss her into mindless submission. He was pleased when she softened beneath his touch, responding despite what he surmised had been her determination to resist. He wanted to take her then, to lay her back on the bed and find their pleasure, but he was certain that would draw from her a vehement objection. He could be patient. At least for a while.

When he ended the kiss, Sarah blinked twice and then pushed at his chest with her hand. "My lord! I am not a wench to be trifled with. Is not Aethel enough for you?"

He had expected her comment about the dark-haired serving woman. He delighted in what appeared to be her woman's jealousy. "I am not trifling, woman. I told you from the first that I want you in my bed. Your body tells me you want me as well. Do you not feel it?"

"I feel nothing!" she protested, though from her passion glazed eyes and kiss-swollen lips he knew she lied.

"I think you do. I like the feel of you in my arms, Sarah. Why do you resist so?"

"I am an English maiden, my lord. There can be nothing between me and a Norman, unless you would take me by force, which you have vowed not to do."

Growing irritated with her continued refusal and her reminder of his promise to the women, he stepped back. Never before had his resolve to protect the virtue of women been so sorely tested. Studying her angry violet eyes, he controlled his voice. "We shall see."

Tamping down his desire and forcing his body to calm, he returned to the trestle table. When he did not hear her footsteps, he looked up to see her still standing by the bed, staring at nothing as if she did not know what to do. He flicked his fingers in dismissal.

"You may go about your work, Sarah. I shall not pursue you again this day."

* * *

Several days later, Renaud sat in the hall, his eyes fixed on Geoff's mouth as the knight engulfed a thick slice of bread dripping with butter and honey. "You keep eating like that, Geoff, and you will be as round as our cook."

"I need my strength for the ride to the west manor."

Renaud rolled his eyes. "So soon you would return?"

"With your permission, I intend to call upon the widow Eawyn this day to see how she fares."

Renaud chuckled. "She is a lovely woman. You could do worse than that one. And fortunate it is for you she comes with a manor house."

A surprised expression crossed Geoff's face. "You would give me the lady *and* the manor?"

"I might." Renaud could feel the corners of his mouth turn up. He slapped his fellow knight on the back. "You seem bewitched by the woman's beauty—and her cooking. I am of a mind to reward you for all those years you have ridden at my side."

Geoff paused, holding the bread in front of his open mouth. A drop of honey fell to his trencher. "I hardly know what to say, Ren. 'Tis a great boon."

"It carries a condition, of course. I would expect you to come at my call if ever I have need of your sword. Mayhap when the castle is completed, you might finish your courtship and we could celebrate both the castle and a wedding. Does the timing appeal?"

"Yea, Ren, it does." Geoff fairly glowed with his fervent ardor for the young widow. "If the lady could be made willing, I would make her mine. Her husband was nay killed by Normans, so it is possible I do not offend with my interest."

"In time I'm certain you can charm her from her widow's state, but before you leave to see Eawyn, I have a few tasks for you, my well-fed friend. And, mind your sudden taste for bread spread with honey. Maggie tells me someone has been sneaking into the kitchen at night depleting her supply."

Geoff looked down at the bread, thick with honey, still in his hand. Renaud detected a look of guilt. Neither said a word, for no words were necessary.

Renaud finished his meal and with Geoff trailing behind, stepped into the yard. The day promised to be fair after the night's rain. Renaud spotted the boy with the pale blond hair and ruddy cheeks he had spoken with at the archery contest. The lad was sitting on a cask next to the manor poking a stick into the soft dirt.

"Jamie."

The boy looked up at the sound of his name then leapt to his feet, dropping his stick.

"Is not that your name, lad?" Renaud asked, stopping in front of him.

"Aye, m'lord. May I be of service to ye?"

Renaud smiled at the boy's eager desire to please and reached down to muss his curly blond hair. "Jamie, I might be in need of a page. Would you like the position?"

"Yea, m'lord! I would!" The boy was nearly dancing he was so excited. The look on his face told Renaud he had offered the lad a much-desired prize.

"Can you point out your parents so I may speak to them?"

"I have no parents, m'lord," the boy said with downcast eyes. "Sarah watches out for me and sees I am fed and have clothes."

It was as he'd suspected. He had seen the boy with the servant girl but no mother or father. So, Sarah had a young charge whose needs she met. She might hate Normans but she could be kind to young English lads.

"Well then, I will speak to Sarah, but I am certain she will approve. Being a page is the first step to becoming a knight. Go see Mathieu, my squire, and tell him of your new position. He will assign you tasks and see you have proper clothing. Unless you are in work clothes, you will wear the wolf on your tunic."

"Thank ye, sir!" The boy's eyes shone as he turned and ran toward the armory.

"Do you know where you are going lad?" Renaud called after him.

The boy stopped and turned. "Aye, sir. I watch yer squire clean yer armor each day."

"Well, then, be off with you." Renaud's eyes followed the boy as he hurried off.

"That was kind of you, Ren," said Geoff. "You bestow an honor on the lad far above his station. Better take care or the people will think the Red Wolf has a soft heart."

"I have watched him each day with nothing to do but a few chores, and no one to care for him except Sarah, who walks with him to the stables. If he can be groomed to become a squire, one day he might be a loyal knight. I like the lad. And he seems intelligent enough."

* * *

Serena looked into the yard from the roof walk where she observed the knights talking to Jamie. She could not hear their words but she noted the Red Wolf run his hands through the boy's sun bleached locks as if teasing him. The Norman was proving to be different than the cold, cruel knight she had envisioned. Often arrogant, and at times short with his words, he held to a code of honor she grudgingly admired. Though his coming had stripped her people of their freedom and their rights under Anglo-Saxon laws, he had not taxed them overmuch. At least not yet. She knew when the work on the castle began he would compel

Talisand's men to build it. Such a task would not go down well with her people.

She grew angry at the reminder he had all of Talisand under his thumb. Yet she remembered his gentleness when he'd kissed her, a kiss she was trying hard to forget. She remembered the heat of his powerful body when he held her close. She had wanted him to touch her. Yet she hated her attraction to the powerful Norman knight for he was her enemy.

And now he was being kind to the boy she loved.

* * *

"Would it be so bad to be the Norman's wife, to again be the Lady of Talisand?" Cassie asked softly, looking at Serena with hopeful eyes. Serena had gone to help her friend in the folding of linens in the back room of the washing area where they were alone for the moment. "He seems an honorable knight, even if he is a Norman, and a bit…fearsome. He's so *tall*. Even Sir Maurin is nay so tall."

Serena stared at her friend, disbelieving. "Cassie! That 'honorable knight' you find frightening is among the men who killed my father and our King Harold and ravaged half of England. I cannot believe you would have me wed one of them. Have you forgotten they have taken our land by force? Slain thousands of Saxon men *and* women? And now he claims the people of Talisand as his serfs!"

"Nay, I havna forgotten, but ye canna change the past, m'lady. Ye must look to the future. I say this as yer friend. The Red Wolf is the new lord and there be a new king in England who, though he is a Norman, seems to be staying whether we like it or no. Ye'll want bairns one day, no?" Not waiting for Serena's answer, the handmaiden continued. "Talisand will need an heir, and it willna come from Steinar as we had thought."

"I'd not have a Norman heir for Talisand, Cassie."

"Would a bairn of yers born in England be a Norman?"

Serena pondered her handmaiden's words. "He'd be at least half Norman."

"If the tales we heard be true, there will be many bairns born in England this year who are only half English. At least ye would have the status of wife—and a countess. Many of those mothers have no husbands at all and will bear only Norman bastards."

"Oh, Cassie. I am still hoping to escape to Scotland and join Steinar. Rhodri tells me many English have fled across the border, waiting to fight the Normans. Good and true men who have not surrendered all. He says it was fear of an uprising that brought the Norman king back from Normandy late last year. Why should I give in if there is still hope? The Red Wolf's knights do not even speak our language!"

"They are making an effort," insisted Cassie. "Sir Maurin's understanding of English has improved much." Setting down the cloth she was folding, the handmaiden said wistfully, "He has been verra kind to me."

Though the Norman knights and men-at-arms were making an effort to learn the English tongue, mostly to speak to the young women and give orders to the old thegn's men, Serena recalled they spent evenings in the hall drinking Talisand's ale and telling jokes in their own language. Her knowledge of the Norman tongue had given her the ability to understand much of what they said. Many times she had grimaced at their ribald jokes and their slurs against the Saxons they had defeated in the south. Each night she tried to convince herself it was England, not Normandy, she was living in.

"I have seen Sir Maurin smile at you, Cassie...would you marry one of them?"

Cassie looked off into the distance. "I might. I, too, want bairns, m'lady. Sir Maurin is older than the others, 'tis true, and his face shows signs of a hard life, but he is a man with a good heart. And though he is a knight, he does nay seem to mind I am not high born. Besides, there are nay any others at Talisand left that I would wed."

"But there are many who would have you as wife, Cassie."

With the death of many of Talisand's young men at Hastings, her lovely handmaiden had fewer choices, though many who remained lusted after the redhead. That her father was the beefy blacksmith kept them at bay. Serena wanted to see her friend wed and happy. Raised together, they were more like sisters than lady and servant. She enjoyed Cassie's honest bantering. Very much her mother's daughter, Cassie freely spoke her mind.

Serena stared at the dust motes in the sunlight pouring in through the open door while her hands worked independently to fold the drying cloths. Her mind drifted to the past and to a time when a tall English guard who worked for her father had captured her interest. For a while, they had walked the river bank together in the afternoons. He'd even stolen a kiss once. Oswine was killed at Hastings defending his thegn. Though it had been the love of a young girl, it might have grown into more in time. Alas, she would never know.

She thought it was probably inevitable that some of Talisand's women would marry Normans. God knew there were widows enough. But if she were to accept the fate the Norman king had willed for her, it would be a sign to all she had given up the fight for England and for Talisand. She shook her head and set her lips in a thin line. *No, I will not do it.*

"If ye willna have a Norman, m'lady, even the new lord, what about young Morcar? When he was still Earl of Northumbria, wasna he one of the men yer father was considering for yer hand? A most handsome and charming man to me memory."

"Aye, Morcar is fair of face and charming, but he has only a few years more than me." She was thinking of the Red Wolf who was older and more virile than the younger Mercian, who she remembered with fondness. The Mercian had paid several visits to her father before he had gone to fight against the King of Norway but her father had not promised her hand to him. Morcar laughed easily and his people loved him, but she did not. Even if she had wanted to wed him, could she do so when she had been given to the Norman lord? "And he lost his lands with the coming of the Normans."

"I often wonder what might have happened," said Cassie thoughtfully, "if he and his brother had not been so eager to rid themselves of King Harold. They held back their men, hoping, I believe, the Normans would defeat Harold at Hastings. With the men Morcar and his brother could have called to fight, we might have driven the Normans back into the sea."

"More important, Cassie, would they fight now?"

"Sir Maurin told me that Morcar and his older brother, Edwin, still the Earl of Mercia, have submitted to the Norman king."

"If 'tis true," said Serena, "I doubt Edwin is sincere. He cannot love serving such a one."

"I suppose ye are right," Cassie said sadly.

"Even if Morcar were to defy the Norman king," Serena speculated, "I cannot imagine him taking me to wife with Talisand given to the Bastard's knight. I no longer have a dowry."

"But he cared for ye, m'lady. I remember the way he looked at ye."

"So much has changed," lamented Serena. "While an English woman cannot be forced to wed a man she'll not have, it is not so with the Normans. The Norman king can force me to accept the Red Wolf if I am discovered. He has only to consummate the relationship." The thought caused Serena to shiver. "Then, too, Morcar is young and impatient. He may have set his eyes on another."

"Morcar is a Mercian," Cassie encouraged. "That has to mean something. It was his brother Edwin who posed the idea of a match between the two of ye to yer father. Me mother heard them talking."

"It was to make me happy my father delayed a betrothal."

"Yea," said Cassie, "and to satisfy a lonely man's heart. Me mother told me he'd not send ye away before he must."

Serena had thought little of Morcar in the past months. In truth, with the coming of the Red Wolf, thoughts of any other man rarely came to her mind. She had not forgotten the kiss the Norman had stolen. Or the feel of his hard chest pressed against her breasts. He was a seasoned warrior, virile and strong. By his sword, the Red Wolf had gained a place of favor with the Norman king and was admired by his men. He seemed so much more a man than the young Mercian earl or even Oswine.

The handmaiden's eyes suddenly grew bright. "What about Eadric? Yer father liked him well enough. I have heard our men talking about him. They say he was able to keep his lands in the south since he wasna at Hastings."

"I have heard the Normans speak of him in the hall, too," said Serena, thinking of the conversation she'd overheard. "They call him Eadric the Wild since he stays in the woods with his men, fighting some Norman to the south. The Welsh king supports him, according to Rhodri." Serena remembered Eadric, the wealthy Saxon thegn from Shropshire, who had come to Talisand seeking her hand. A tall warrior with broad shoulders and a full beard. "Though I cannot imagine Eadric would want to take a bride if he is living with his men in the woods. And, Cassie, if I were to come out in the open, as I must to wed Morcar or Eadric, think how the Red Wolf would react. He would be incensed at losing what he sees as his. Pride would demand he hunt me down, even if only to hold me prisoner. No, it would not do for me to marry a Saxon while still in England for I have been given by the Norman king to one of his own. You see? I must leave and seek my future in Scotland."

"Yea, I suppose 'tis true. I dinna want ye to go. But it seems yer only future at Talisand is as the Red Wolf's bride."

"I shall never choose to be his wife," Serena insisted, all the while shivering at the prospect, whether from anticipation or dread she could not say.

CHAPTER 7

Geoffroi was just leaving the stables the next day on his way to the hall, hungry for the midday meal, when he heard the boy Eric shouting to one of the cottars who had come to the manor to sell his wares. "Dunn, did ye hear the news? Rhodri has returned to Talisand!"

The cottar looked up from his cart of kettles. "Has he now? When?"

"A few days ago. He has said he will play for us tonight after the evening meal. Steward Hunstan told me all who would come are invited. 'Twill be almost like it was ere the Normans came."

By now Geoffroi knew enough English to understand their conversation. At his approach, the boy's face turned scarlet as he realized the Red Wolf's man overheard what he was saying. "Eric, are you talking about the Welsh bard who was here before?"

"Yea, sir." The boy's posture relaxed, possibly because he was grateful not to be scolded.

"I should like to hear this bard entertain us in the hall this eve. Is there a singer at Talisand who could join him?"

"Well…" he hesitated, "Sarah can sing. She and the bard often sang together."

"Indeed? You may tell Sarah her new master would have her sing with the bard tonight." Geoff had observed the way Ren looked at the servant girl. At least her singing would take his mind from the missing Lady Serena about whom he had brooded overmuch. And some entertainment for the men would not go amiss. "I will look forward to hearing her myself."

"I will tell her, sir. Ye willna be disappointed. She has the voice of an angel!"

* * *

Occupied with plans for the castle all afternoon, Renaud rose from the trestle table in his chamber, comfortable with his decision. He had finally chosen the site for the castle, though in truth the location had been in his mind all along. The same bend in the river that protected Talisand's manor would become the source of his castle's moat. And the motte that would rise from the yard to form the foundation for the timbered structure would look down on the manor. From the top of the new *donjon*, he and his men would have a view of the entire countryside.

A knock sounded, interrupting his musings.

"Enter."

His chamber door opened and Geoff strolled in. "Are you still wanting to review the changes to the stables?"

"Aye, I'm long ready."

"Then I've good news. The work is done. Sir Niel awaits your examination of the new building. I think you will be pleased. There is room for all the horses and the groom and stable boys."

"Splendid!" He strode to the door, eager for a chance to stretch his legs. "We will have need of it as I fear Talisand will have harsh winters."

Renaud descended the stairs, Geoff on his heels. Looking into the hall as they passed, Renaud saw the long tables crowded with knights and men-at-arms sitting down to the evening meal. He would delay his dinner to see the new stables.

The smell of freshly cut wood filled Renaud's nostrils as he entered the new structure, along with the scent of hay and horse, familiar smells to a knight.

"This will serve us well," he said to the young Sir Niel, standing inside the large open door where he waited for his lord. Niel had been Renaud's squire before Mathieu and knighted only a few years before Hastings. The scar on his jaw was a lasting reminder of his bravery in that battle, but with his light brown hair and blue eyes, he was still attractive to woman, mayhap more so.

Fresh hay had already been laid in the stalls and stable boys were leading in some of the horses. Renaud strolled down the middle aisle, taking in the new construction that provided more than a dozen timbered partitions on each side. As he walked along, his gaze drifted up to the second level where a large hayloft had been added.

"There's enough room above to house the stable boys," said Sir Niel, "and a separate chamber for the groom below."

Renaud rested his hand on the knight's shoulder. "The work appears sound, the structure proof against the cold drafts of winter. The men have done well."

"Your knights and their squires are content the horses will nay freeze come Christmastide, my lord," said a grinning Sir Niel.

Renaud nodded as Mathieu joined them. "I've already brought your horses in, my lord," said the squire. "They are fed and groomed and in the far stalls. We have oats aplenty."

"Good work, Mathieu. And where is my young page?"

"Polishing your sword and cleaning your shield, and before that he helped with the horses. He's a good lad, Jamie is."

"Aye, he is. See that you both eat. The meal has begun." Geoff cast a longing look toward the hall, causing Renaud to add, "And have Maggie send some food for Sir Geoffroi and me. We will eat here."

"Yea, sir." The squire dipped his head and took his slim body off toward the armory.

Renaud turned to Niel. "You as well. Go eat your supper. The groom and stable boys can answer any questions we might have." He wanted the opportunity to get to know the lads who'd been retained to care for the knights' horses.

"It feels like those times we rode with Duke William," said Geoff, when some while later, they sat on crates eating their meal.

"Aye, it seems a familiar pastime," agreed Renaud.

An hour later, Renaud had finished the meal Maggie had sent him. The rabbit stew had been tasty. And the conversation he and Geoff had shared with the stable lads had filled him with excitement. He would breed Belasco, his gray stallion, to some of the English horses for a stronger stable of horses.

Content the new stable met all his requirements, he stood to go. "You can release the carpenters to turn their attention to William's castle," he told Geoff. "Come, let us leave the lads to the horses. I have a craving for a drink."

"Aye, that would be most welcome."

Renaud crossed the yard, hearing faint music coming from the hall. Opening the door he was confronted with a voice from heaven itself. The hall was dark save for the light from the central hearth and the torches still burning at the edges of the large rectangular room. He and Geoff stood in the shadows, listening.

Aethel, who had apparently been watching for him, walked in their direction carrying tankards of ale. Her brown eyes conveyed the same invitation Renaud had seen before, but gaining no different reaction from him, she took her leave. Renaud drank deeply having grown accustomed to the dark brew and turned his attention to the picture before him.

Sarah sat on a stool in front of the hearth, singing in a foreign tongue.

It might be Welsh as he had heard the language before. Her long brown plait lay over one shoulder, drawing his attention as she inclined her head with the song. The light of the fire reflected on her face, rendering her skin the color of honey. Facing her, on another stool, sat a man with curly black hair and short-cropped beard. He was clothed in the colors of the forest over which he'd donned a brown leather jerkin. In his arms he held a small harp, his fingers moving rapidly over the strings as he plucked a lively tune.

A circle of children sat at their feet, many with chins resting in their upturned palms, their elbows braced on their crossed legs while they listened with rapt attention.

Sarah's voice lifted high then dipped low, sending notes flowing about the room like magical ribbons of sound. When the man's tenor voice joined hers, the two voices entwined like lovers as they smiled at the children and at each other.

Renaud watched transfixed. The servant girl was more beautiful, more animated than he had seen her before. Her hand reached out to caress the cheek of a child. There was love in her eyes. *She will make a good mother.*

Without turning his head, he asked Geoff, "Who is that singing with Sarah?"

"It must be the Welsh bard, Rhodri. I had heard he arrived and intended to provide us with entertainment. We were so consumed by the work on the stables I forgot to mention it. You remember, Ren. He is the one who was here before at the old lord's invitation. The boy Eric told me the girl had the voice of an angel. He was nay wrong."

"You understand the Welsh tongue—of what do they sing?"

"'Tis a traveling song. She sings of the beauty of the hills and valleys and the adventure of the road. He joins her, but sings of the love left behind."

Renaud could not dismiss the thought that troubled him. What servant would understand the Welsh tongue well enough to sing it? Had the bard taught her whilst their heads rested on the same pillow? He frowned. "It seems the Welshman taught the people more than the bow."

"'Tis a bit of talent he has," said Geoff. "I have never heard the ballad sung so well."

Renaud's eyes narrowed as he continued to gaze at the two singing, their heads close together like two lovers exchanging endearments. The Welshman gazed intently at Sarah, and she returned his regard. Clearly they shared a great affection for each other. So it was not only the old lord's son for whom she made room in her heart. Did she also make room for the Welshman in her bed? Notwithstanding her protests, he wondered if she was a maiden still. How could a woman so lovely be left alone for so long?

As her voice rose with the song, Sarah smiled at the children sitting at her feet. He had never seen her smile like that. It was a dazzling smile. She was beautiful, bewitching—happy. The lovely sound of her clear voice wrapped around him like a warm cloak, filling him with a sudden desire to possess her.

Renaud's body tensed like hard steel when he looked at the faces of his men. They were enthralled with the English servant girl, whose skin glowed in the firelight, and whose eyes danced with the song. A wave of jealousy flowed over him.

When the song ended and another began, Renaud set his face in firm resolve and turned to Geoff. "Ask the seneschal to send up my bath and some wine. When the singing ends, have Sarah sent to my room. I would have a word with her."

"Aye, Ren. I will see it done."

Geoff turned to carry out the orders, and Renaud said over his shoulder, "See that none of the men touch her."

* * *

Serena paused at the bottom of the stairs leading to the chambers above...to *his* chamber. It was late and she had never gone to his chamber at night. But refusing his command would only arouse suspicion. A servant was bound to obey. Her heart raced and she wiped her damp palms on her tunic. What did his summons mean?

She had been dismayed when they'd asked her to sing, aware it would put her in front of the Norman men and remind the people their lady was still among them. Soon one of them would make the mistake of calling her by her real name. It had almost happened with the children. Though singing with Rhodri presented risks, in the end she was glad she had done it for it reminded her of happier times when she and Rhodri had sung for her father and Steinar, when such evenings were common at Talisand.

Her father had loved the music of the Welsh bard and had encouraged the people to embrace the songs Rhodri brought to their hall. The songs and languages of many cultures had found a place at Talisand. Even the Norman food and language had been of interest to the old thegn since the time when King Edward had invited Normans to England. Her family had never seen them as enemies, not until the Bastard Duke decided to assert his claim to the throne.

Serena had not seen the Red Wolf in the hall while she and Rhodri sang; she hoped he had missed the performance. She did not wish to be the object of the gray eyes that increasingly followed her every movement, desire reflected in their depths.

Within her, hate warred with reluctant respect. Resistance warred with desire. Though he was one of the dreaded Normans, he was a fair master and a defender of women. She was drawn to him, albeit against her will, whenever he was near. Now summoned to his chamber, her heart leaped within her chest. What did he intend?

Resigned, she slowly ascended the stairs.

Her knock sounded softly on the wooden door, the door that had once led to her father's chamber.

"Come." At his deep voice, she nearly jumped.

Carefully, she opened the door and stepped inside, closing it behind her. She scanned the room looking for the tall knight with the chestnut hair. At first she did not see him but a movement drew her gaze to the large bathing tub on the floor. He was sitting in the water with his back to her, his knees drawn up to his chest. The dark rust of his hair captured the light from the candles causing it to glisten with streaks of amber.

"Please forgive me, my lord. I did not realize you were bathing." She turned to leave.

"I would speak with you, Sarah," he said without turning. "You can wash my back while we talk."

Serena's heart sped. While it was not unusual for the lord to ask a servant girl to assist with his bathing, her father had never allowed her to undertake such a task with any of their guests. She did not want to be close to the man, especially knowing he was naked, but a servant could not refuse her lord such a request.

"Yea, my lord."

Taking up the cloth and soap, she knelt behind him, dipped them both in the water and, working in the soap, began to scrub his back. The muscles of his broad shoulders rippled as she dipped the soapy cloth in the water and ran it over his bronzed skin. His was a knight's body, one that had wielded a weapon against her people. Despite all that, she wanted to touch him, to smooth her hand over his muscles and the jagged scar on his shoulder. It troubled her that the body of her enemy could arouse her senses so.

Her hands continued to work the soap into his skin, scrubbing with force lest she be lulled into touching him with gentle strokes. She tried to erase the thoughts that swirled through her mind. She supposed many women would want such a man. *Aethel had wanted him.* While his men told ribald jests at the evening meal, some had spoken of the many women who sought the Red Wolf's bed. It was easy to see why Aethel had desired him. The scene she had witnessed that night in his chamber when she had found them together was still vivid in her mind. Her hand slowed when his right hand gripped the side of the tub. A jagged scar slashed across the skin of his wrist. Was it the mark of the beast he had killed?

The Red Wolf let his head drop forward and he uttered a soft moan, causing her to lift the cloth from his back.

"You have a beautiful voice, Sarah," he said in a lethargic voice. "Did the Welshman teach you the songs?"

She forced a thank you from her lips, and resumed scrubbing his back. "Yea, Rhodri taught me his music."

He reached back, took her hand that held the cloth and drew it to his chest. "Sarah, I would have you also scrub my chest." He was deliberately forcing her to confront his maleness, to put her hands on the dark hair that covered his chest. She kept her eyes above the water even as her breathing became more strained. She had to fight her own attraction for him in order to keep her distance.

He took the cloth from her and finished scrubbing his legs and what lay beneath the water. She was grateful she would not have to touch that part of his body.

"What is the Welshman to you, Sarah?"

The question surprised her. *Why would he care?* Reaching for the pail of rinse water, she considered how to answer. She did not look at his naked form but her fingertips touched his warm flesh as she poured the water over his hair and his back. The heat of his body made her keenly aware they were alone in his chamber and he was unclothed. She had never touched a man like this, never felt her heart race at the nearness of so powerful a warrior.

She managed to say, "He is a friend and my teacher of the bow as he is to many at Talisand."

"Nothing more?"

"Nay, my lord." Her voice was calm but his words caused her anger to rise. What business of his was her relationship to the Welsh bard? But a servant would not ask so she said naught.

"That is good."

Still behind him, Serena reached for the drying cloth, bringing her head near to his. He turned to look at her. His eyes, only a hand's width away, flashed liquid silver, and in them she glimpsed raw desire. Like a mouse caught in the fixed glare of a snake, she was unable to move. The drying cloth slipped from her hand.

His gaze fell to her lips. "Sarah…"

He reached out his hand and pulled her towards him as his mouth closed the short distance to hers. His lips touched her own ever so lightly. His tongue followed the curve of her bottom lip, causing her skin to tingle. Had he tried to force her she might have fought, she might have fled, but his slow seduction lulled her into remaining still. His hand moved to her nape where his fingers curved around the tingling skin and held her tenderly. She responded, willingly offering her mouth to him and closed her eyes.

A feeling of pleasure she had never experienced swept over her as his lips softly teased and his tongue slipped between her parted lips to freely explore her mouth. His slow deliberate movements tantalized as they promised pleasure, a pleasure for the first time she very much wanted. She entwined her tongue with his and moaned.

When he pulled her tightly against his chest, the touch of his wet skin and the edge of the tub pressed against her breasts awakened her to what was happening. She wrenched back, frightened at how close she had come to giving him what he sought and angry with herself for allowing such intimacy.

"My lord!" Still on her knees, she scurried backward and hastily rose.

"Sarah..." His voice was deep and coaxing. "Come back."

"Nay!"

She raced to the door, flung it open and fled, letting it slam behind her. He called her name but she did not respond. Flattening herself against the wall next to the door to what had once been her chamber, her heart pounded in her chest. Pressing her palms against the wall, she willed her heart to slow.

Her mind reeled, alarmed at what had transpired. No man had ever kissed her like the Norman had—no man had ever made her want him.

How could the Norman knight affect her so?

She reached one hand to her lips; the soft flesh still throbbed from his kiss. Hearing voices below, she stepped away from the wall to peer into the entry where a few men lingered. One of them looked up at her. *Maugris.* The old man's gaze held hers and a slow smile spread across his face. She fell back against the wall, her heart still racing as she sought to hide in the shadows. Did the old man know what had transpired?

CHAPTER 8

The sun was nearly at its zenith when Renaud set aside his sword and wiped his face with the back of his hand. After the night before when Sarah had fled his bedchamber, leaving him hard and wanting, he relished the physical activity of sword practice with his men. Besides, he would need to keep up his skills for battle.

"Good work, Alain. You have wearied me," said Renaud.

His banner carrier, the knight who always reminded him of a large bear, smiled. "And you have me sweating like a pig in a slaughterhouse, my lord," said Alain, sheathing his sword.

Renaud looked around at his other knights. All were sweating in the heat of the midday sun from hours of heaving their swords in mock battle.

"Take a break and get some food," Renaud urged his men. "This afternoon, some of you will hunt while others have duties supervising the motte construction." Then to Geoff, who had just sheathed his sword, "The men appear ready, even eager for an engagement."

"Aye, they do. They enjoy the peace they have found here, but they are trained for war, so a short excursion to join in one of William's campaigns would appeal. Do you think it will be long ere the king calls us to attend him in some skirmish?"

"There are rumors of rebellions in the south, so it might not be long." William had not conquered all of England and, knowing his sire, Renaud thought it was only a matter of time before they were summoned to put down some rebellion. In the meantime, he had duties here.

"Geoff, this afternoon I would see the village. I intend to take Maugris with me, but I need someone who can accompany me who knows the villeins well. Can you identify such a one?"

"Maggie knows everyone. She will have a name."

"I will bathe first, then join you in the hall. And, yea, ask Maggie." Renaud liked the cook and her easy acceptance of him and his knights. She could have poisoned them all, but instead, she fed them well.

On his way back to the manor, Renaud passed the Welsh bard as he was going through the gate. "I would have a word, Welshman."

The bard stopped. "Yea, my lord?"

"I am a bit confused as to who you are. Be you bard, Welsh warrior or something else?"

For a moment, Renaud thought he saw a flicker of concern in the bard's dark eyes. But it was gone as quickly as it had come.

"Merely a bard, my lord, who entertains along the road. When I first visited Talisand, the old thegn saw me practicing the bow and asked me to train any who would learn."

Renaud suspected there was more to the story. "And why do you return now?"

"I am merely passing through. I did not know the thegn was dead and thought to visit him."

An unlikely story. "Know you aught of Lady Serena, where she might be, for instance?"

"I have not seen her on my travels, my lord. The people say she has followed her brother to Scotland."

"Yea, that is what they say." Renaud considered the Welshman, the bard who could fashion a bow that competed well with those of his archers, and his suspicions were raised. "Do you train with my archers this afternoon?"

"If you would desire it, my lord, I would be willing."

"It may be you can teach them something."

"Or, I might learn from them," the Welshman said with a grin.

As the bard, who Renaud suspected was more than a bard, started to walk away, Renaud called him back. "Rhodri, there is another matter I would address."

"Yea, my lord?"

"What is your relationship with the servant girl Sarah?"

The Welshman paused before answering. "Why, I am but her instructor of the bow and her friend. And sometimes her partner in song."

Renaud rubbed his fingers over his chin as the bard bowed and sauntered through the palisade gate. There was more to the man than music and arrows, he was certain of it.

* * *

Geoffroi strolled into the kitchen to find Maggie and her daughter Cassandra hard at work putting the finishing touches on the midday meal, while one of the lads stirred the contents of a large kettle suspended over the central hearth. Smells of a rich stew rose in the air making his stomach growl.

"Good day, Sir Geoffroi. Can I help ye?" Maggie paused in her work setting fresh loaves of bread on platters.

"Good day to you, Maggie, Cassandra," he said with a nod toward each of the women. "I need your recommendation for someone to accompany the lord on his walk through the village this afternoon. It would be best if it were a person who is familiar with the people and their needs...someone who can assist with introductions."

Maggie wiped her hands on her apron and exchanged a glance with her daughter. Drawing her brows together, she appeared to ponder his request while her daughter continued in her work, and the lad stirred the kettle that was the source of the spicy aroma. Geoff's mouth watered.

Cassandra's eyes never left her mother. Suddenly a smile spread across Maggie's face.

"Well, now, the best be steward Hunstan, but he is nay here today. The lord sent him to the far manors to see what workers could be had for the building of his castle."

She must have seen the disappointment on his face, because she quickly added, "But there be another who is perfect for the task."

Geoffroi raised his brows expectantly.

"'Tis the maid, Sarah. She knows the people well and often carried Lady Serena's wishes to the village."

He thought for a moment. It did seem that the girl Sarah spoke well and she had the friendship of Eawyn. And Ren had a personal interest in the servant girl, of that he had no doubt. Yea, she might be just the one to introduce the Red Wolf to the people. "'Tis a grand idea, Maggie. See that she is available this afternoon. I will tell the lord."

* * *

Serena stepped into the dirt path leading to the village, the Red Wolf on her right and Maugris on her other side. The village was close to the manor so they had no need of horses, which was good, as she did not want the Normans to know she could ride well. She missed her daily rides on Elfleda, the white mare her father had given her in her fourteenth year, but it could not be helped.

A boy chasing a squawking copper feathered chicken ran in front of them and missed when he reached down to grab the panicked fowl. The

Red Wolf laughed, his deep voice bringing back the memory of their encounter in his chamber the night before. Serena shivered though the sun on her head was warm. The memory of his lips on hers brought back exciting sensations. Her fingers twitched as she recalled the feel of him and the smell of his wet skin.

How foolish she was to think of such things when this man, she reminded herself, was one of the Bastard's knights.

She had argued with Maggie saying that going to the village with the Red Wolf was not a wise thing. But her words had only drawn a smile from the older woman, who insisted the new lord had need of the servant girl Sarah. Thankfully she had dyed her new hair growth that morning.

The thought of being so close to him after what happened the night before left her anxious and unsettled, her stomach churning as if two cats fought within it. After successfully avoiding the man all morning, she was to be with him all afternoon. It was not just his nearness that plagued her, though that was surely enough cause for concern. Nay, visiting the men and women of the village was something she had often done with her father and Steinar. Seeing her with the new lord would surely remind the villeins that she was their lady. She prayed none revealed her identity.

Other lads joined the boy who had chased the chicken, the group of them pausing at the side of the path to gape at the tall knight, who bore the name of the wolf he had killed with his bare hands, and the old man the whole village thought of as a wizard.

The boys' openmouthed gazes lingered on the Red Wolf's dark blue tunic circled with a silver-studded belt at his waist from which hung a deadly short sword that glistened in the afternoon sun. His hosen were brown as were the leather straps that crossed them. Even without a hauberk or the wolf's pelt, he appeared dangerous. The children's wide-eyed stares followed him as though they were watching a mythical god. He was so different from the English thegn they had known with his long fair hair and graying beard.

The Red Wolf cast a glance at the young ones, then paused, his gaze lingering on the cottages with their neat thatched roofs extending nearly to the ground. "The cottages seem well kept. Though some of the thatch needs to be repaired. Maugris, see that Sir Geoffroi knows of this task."

Before Maugris could answer, Serena said, "Those are repairs we make before winter, my lord."

He raised an eyebrow but Maugris only looked amused. Instantly, she realized she had stepped outside a servant's demeanor.

"You are an impudent one for a servant, Sarah. Do you think I would not know that?"

"Nay, but 'tis not time for the repairs while spring is still upon us. New thatch will be laid after harvest. And some repairs have been delayed for lack of men to complete them." *Men the Normans have taken from us.*

As if to make peace between her and his lord, Maugris inquired, "Are all these cottages homes?"

"Nay," replied Serena politely, "some are the workshops of the men and women who provide what Talisand needs. The tools, wooden implements, cloth and cooking kettles. And the smith, of course. The mill lies on the river just north of the village." She pointed into the distance to a larger thatched structure rising amidst the trees.

"Is it the same in Normandy?" she asked, curious.

"Aye," said the old man, "'tis similar, but there are some differences."

Serena hoped the Norman knight appreciated what a well-tended village Talisand had. Did the knight fail to notice how the people were well clothed and the children well fed notwithstanding all the fathers they were missing?

"How many slaves are in the village?" asked the Red Wolf. "I have seen few in the manor."

"There are no slaves in the village, nor in the manor," she answered with pride. "All those the old lord brought here he freed." That was one of the reasons her father was so loved. He brought those to Talisand who had skills to share, and the people produced much from the pure joy of building lives they were proud of, of working their own land.

The Red Wolf seemed to consider her words. "It seems a waste to me, but then he was an unusual thegn."

Serena could feel her anger rise but she quickly damped it down. As if explaining to a child, she said, "It is because they are free, my lord, that the people work so hard. They work for the future of their sons and daughters. They were happy to give back to the thegn who gave them so much. To now become serfs does not sit well." Inwardly she cringed, knowing she had again stepped over the bounds of a servant, but it was important to convince this Norman her father's ways were best. Obviously he knew little of caring for villeins.

His gray eyes seemed to study her for a moment. She felt uncomfortable beneath his intense gaze. Then, in a deep voice he said, "Lead the way to the blacksmith, Sarah. It is time that I meet him."

Serena dropped her head as Cassie had instructed, though the gesture ran against her nature. "Yea, my lord. His name is Angus. His cottage is a short way ahead."

Maugris smiled.

She pointed toward the cottage set off from the others. The small building they entered was open on one end where the breeze from the large door fanned the fire in the forge. A wave of heat billowed out to meet them as she spotted the stocky man with bright red hair sitting on a stool, sweat rolling off his soot-smudged face. In one hand he held tongs that gripped a bar of iron he forced into the fire. In his other hand was a large hammer, which he used to pound the red hot metal, the clanking sound resonating as sparks flew upward.

Angus paused in his work to thrust the glowing bar into a vat of water sending steam shooting into the air as the tortured metal screamed. As Serena approached, he set aside the cooling bar and rose, wiping his powerful hands on his leather apron.

The Red Wolf followed her through the door, bending his head to avoid hitting the lintel. Maugris was close on his heels.

"Greetings, Angus. 'Tis Sarah," she said, careful to remind him of the name she had taken, hoping the Normans did not think it odd. "The new lord and his wise man have come to meet you."

"Aye," said Angus, looking at the tall knight and Maugris behind him. "Maggie told me ye would be coming. Yer men are keeping my forge busy, m'lord."

"My men have much need for a smith's services," remarked the Red Wolf. "I trust you can keep up. We'll need the horses shod and some armor repaired. Then there will be fittings for the castle."

"The forge and workers I have willna be enough."

"Then you must build another and hire more men," said the Red Wolf shortly, "or I'll send for a smith who can."

"My lord," Serena interrupted, "Angus can do it but he will need coin to pay for materials and for the workers required for a second forge. Talisand does not have such resources."

The Red Wolf's eyes flashed in anger.

"Aye, I will need more iron and more workers," echoed the smith, running his hands through his tousled red hair. "There be some lads in the next village who can be put to the task."

The Red Wolf's brow furrowed as his gaze came to rest on the forge. "I will see you have coin for the workers and the iron you need. Let Sir Geoffroi know your requirements, and you will have them."

Angus dipped his head. "Aye, I shall do as ye say." He winked at Serena and she breathed a sigh of relief. Though she had incurred the Red Wolf's anger to do it, she had helped the Norman understand what Angus needed and for that she was glad.

"Would you want to see the chapel?" Serena asked as they left the smith's workshop.

Renaud looked at her disbelieving. "Talisand has a chapel?"

"Yea, a proper stone chapel. The old lord observed many on his travels and wanted his people to have a place both to worship and to keep the holy days."

"Where is it?" Maugris inquired.

"Just a short walk from the end of the village. We can return to see the other workshops, but as long as we are here, the chapel is best seen now."

"Lead on." The Red Wolf gestured them forward.

The chapel was nestled in a copse of oak trees. A mood of calm spread over Serena as it always did when she came to the beautiful structure built by her father's men. They entered through two heavy oaken doors, each with an iron ring handle. Inside, small arched windows on the side of the structure in the shape of a cross allowed narrow shafts of light to fall on the stone floor.

As she walked down the center toward the nave, the sun cast its meager rays across her path in failed warmth. It had always been cool in the chapel. She looked up to the window at the far end of the nave, the one that had brought her father so much pride. The arched opening was large in comparison to the scale of the chapel. Small pieces of heavy glass separated by strips of metal revealed the green of the trees outside. The walls of the chapel were painted in bright colors of red, blue, yellow and orange depicting Bible scenes that reminded the people of their faith.

Even for Talisand, the chapel was unusual, and for Serena, it was a very special place. She had come here to pray for her father and Steinar and for all the men of Talisand who had gone to fight for King Harold. It had been here she had wept 'til there were no tears left when she'd learned of her father's death. And it was here she had one day hoped to wed a man of her father's choosing.

She forced back the tears that could so easily fall. "'Tis quite beautiful, my lord, is it not?" she asked in a weak voice.

With a look of wonder on his face, Maugris gazed at the large window and the brightly colored paintings covering the whitewashed walls. As if he could read her thoughts, he said, "'Tis beautiful. A fine place for a wedding."

"Ah but that would require a bride, oh wise one," said the Red Wolf in a sarcastic tone, disrupting Serena's mood.

Maugris seemed unaffected. "I dare say one will be found, my lord."

Serena glanced back at the two men and wondered at the curious exchange. Were they talking about her, the Lady of Talisand? Or, might he have given up the hunt and now sought another? She felt a sudden chill as she considered what might be her fate were he to wed another. Would she lose all she had hoped to regain? Perplexed, and becoming increasingly uncomfortable, she walked toward one side of the small chapel and out of the corner of her eye saw the Norman knight run his hand over a wooden railing.

"Excellent workmanship. 'Tis walnut, is it not?

"Yea, my lord," she answered. "The wood comes from Talisand's forests."

"I would not have expected it in a small village." He sounded surprised. "Is Talisand blessed with artisans and masons?"

"We have a man who is trained in masonry, my lord, and some who work in wood, but the old lord also brought skilled workers and craftsmen to Talisand to construct the chapel. They worked with him to conceive the plans for what he wanted."

"'Tis a fine job," said Maugris.

"Does the chapel come with a priest?" asked the Red Wolf.

Serena fought a smile. Of course her father would have seen to a priest. "Talisand shares a priest with other villages. Father Bernard travels among them, hearing confessions, saying mass and blessing marriages. Even when he is gone, the people come here to pray so the chapel is always open." She was glad the priest was away. He was aware she was to marry the Norman and would not have approved her deception. She had decided to stay long enough to see how the Red Wolf treated her people, but the time was growing short for her to leave.

Maugris faced the knight. "You have a need to see the priest?"

"Nay," the Red Wolf hastened to answer, "but a warrior never knows when he'll have need of one so I am glad he is often here."

Serena knew well the meaning of his words. A knight would think of needing a priest. Many of Talisand's men had died in battle, unshriven of their sins. The thought of the Norman knight needing a priest for last rites gave her pause. She was surprised to realize she would feel regret at his death.

Maugris nodded. "'Tis true, my lord. I recall that priest at the church in *Dives-sur-Mer* who prayed for you and William's other knights before you left for England. Mayhap his prayer gave you victory. Certainly God, who raises up kings, was with the duke that day."

The Red Wolf lifted his head and stared at the glass window, a frown appearing on his face. "Since you brought up the subject of prayer, Maugris, when he returns you might ask Talisand's priest to pray we will soon find my lady, before I am forced to ask William for another."

"Those prayers have been said, my lord, at least by me," answered the old man, "and I am confident they will be answered."

Serena was suddenly anxious to leave the chapel. "Would you want to see Talisand's weavers?"

"Do you mean the women of the village?" asked Maugris.

"I had in mind two who are most special." Serena walked to the door of the chapel, leading them back into the warmth of the afternoon sun.

As they returned to the main part of the village, the same boys who had earlier stared at the Norman knight followed them.

The old man drew his lord aside to show him some damage to one of the thatched roofs. A boy with sun streaked brown hair ran up to Serena.

"M'lady," he said, his dark eyes beseeching while he tugged on her sleeve, "I've something to tell ye." Fortunately, the boy spoke hardly above a whisper.

She whispered in return as she took his hand and squeezed it. "'Tis Sarah, Beorn, remember?"

"Oh," he said, covering his mouth with his hand, his eyes bright and a smile on his lips. "I forgot." Then taking a deep breath, he began again. "Sarah, have ye heard about Dunn's father? He died two days ago and now the cottage and land will nay be Dunn's, but will belong to the Norman lord."

Sarah looked to where the Red Wolf and his wise man were talking amongst themselves before she turned back to the boy. Letting out a breath, she said, "Yea, I knew of Dunn's father's passing. Dunn and his mother may remain in the cottage. But all of Talisand, its lands and manors, now belong to the Red Wolf, Beorn. The Norman king has claimed England for his own and doles out parts of it to his barons and knights. The Red Wolf is one of them."

"I like it not," said Beorn, a frown creasing his young forehead.

She sighed. What could she say? "I know. I feel the same. But 'tis the way of it now." She did not want to give him hope the situation might change though she held onto that slim thread of hope herself.

Serena let go of the boy's hand, and he rejoined his companions. Beorn thought she could work miracles. Much as she wanted to, she could not.

She returned to the two men. When their conversation ended, she directed them to the cottage where a short piece of cloth hung over the open door announced to all in the village the weavers were working.

"Good day to you, Ingrith, Annis," she said as she led the men through the door. "'Tis Sarah and I've brought with me the new lord and his wise man to see your fine work." She turned to the Red Wolf who was standing close behind her, his nearness unsettling. "Ingrith and Annis weave for the whole village, my lord, nay just themselves."

"Talisand has women who weave for the others?" he asked with a puzzled look.

"All the women can weave," Serena proudly replied. In any village the women would know how to weave cloth. "But Ingrith and Annis became so skilled at weaving the fine wool of Talisand's sheep that the old thegn encouraged them to do only that. 'Twas he who had this workshop built for them." Dark-haired Ingrith smiled at Serena from behind a large loom in the corner, while Annis with her lighter hair and green eyes sat looking on from another loom to the side. "The villagers pay Ingrith and Annis for their cloth in trade for things the two women and their families require."

Serena walked to the table that held folded lengths of cloth in colors of blue, rust, brown and green. "You can see the cloth is very fine."

The Red Wolf observed the two women working at their looms. His size made the cottage seem small. It was no wonder he wanted a castle; his body was made for such a grand structure. But she knew his king's demands were for more than shelter. Castles would tell all of England the Normans were here to stay.

After a moment, the knight's gaze shifted to Serena as though he had sensed her eyes upon him. Heat rose in her cheeks and she averted her gaze. She did not want him to know her thoughts were of him.

Maugris walked to the table where the finished cloth lay, running his fingers over the woolen fabric. "My lord." He looked to the Red Wolf. "'Tis softer than velvet."

Happy to have another subject to fill her mind, Serena said, "Ingrith and Annis provided the cloth for the tunics worn by the old lord's family. And the thegn traded Talisand's woolen cloth for goods the villagers did not make and for the treasures he sought from other lands."

Maugris glanced at Serena's simple tunic. His smile, as if he were amused, caused her brow to wrinkle. What did the old man see? Was he amused by her ill-fitting servant's attire?

The Red Wolf was still studying Ingrith working at the loom and Serena breathed a sigh of relief that he had not witnessed his wise one's mirth.

"I have need of a new tunic," the Red Wolf said to Ingrith. "Some of your cloth in dark blue would do nicely." He reached for a folded piece on the table. "I'll send my squire for several lengths of the other colors."

"But my lord," interjected Serena, "they *trade* for their wool. You cannot just take it!"

His glower was sharp evidence of his displeasure. "This is now my land and Ingrith is my serf. You would do well to remember it, Sarah. A wise servant does not disagree with her lord."

Serena bowed her head. "Yea, my lord." She had already crossed the line from servant to something more. It would not do for her to fight him on this. But inside she was shocked. Did he mean to disrupt the system her father had worked so diligently to establish?

Maugris exchanged a look with his master, but it brought no change in the Red Wolf's expression. He seemed determined to take what he considered to be his.

With regret, Serena bid the weavers good day and left with the men to continue their advance through the village. The Red Wolf handed the blue cloth to his wise one as they approached the next workshop.

A goose followed by her goslings crossed the road, hurrying at the sound of the knight's heavy footfalls. The familiar bark of a dog sounded in the distance. When Maugris looked at her in question, she said, "The sheep grazing in the far pasture are being brought in for the night. The dog you hear is one the shepherds use."

"Where do you keep the sheep after gloaming?" he inquired.

"There are pens at the far end of the village and on the south side of the manor, where the sheep are protected from wolves and other beasts."

Maugris's mouth hitched up in a grin aimed at his master, but the Norman knight did not see the old man's smile. It was then Serena realized what she had said. A wolf was a predator, a beast all feared. Had she brought to the old one's mind the Norman knight he served? Serena cared not if her comment displeased the Red Wolf. After all, he was the one who had chosen to wear the wolf's pelt. Observing his fierce countenance, she thought the name he had taken suited him well.

As the afternoon lengthened, Serena observed the Norman knight's interest grow in the village and its people, though his regard was not always returned. In response to his presence, she glimpsed fear in the eyes of some.

Was the Norman impressed with the lands his king had bestowed upon him? Talisand was a prosperous holding, a place of peace in a land that had often known war. He was a warrior far from home who had followed his duke, now his king, to a distant land. All knights wanted land, did they not? But it was not just any land he had taken, it was her land.

As she walked through the village, Serena had to fight the desire to act the thegn's daughter and the lady of her people, planning the things she knew were needed for the winter to come, inquiring about their families and seeing to their needs. They were good people, trying to do the best for their children and she wanted to help them. Playing the servant limited her role. Could she do more if she accepted the marriage foisted upon her? Or, could she better serve the people by seeking Steinar's aid to one day reclaim their lands? Aid that might only bring war to Talisand. The desire to flee and the desire to stay warred within her.

Introducing the Red Wolf to the villagers had a strange effect upon her. While being deferential to him, as a servant must be to her lord, the hatred she'd held onto so tightly began to ebb. It was easy to hate the dreaded Norman king who had conquered England with his army of knights and mercenaries, but it was not so easy to hate the knight who talked with her people. He needed her help to understand their needs. Though she had been angry at his ignorance of their ways and had bristled at his rebuke, she could not forget his kiss. His reputation was that of a ruthless warrior, as vicious as the wolf he had slain. Yet he'd been gentle with her. She fought to remember the steel gray of his eyes and the firm set of his jaw when he gave orders to his men, and when he had claimed the blue cloth he believed was his by right. She fought to remember he was her enemy, but she could not fight the desire that welled up inside her.

The Red Wolf bent to greet a village lad and images of his naked back from the night before flooded her mind. She remembered the scar on his shoulder and the one on his wrist. He is not invincible. He is only a man, imperfect and vulnerable. Mayhap he wore his tunic and weapons more confidently than most, his stance prouder, more sure. And he was more handsome to her mind with his dark hair and olive skin, bronzed from the sun. But for all that, he was just a man. And her fascination with him was disturbing.

A loud boom violently rent the air like a thunderclap. Serena jerked her head in the direction of the noise. With lightning speed, the Red Wolf shoved her behind him and drew his sword from its sheath.

"What was that?" Maugris shouted.

"I know not," said the Red Wolf. Then to Serena, "Wait here until I see what has happened."

"It came from the potter's workshop," she said. Ignoring the Red Wolf's order for her to wait, she followed him as he strode toward the cottage. Behind the cottage, dark smoke belched into the air.

At the open door, the Red Wolf turned to face her. "I told you to wait!"

"But my lord, I know these people."

He scowled, sheathed his sword and proceeded into the cottage. Again, Serena followed, holding her hand over her nose against the smoke filling the small space. It made her eyes water. As the smoke cleared, she gazed around the workshop. It appeared unaffected, pots lining the walls and blocks of clay and tools piled on a work table as they always were.

The potter's wife, Hulda, leaned against the doorpost at the back of the cottage. She looked about to faint. The door to the rear yard stood open. Hulda stepped aside to let the Red Wolf pass. Serena put her arm around the distraught woman and watched the knight kneel beside the girl lying on the ground in front of the kiln. Black soot covered her face and blood tricked from her neck and arms where flying shards of pottery had sliced through her skin. The ground was covered with pieces of burnt and broken pots.

"Be Edith alive, m'lord?" Hulda asked tentatively.

"Yea, but she's hurt badly," said the Red Wolf. "Is there a place I can lay her?"

"Yea, my lord," said Hulda, "just inside."

Carefully lifting the girl in his arms, the Red Wolf carried young Edith into the cottage and laid her on the straw pallet that Hulda directed him to.

Maugris, who had entered the cottage, stood next to Hulda as she explained, "My husband Godfrith is away so Edith worked alone. She must have failed to dry the pots she was firing. The lass is new at the craft. I was afeard something like this might happen." Shaking her head and wiping her hands on her tunic, she added, "She was nay always careful."

The Red Wolf faced the older woman, his eyes reflecting concern. "Is there a healer among you...someone who can clean and tend her wounds? It is best done while she is unconscious."

Hulda shot a glance at Serena for all the villagers knew, along with Aethel who had the knowledge of herbs, the Lady of Talisand could treat wounds.

"I will see to the girl," said Serena before the woman could answer. "Have you clean cloths and water, Hulda?"

While they waited for the needed provisions, the knight knelt before the girl and began to remove the broken pottery shards from her clothing. Serena was surprised he would do so.

She knelt beside him. "I can see to her, my lord."

"Nay, we can work together until the woman returns with the cloths and water. It will not be the first time I have picked sharp objects from a wounded body, right Maugris?"

"Yea, more than once," the silver-haired man answered.

Serena worked alongside the Red Wolf at the difficult task. The shards were stuck in the young woman's tunic and had to be carefully lifted out. For the moment Edith was not aware, which was a blessing. In some places, the jagged pieces of pottery were still lodged in her skin.

Maugris hovered behind them. Serena could feel his eyes upon her and wondered what he was thinking.

A few minutes later, Hulda returned with the water and clean clothes.

By then, most of the shards had been removed from Edith's tunic. Serena rose. "I must go to the manor for the salves Maggie keeps in the kitchen."

"Nay," said Maugris, "You stay, Sarah. I will ask Maggie for the salves."

Serena nodded and the old one left the cottage. "I will need to cut her clothing from her," she said to Hulda. The Red Wolf rose, handed her the knife from his belt and waited on the other side of the small cottage while she and Hulda carefully cut away the girl's ruined tunic. There were some cuts on her face and arms but her outer garments had protected most of her body.

Serena cleaned the cuts, staunching the blood, and wiping the soot from Edith's exposed skin. Once that was done, Hulda covered the girl with a large drying cloth.

Maugris returned and handed Serena the salve Maggie had made, which Serena applied as gently as she could.

"Will Edith recover?" asked Hulda hopefully.

"I have done all I can for her," Serena said, rising from where she had sat upon her knees and dusted off her tunic. "The wounds are cleaned. We can pray there will be no fever. I will leave the salve and ask Aethel for herbs to help with the pain. Send for me or Maggie if you need us."

"I am thankful to ye," said Hulda. Then looking up at the Red Wolf, she said, "M'lord, 'tis a sorry welcome I've given ye. I'm in yer debt for yer kindness shown Edith this day."

"Do not concern yourself with any welcome, madame. I came to meet the people of Talisand, and to see to the needs of the village."

"And so ye have done, m'lord."

It appeared to Serena the Red Wolf had won at least one of Talisand's people to his cause. She was glad the afternoon was over as she left the cottage with the two men. Weary in body, she was lifted in spirit by the actions of the Red Wolf. When he could have left her to tend the potter's assistant alone, he had lingered and done more; he had helped. It had meant a lot to Hulda.

It meant a lot to her lady.

CHAPTER 9

Renaud returned to the manor, the sun now lower in the sky. Maugris was still with him but he had dismissed Sarah to her evening tasks. Yet he could not free his mind from thoughts about the servant girl. All day he had struggled to concentrate on the village and its people, to assess the lands William had given him, but Sarah had proved most distracting.

Walking before him, her long brown plait moving from side to side, his eyes were drawn to her swaying hips. He wanted to reach out and pull her to him as he had the night before. To kiss again her soft lips. He vowed he would do so and soon; it was merely a matter of time's passage.

Her effect upon the villeins had been remarkable, making him wonder how a handmaiden had garnered such respect. Mayhap she undertook errands for Lady Serena as Geoff had suggested. Was the handmaiden more accomplished than the lady herself? He considered the possibility for the people deferred to the servant girl, not once mentioning the missing Lady Serena. Not for the first time, he wondered at the girl with the violet eyes. Could she be more than she seemed? Sarah had been quick to help the wounded potter and brave enough to confront him when she thought he was wrong. He respected such qualities in a warrior and coveted them in a woman. But in a servant, it was most unusual. And it made him wonder.

Occasionally, when Sarah had leaned in to explain something, Renaud had caught a whiff of her flowery scent. He had tried to suppress his desire for her and found it impossible. He was drawn to her as a bear to the delectable smell of ripe berries. And because of her, he'd lost interest in the other women at Talisand who might have met his physical needs. He wanted only her as his leman. His patience was wearing thin, the scowl on his face proof of his frustration.

Maugris chuckled under his breath.

"Do you find something humorous, wise one?" Renaud asked as they entered the hall and he waived away a tankard of ale offered by a servant.

Maugris just smiled and refused the tankard he was offered. "Naught, my lord...and everything."

"You would be mysterious?"

"I would be an observer. But to see all does not mean I tell all."

"As you will. But join me by the hearth fire for wine and conversation. I would tell you of my plans for William's castle."

"Of course," said Maugris.

Renaud stepped into the hall, Maugris at his side. The wise one's hidden ways could annoy Renaud at times, but the old man's wisdom impressed even the doubtful among his men, thus he rarely questioned him when he was like this. He had learned his questions would avail him little.

* * *

Serena woke in a cold sweat with an image in her mind of the Red Wolf's deep gray eyes staring intently at her as if he knew the truth of who she really was. It was her greatest fear.

Rising from her pallet where she slept among the servants, she donned her tunic and shawl and slipped outside into the dull light of an early morning without sun. Above her, dark threatening clouds covered the sky like a heavy blanket. It would rain this day. Gathering her shawl tightly around her against the chill, she walked to the river's edge and stood looking down at the smooth rocks scattered on the small shore, content to be alone with her thoughts. Often she had come here to think. After Hastings, sometimes she came to shed tears away from the eyes of others.

The honking of a flock of geese above her drew her attention as they winged their way north toward Scotland where Steinar was. Where she should be even now.

Returning her gaze to the river, she stared at the water flowing with nary a sound. The wide rippling thread reflected the color of the sky, only a deeper shade of gray—the color of the eyes in her dream, just as deep and just as mysterious.

The eyes of the Red Wolf.

His coming had changed everything. For a moment, she was overwhelmed with a deep regret that brought tears to her eyes, a few escaping down her cheeks. She brushed them away as thoughts of her father and Steinar filled her mind. They had been her strength, her protection, but they had abandoned her, leaving her alone and vulnerable. They had not meant to leave her but still they were gone.

No sound warned of his approach, but the uneasy feeling of being watched made Serena turn in nervous anticipation to see Maugris silently walking toward her.

"Oh, 'tis you." She let out the breath she'd been holding as her heart slowly returned to its normal cadence. The wise one did not threaten her.

"Yea, only Maugris," he said with a warm smile as he joined her to stand by the river.

She snuck a glance at him. He was looking straight ahead. "They say you are his wizard."

"I am no wizard for I worship the Master of the Heavens the same as you."

"What are you to the Norman lord, then?" She had wondered many times about the nature of their relationship.

"Merely his advisor and I think a friend."

"He is fortunate to have you, sir, for I perceive you are wise and surely a man such as the Red Wolf would need your wisdom."

"You, too, were helpful to him yesterday in the village. Do you always have such care for the villeins that you would step in the path of a wolf?"

"I suppose I do."

"And do the people always defer to you?"

She hesitated, fearing the question. "As a handmaiden to their lady—"

"It is possible a handmaiden could rise to that level," he interrupted, "but it is not common. You were not merely passing messages yesterday, but speaking as one whose words are heeded in her own right."

Serena was uneasy at the turn of their conversation. What was he suggesting?

His pale blue eyes suddenly bore into hers with new fervor. "Your defense of the woman who was nearly violated by Sir Hugue was the action of one who assumes responsibility for the maidens of Talisand. A servant might have run away, glad to have been the one spared, but from what I heard, you would have killed the knight had not Sir Geoffroi stopped you."

"In the absence of Lady Serena, surely I must defend the women."

"Indeed, my lady, I well understand."

She inhaled sharply at his words. "Why do you call me 'lady' good sir?"

"I call you 'lady' for that is what you are...*Lady* Serena."

She gasped at his revelation of her true identity, and quickly looked around to see if anyone had heard. She was relieved to see they stood alone on the river bank. Lowering her voice to a whisper, she asked, "How do you know this?"

"I have the gift of visions and of the sight and discern many things others do not. The first time I saw you, I doubted you were a servant."

"Was it my temper? I have worried it might draw attention to me. Servants are meek and compliant."

He smiled. "Nay, not all servants are compliant."

"What then?" Serena had to know what had given her away for she would change it.

"There were many things that told me you were the Lady of Talisand. To begin with, your eyes flare in anger like a fire fed by the wind when you witness wrongs against your people. Only one who has carried the weight of justice for them would react so." Shrugging, he added, "There were other signs as well. The way you carry yourself, for one. 'Tis more like a young queen than one who does laundry. Then, too, your performance with the bow was telling. The Lady of Talisand is known to be proficient at the bow. The villagers nearly gave you away with their disappointment at your miss. The Red Wolf took note of it. He has also observed the way the other servants defer to you with their eyes whenever you speak. He will soon have your identity, my lady. Even now he is close to the truth."

Serena was horrified that this servant of the Red Wolf had seen so much. Mayhap he was right. The Norman lord might soon know who she was. The thought was frightening. "But you have not told your master who I am, though you know he searches for me. You have kept my secret. Why?"

"He must discern the truth for himself. But know this, the day is not far off when he recognizes the jewel hidden among the stones."

Serena wondered at his strange words as a sudden foreboding came over her like an ever-tightening rope about her neck. She had wanted to stay to be assured her people fared well. But now it was clear she had stayed overlong. Had she stayed for more than her people? Had she lingered for the Norman lord? Panic rose in her throat. She bit her lower lip with rising dismay. She must leave before the Red Wolf could discover her. Before the Norman knight claimed her.

The old man's intense blue eyes watched her closely. "The Red Wolf has a great destiny, my lady. You are a part of it. I have seen it. Do not fight this. You are meant to be his lady, to be the mother of his cubs."

"No...never!"

The old man shook his head, a look of regret in his benevolent eyes. Though he was one of the dreaded Normans, she could feel no anger for him. He had kept her secret. *But for how long?*

Hastily bidding him good day, she took her leave. As she ran back to the manor, her mind spun with plans for escape. For too many days she had lingered. It was time to leave.

Lost in her thoughts, Serena did not see Aethel and nearly collided with the dark-haired woman standing near the entrance to the kitchen. "Oh, Aethel. Forgive me, I did not see you." Serena held her hand over her racing heart.

Aethel leaned back against the manor, her arms folded under her ample bosom, and smiled. "So, m'lady. Why be ye in such a hurry so early this morn?"

Looking around to assure herself they were alone, Serena cautioned, "Aethel, do not give away my station. I am not your lady at the moment, but a mere servant. You know this."

"Aye, I know it but ye do not wear the disguise well. 'Tis not natural for ye."

"Mayhap you are right, but for now, it serves. I expect you to say nothing."

"Heavens, no, m'lady! Think ye I am daft? Ye hide from the Norman lord when he would have ye to wife where I would be pleased to share his bed as I did yer father's."

Serena inwardly cringed at the woman's bold statement. It had been hard for her to accept that her father had taken Aethel to his bed. Yet she knew he'd been lonely, and so Serena was unsurprised when he'd sought out the dark-haired beauty. But remembering the night she had discovered Aethel in the Red Wolf's bedchamber, she bristled. It did not please Serena that Aethel desired to be the new lord's leman. But how could she object?

"You are welcome to him, Aethel. Surely he has accepted your favors."

"Nay, he has not. But that could change if ye were gone."

It gladdened Serena's heart to know that despite what she'd seen, the Red Wolf had rejected Aethel's attentions. "Whatever happens, Aethel, I thank you for keeping my secret."

"I would do more, m'lady. I would help ye leave."

* * *

Thwack! Morcar angrily plunged the dagger into the wooden table and the harsh sound echoed around the chamber. "Damn William for taking

Northumbria from me! Else Serena would be mine."

"Calm yourself, brother," Edwin said, leaning his elbows on the wooden table where he relaxed with a tankard of ale. "You must be practical. Even if you still had Northumbria, it may not have been enough. As Earl of Mercia, William promised me his daughter, Alice. Yet he was happy enough to change his mind when the greedy Normans he surrounds himself with urged him to renounce his pledge. We were fools to give him our fealty thinking he wanted only Wessex. We should have realized he wanted all of England."

"He will not stop 'til he has given it all to his barons and knights. But Serena…" He paused, remembering the woman of his dreams. "I still want her."

"There will be other women, Morcar. At least that is what I have tried to tell myself."

Morcar paced in the solar of his brother's Mercian manor. "Aye, he was unworthy of our fealty. But there are no other women so fair as the Lady of Talisand. I would have her still be she unwed. I have heard her brother Steinar lives; mayhap he'll consent to the match. If William had not dragged us off to Normandy, I might have seen to it ere now." Morcar burned with resentment for the Norman king who had taken Northumbria from him. "I am still Earl Morcar. I will go to Talisand and seek her hand."

"Nay, the country is too uncertain and William might think you travel north to retake Northumbria."

"Mayhap I do, brother." He grinned. "York is not far." He allowed a smirk to slide across his face as he considered the possibility. "Though Edgar Ætheling bides his time, he might be persuaded to join in a fight that would give him the throne. Many in the north would rally to support his claim to the crown."

"We can only hope. But it will take time for us to gather sufficient support to confront the Bastard in battle. As for Lady Serena, I bid you wait. 'Twould be best to send someone to Talisand who will not draw attention to himself, one who can quietly inquire if Talisand is still in Steinar's hands or if William has bestowed it upon one of his knights. Though the lands are far to the north of London, you cannot be certain the old thegn's lands have not fallen to one of them. They are too rich for William to ignore."

Morcar considered his brother's advice. Though he was still angry for all he had lost, and the shame William had heaped upon them in Normandy, parading them about as his guests when they were no more than prisoners, he could not dismiss the wisdom in Edwin's words.

"There was a wench who was the old thegn's leman. I spoke to her when last we visited Talisand," Edwin said, rubbing his bearded jaw. "Her name is Aethel. I can send a messenger to speak with her. The servants will know all that has happened at the manor. And in the meantime, you can make your inquiries of Edgar."

"'Tis a good idea," mumbled Morcar, wondering how it might be accomplished.

"Do you remember that the old thegn was known for entertaining artists and those skilled in crafts and fine wares?" asked his brother.

"Aye. We were well entertained when we were there and Serena was always lavishly gowned. What do you suggest?"

"Let us send a man disguised as one of them," offered Edwin, "and you will have the information you seek without anyone aware who is asking, save this woman Aethel."

"Aye, 'twill serve. Soon I will have Lady Serena here in Mercia, and mayhap information from her brother."

* * *

It was dark when Serena woke. With haste, she donned the clothes Rhodri had given her the night before as he told her of Eadric the Wild and his alliance with King Bleddyn of Wales. What did it bode for their chance to regain England?

Only a day had passed since she had talked with Maugris at the edge of the river, and the words of the old man continued to haunt her. The desire to be with Steinar pulled her toward Scotland at the same time her fear of discovery and her growing attraction for the Red Wolf prodded her to go.

Her people would survive. Though he might be arrogant and demanding, she was convinced the Red Wolf would do nothing to harm them.

As she made ready her escape, she told only Cassie, Rhodri and Aethel, who for her own reasons, had offered to help. Though the Welsh bard had counseled against it, Serena had decided to take no one with her. She would risk no one save herself.

Securing her long plait on top of her head, she pulled the brown cap over her ears. With great care, she stole from the servants' sleeping quarters, waking no one. Her soft boots made no sound as she crept into the kitchen and took her bow and quiver of arrows from behind the cabinet where Maggie had hidden them. Jamie had recovered her seax and once more the blade was secured at her waist. The bread and cheese saved from yesterday's meals would last her a day and then she would hunt. It was early summer and there would be plenty of game.

Keeping to the darkest shadows, she crept through the door leading to the kitchen garden. As she stepped over the threshold, she was startled to find Rhodri waiting for her.

"Serena, I would go with you," he whispered. "Steinar would expect it." The Welshman carried a small sack and his bow was slung over his shoulder.

"Nay, Rhodri," she insisted, "I would go alone. You are needed here."

His black curls fell onto his forehead and he frowned as he stepped back and bowed. "As you wish, my lady."

Serena could feel him watching her when she slipped silently to the stables. He still had his doubts, she knew. As Serena had expected, the stable boys slept soundly in the loft above, and the groom in his own alcove, so her soft footfalls did not wake them. Elfleda whinnied softly. Serena quickly walked to her stall and saddled the mare, leading her from the stables while keeping to the edge of the yard. Soon she was through the postern gate. The loud snores coming from the guard gave proof to the sleeping draft Aethel had supplied him the night before with his ale. He would not wake to stop her.

Once the woods engulfed her, Serena mounted her mare and rode north, slowly at first, winding her way through the dense stands of trees, and then at a gallop in open country. The rising sun painted the sky with gold streaks and she smiled with her success at getting away unnoticed. But she was less certain of her feelings at leaving the Norman whose very presence pulled her to him. She did not want to like the knight for the man he was, to remember the way he had kissed her, to see his gray eyes in her dreams. She wanted to remember only the Norman king he served. But in her heart, she already missed the Red Wolf.

She rode all day, stopping only briefly to water her horse and eat some of her food. The night brought her to a copse of trees near a large boulder. Exhausted, she drew her warm cloak around her, and with her arrows and seax held close, she curled up with the rock at her back and sought sleep.

CHAPTER 10

Renaud stormed down the stairs of the manor and seeing Geoff, drew the knight to one side. "Have you seen the servant girl Sarah? This time of day she is usually above stairs, but she has not yet come."

Although the morning meal had ended long ago, Renaud had not observed Sarah around the manor. Without realizing it, he had become familiar with her pattern of work, looking for the brown plait and violet eyes, pleased when he spotted her. He had noticed when the boy Jamie, now his page, walked to the stables alone that morning. Most days, Sarah would have been with him. And now she was absent from his chamber when she should have been freshening the linens.

"Now that you bring her to mind," said Geoff, his brows drawing together, "I cannot recall seeing her."

Renaud frowned but did not answer immediately. "I sense something is awry. See if Maggie knows of the girl. She may be unwell. I will be working in my chamber."

As he ascended the stairs, he could hear Geoff in the hall talking to Maggie while she and the serving girls cleared the trestle tables. "Maggie, have you seen Sarah? The lord is asking for her."

"M'lord, I know not where she is keeping herself. I've nay seen the girl all day. Ye might ask the boy Jamie."

A feeling of unease settled over Renaud as he entered his chamber. He was not able to concentrate on the drawings of the castle on his work table. Could one of his men have defied him and taken the girl? Certainly none would be so foolish, not after Sir Hugue's banishment. More likely she had gone to hunt rabbits and lay in the woods harmed by some beast. The image of Sarah's crumpled form lying still in the woods made him mad with anxiety.

By the time Geoff appeared at his door, Renaud was beside himself.

"Ren, the housekeeper has no knowledge of the girl, and the others we've questioned have nay caught a glimpse of her all day."

"Take some of the men and search the village, the woods. Find her!"

His friend knew him too well to question the order. "As you wish."

It was later that afternoon when Renaud sought distraction in swordplay with some of his men, taking out his frustration and his worry on the clash of metal against metal. Seeing Geoff approach with a worried look, Renaud waved off Sir Maurin with whom he'd been sparring and sheathed his sword. He knew immediately they'd not found the girl.

"She is not in the manor or the outbuildings. The village and the woods have been searched and she is nay there. On my way here, one of the stable lads came to tell me the mare belonging to Lady Serena is missing. Assuming the servant took the horse, she has stolen a fine one."

"When did the lad notice the horse missing?"

"He told me it was when he was feeding the horses this morning."

"And he said naught of it?"

"He assumed one of the men had taken the horse and would return it. He said he would have reported the horse missing if it had not been brought back. I think he felt badly he had not done so earlier."

His mood somber, Renaud wiped the sweat from his brow and chest and donned his tunic. "Let us return to the manor." Once bathed, and still brooding over the girl's disappearance, he joined the men in the hall where they were beginning the evening meal. She was only a servant, albeit a comely one. Why should he care if she took to the road? Mayhap the loss of the palfrey should concern him more.

Renaud could summon no appetite, so he strolled out to the yard, gazing through the gate to the dark green of the forest. She was gone. He had known in his heart it was so, but had hoped he was wrong.

Had she left on her own or had she received help from another?

After a few minutes, Geoff joined him.

"Have you seen the Welshman today, Geoff?"

"Nay, I have not."

Renaud wondered if they'd left together. He had never trusted the bard.

But why would she leave? The answer came quickly. It had been his attempts to woo her to his bed. She had made clear her hatred for Normans and likely feared he would force her. Or, mayhap it was more. Did she fear her own desire, that in time she would, of her own accord, come to his bed? After all, she had surrendered to his kisses. Even she could not deny the passion flowing between them when their lips touched. Because of her disdain for Normans, she would try and deny that passion.

"I am going after her." Renaud spoke his intention aloud. "There is still sun enough to travel for some hours yet."

"I'll gather some of the men and be ready to leave immediately," Geoff proffered.

As Geoff turned back to the hall, Renaud said, "Nay. This I do alone. The young fool left to avoid me. Without knowledge of how to ride, she may be lying hurt somewhere. It must be me who brings her back." His tone had been harsh though he was not angry with Geoff; he was angry with himself. And if, as he surmised, she had chosen to leave him because of what lay between them, he'd be angry with Sarah. And Rhodri if he aided her.

"When last she fled," Geoff said, "she rode north. She might have done so again. I doubt she has traveled far."

"I will ride the night if I must, but I will find her. Of that you can be certain."

As Renaud rode out of the gate, he passed the bard Rhodri coming in. They exchanged a slow look as Renaud rode past him.

So, she rides alone.

* * *

Serena shivered where she lay on the cold ground and pulled her blanket more tightly around her as the dream faded. The morning brought a pale sun and cold air nipped at her face. She had managed to sleep a few hours, but from the dull ache in her head, it was not enough. When night had fallen, she had listened for sounds that might warn her of men in the woods or beasts that would see her as prey. Thankfully, there had been none, but she'd listened all the same as she lay shivering in the night.

When she had slept, it was only to wake with the image of the Red Wolf in her mind. There was anger in his gray eyes, as she knew there would be when he learned of her escape. But it was needful she leave before she succumbed to his masculine lure, before he could claim her as his. If he took her maidenhead, she would belong to him forever, no matter the priest had said no blessing.

A rustle of leaves drew her gaze, but when she cautiously surveyed the woods around her, she saw nothing unusual, and heard only the birds greeting the morning.

Rising from the hard earth, she dusted off her clothes. She would ride for a while before breaking her fast. Mayhap it would clear her mind. Today she must hunt.

She had traveled only a few hours when, seeing a fast flowing stream, she decided to stop. If the stream was bountiful, she might catch some fish. But first she would hunt rabbits. She could cook the meat, eat some and carry the rest with her for her evening meal.

Leaving her horse tied in the sheltering oaks, she crept on silent feet, making her way through the sun-dappled forest in search of her prey. Long ago Rhodri had taught her to move as one of the creatures of the woodland, confident none would hear.

* * *

Renaud had ridden Belasco through the night, determined to find the girl. Before he lost the light, he had identified a trail heading north. When the sun sank and its glow of scarlet and gold gone from the sky, he gingerly made his way by the light of the moon. His body was now crying for rest but he was used to ignoring its demands. As a knight in William's service, he had gone days without sleep.

All during the night, thoughts of Sarah had run through his weary mind. Why was he so fascinated with the girl? All he had wanted at the end of war was peace, to find his joy in the land, as had his father and grandfather before him. Though, in truth, he knew little of the demands of a *demesne* such as Talisand, as Sarah in her impudence had informed him. But he could learn, and he would. And beside him he wanted the English girl, no matter she was a servant. He was certain he had been right in thinking she left because of him. Telling the women he would allow none of his men to force them was a truth. But he would never have to force Sarah. She had softened in his arms and returned his kisses, no matter how it shamed her to do so. She was only a servant and he was a Norman knight, now made an earl by his king. How much longer could she have refused him? Not long, he thought.

Anger warred with worry as he plodded on, concerned all the while what might have befallen her for her reckless leave-taking. Would he find her lying hurt somewhere? Thinking the worst, with the rising sun, he urged Belasco to a faster pace.

The sound of the running stream shook him out of his musings and reminded him both he and his horse were sorely in need of water and rest.

He led the gray stallion toward the sound of the gurgling water, and loosely wrapped Belasco's reins over a log near the stream's bank. But he walked on some distance until he spotted a large flat rock near the edge of the water. Kneeling, he leaned over the edge and brought the cold water to his mouth.

A snapping twig brought his head up. He stilled, searching the forest for the source of the sound. Brown and yellow leaves strewn about the gray rocks beneath the trees soaked up the sun's rays. A labyrinth of fallen logs and tree trunks lay before him. Anything could hide there.

The cause of the snapping twigs soon became apparent when he spotted movement. A slim lad, dressed in the colors of the forest, crouched at the edge of a small clearing, focused intently on the broad base of a tree where three rabbits foraged, as yet unaware of the lad's presence.

Without a sound, the lad nocked an arrow and pulled back the shaft. The first arrow flew with a whooshing sound. Then, so fast Renaud could not see the movements clearly, the lad nocked the second arrow, and fired off another shot, then another.

At the base of the tree, three rabbits lay dead.

He had never seen an archer so fast or so accurate. In truth, such skill was unknown to him. Mayhap he could recruit the young man to join his archers for he doubted if any of them could match the lad's speed.

Renaud watched as the lad walked to the base of the tree and leaned down to gather his kill. As he reached to pick up the first animal, his cap fell from his head and a thick brown plait tumbled toward the ground. A curse escaped Renaud's lips in a low hiss.

Sarah!

Then, into his mind came unbidden the words spoken by Jamie at the archery contest.

Her arm is so fast 'tis as if the bow is part of her, as if they are one.

Not Sarah. *Serena!*

With sudden clarity, he realized he'd been played the fool. Rage filled him as he slowly rose. The lady had deceived him, living beneath his nose disguised as a servant, determined to thwart his claim to her. Well, her deception was at an end.

Uncaring if she heard him, he boldly stomped toward her.

* * *

Startled by the sound of heavy footfalls crushing leaves and rattling stones, Serena whirled drawing her seax. Like an angry beast robbed of its kill, the Red Wolf stalked toward her, his hands curved into fists at his side. Fear gripped her as his cold gray eyes made clear his intent. Rising, she retreated until her back hit the broad trunk of the tree. Like a doe held in the fixed gaze of a wolf, she froze.

Knocking the knife from her hand, he clasped one arm around her waist and the other under her legs, sweeping her into his arms, and carried her toward the stream. The tension in his hard muscles and the set of his jaw shouted his anger. The force of his hold told her to struggle was futile.

"Where are you taking me?" she cried, aware they were alone in the forest.

"To prove to both of us just what I have found."

Without another word, at the edge of the stream he tipped her head down, causing her plait to splash into the flowing water. Holding her fast to his chest, the Red Wolf stared beyond her to the stream. Fearful of falling, she wrapped her hands tightly around his neck and looked back, her head only a foot above the rippling swirls. Her long brown plait drifted in the water. A feeling of dread came over her as she saw the brown color running from her hair to be carried away by the swift current. Parts of the plait were now flaxen where the walnut dye had deserted the pale strands.

Slowly she turned to look at him, his face mere inches from hers. Realization and anger glared from his cold gray eyes like a storm about to break.

He knows.

Setting her on her feet, he clamped his hands around her upper arms. "What is this deceit you have wrought? You are mine, Serena, by William's decree!"

"Never!" She pushed against his chest. "Never will I accept your claim or your king's decree." Though she knew the Normans counted women only as possessions, something to be bartered and given away like her lands, she was determined to fight. Within her raged a battle between dread and desire. But to give in to the desire seemed a betrayal of her father, her brother and all she held dear.

As if she weighed but a *sou*, he lifted her into his arms and carried her the short distance to the clearing. Setting her once again on her feet, he threw his cloak on the ground and forced her down upon it.

"What are you doing? Let me go!" She tried to stand, but his hand on her shoulder held her down. Squirming, she tried to fight off his hands but he fell upon her, his heavy weight pinning her to the ground. He captured her hands in his and held them above her head, as he looked into her eyes. Captivated by the desire she saw in his darkening gaze, both fear and excitement rose within her.

"No, Serena. I'll not let you go, not before I show you what lies between us. What you seek to deny. The reason for your flight. You cannot bear to want me, a Norman, can you?"

Before she could think to move, his lips were upon hers. She jerked her head away only to have him take her hands in his and raise them above her head. He took both her hands into one of his and grasped her chin with the other, forcing her to face him while she was pinned beneath his long muscled body.

The kiss was punishing. His tongue invaded her mouth, compelling her to accept him. Her body responded, her breasts sensitive to the weight of his powerful chest and her senses reeling from his warmth and his masculine scent, now so familiar. He lifted his mouth from hers, and leaving her gasping, rained kisses down her neck. He murmured words in French she could not discern, his voice a low seductive growl.

When his teeth grazed the base of her neck she moaned. He slid his hand to her breast where his touch rendered her nipple sensitive beyond enduring.

She could not help but reach her fingers to the thick chestnut waves of his hair.

His palm swept beneath her short tunic to cover her naked breast and she quivered as her nipples reacted, producing a tingling sensation that echoed through her body. His kiss was deep, his tongue moving like a flame, branding her as his. In spite of the all-consuming heat from their passion, she shivered as an unfamiliar ache arose in her most intimate flesh.

Overcome by the new sensations, every soft curve of hers embraced his hard body. He continued to kiss her while settling his lower body between her thighs. Moving his hips with a slow rocking motion, she was suddenly aware of his hard shaft pressing against her woman's center, demanding to claim what was his.

She knew enough about the mating of men and women to know his intent. "Nay!" she shouted. With her hands, she pushed against him with all of her strength, squirming to be free.

"You only entice me with your movements, Serena." The depth and huskiness of his voice told her he spoke truth. His lips brushed her ear.

Ignoring her protests, he pressed warm kisses to her neck just beneath her ear. Without meaning to, she bent her head to his, melting with the touch of his lips on her skin.

He raised his head. "Do you see how we are together, Serena? You have always been mine. You were given to me afore I ever came to Talisand. And now I will have you as my wife."

"But I will not have you!" Serena struggled to find the will to match her actions to her words, but her resolve was fading with his whispered words of love and his seductive movements.

She gripped his hair to pull him from her, but he kissed her again and soon her hands threaded through his thick locks and she ceased fighting and allowed her body to respond fully to his. She wrapped her arms around him and held onto his strength.

The Red Wolf moved his hands to the open laces of her tunic and then to her linen shirt, moving the cloth aside to expose her breasts to his eyes. "You are beautiful, Serena, as I imagined you would be." He forced another sigh from her when he cupped her naked breast and the warmth of his hand made her pull him closer.

Taking her nipple into his mouth, he gently sucked.

She shivered, then sighed. "Nay…" But it was only a weak plea.

Suddenly he rose up on his elbows. "Look at me, Serena." Her eyes fluttered open. In his silvered eyes she saw unrestrained passion. "You belong to me by the king's decree. Why do you not give to me what is mine to take?"

"Your king, not mine," she protested. Then looking away, "Take another for your wife."

"Nay. I wanted you as my leman ere I knew you were my bride, and I intend to have you and no other."

He bent his head to her breast, his tongue stroked her nipple, leaving her boneless and craving more. Against his strength, her weak efforts to resist availed little. In her woman's flesh the ache grew demanding.

His hand slid down to her braies and quickly stripped them down. The feel of his searching hand on the bare skin of her thigh was both alarming and enticing. He was moving ever closer to—

She panicked. "You would force me?" she asked breathlessly knowing only his own rules could stop him now.

At her words, he stilled, hovering over her, his breathing rapid as he stared into her eyes. Then, with sudden force, he pushed from her and sat back on his knees, breathing hard. He ran his hand through his hair.

"Though you say me nay, Serena, your body tells me something else."

"I am an innocent. You would seduce me against my will?"

"I would make you my wife in truth. For that is what you will be, no matter your anger at being wed to a Norman. You are mine by right." He let out a breath in a deep sigh. "But I would not take you here upon the hard ground. Talisand has beds enough. And you and I will find pleasure in them, have no doubt."

Still flushed with the pleasure he had called forth from her innocent flesh, Serena experienced a wave of relief. Every time he touched her, whether as Sarah or as Serena, he created a desire for more. His words only made clear how close she had come to submitting. How much she already had.

* * *

Renaud looked down at his bride where she sat upon the grass pulling her clothing together. He was glad her words had brought a halt to his fevered consummation. Her eyes told him she was bewildered by her own reaction. Serena had meant to fight, he knew, but was defeated by the passion between them. A passion that pleased him. If that is all they had to begin their marriage, he was content. It was more than most marriages of state had when they began. He would use it to hold her. But he would not take her here, even though she was his to take. He wanted the memory of their first joining to be a pleasant one.

"I will give you time to get used to the idea but know this, Serena: it will not be long. Your resistance and your deception are at an end, my lady." The irony of it was that while his rules kept him from forcing the servant girl Sarah, a wife was another matter.

He retrieved the rabbits Serena had killed, and her seax, fixing them to the saddle on the white palfrey he found standing among the trees. Whistling for his horse, he waited only a moment before Belasco entered the clearing and nuzzled his master's shoulder. Renaud reached for the satchel of food tied to the saddle.

"Here," he said handing her some dried venison. "Eat. You must be hungry if you are hunting. But I do not want to take time to cook the rabbits now."

With a look of resignation, she took the dried deer meat and chewed in silence.

"It was your speed with the bow that told me you were Lady Serena. You hid well your skill in the shooting match, but not so well I did not think something amiss."

He tied the reins of her white mare to Belasco's saddle while continuing to glance at her where she sat upon the ground. Even with her wet plait, now half brown and half flaxen, and her disheveled state, she was beautiful and the knowledge that in finding her he had found both the servant girl he desired and the woman promised to him produced a feeling of deep satisfaction. A wife and a leman in one woman, and in one day. Even his anger at her deception could not destroy his joy at so great a find.

Serena slowly rose, and without a word or a glance at him, walked toward her horse as if in a daze. He reached for her arm and pulled her toward Belasco.

Defiantly, she wrenched away. "I can ride my own horse!"

"Nay, you'll ride with me. I want you close." In truth, he did not want to be so far from her he could not touch her.

He lifted her to his saddle and leapt up behind her, repositioning her onto his lap. She kept her back stiff, even when he drew her body against his chest.

Taking the reins in his free hand, he swung Belasco toward the south and Talisand, urging the stallion to a fast pace with his knees. Serena looked straight ahead, her hand clenched on the pommel of the saddle.

He bent his mouth to her ear. "Serena, you must accept the truth of it. England is conquered, your lands are conquered, and you are conquered. God must have willed it for William has prevailed, as have I. He is king by conquest as I am your lord. You will become my wife and bear my sons. You are mine as Talisand is mine."

She tensed against him keeping her gaze fixed ahead as she spoke. "You may have conquered my lands, my lord, and I may be forced to birth your sons, but I shall never be content to be a Norman's wife. I…I hate you!"

"Nay, Serena, I think not. You hate only yourself for wanting me. Mayhap one day you will even be content to belong to me."

"You are wrong!" She spit out the words with great force, as if trying to convince herself they were true.

He experienced a sudden twinge of remorse seeing the girl's broken spirit. She had tried so hard to escape her fate. A proud, courageous woman who loved her people. As she had told him the first day they met, she would have fought alongside her father had she been a son. But she had seen him with her people and had to know he would not treat them ill.

She might hate what he represented, but she could not deny what lay between them. He was certain if he touched her again, as he intended to, she would respond as she had before. Only next time he would not rein in his passion. He would make her his in all ways.

He had not expected to find a woman of such fire in the English maiden William had given him, but he was glad of it. Their winter nights would be warm and their children would be many and strong.

In one sweep of his arm, Renaud wrapped his cloak about her and held her fast, declaring his intention to possess and protect what was his. Her days of hiding from him were over.

The Lady of Talisand was coming home.

CHAPTER 11

Serena woke to the movement of the horse beneath her and the Red Wolf shouting orders as they rode into the yard. Sometime during the long ride back, she had fallen asleep against his warm chest where his strong arm now held her. For hours she had fought to stay awake as the knight drove his horse at a maddening pace. Finally exhausted, she had succumbed to the sweet oblivion of sleep. Now fully awake, she sat up to see they had reined in before the manor where a crowd was gathering to greet them.

The Red Wolf dismounted and reached for her. She did not fight him when his hands circled her waist and he lifted her down, but when he again swept her up into his arms, she protested. "Put me down! I can walk."

"Not just yet," the Red Wolf replied stonily. Then to Eric, "See to the horses, lad. A good rub down and oats. It was a long ride home and Belasco did well."

"Aye, m'lord," said the boy, accepting the reins.

Serena twisted in the arms of the Red Wolf, embarrassed at being treated like an errant child in front of her people who watched with curious eyes.

Jamie ran up to his master, smiled at her, and awaited his lord's instructions. Though his blond curls were in disarray, Jamie now wore with pride the dark blue tunic displaying a snarling red wolf.

"Jamie," the Red Wolf looked down at his page, "see that Maggie gets the rabbits."

"Yea, sir, I will. Welcome back, m'lord."

Serena could feel the tension in the Norman's body as he held her. She gave up struggling, realizing he intended to carry her into the manor whether she liked it or no. The Norman knights who had come to greet their returning lord gazed intently at the woman in his arms who was dressed like a Welshman. Serena's plait was under the cloak he'd wrapped around her, so none yet observed the change in the color of her hair. They knew only what they observed: the maid Sarah had tried to run away disguised as a boy, and had been found by their lord who was now carrying her close to his chest. She could only imagine what they were thinking took place in the woods.

With her in his arms, the Red Wolf closed the short distance to the manor's door. She spotted Rhodri standing to one side, his clothes soiled as if he, too, had been in the woods. He watched her with concern in his dark eyes. Where had he been? Had he followed the Red Wolf? Next to Rhodri stood a few of Talisand's women who looked at her with questioning eyes. She wondered, as mayhap some of them did, in what manner she had returned? Prisoner? Bride? Or both?

The Red Wolf carried her inside and dumped her onto the bench. She shot him a glare just as Maggie rushed to meet them.

"M'lord?" the housekeeper said, a worried look on her face as her gaze shifted from the Red Wolf to Serena. Both were wearing a scowl.

"See that your lady has a bath and something to eat," he ordered shortly.

A startled look crossed the housekeeper's face as recognition dawned. "Yea, m'lord." Maggie's eyes took in Serena's bedraggled appearance. "Come, m'lady, I'll see to ye meself." Maggie wrapped a comforting arm around her and led her toward the stairs.

"So he knows, does he?" Maggie whispered.

"Aye." Serena let out a sigh. She was tired but her desire to fight was changing into a new resolve. It was no use fighting the inevitable. Mayhap it was time to resume her position as the Lady of Talisand even if she had to become a Norman's wife to do it.

They started up the stairs, and from behind them, the Red Wolf shouted to Maggie, "See that her hair is washed and that dreadful color of dirt gone from it. I will have a tray sent up."

Maggie looked over her shoulder. "Yea, m'lord."

Nearly to the top of the stairs, Serena heard the Red Wolf order Sir Niel to guard her door.

So it was to be a prisoner, after all.

* * *

Renaud took a deep drink of his wine, forcing himself to calm as the evening meal commenced. He was fighting exhaustion but he was pleased his bride was now in her chamber behind a guarded door.

Sitting on his left, Geoff speared a large piece of venison on the point of his eating knife. "Is it true?" he asked, holding the meat before his mouth. "You have found not only Sarah, but your bride?" At Renaud's nod, he continued, "I can scarce believe it, Ren. All this time Lady Serena living among us. I must say, she fooled me. I failed to recognize the lady in the servant's garb."

"As did I," Renaud muttered as he circled his goblet with his hand. Something was nagging at him, a thought that had not left him since he had nearly taken her at the edge of the stream. She was clever in deceiving him, disguised first as a maid and then as a lad. On the ride home she had fallen asleep, curled against him like a protected child. But she was no child. She was a woman full grown and he could not hold her without his body stirring. He had wanted the violet-eyed beauty since the day he had first seen her, and now she was returned as his bride. One day she would be the mother of his sons, would she prefer it or no. Still, he has no illusions. She might try and escape again if she could. The desire he had awakened in her, he was certain, did not alter her feelings for Normans. He had to remember the battle was not over.

"Why are you so sullen?" Geoff needled. "This sudden turn of events should please you." The blond knight snatched the venison off the knife with his teeth.

"Aye, it does, but I'll not celebrate the marriage just yet. Something tells me the fight for the lady's hand is not over. I cannot trust her, Geoff. As you observed yourself, the woman has only disdain for Normans. And she is clever at escape. Hence, I have posted Sir Niel at her door. I want her watched at all times Mayhap the next days will disclose her intent. I expect she may yet try to flee."

Renaud gazed about the room. Some of his knights still lingered over their meal. Others diced or played *échecs*, the game of skill with carved pieces, occasionally letting out a yell when one won a round. The red-haired serving girl he recognized as Maggie's daughter was smiling at Sir Maurin as she filled his tankard with ale, and the knight smiled back. Mayhap there would be more weddings celebrated ere midwinter was upon them.

"Would it help to recall that you need no priest's blessing to claim what William has given you, Ren?"

"That may be, but I would have our marriage blessed by the church. Best send for the priest, or the bishop, if near. I want the people to know we are wed according to God's law, not just William's command."

"Have you forgotten? Father Bernard left some time ago, not to return for a fortnight. Sarah...that is, Lady Serena said he is seeing to the needs of other villages. And the nearest bishop is Ealdred, Archbishop of York to the east."

"Ah, so it is. I remember now, the chapel was missing a priest. Mayhap 'twould be best if I await his return. Still, I would keep her guarded until the marriage ceremony, no matter she shares my bed. Tell the men she may have free run of the manor and the yard as long as her movements are watched. She may not ride unescorted."

"Get her with child and she will nay travel far."

"'Tis my plan." Renaud had thought of little else on his ride back to Talisand. Now that he had his bride, he need not woo the servant girl. And he wanted no other. Serena had ruined him for any other woman. Geoff and Sir Maurin were not the only knights at Talisand who were besotted with English women. But Renaud knew well he would have to hide his weakness for his bride. If she were not loyal, she could do him great harm.

He drank deeply of his wine and pushed back from the table, bidding Geoff a good night. He was barely able to keep his eyes open, yet he was eager to see the lady who had so long eluded him. Likely, she was still angry with her Norman captor. He was angry as well for her deceit had disturbed him.

As he dragged his tired body from the hall, Maugris intercepted him at the bottom of the stairs.

"My lord, I understand the Lady of Talisand has returned...is it so?"

"Yea, I hunted the servant girl, Sarah, but found the Lady Serena. It seems she has been deceiving all of us." Renaud studied the wise one's face and realized from his knowing smile he had been aware.

"'Twas nimble witted, you must admit," the old man said with amusement dancing in his ancient blue eyes. "Me thinks she is a worthy mate for the Red Wolf."

"I did not find her behavior praiseworthy, wise one. Though I am certain it brought smiles to the faces of the villeins. They knew, all of them. To fool the Normans who went about their business unaware the lady of the manor was living under their noses as a mere servant must have amused them. And you, my *own* advisor—you knew, yet did not tell me!"

Maugris's smile faded. "No, I did not. I knew from my vision it was you who had to find the jewel among the stones. And I had confidence you would find her, though you had to reason it on your own if you were to be her mate. Think, my lord. She was angry and afraid, and only fled for her honor and that of the other maidens. Do you not remember?"

"Aye, I remember the women." Renaud could not find fault with the servant girls who had fled that first day. Mayhap Serena was only doing what she thought was right. But when she learned he would be honorable toward her people, she had not revealed herself. Instead, she had sought to escape again.

The old man's blue eyes stared at Renaud. "You have but to hold her close, my lord, and she will be yours."

"Oh, I intend to do that, Maugris." Renaud's gaze traveled up the stairs. "Very close."

"I will leave you then to your bride." Maugris grinned and headed toward the hall.

Renaud could still hear the sounds of his men indulging in their entertainments but he had no tolerance for games or small talk this night. His head was pounding, and he was more exhausted than he could remember being. But he still had one last task.

Climbing the stairs to Serena's chamber, he sent Sir Niel to his dinner and to his pallet. Renaud entered to find the room dark, save for one candle. He recognized the flowery scent and chided himself for not identifying it before. It was *her* scent.

Flickering golden light bathed the lone figure curled up on the furs at the end of the bed. Dressed, from all appearances, only in a white robe, her eyes were closed and her head rested on her hand. A cloth was clasped in her other hand. She must have fallen asleep while drying her hair.

She had the face of an angel with delicate features, ivory skin and rose-colored lips. Her long flaxen hair fell around her, glistening in the candlelight, a crowning glory so magnificent it could have hidden wings had she possessed them. Certainly his woman, soon his bride, was an otherworldly creature. Fierce with a bow, quick with her tongue and the voice of heaven in her throat when she sang. And curves to entice the most monkish of knights. No man, be he warrior priest or no, could resist her when she lay like this.

William had given him no ordinary woman. Renaud had only to claim her.

Quietly he approached the sleeping girl and lifted her into his arms. She stirred but did not wake as he carried her to his own chamber, her pale hair falling over his arm nearly to the floor.

Laying her down on his bed, her robe fell open revealing the full breasts he had feasted upon next to the stream. His manhood stirred. Brushing her long silvered hair to one side, he shed his clothes and climbed into the bed to lie beside her, pulling her body into the curve of his own. He drew the cover over them and his body responded to her softness, his aroused flesh eager to sink into her sheath. Serena softly moaned in her sleep as he cupped a warm breast. But it was more than lust he felt. He wanted to protect her, to care for her, feelings he'd never had for another woman.

He doubted he had won her fully. Mayhap their sons would bind her to him, as the king's decree could not.

Renaud had intended to wake her to his lovemaking, but he was so exhausted after riding hard without sleep for so long, his last waking thought was to shut his eyes for a few minutes. Then he would wake and claim his bride.

* * *

A pounding on the door woke Serena from a deep sleep.

Still groggy, she heard a voice shout, "My lord, a messenger from the king!"

The arm that held her slipped away and the bed cushion beneath her was jostled, making Serena realize she was not alone. The one sleeping next to her lifted from the bed. She opened her eyes, surprised to see she was in the lord's chamber—and in the Red Wolf's bed. She caught only a glimpse of his naked form as he reached for a dark blue robe.

His body was that of a warrior, his powerful muscles beneath his skin rippling as he moved. As she had observed when she'd helped him with his bath, his back was bronze to his waist. But his muscled buttocks and long legs were a lighter shade. A man to make any maiden blush.

She'd not seen the scars on his midsection before. So, he had not always fought wearing mail.

Donning his robe, he opened the door a slit. What she could see of Sir Geoffroi's face bore a grave expression. "The king summons you," he said to the Red Wolf. "His messenger awaits below."

"I'll join you as soon as I am clothed."

The Red Wolf closed the door and turned. Serena pulled the covers under her chin and kept her eyes on his face.

"My lady," he said, taking off his robe. He seemed entirely comfortable in just his skin. "I would we had this morning to lie abed and become better acquainted, but as you heard, I am summoned. The consummation of our marriage must wait upon the king's needs." Reaching for his hosen, linen shirt and tunic, he leaned over the bed and kissed her forehead.

Her eyes slid to the dark thatch of hair at his groin and to his large manhood.

"If you keep staring at me like that I will find myself in trouble with the king."

Embarrassed that he had caught her staring, Serena's cheeks burned.

"'Twould be best if you dress quickly and join me below. It is time my men met their lady."

Once he was dressed, he left, the door closing behind him.

Serena lay back against the pillow, thinking of all that had happened. There had been no words between them after they had returned to the manor the evening before. Her last memories were of his harsh words on the ride home and his instructions to Maggie. But his kiss on her forehead a few moments before had been tender. Did he assume she was now resigned to being his bride?

Was she?

Twice she had tried to escape. Twice she had failed. She had fought her attraction to him as the servant girl Sarah, but in that, too, she had not succeeded. She might fight him still if it would change her fate or that of her people. Sadly, she believed it would not. Thoughts of Steinar filled her mind. Was he still in Scotland? Though she was reluctant to admit it, she had little desire to flee again. She had shouted her hatred of the Norman knight, but even in that she had not been sincere. He had raised a desire within her no other man had. No man had ever touched her the way he did, and caused her to want him. As a Norman he might repulse her, but as a man he entranced her. Even as she had ridden from Talisand, she had missed him. When he had discovered her in the woods, a part of her had been relieved the ruse was over.

The Red Wolf had ordered a guard at her door, so little was his trust of her. No longer the maid Sarah or the thegn's daughter, she belonged to the Norman knight. Yet neither fully trusted the other. She reminded herself of her new resolve. For the sake of her people, she would take her place at his side. He was right when he said not only her country had been conquered, but that she had been conquered. Conflicting emotions warred within her. She was the proud daughter of a thegn, and only reluctantly did she accept her fate as the wife of the powerful Red Wolf.

Serena slowly climbed from the bed, and reached for her robe lying at the foot of the bed. Once she was sufficiently covered, she returned to her chamber, hugging the wall of the corridor so that none below could see her. She could hear the knights speaking, their murmurs loud enough to reach her. They seemed excited about something, mayhap the messenger who had come from their king.

She opened the door to her chamber to find Cassie waiting.

"M'lady!" The handmaiden ran to Serena and embraced her. "Me mother told me last night ye were brought back by the Red Wolf. He has sent me to help dress ye, and not, as ye might imagine, in the clothes of a servant. He asks ye to wear the gowns of yer station as the Lady of Talisand."

Serena sank onto the edge of her bed, twining her fingers through her now flaxen tresses. "Yea, 'tis nay something I can escape this time."

"Did he hurt ye, m'lady?" Cassie asked with a worried look as her gaze roamed over Serena.

"Nay." At Cassie's surprised expression, Serena added, "I did not wake when he carried me to his chamber last night. We shared a bed but naught more. He was likely as drained of strength as was I. Sir Geoffroi awakened us both. I do not doubt the Red Wolf would have done more but for the messenger. He said as much."

"Yea, a messenger arrived from the Norman king. Sir Maurin and the others were called together as I was coming up for ye. Ye'd best dress, m'lady. Something is afoot."

Serena rose. "This time I must face them as the thegn's daughter."

Her handmaiden smiled. "Come, let us show the Red Wolf's men the real Lady of Talisand." Pride gleamed in Cassie's green eyes. "I think the purple gown of fine wool, embroidered with the golden silk thread yer father gave ye, would be fitting. 'Tis nearly the color of yer eyes."

Serena washed her face and slipped on her linen undertunic, happy to have the fine cloth next to her body once again. Cassie lifted the elegant gown over Serena's head and let it fall in soft folds about her. Her handmaiden pulled the lacings tight so that the gown hugged her slender form. Brushing her hair 'til it shown like moonlight, Cassie sat back with admiring eyes and then began to braid it.

"Nay, Cassie. This day I will wear my hair unbound and uncovered. It may well be the last time."

"Then let me secure it with the circlet yer father gave ye."

Cassie opened the chest at the foot of the bed and pulled from it the precious circlet of silver woven with intricate gold leaves and set with amethyst stones.

Standing back, the handmaiden smiled. "Now ye look like yerself, m'lady. Willna all of Talisand be happy to see such a grand sight?"

"In truth, I cannot say. It is not what I wanted, Cassie, but it might be for the best. If it is my fate to serve the people at the Norman's side, so be it. It is my fervent hope I can help him understand their needs."

"Ye can lift yer head high, m'lady. Never forget ye are a powerful thegn's daughter."

"I never shall." She hugged her childhood friend, straightened her shoulders and raised her chin. It was time to greet the Red Wolf and his men.

CHAPTER 12

Standing in the manor's entry, Renaud crumpled the parchment in his hand and exchanged a look with Sir Maurin. "William's summons comes at an inconvenient time, but our sire has need of us, so we must go." He shifted his gaze to the young messenger dressed in the king's livery. "Get some food and then be on your way. You may tell the king the Red Wolf rides this day to join him."

The messenger bowed, then headed toward the kitchen. Flanked by Geoff and Sir Maurin, Renaud stood watching his men breaking their fast, wondering what he should tell them.

"Where are we bound, Ren?" asked Geoff.

"To Exeter. It seems Gytha, mother of the dead Harold, has stirred the city to resist William's increase in annual tribute and his demand for fealty. He has marched on the city intending to lay siege and summons me to add my men to his army."

"I'll ready the men," Geoff said solemnly, and together with Sir Maurin, turned toward the hall.

Renaud reached his hand to Geoff's arm to stop him, but allowed Sir Maurin to continue on his way. "I will address the men, Geoff. There is Talisand to see to as we may be away for some time."

Renaud stepped to the large doorway leading into the hall. His presence silenced the men's conversations as all eyes turned toward him. In addition to his knights and retainers, there were a number of Talisand's men in the hall. The Welsh bard, Rhodri stood to one side looking on with furrowed brows.

"The king has summoned us to join him in the south for a siege," he announced.

The men cheered.

When they quieted, he continued. "Knights and archers be prepared to ride at the sixth hour." Nodding heads and smiles on the faces of his men displayed their approval of the new orders. "Sir Maurin will remain here with enough men to defend the manor and village. Now that I have chosen a site for the castle, and the plans are drawn, the building will proceed apace with Sir Maurin as overseer in my absence. Talisand's men and the carpenters we brought with us will see the task done."

Sir Maurin nodded from where he stood amidst the others, and Renaud was reminded he must speak to the knight about the guard he had appointed for his errant bride.

As Renaud gave further instructions for their travel to Exeter, the continued smiles on the faces before him made clear his men were eager for battle. It was what they had trained for, and the past months had shown them little action.

In the midst of the men's murmurs, all sounds suddenly died away and the eyes of his knights fixed on a point behind him as they rose from their seats.

Renaud sensed her presence even before he turned.

Serena.

No longer dressed as a servant, his bride stood adorned like a queen. Stunned by her beauty, his eyes took in the elegant purple gown that hugged her curves not revealed by the servant's attire she had worn before.

A fitting mate indeed.

Her unplaited flaxen hair, crowned by a silver and gold circlet, announced to all she was a maiden still, making him regret again that the king's summons that had forced him from his bed.

Stepping aside, he gestured her forward. As she approached, there were gasps from some of his men who, looking more closely, realized for the first time who the servant girl Sarah really was.

She stood proudly, her violet eyes shining with a light of determination.

"Good knights and men of Talisand," Renaud said loudly, first in Norman French and then in English, "I give you my lady, Serena of Talisand." For a moment the hall was silent. Then his knights dropped to one knee, each bringing his fist to his heart, silently pledging fealty and protection to the woman who was to be their lord's wife.

Serena stood for a moment, her eyes traveling over his men, a slight smile on her lips. Then, to his great surprise, she spoke in perfect Norman French.

"I thank you for your obeisance. But lest you believe otherwise, know this: Talisand is the rich *demesne* you see today because of the foresight and wisdom of an English thegn, my father, Sigmund. I would ask that you respect his memory and treat well the people of Talisand he loved, for they have lost much and I would restore it to them if I could."

She paused for a moment and then stepped back into the manor's entry, and smiled at him briefly before saying, "My lord," and hastening through the door to the yard that Sir Niel held open for her. The knight nodded to Renaud and followed after her.

Renaud faced his men, his knights having risen from their knees to stand.

"Heed my lady's words. I would have no disparagement of the old lord. He is the grandsire of the sons Lady Serena will one day give me."

To Renaud's ear came the sound of a loud cheer from the yard outside. He turned and strode to the front door. The yard was bathed in sunlight. Serena, her back to him, stood before a large gathering of English men and women. Unwilling to interfere, he waited, wondering what she would say.

She raised her hands to still their murmured praises.

"Good people of Talisand, I am once again among you as your lady." A cheer rose up from the crowd. It seemed to Renaud this was no conquered English maiden. More like a queen returning from a forced absence to greet her subjects.

"I seek only to serve you and to help ease the pain of your loss—the husbands, fathers and sons who are gone from us forever—and the independence my father had granted you. Though we have lost much, we must thank the Master of the Heavens for what we still have and for the coming harvest. I thank you, as well, for your loyalty, your protection and your many kindnesses."

Renaud was pleased to hear her gracious words. Though he was angered at her deception, to his ears she sounded resigned to her role as his countess. He could only hope it was so. Walking forward, he wrapped his arm around her shoulder, claiming her before the people. She stiffened slightly but did not pull away. Mayhap if he were gracious, he could end the acrimony between them.

Speaking to those gathered, he said, "I have told my men that Serena is my lady and soon, my wife and countess. They are to respect her as such. May we all prosper because she is returned to you." The people listened, but remained silent at his words. To them he was still the foreign invader. Then, too, some would be called to battle this very day at his orders. But before they left, he would have them know he respected their lady.

Renaud faced Serena and spoke in a softer voice for her ears alone. "Join me at my table for the morning meal, my lady, and then I must depart to join William."

"You go to fight again?" she asked anxiously.

He hoped it was worry he saw in her beautiful eyes yet he dared not believe she might truly care about the husband forced upon her. There was passion between them, he knew that well, yet he was still the Norman who had claimed her lands. "Yea, I go to Exeter in Devon."

Frowning, she said, "Gytha, the queen mother lives there."

"She is no longer the mother of a king, Serena, and because she has stirred the men of the city to rise against William, they will once again know his wrath."

Serena looked down, but he doubted it was in resignation.

In a subdued voice, she said, "Four of Gytha's eight children died the year your king claimed England; she lost three sons at Hastings alone."

"And the other—Tostig—was a brother of treachery."

"Yea," she said raising her head and staring into his eyes, "he fought his brother Harold and fell at Stamford Bridge. So did Ulrich, husband of Lady Eawyn, who fought against the invader from Norway. But after Hastings, Gytha pleaded with your William for the body of her son Harold. The Norman king rejected her plea. Is it not understandable she should inspire the Saxons to rise against a man who would deny a Christian burial to their king?"

"It is the way of war, my lady. William had his reasons. But one day the fighting will end. You must look forward to that day, as I do." How he longed for the day when he could be concerned only with his lands, his lady and his sons, and claim the peace so long denied him. Yet he feared he would never know that peace.

"*Will* the fighting end?" she asked. "I wonder. Your king is still challenged by many. And do not forget that Edgar Ætheling, the Saxon who would sit on the English throne, is now safely ensconced in Scotland with my brother."

He had not known that Steinar was with Edgar Ætheling, the young English contender for the throne, but it made sense. "I have not forgotten where your loyalties lie, my lady." Renaud was unhappy to be reminded that the woman he would take to wife was not loyal to William. But he had no desire to argue with her just before he rode to battle. "Come," he said as he led her inside the manor, the people having dispersed, "I would share a meal with you, Serena, lest we argue ere I ride, mayhap to my death." Serena placed her hand on his offered arm and another question occurred to him. "Would you mourn the loss of your future husband?"

* * *

112

Still pondering his question, Serena took her place at the Red Wolf's table for the first time since the Normans had come. She sat on his right, Sir Geoffroi on his left and Maugris on her other side. Though there was still much activity in the hall, some of the men had already left, presumably to prepare for their soon departure. Rhodri looked at her from where he sat at one of the long tables, a question in his eyes. She knew he wondered if this had truly been her decision or if she had been forced. The Welshman and Steinar were close, and to her, Rhodri wore the look her brother would have worn had he been here. A look of incredulity. How could she agree to wed a Norman?

Staring at the trencher she shared with the Red Wolf, she took a bite of the brown bread spread with butter and then a piece of the cooked white fish taken from the river that ran next to the manor. Wild strawberries were piled high in a small bowl set to one side.

She picked up a berry, the color of fresh blood, and worried it in her fingers. Would it matter if the Red Wolf were slain in this battle he was called to by his king? Her anger still burned for the Norman who called himself England's ruler, the one who had robbed her of her father, but no matter her words the day before, she could not bring herself to hate the knight who would take her to wife. She would miss him were he to be slain. And, if he were killed, the Norman king would only force her to wed another of his men, one she might like less well than the Red Wolf.

"I would see you return from Exeter, my lord."

He studied her face. "You tarried long in coming to that answer, my lady."

She looked into his gray eyes framed by the thick russet waves of his hair. Was it concern she saw in them? He was a handsome knight, she had to admit, and though oft stern, an honorable one. If she were honest with herself, she would have to acknowledge she cared for him.

"I had much to ponder, my lord. But when the time comes for you to leave, know that I will wish you Godspeed."

He smiled and reached for the goblet of ale set between them, taking a long draw. "For that I am grateful, my lady. Hopefully I shall not tarry long in the south. While I am gone, you can prepare for our wedding feast."

"As you wish, my lord."

"Ah, the obedient Lady of Talisand. I wonder if this change is to be believed."

Serena said nothing. She wondered herself.

"I hope it is," he said, studying her somber face. "Meanwhile, when I return, the castle should be well underway. I have chosen the site next to the manor. What think you of that? It will mean we can incorporate the existing structures into the larger bailey."

"It pleases me, my lord. I would like to retain what has been my home."

"I thought you might," he said, mirth reflected in his sparkling gray eyes.

Now that he'd found her and she had agreed to become his wife, he seemed to have softened toward her, evidenced by the new light in his eyes. "You did it for me?" She had never considered the possibility he took her desires into account, particularly when at the time he made those plans he thought the Lady Serena was in Scotland.

"I had to consider a place that could be defended, of course, but your father had obviously chosen well, locating the manor in the bend of the river as he did. It made sense to follow his lead. I also believed Lady Serena would want her home to be part of the castle grounds."

"I thank you," she said, taking a drink of ale from the cup he passed her. "It will please the people as it pleases me."

* * *

Aethel brushed her long dark plait over her shoulder and picked up the pitcher. Slowly she walked toward the kitchen. The knight's eyes followed her from the corner of the hall where he stood leaning against the wall with his arms crossed over his broad chest. Sir Alain de Roux, the largest of the Norman knights, the one who carried the Red Wolf's banner, was staring at her as he often did. There were other men who looked at her, but his intense perusal was different. More possessive somehow.

She had been with no man since the old thegn died, having been rejected by the new lord. And she wanted none. So, she ignored them all. Still, the big knight intrigued her, his penetrating gaze following her about the hall as she served the evening meal. Was it lust she saw in his eyes or something else? Something more?

He walked slowly toward her and her pulse sped. The man rarely said much, even to the other knights, so she was surprised when he came to stand before her and leaned in to whisper in English, "You are better than what you think of yourself, Aethel."

His hazel eyes had sparks of green and his dark brown hair was wavy to his nape, a sensual man with a face that said he'd experienced much of life. "What know ye of what I think, sir knight?"

"I know you were jealous of Lady Serena even when we all thought her to be a servant. It need not be so. You are a beautiful woman and should have a man of your own."

Aethel hardly knew what to say. She had played second choice for so long she had become used to the role though, in truth, she had always wanted more. "A man like ye, sir knight?" she teased, assuming he was not serious. With his large muscled chest and arms, he was a giant of a man. And not unattractive. "Would ye be wanting me for a night?" She had no intention of giving herself to this man, if that is what he sought, but she would know.

"Nay, Aethel. I would have you for more."

Aethel shivered at the heat she observed in his eyes, a fierce look that seemed to peel away all her layers of defense.

"I would have you for my wife."

"Wife?" Was the Red Wolf's banner man sincere? Though men had desired her, even some of the Red Wolf's men, Aethel had never been offered marriage. And since Theodric had rejected her love, and she'd gone to the old thegn's bed, she thought she would never have a husband or children of her own. She knew enough of herbs to assure she would not birth a bastard. But as a child, she'd had dreams. Always they were of the fair-haired Theodric, captain of the thegn's guard, who she'd watched at swordplay from the time they were both children. But those dreams died years ago.

"Aye, *wife*." His gaze did not falter and in his eyes she saw a challenge. He meant what he said!

"Ye seem very certain of me when ye know me not at all, Sir Alain."

"I know this, Aethel: you would make me a fine wife. Though I have seen you make eyes at the Red Wolf, you have been with no man, be he knight or villein, since I came to Talisand. I want a family and I want a woman I desire above others to birth my sons. You will be that woman."

A shyness suddenly came over Aethel, as if he had stripped away the crust she had formed to protect her broken heart. Glancing down at her feet, she whispered, "I am not worthy. Ye should have a fine lady, one who has known no other man."

"I shall have the woman I want, Aethel." Taking her hand, he lifted her fingers to his lips and pressed a kiss on her knuckles. "And I want you."

* * *

Standing in the yard, Serena's gaze followed the Red Wolf as he departed Talisand, sitting tall on his gray stallion at the head of the column of knights and retainers. A sudden jolt of pride made her chest swell knowing he was hers, yet that pride warred with the knowledge he rode to battle against yet another English city.

Brown hosen covered his long muscled legs, crisscrossed by leather straps from his ankles to just below the knee where they were met by tunic and mail. Over his mail, beneath his cloak, he had donned the pelt of the beast, announcing to all he rode as William's knight.

Though the knights rode palfreys and other horses, their powerful destriers traveled with them, ready for battle. The Red Wolf's banner, held high by the burly knight, Sir Alain, waved in the breeze, a snarling red wolf on a dark blue field.

Jamie now rode in the Red Wolf's personal attachment. When she'd bid the boy safe travels, his smile beamed from where he'd sat atop the small horse, delighted to be accompanying his master to battle. A foreboding swept over Serena as she thought of the terrible scenes the boy might witness, battles where a small boy might be caught in the fray. Jamie had never seen war, though he knew well men could be slain and never return. The Red Wolf had assured her he would keep the boy safe, but she had witnessed the knights in their mail securing their shields and lances to their saddles and experienced the unease of one who has bidden warriors farewell never to see them again.

As she had said she would, she had wished the Red Wolf "Godspeed" from where she stood next to his stallion in the yard. In response, with his chestnut hair blowing across his forehead, he reached down, wrapped his arm around her waist and lifted her to him, soundly kissing her for all to see. The kiss was possessive and nearly punishing, but it roused within her a longing she could not deny as she brought her arms around his neck to hold him close and return his kiss. When he had set her feet on the ground, she had flushed with embarrassment seeing the smiles on the faces of his knights.

Aethel and Cassie had been in the yard as well, but they had been looking at other knights. Cassie had eyes only for Sir Maurin, and to Serena's surprise, Aethel was waving to a smiling Sir Alain who rode behind the Red Wolf.

The column of knights grew smaller and began to disappear over the hill in the distance when Serena climbed to the roof walk. Raising her hand to shelter her eyes against the midday sun, she gazed at the men and their horses fading from sight. She felt a deep sadness at the Red Wolf's going, and that surprised her. Embarrassed by her feelings for the Norman knight, she dropped her hand, intent on returning to her duties as the Lady of Talisand. She would stay busy and soon he would return.

The sound of a hammer striking wood drew her attention to the yard below where a man mended a wooden sheep's pen. A boy walked toward the kitchen, carrying a catch of fish. And a few chickens squawked as they found themselves in the path of a tinker and his cart pulled by a donkey slowly plodding through the gate.

The traveling merchant was clearly English, his beard showing below the wide brimmed straw hat he wore upon his head. From beneath the cart's cover, she observed a flash of bright sapphire blue, and next to it, a deep shade of crimson, bolts of cloth he had come to sell. 'Twas most unusual to see such cloth in a tinker's cart, but now that she was once again wearing the clothes of the Lady of Talisand, she needed a new cloak and a few gowns for she'd had no new ones since before her father left for Hastings.

Descending to her chamber, she found Cassie attending the room. "Cassie, a tinker has come and his wares look more like those of a mercer. Perchance he will have some velvet for us to see."

Her handmaiden set aside the linens she was folding. "He might have silks as well. Ye should have a fine silk gown for yer wedding and also one for court. Sir Maurin told me the Norman king favors the Red Wolf. Ye may be asked to go with him now that ye'll be his countess."

"Oh, Cassie," she sighed, sinking onto the chest at the foot of her bed. "I have no desire to dance attendance on the Norman king I despise, but I will go with you to see the tinker's cloth. Mayhap he will have a riband or two for us."

Cassie's eyes lit up. "I would love a new one!"

When Serena and her handmaiden reached the yard, they found it filling with women who had left off their chores to peruse the wares of the traveling merchant. The weavers, Ingrith and Annis, appeared especially curious to compare the woolens he had with their fine cloth. Aethel, who had been distant since Serena had returned to Talisand with the Red Wolf, seemed remarkably cheerful as she examined some ribands in colors of scarlet and emerald green.

Hulda, the potter's wife, and her young assistant, Edith, who had been injured in the kiln accident, were peering eagerly into the merchant's cart.

"Are you well, Edith?" asked Serena. She had not seen the girl since being told she would recover.

"Aye, m'lady. I am. A few scars that will nay go away, but 'twas to be expected. I thank ye for what ye and the Norman lord did fer me. Hulda told me of yer kindness. I'm making a special bowl fer yer wedding feast. This time," she said with a blush, "I'll be asking fer Godfrith's help."

Serena's cheeks warmed at the reminder that the day was not far off that would bind her to the Norman for the rest of her life. That is, if he returned from Exeter. But she refused to consider he might not. Instead, she thought of her people who seemed to be looking toward the future. A wedding blessing and a feast would be expected for the lord and his bride.

"'Tis most kind of you to think of me, Edith."

Cassie fingered the blue silk the man had spread out on top of the other bolts.

"My lady," she directed her comment to Serena, "this would make a fine wedding gown."

"Aye, it would." Serena stroked the shimmering cloth and looked at the merchant. "You have brought us rich wares, good sir."

He glanced at the silver and gold circlet that still graced the crown of her head. "Me name's Fugol, m'lady. Be ye the Lady of Talisand?"

"Aye, I am Lady Serena. Do you travel far?"

"From Mercia, m'lady."

Serena knew Mercia to be the lands of Earl Edwin, but she would not speak his name to this man. "'Tis a far distance you've come."

"Not so far, m'lady. No more than few days' ride. Though my cart travels more slowly, 'o course. I had heard the old lord of Talisand clothed his people well and loved his daughter much. 'Twas why I came. I thought mayhap ye'd want some of me fine velvets and silks."

She smiled at the merchant. "You are correct, good sir." Running her hands over the shimmering cloth, Serena glanced at the women of Talisand standing around the cart, captivated by the rich fabrics the likes of which were rarely seen in the village. "Though my father is no longer with us. We lost him at Hastings."

"You have me sympathy, m'lady. England lost many good men that awful day."

She nodded sadly and let out a sigh. But it was no use dwelling on the past or the father she would not see again in this life.

She perused the silks among the mercer's wares. They were too fine for daily wear, but Cassie was right, she would need a wedding gown. Such a gown would be needful when she entertained the Red Wolf's guests. "Some ribands and some silk for a gown would serve well, good sir."

Serena made a selection and gave Fugol the coins to buy the blue silk that Cassie had found for her, some emerald silk for another gown and some ribands for her handmaiden. While Cassie was engaged in a conversation with one of the village women, Serena also bought some green velvet and a fabric of the same color green to go with it that was imprinted with a gold pattern. They would make a lovely wedding dress for Cassie with her red hair. Perfect for a harvest wedding, though she did not tell her friend of her thinking.

Sir Maurin was spending the time that was his own with Cassie, and though the handmaiden had said nothing, Serena believed the two were falling in love. She had never considered the possibility either she or Cassie would wed Normans, but it seemed her thoughts mattered little. For Cassie to marry a knight was a good match, more than she might have expected. Sir Maurin was no fool. Anyone could see Cassie was a woman to treasure.

Two weeks passed with no word from the knights who had ridden south. Serena anxiously awaited a messenger while working hard at her duties, and sewing with Cassie the gowns they were making together. The stands of wheat grew high and turned golden in the long days of summer. The orchards were showing the new apples they would harvest in the fall. And rising above the manor to the south was the wooden castle set on the large motte of earth.

Rhodri lingered at Talisand and he and Serena sang for the people in the evenings. It was almost like the days of her youth except that Norman French could be heard in the hall and Normans sat at the high table.

As summer lingered, Serena struggled with her emotions. Most of her people appeared resigned to their new lord now that she was to be his bride. But a niggling question persisted in her mind. Was she?

CHAPTER 13

Morcar was eager for news. "What did you learn?" he anxiously asked Fugol while his brother looked on. "Does she remain unwed?"

"My lord," said the brown-haired Saxon, his beard now trimmed and his attire resembling that of a freeman in the employ of a wealthy earl, "I met Lady Serena when she came to see the wares ye gave me to sell. She wore no ring and her hair was uncovered, but the people spoke of a coming wedding to the Norman who has been given Talisand."

"I knew it!" shouted Morcar, slamming his fist on the table, the sound reverberating off the walls of Edwin's solar in Mercia. "Damn William for promising one of the fairest English maidens to one of his knights when her father would have given her to me."

"Not just any knight, my lord," added Fugol. "'Tis Sir Renaud, the one they call the Red Wolf."

"I know of him," said Edwin from where he sat at the end of the table stroking his beard. "He has long fought at William's side. When we were dragged off to Normandy as William's *guests*, the Red Wolf was one of the senior knights the king left in London, one he trusted with his affairs."

"Yea, and I seem to recall him when we were still at William's court," said Morcar. His eyes narrowed on the spy. "He wore that pelt that has branded him as vicious as the animal he killed. Was he at Talisand?"

"Nay," said Fugol. "He and most of his knights and men-at-arms were gone ere I came, summoned by William to Exeter to join him in a siege of that city where some Saxons are holding out against him."

"I pity the good citizens of Exeter," said Edwin.

"The only Normans left at Talisand," said Fugol, "are guards or those supervising the work on the castle they are building."

Directing his words to his brother, Morcar said, "It seems William is intent on leaving his mark all over England with those infernal castles. Our hopes to be left alone to rule the north are crumbling to nothing."

"I still hold Mercia," said Edwin, "though for how long I cannot say."

Morcar shifted his gaze to Fugol. "What about her brother Steinar?"

"He's no longer at Talisand, my lord. According to the woman Aethel, he is in Scotland."

Morcar traded looks with his brother. They had been in contact with Edgar who was safely ensconced across the border, waiting for an opportunity to return to reclaim the English throne. And they knew Steinar must be with him.

Returning his attention to the spy, Morcar asked, "Can the lady be taken?"

"Aye." The spy smiled. "As I told ye, there be few guards, though one of the Norman knights follows her about and sits near when she dines at the high table with Sir Maurin, the knight left in charge. The wench ye sent me to, Aethel, may know how best to get in and out of the manor unseen. She seemed willing enough to help. She told me Lady Serena had twice tried to escape, but was brought back each time."

"She sought to escape?" asked Edwin.

"Aye, she did," said Fugol. "Brave lady that she is. But when I was there, she bought silk for a wedding gown from my cart."

"Mayhap she feels she has no other choice," said Morcar. He would give her another choice and soon. "Ye said naught to Lady Serena?" He wanted to limit those who were aware of his plans. Though he knew Serena must be unhappy at the prospect of being forced to wed a Norman, he did not want his spy's presence to become known.

"To Lady Serena, I spoke only about the cloth I sold. About my mission I spoke only to Aethel."

Rising, Morcar faced his brother. "Then we go forward as planned. As it happens, there is a Norman mercenary knight who only a few days ago approached me offering his sword. Though I trust not a turncoat, this one by fortune's chance has been at Talisand and may be of use. It seems he rode with the Red Wolf only a short while ago. They disagreed over some matter leaving the mercenary bitter."

"Oh?" Edwin raised a brow. "And who might he be?"

"He gave the name Sir Hugue."

* * *

Renaud and his men neared Exeter and still his thoughts lingered on

Lady Serena as they had on the long journey south. He had not wanted to leave her; their relationship was too new, too tenuous. But William's summons could not be refused.

The sounds of the siege filled the air, interrupting his thoughts, even before he and his knights were close enough to see the old Roman walls. The projectiles shooting from the Norman catapult made a loud whooshing sound renting the stillness of the countryside. Close up, he knew the noise would be deafening.

As he and his men drew nearer, he heard the clash of steel upon shields a short distance away. The Norman knights were practicing the skills they would need when the siege broke through the ancient walls. Even now, William's men assaulted those walls, and Renaud paused to study the effects of their efforts.

From where he sat on Belasco, hundreds of knights and men-at-arms circled the red walls. Arrows rained down from the battlements on those close enough to be within range. In response, William's archers launched a blast of arrows tipped in flaming oil. The sound of the flying shafts was like a rushing wind. The odor of the pungent oil rose to his nostrils.

Some of William's men attempted to scale the walls. From this distance, they looked like ants climbing over a mound of earth, only to be repelled by the defenders at the top with kettles of rocks and scalding oil. Shrieks of men sent plunging to their deaths reminded him of the ugliness of war. Though it had been his life for nearly two decades, he longed to see the end of it.

It looked as if William was throwing everything he had at the English rebels, yet still the stubborn walls stood.

Surely there must be a way...

"Look! There lies William's tent," shouted Geoff over the tumult.

Renaud turned his attention to the golden leopards on a field of red flying above the largest tent in the middle of those housing William's army.

"Have Sir Alain and the men find a place for our tents while you and I report to William."

Geoff passed the orders to the banner man as Renaud made his way toward the tent displaying the royal standard.

He dismounted as Geoff caught up with him. They entered the striped tent together to find William, wearing his hauberk, standing over a table. Several of his closest advisors and knights huddled around him as the king studied a drawing of the walled city.

"Sire." Renaud dropped to one knee and Geoff followed suit.

"Ah, the wolf comes!" said the king. "Rise, Lord Talisand. We are glad you are here. We have need of you and your men." With a nod to

Geoff, William continued. "As you have no doubt seen," he gestured in the direction of the city, "we assault the walls of Exeter and yet the stubborn English remain, over two thousand of them defying our request for their oath of fealty and payment of tribute."

"I am surprised they refused," Renaud said. "After all, you have conquered half of England."

"Humph. We have been up and down with that," said William. "First the chief citizens sent a message saying they would not swear allegiance to us, though they would condescend to pay a tribute 'according to ancient custom'. We suppose they did not get our message when we sacked the towns of Devon on our way here."

Renaud heard the sarcasm in his king's voice and knew well enough the citizens had made a grievous error ignoring such warnings. William would show them no mercy if they persisted. "Surely they could not be thinking to hold out against you."

"Well, they did, mayhap spurred on by the English who joined them from Somerset and Dorset. Then there is Gytha, the mother of Harold Godwinson, to consider. No doubt she has stirred the Saxons to a fervor in their rebellion."

Renaud remembered Serena's words describing the woman's urgent request for her son's body. A request William had denied.

"We told them their offer of tribute according to ancient custom does not suit," the king continued. "We will not have subjects on such conditions. We will have no conditions at all!"

"And what of your army?" Renaud asked, incredulous. "Did not the English fear so many?"

"Oh, yea," said William. "When they heard we had an army, they changed their course. The elders of the city came out to meet us, crying peace, offering hostages and swearing they would do all we asked. But the good citizens within must have disagreed for when we approached the city, we found the gates locked against us. We had the eyes of one hostage put out, and another hanged, all to no avail. The stubborn English have tried our patience overmuch."

Renaud inwardly cringed at the memory of revenge he had seen William exact when his will had been defied.

"So we brought our army to the city and laid siege. Yet, as you see, the walls still stand. We must have those walls down!"

It was clear to Renaud the affair had put his sire in a most foul mood. The siege must be brought to a successful conclusion, and soon, if any of the English behind the walls were to be spared. He did not want to tell Serena of another bloodbath.

"One of the English had the audacity to insult the king," said the knight Renaud recognized as Sir Baldwin de Meules, "dropping his chausses and loudly breaking wind."

The dour look on William's face told Renaud it had been the final insult.

"How long has the siege gone on?" Renaud asked.

"We ordered the siege begun nearly two weeks ago," said the king. "The English have manned the walls continuously ever since. Their missiles have taken a toll on our army. With God's help, I mean to see them pay."

"How many have we left?" Renaud asked Sir Baldwin.

"Two hundred on horse and more on foot. Some over-hasty assaults early on by enthusiastic knights led to many losses."

William shrugged at the news of the men he had lost.

"You are just in time to lead a task we've in mind," said William, his mouth set in grim determination. Renaud had seen that look before. It did not bode well for the Saxons behind Exeter's walls.

"As you wish, Sire."

The king was in his element. His sun bleached brown hair was in slight disarray beneath his crown as he fingered his mustache. His intense blue eyes focused on the parchment spread before him. "We've been studying this drawing with the idea of undermining the walls from beneath," said William, shoving a chart toward Renaud. "What think you?"

Renaud carefully examined the drawing, remembering what he had seen as he'd scrutinized the old walls on his approach. Pointing to the East Gate, he said, "It seems like this might be a weak place worthy of your attention, Sire."

"We thought so," said the king with a gleam in his eye. "But we are glad to have you confirm it. That is where the dry moat lies."

"We'll need protection from their arrows and boiling oil, of course," Renaud said, speaking his mental list aloud, "and your engineers to dig the tunnels. But it can be done."

"His Grace has ordered the protection you speak of and his engineers stand ready," offered Sir Baldwin.

"See to it, Lord Talisand," ordered William. "We want those walls down!"

The last thing Renaud wanted was to slay more English. The people of Talisand were now his people, their lady soon to be his lady. If he could undermine the wall, the city could be taken with fewer casualties and William might be persuaded to grant clemency.

It took nearly a week before they began to see the progress in the tunnel that Renaud had been hoping for. In the meantime, William's army continued the assault with the utmost force, Renaud's own men joining the attacks on the English stationed on the walls while the engineers supervised the digging to provide them access from beneath.

The thirty-foot siege tunnel under the East Gate was nearly complete when Renaud thought to add another, smaller tunnel, this one under the wall itself. It might weaken the structure enough to bring down the wall. It had just been completed this morning.

"M'lord, ye must see it!" said Jamie excitedly as he ran to where Renaud was honing his skills in the practice field. "A huge cloud of dust rises where the wall has collapsed from yer tunnel!"

Handing his shield to Mathieu, Renaud signaled Geoff to follow him. "Aye, Jamie, I will see it."

The two knights ventured forth, Jamie running before them. As they neared the red walls, his page pointed and shouted, "See how the wall caves, m'lord!"

In the distance, Renaud saw the remnants of the wall laying in a ruble and the cloud of dust settling over the debris. At that moment, he heard the launch of arrows from atop the city walls. The lad ran ahead, unaware of the danger that streaked toward him.

Geoff shouted, "Jamie, no!"

Renaud yelled, "To me, Jamie, to me!" The boy turned to obey his lord's command. Sensing his page would not be fast enough to outrun the arrows streaking toward him, Renaud broke into a run, his longer stride quickly closing the distance between them. He leaped upon the boy, dropping them both to the earth just as an arrow sliced through Renaud's mail into the back of his arm.

He flinched as the jolt of pain reverberated through his body. Only a bodkin arrowhead could have pierced his hauberk, but the English had learned the importance of such arrows at Hastings and now used them to great effect. Realizing Jamie's slight chest was beneath his arm, Renaud gave thanks his action had kept the arrow from the boy's heart.

Grunting in pain, he rolled off the boy who sat up and stared in confusion. With Geoff's help, Renaud rose from the ground.

The arrow had gone through his arm, the tip just piercing the other side. "Break it off!" he commanded Geoff. His knight obeyed as Renaud bit down on the leather sheath of his scramaseax.

"Come, Ren," Geoff urged. "A doctor of phisyk awaits in yon tent to pull the arrow through. It must come out."

Jamie was distraught, pacing alongside Renaud as he headed toward the tent that had been allocated to the healers. "M'lord, I am so sorry. 'Tis all my fault."

"Next time you will know, boy," Geoff scolded. "You'd be dead if it were not for your lord's sacrificing himself."

The page dropped his head. Renaud reached out with his uninjured arm and placed his hand on the lad's shoulder. "We've all had to learn such lessons, son."

Jamie looked up at him with adoring eyes. "Yea, sir."

While Renaud suffered the ministrations of the king's physic, the city elders, seeing the walls collapsing, had shouted their surrender. Over the objections of Geoff, who had brought him the news, when the stitching was done and the wound bandaged, Renaud traveled the short distance to the king's tent. He had to do what he could to spare the English his sire's wrath.

Still smarting from the wound in his arm, Renaud entered the tent just as the king was preparing to leave for the city gates.

"Sire, might I suggest a gracious act of mercy to the English if they but concede to your demands?"

"We will consider it," William said, looking doubtful. "First we must see for ourselves what groveling the good citizens of Exeter may offer to appease our anger." They walked out together, the king's retinue following. All sounds of the battle had ceased. Renaud found the quiet after so much noise unnerving.

Glancing at Renaud's arm, the king observed, "Our sympathy for your arm, Lord Talisand. We heard you saved your page a more grievous wound."

Renaud acknowledge the king's words with a shrug. He was not without some feelings of guilt for the actions of the untrained youth who had followed his lord to battle.

The king's entourage approached the city and the gates opened to allow a procession through the wide opening. Included among the party coming to greet them were beautiful young maidens dressed in colorful silk gowns, their long hair flowing down their backs. These were followed by the elders of the city, and Bishop Leofric and his clergy, carrying sacred books and holy ornaments.

Prostrating themselves at William's feet, they begged for mercy. "My Lord, we beg you to swear a holy oath on the Bible that you will not harm the city and its people."

With a glance toward Renaud, the king let out a deep breath and relented. "Rise. Since you make such a grand display of your repentance, we grant you the mercy you seek." When the clergymen stood, William gave them a stern look. "Every last man will swear fealty to us and you will pay the new tribute we demand."

The city fathers were quick to nod their heads in agreement.

"And henceforth you will have our royal presence within the city," announced William.

The city elders looked startled but wisely chose to say nothing.

Later, Renaud discovered that Gytha had escaped through the Water Gate, taking the River Exe to the sea. It was only when her safe escape had been assured that the city's leaders had surrendered. By the time the king learned of this, he had already granted clemency and, to Renaud's relief, did not withdraw it.

William posted some of his soldiers at the city gates so his army would not be tempted to plunder the hapless English. This pleased Renaud for he did not wish to answer Serena's questions as to what transpired after the siege only to have to admit his fellow Normans had raped and pillaged.

The siege had lasted eighteen days from its beginning to William's victory, which came the day Renaud took the arrow. Smiling to himself as he congratulated the king and walked back to his own tent, Renaud realized it was no longer Normandy that held his heart, but Talisand, and he was anxious to return to his English bride with the violet eyes.

The day after the surrender, William came to Renaud's tent where he was resting while his men prepared to leave. His wound had not festered but was still tender and gave him much grief. It would be a while before he could hold a shield with that arm. It could have been worse, he knew. At least it was not his sword arm.

Still wearing his hauberk, the king inquired, "Is the heroic wolf able to leave his den to help us select a site for our new castle we intend to construct within the city's walls?"

"Yea, Sire," he said, rising. Jamie was at his side, for the boy had not left him since Renaud had taken the arrow. "I will gladly serve you in that task."

With Sir Baldwin and Geoff accompanying them, William and Renaud walked to the city gates, which now lay open but guarded.

They surveyed the possible locations for a castle. Finally, William settled on the northeast corner of the Roman wall lying next to a steep bank.

Renaud conferred with Sir Baldwin on an idea he had before saying, "Sire, with a deep ditch between the northwestern and northeastern walls and the addition of an internal rampart, you would have a square bailey for the castle."

"We think that a fine idea!" exclaimed the king, obviously eager to see his castle constructed. Then looking to Sir Baldwin, "We leave you in charge of razing the homes that stand in the way and building the castle, sir knight. Enough of our army will stay behind to provide a garrison. Henceforth, you shall be our castellan and High Sheriff of

Devonshire."

Sir Baldwin dipped his head and smiled, appearing pleased at the honor bestowed upon him. "As you wish, My King."

And so it was done. The king had his victory and Renaud had lost not a man. Best of all, he would have good news for Serena: Jamie and the men of Talisand were safe. Renaud would not share with her his certain belief that in the future the king intended to give every Englishman's land to a Norman for William no longer trusted the fealty of those he had conquered.

Though the Talisand archers had remained true despite having to fight on the side of their Norman lord, Renaud did not doubt their loyalty was aided by the presence of English among the ranks of William's army. As more and more English fought on the side of the Norman king, the resistance would grow weaker.

Because Renaud was still healing, William allowed him to return to Talisand.

"We bid you leave to go," said the king, "to see our castle built at Talisand and to get an heir on that English maiden we have given you. But know we shall call upon you again. You served us well."

Renaud bowed before the king, grateful to be going.

The next morning, the column of Renaud's men formed behind him. Mounting his great gray stallion, he gave the signal to move forward and turned his face to the north—and his thoughts to Lady Serena.

Would his bride be waiting for him? Twice she had deceived him. He could not help but wonder if the magnificently gowned lady who had so mesmerized him the day he had left was yet another of her disguises, mayhap the most devious of all. He had not known Serena could speak the Norman tongue until she had addressed his men. What other abilities had she hidden from him? Was it possible the English maiden who hated all Normans had succumbed to his kisses and would now bow to the king's decree to become the wife of the Red Wolf? Or, had she only been biding her time until he had gone so that she could escape once again?

CHAPTER 14

Serena sat at the high table barely listening to the conversations around her as the evening wore on. Outside, the summer sun still lingered in the sky, its last rays finding their way through the open shutters to pool among the rushes.

Maugris, who had stayed behind when his master rode south, now joined her for meals, he on her left and Sir Maurin on her right. Since he had learned she spoke Norman French, Sir Maurin often slipped from English, of which he knew only a little, into the language of his birth. But Maugris spoke English nearly as well as Serena. And though his words might be few, what he said was often worth hearing. Serena did not mind his company. The wise one was a gentle soul and so unlike the Red Wolf's knights with their rough warrior ways, she had ceased to think of him as Norman at all. His tunics were now made of the fine wool woven by Ingrith and Annis, and the children of Talisand looked upon him as a kind of grandfather, eager for the stories he told around the hearth fire each night.

Her mind dulled to sounds of men eating and joking as her thoughts drifted to the past. So many men were gone from the hall forever, good men who had fought with her father, men who died defending the Saxon king. The ones who remained were now compelled to construct a castle for their conquerors, the timbered structure that was the symbol of the Norman domination. She knew some of Talisand's men resented being pressed into the work, but others considered themselves fortunate to have a lord who was powerful enough to protect their families from future attacks. They worried only about their crops and feeding their children. She could hardly blame them. To survive was in some way to succeed.

Looking around the hall, it was as if she could see the ghosts of those whose laughter had once filled the large space: Sigmund, her father, Oswine, the dark-haired young guard to whom she had once given her heart and the men who had followed them to Hastings. She remembered Oswine teasing her for the shorter bow Rhodri had made her. His voice, along with the others, faded now, never to be heard again in the hall, but she would remember their courage and their sacrifice for as long as she lived.

Those who had survived the coming of the Normans would never forget, as she never would. It had changed their lives forever.

Sighing, she chided herself for dwelling on the past. She took a deep breath and brought herself to the present and focused on the evening meal.

The mutton stew set before her was hearty and the aroma of the well-seasoned broth made her mouth water. She had not eaten since breaking her fast and that had been only bread and cheese. From their murmurings in Norman French, Serena discerned that Maggie had once again impressed the Red Wolf's men with her cooking. Having worked all day on the castle, they consumed with relish the stew and hot bread fresh from the oven. More and more the Normans drank the English ale now.

Sir Niel, her constant shadow, sat at one of the long tables laughing with another knight. Although he appeared unaware of her, she knew if she were to rise, the knight, whose hair failed to cover the jagged scar that marred his handsome face, would do so as well.

Serena understood the lack of trust between her and the Red Wolf that had led to the guard. How could they know she was resigned to her fate when there were times she doubted it herself? The gesture she had made to greet them in her fine gown and circlet of silver and gold had, even then, seemed a betrayal of her father. It was why she had spoken of him when she addressed the Red Wolf's men. Why she had insisted the Normans pay the old thegn respect.

What would he say if he were alive to see her acceptance of the Norman king's bidding? What would Steinar say if he knew she would soon be the Red Wolf's wife?

Of Talisand's men, tonight the hall was missing Theodric, the captain of her father's guard, now one of the Red Wolf's men. Though Theodric was married and lived in one of the manors, he often dined in the hall if he spent the day at the manor. Leppe and Alec, who had guided their small band into the woods the first time she had tried to escape, now served their new lord as archers. Their sworn fealty required them to join the Red Wolf in battle if he had need of them. Mayhap it was for the best. If they were to prosper, they must show loyalty to the new lord.

And so must she.

The Red Wolf was a warrior unschooled in all that must be done for the smooth running of Talisand's lands. For her people's sake, she must help him and turn her attention to the harvest if they were to eat this coming winter.

"My lady," said Maugris, his forehead wrinkled in concern, "you speak little this eve, yet your face tells me you ponder much. Is something amiss?" His ancient eyes, fathomless pools of pale blue, lingered on her, making her wonder what he might see that others did not.

"Sometimes, I think of how things were."

"It is unwise, my child, to look too long behind you, else you will miss the future that lies before you. Though the wounds of the past are deep, let your heart find solace in the knowledge it has loved well."

"I know you speak the truth, wise one, and I have told myself the same. But if we are to speak of the future, I must tell you I am worried about all that must be done to bring in the harvest and prepare the cottages for winter now that we have fewer men. Your lord took some of the strongest, while others have been compelled to build his castle."

"When the time comes, the Red Wolf's men will help, my lady. You have only to ask. The lord will withhold naught you require."

"The villagers will be relieved to hear it," she said gratefully, turning to face him. "I thank you."

The rest of the evening meal passed with only brief comments about the progress of the castle. On the south side of the manor, where nothing had stood before save shelters for the sheep, there was now a huge mound of earth and, on its flat top, a half constructed tower.

"Soon the castle will be finished," said Sir Maurin cheerfully, slipping into Norman French. "When the harvest is ripe, the men of Talisand will be free to work the fields."

"That is good for we will need them to bring in the wheat and the other crops. And for the hunting and butchering that must be done before winter."

The senior knight the Red Wolf had left in charge was consumed with plans for the castle. "Have you seen the drawings, my lady?" asked Sir Maurin.

"Nay, but I have heard the hammers and seen the ditch created from the huge mound of earth that supports the new timbered structure."

"There will be a keep with a larger hall at its base and a small chapel, as well as the lord's solar and chambers for others. 'Twill be larger than some built by William's command but not so fine as the home of the Red Wolf family in Normandy."

Serena wondered about the home the Red Wolf had left in order to seek his fortune in distant England. He had yet to speak of it. And she wondered, too, how it would feel to be the lady of the new castle—to be the wife of the unbending knight. Not wishing to dwell on the future rushing toward her, she asked instead, "Why another chapel?"

"Knowing the Red Wolf," Sir Maurin said with a smile, "he would want one close for he is a man of faith. But 'twill also serve to satisfy the penance decreed for Norman soldiers who took lives at Hastings." At her puzzled expression, he explained, "One year's penance for each man the knight killed or, if he does not know the number, then he must do a penance one day a week for the rest of his life, or he may build a church."

"I see." *New churches must be rising all over England.* "The Red Wolf does not know how many Saxons he killed, does he?"

"Nay, my lady," the knight said with a guilty expression. "Few of us have a count."

Serena was not surprised with so many dead at Hastings and all over the south of England. The Norman king had been ruthless. And she expected the Red Wolf was adding to his number even now at Exeter. She shuddered at the thought of what the battlefield must look like.

Sir Maurin's gaze followed Cassie as the comely redhead helped to serve in the hall. Serena had observed the two of them walking near the river, so enthralled with each other they appeared ignorant of any who watched. She was happy for Cassie if that is what her handmaiden wanted. Sir Maurin was a good man, even though he was a Norman. And how could she criticize Cassie when she herself would soon be sharing the bed of a Norman knight?

Aethel approached the high table and began refilling the goblets from the pitcher she carried. Thanking her for the ale, Serena drank her fill, letting out a sigh. Was Aethel still enamored of the Red Wolf? There was no love involved, of that Serena was certain. In fact, since Theodric had wed another, Aethel seemed to care for no one, not even the old thegn whose bed she had shared. But remembering the way she had waved at Sir Alain as he had departed for Exeter, Serena thought one day Aethel might find a man to please her, even a Norman knight.

Just not the Red Wolf.

* * *

The hall was quiet, the tables cleaned and moved against the walls and the knights and men-at-arms asleep on their pallets when Aethel stood in the shadows of the entry, waiting for the next step in her plan. The only noises now were the men's snoring where they slept. It was unusually warm, so there had been no hearth fire that night, and the torches were long since snuffed. A lone candle stood vigil in the manor's entry.

Cassie came from the kitchen and climbed the stairs, carrying a tankard of ale to Sir Niel, the knight who guarded Serena's door. The long summer days were upon them and, by evening, the air in the manor was still. Aethel had known the drink would be welcomed and made certain each night for a sennight a different serving woman had carried him the drink. But tonight the tankard held more than the amber liquid that would quench the knight's thirst.

Aethel's knowledge of herbs, learned from her grandmother, made adding a sleeping potion a small matter. And she had done so without Cassie being aware. Nor would the knight detect any difference in taste, just as Serena had not in the ale Aethel had served her at the evening meal. The potion would only bring sleep. Neither would be harmed.

Aethel listened to the conversation between the handmaiden and the young knight.

"Good eve, Sir Niel," Cassie said as she handed him the tankard.

"Good eve to you, Cassandra. 'Tis the end of a long day." He accepted the drink. "The ale is appreciated."

"It is nay more than we did for the old lord and his men, sir knight."

Sir Niel finished the drink and Cassie took the empty tankard and descended the stairs.

Still in the shadows, Aethel watched expectantly. Since the Mercian seller of cloth had departed, she'd been waiting for his return. He had told her Earl Morcar had sent him, and she doubted it not for she knew well Morcar's purpose. She had seen the look in the eyes of the tall blond Mercian as he gazed upon Serena when he had last visited the old thegn. And then a few days ago the message had come, telling her to be prepared for this night.

Aethel told herself she was helping Lady Serena find a better fate than the Red Wolf. After all, there was so little trust between the two of them a guard trailed her every move. And Serena had tried to escape more than once. So Aethel had planned to help her lady escape again.

She slipped out of the manor, heading toward the postern gate, secure in the belief Serena would be pleased to wed the handsome Mercian earl. Knowing Serena wanted to leave soothed Aethel's conscience for Sir Alain had been right. She had been jealous. Even as a young girl, her own dark beauty had never drawn the boys' stares as had Serena's flaxen hair and unusual violet eyes. Aethel had wanted Theodric, yet his gaze always followed Serena. But the thegn would never give his daughter to Theodric, allowing Aethel's hopes for a future with him to rise. It had all been for naught.

Knowing the thegn was lonely and had wanted her for a long while, it seemed the easier path to become his leman than to take a lesser man as husband. And, though there was no love in the coupling, for a while it had been enough. Sigmund had been kind and Aethel came to care for him. But when the thegn was killed, Aethel lost more than a man in her bed; she lost her status among the people and the hope Sigmund would one day marry her. Thinking to regain her position, she had sought the bed of the new Norman lord. But the Red Wolf held himself apart from all the women at Talisand, save for one. One who did not want him. One who hated Normans. One who would be pleased to leave. For Aethel did not believe the grand display Serena had put on for the benefit of her Norman captors.

Now Aethel would make two people happy, Lady Serena and Morcar, who would claim her as his bride. What did it matter if she angered the Red Wolf? He would never know it had been she who helped to rob him of his bride. Yet even as she told herself all this, a thought rumbled around in her head. Since the night Sir Alain had made his intentions known, she had watched the brawny knight who carried the Red Wolf's standard. That such a man would want her as his wife gave her new hope.

But would he understand why she had aided Serena's attempt to flee his lord?

* * *

A short time later, Aethel arrived at the postern gate, gratified to see the guard leaning against the palisade timbers softly snoring. She did not have long to wait. In a matter of moments, a man approached dressed as a knight, his cloak falling over his tunic and mail like a dark shadow. In the dim light of the half-moon she did not recognize him at first but she knew who had sent him for he was expected.

As the moonlight fell across the face of the saturnine knight with the dark hair and beard, she stepped back, exclaiming in a harsh whisper, "Sir Hugue!"

"Aye, Aethel. 'Tis I."

"What are *ye* doing here? I was expecting a man from Mercia!" Now she was worried. Why would the mercenary sent away in disgrace return on this night?

"I have been sent by Earl Morcar. I do his bidding now," he said shortly. "Is all ready?"

Aethel had never trusted the mercenary who had tried to rape Eawyn. Yet there was little she could do at this point if Morcar had dispatched him to fetch Serena. "Yea, all is ready. But first I must have yer word that ye will not harm my lady."

"Do you think me a fool, woman? Earl Morcar would not pay me the coin he has promised if I harmed his lady. Nay, I will touch her only to carry her to him."

"Then ye may take her," she said, still feeling some trepidation. "But ye must be careful to follow me and do all I say. Should he awake, Sir Maurin would not be pleased to see ye here at Talisand. Sir Niel guards the lady's door but he is sleeping from a potion just like this guard." She looked down at the snoring man at her feet. "But others in the hall and in yonder tents have not received the drink and will hear us if we are not careful."

Avoiding the hall, they entered the front door of the manor and crept up the stairs illuminated by the single light left burning. Sir Niel was sprawled against the wall next to Serena's chamber where she slept unaware of what was happening around her. As they were about to enter her chamber, a man stumbled from the hall to the manor's entry below. Sir Hugue flattened himself against the wall, pulling his dagger from his belt and held it aloft, ready to strike.

Aethel drew in her breath as her heart raced. Shaking her head at the mercenary, she frowned, silently cautioning him. Sir Hugue sheathed his dagger but kept his eyes on the man in the entry whose unsure steps told Aethel he had indulged in too much ale. Weaving his way to the door, he stumbled from the manor, no doubt heading toward the privy.

Breathing a sigh of relief, Aethel gestured to the mercenary to follow her as she carefully opened Serena's door and entered. She walked to the bed and held aside the curtain, as Sir Hugue peeled back the cover, revealing Serena asleep in her night tunic.

"So this is the Lady Serena," he whispered. "She is a comely woman and looks a mite familiar."

"She was disguised as the servant Sarah."

"Aye, now I remember. The wench who shot an arrow into my arm."

"She is no wench, sir. She is the Lady of Talisand. Ye'd best be respecting her."

"Aye, my new lord requires it." His smile made Aethel cringe. "'Twill be good to see the Red Wolf lose this prize."

"Be quick or we will be discovered!" She had no time for this and did not like the way the knight's eyes roved over the sleeping woman. Aethel had a pang of regret and wondered if she should be doing this.

Turning his attention to his task, Sir Hugue lifted Serena, and carried her toward the open bedchamber door.

At the bottom of the stairs Aethel paused, waiting for any sounds that would tell her if someone might still be awake. Hearing nothing, she retrieved the small bundle of clothing she had prepared for Serena, hidden at the base of the stairs. Walking in front of Sir Hugue, she opened the manor door and stepped into the night. The Norman followed with Serena in his arms. Aethel closed the door and carefully draped her lady's cloak over her.

A sheep dog barked in the distance and once again Aethel froze, listening. The man who had stumbled out of the manor moments before now ambled his way back. Aethel, followed by Sir Hugue, pressed into the shadows.

The drunken man noticed nothing.

They waited for him to enter the manor, and once he did, Aethel motioned the mercenary forward. She saw the guard at the main gate but knew he could not see into the shadows, and his eyes looked outward not behind him.

Finally, they reached the postern gate, where the guard still snored. Aethel began to worry if Sir Hugue could carry Serena on the long ride ahead. In a whispered voice, she asked him, "Are ye alone?"

"Nay, Morcar sent two of his men with me. They wait in yon woods."

"Then I will see ye to them. I want Lady Serena to have this bundle when she awakes."

Aethel followed him into the woods at the edge of the village. Two cloaked men stood, holding the reins of three horses. Their light colored beards and long hair told Aethel the men were Mercians and that brought her comfort. Without a word, she handed the bundle to one of them. Turning to Sir Hugue, she asked in a whisper, "How long will it take ye to reach Morcar?"

"A bit more than a day if we ride hard."

Aethel bit her lower lip, worried. Serena would wake before then. "Ye must give her more potion when she begins to stir." Prepared against such a possibility, Aethel reached into her cloak and drew out a small skin containing ale mixed with more potion, and another skin that contained vegetable broth. "Give her this." She handed the skin with the potion to one of the waiting Mercians. "And then give her this broth if she can be made to take it," she said, handing him the other skin. "It is a broth to give her sustenance while ye travel. When she awakes in Mercia, she will remember nothing."

CHAPTER 15

Serena woke to a pounding in her head and a gnawing hunger in her belly. The dim morning light pierced the narrow opening in the bed curtains. Still groggy, she could barely discern with her half opened eyes what seemed strange about her surroundings. After a moment, she sat up and pulled wide the curtains, startled to realize she was not in her bedchamber, nor in her bed. She had never before seen this room with its stone walls, arched window and high timbered roof.

Where am I, and how did I get here?

Moments later, a knock sounded at the wooden door. Before she could say aught, it opened to reveal an older woman with graying brown hair wearing a servant's tunic. The woman entered carrying clothing Serena recognized as hers.

"My lady, 'tis time ye were up. Earl Morcar has been asking for ye."

Relief swept over Serena. Not a Norman then. She dropped her feet over the side of the bed. "Earl Morcar?"

"Yea, my lady, ye were brought here last night."

"Where is 'here' good woman?" Rubbing her temples helped the pounding in her head to subside. Why would Morcar take her from Talisand and without telling her beforehand?

"Oh, do ye not know? Why, ye are at Adlington, my lady, Earl Edwin's manor in Mercia."

"M...Mercia?" Serena stammered. She had been abducted from her bed and taken south to Mercia? "Why was I brought here?"

"For that ye'll have to ask the earl, my lady. I know only what I've been told. My master, Earl Edwin and his brother Morcar await ye below."

Edwin? Morcar? They abducted her?

139

Serena rose, vaguely aware she was still wearing the garment she had worn to bed. Was it only the night before? She walked to the side table feeling the chill on her feet from the stone floor. The woman had set out a bowl of water and a drying cloth. As she stood before the bowl, a swirling mist filled her mind like a remnant of a bad dream and her temples ached. Why was she so addled? Had they given her a sleeping potion? She tried not to think who might have seen her in her nightclothes.

Splashing water onto her face, she began to feel more herself. She patted her skin dry. The servant replaited her hair. Without a word, the woman efficiently helped her into the pale green undertunic and leaf green gown. The belt at her waist was a simple one of leather woven through a chain. Whoever had arranged this had even remembered her hose and leather shoes, which she was happy to have.

Through the shutters of the window, which the servant had opened, Serena looked out onto rolling hills, green with the rains of summer, stretching far into the distance. Grazing sheep dotted one slope. It was not so different from Talisand. But the why of it was confusing. What did the brother earls intend?

When she was ready, she followed the servant from the room. The old woman gestured to the stairs and then left her. Slowly Serena descended, pausing when she heard men's voices coming from a room off the main entry.

"You may go, Sir Hugue. I will advise you when your talents are needed again."

Sir Hugue? She recognized Morcar's voice as the one speaking, but why would the Norman mercenary be here? Had he been the one who'd abducted her from the manor? A myriad of questions arose in her mind as the Norman knight strode through the entry never seeing her standing on the stairs above him.

Another voice from beyond the doorway said, "At least you should ask Serena if she would have you, Morcar. She is a lady after all, not some wench you can grab in the night and do with as you please."

"I am fully aware of Lady Serena's status, brother. But why should I seek her approval? Have I not spared her a Norman's bed? Nay, I will not ask. I have brought Lady Serena here to wed, and I shall. You know as well as I that before he died her father had warmed to my suit. I have no doubt he would prefer a Mercian earl to one of William's knights were he here to consult with. What I plan for Serena is obviously the right path. She will be willing, I've no doubt."

Reaching the bottom of the stairs, Serena took a step forward, bringing herself into view. Morcar raised his head from where he sat at the table across from his brother. Both men stood.

"My lady," said Morcar. From his expression, Serena judged him delighted. "How good it is to see you and looking so well! You have grown more beautiful than I remember, and I remember quite well how very fair is the Lady of Talisand."

Flattery had never meant so much to Serena as sincere affection. She did not even blush, knowing Morcar's words were calculated to appease her.

The two Mercian men, each with shoulder length blond hair and beards, one an older version of the other, gave her a studied look as she walked toward the table set with an array of food. In the center was a bowl of fruit, reminding her of her hunger.

"Why am I here?" she said impatiently. "You did not extend a proper invitation nor allow me to travel as I might, but dragged me from my bed in the night. Judging from how little I was aware and my aching head, I'd say I was given a potion."

Finding his voice, Morcar offered, "Soon, I will explain. But first, allow my brother Edwin to welcome you to his home."

Serena had met both Morcar and Edwin on their visit to Talisand when Morcar was still the Earl of Northumbria and recalled the older brother as possessing a gracious nature, more mellow than his younger sibling.

Edwin bowed before her. "My lady, 'tis an honor."

"My lord," she said with a faint smile, not extending her hand, "except for the manner of my coming, I would have been happy to see you. But I cannot act as if this is merely a pleasant visit. I was abducted from my bedchamber! I must know why." Having heard their conversation, she had a fair understanding, but she asked to see if they would tell her a different tale.

"First, I would offer you a morning meal." Morcar gestured toward the table heavy with trenchers of food. "I imagine you are quite hungry. And is it not a better way to begin our discussion?"

Reluctantly, she took the seat Morcar offered her. Though she was anxious to know of their plans, she had to admit she was famished. Taking some fruit and bread onto her trencher, she smiled inwardly at the irony of it. All the times she had wanted to escape the Red Wolf, yet when she had finally come to think that her duty, if not her heart, required her to remain at his side, here was escape set before her as if served up on a platter.

In addition to the fruit, the table was laden with cooked pork, eggs, and bread and butter. A male servant poured mead into goblets and, raising the drink to her lips, she sniffed the golden liquid to see if she could detect any unexpected odor. But there was only the sweet scent of honey and familiar spices.

Seeing her do this, Morcar apologized. "I'm sorry, my lady, for the potion given you. It was thought best for the secrecy we needed that you should have no voice to question my men. There was no time for explanations in our rescue."

"Rescue? From Talisand? Surely you jest."

"Nay, my lady, not a rescue from Talisand," his voice rang with sincerity, "but from the Norman who now holds it."

"Ah, I see," she said considering his words as she toyed with the food on her trencher. She supposed she did understand. After all, she had thought to escape the dreaded Normans herself. "But you did not think to warn me?"

Earl Edwin interjected, "We thought it best if you were unaware of our plans."

"And the guard? You did not harm him?" She was concerned for the faithful Sir Niel, whose lord would not be pleased that she had vanished beneath the young knight's watchful eye. If Sir Hugue was involved, after the punishment he had received, he might have been cruel to the Red Wolf's men.

"No one was hurt, my lady," said Edwin. "More than one guard received the same herbs as you in his ale. And, just as you did, all will recover."

Serena's memory of Aethel serving her ale in the hall came to her mind. Was Aethel trying to rid herself of a rival? Did the herb woman think to take her place in the Red Wolf's bed if Serena were to wed another?

"I can explain," said Morcar.

She waited while he took a drink of his mead and set down the silver goblet fingering the carved design as if contemplating carefully his next words.

"You see, word came to me William was going to give you to one of his Norman knights. I was certain you would want to avoid such a marriage. I had asked for your hand when your father, the thegn, still lived. He was favorable in his comments to me. If not for Hastings, we might be wed ere now. I have sent a message to your brother in Scotland, but as yet have heard nothing. It seemed only right we should carry out what would certainly be your father's wishes."

Serena watched the emotions playing across the face of the handsome Mercian who, according to all she had heard, was well liked by the people of Northumbria. Morcar was Steinar's age, only a few years older than she. And while Serena would not have objected had her father betrothed her to him, she was unsure if her father would have done so. Though Morcar likely did express what would have been Steinar's wishes had he known of the matter. Offered the chance, would she wed the Mercian? How could she do so when her heart longed for the Norman knight whose expression was ever stern but whose kisses deprived her of breath?

The Red Wolf might be her enemy, but given all she had observed, he was more a man than Morcar. Older, less compulsive and accustomed to being responsible for the lives of others, he had won her respect in the weeks he'd been at Talisand. Then, too, she remembered that Morcar and his brother, after having been defeated at Fulford by Harald Hardrada of Norway, failed to appear at Hastings when their help was so badly needed.

If she refused Morcar, she knew there were ways he could bring the marriage to pass. The priest may be under his control, and there were potions that could rob her of the will to resist. He had already demonstrated he would use them to aid his cause.

"What about the Norman king?" she asked. "You would defy him?" Here was the essence of it in Serena's mind. She herself had once entertained the possibility of wedding a Saxon, but thought only to do so from the safety of Scotland. She had not believed it wise to marry in defiance of the Norman king while she remained in England. The Bastard's reputation was that of a hard, ruthless man who showed no mercy to those who defied him.

"I would," Earl Morcar said proudly.

He does not intend to serve England's new king! The Mercian earl was naïve if he believed he could succeed in robbing a Norman knight of the bride his king had given him, the king who had conquered England with his hundreds of ships and his thousands of men. It would take more than one Mercian earl to return England to the English.

Morcar's brother moved restlessly in his chair, catching her eye. She turned to look at him. He averted his gaze, making her think he was not comfortable with Morcar's chosen course of action.

"Then you would fight still," she said.

"Yea, I would," Morcar admitted, "and there are others who would fight with me, your brother among them."

Her gaze darted from one brother to the other, searching their faces. "You spoke of Steinar before. Have you word of him?"

The two earls shared a glance before Morcar answered. "I know that he resides with Edgar in Scotland, who even now gathers a force to return. In regards to you and my intention to wed you, I did send Steinar a message. I am certain he would wish this between us, my lady, as did your father. Steinar would never give his sister to a Norman."

Serena's appetite waned and she picked at her food as she again thought of the older brother she loved. Morcar had the right of it. Steinar would never consent to having the Red Wolf as a brother-in-law. "It has been a long while since I've had any message from him," she said sadly.

"I need not await his word to summon the priest and see us wed, Serena. Once 'tis done, we can travel together to join Steinar."

* * *

Two days after Serena disappeared, Cassie began to suspect where her lady had gone. Sir Niel had been dispatched to find Serena the morning after she had disappeared. Sir Maurin believed Serena had arranged to flee once again, and knowing she had gone north before, it was in that direction he sent Sir Niel.

But Cassie cast her gaze to the south. She did not think Serena had escaped. No, her lady had been taken. For Cassie knew once Serena made up her mind to accept the Norman lord as her husband, she was not likely to change. Cassie had seen the way Serena had looked at the Red Wolf, her eyes following the powerful knight as he strode though the yard and lingering on his broad shoulders in the practice yard. Nay, Serena had been preparing for a wedding, not a flight into the woods.

When the cloth merchant from Mercia had left Talisand, Cassie remembered he rode south. But his cart was still full of wares. Why would he return home so soon? Most merchants would have ridden east to the rich purses in York before heading south. She had wondered at the time, and now she again puzzled over his going. The morning after Serena disappeared, her white mare Elfleda was still in her stall. Serena would not have left behind the horse her father had given her.

But who would have abducted Lady Serena? Could it be Morcar? His brother Edwin was Earl of Mercia and she had heard that Morcar, having lost Northumbria, now dwelled with him. Yea, it was possible he had taken her. And Cassie was determined to follow.

As a young girl, Cassie had learned to ride when Serena did, so she could be her lady's companion. Though she rode infrequently and had no horse of her own, Cassie decided to take Elfleda and ride south to search for Serena. She would not tell Sir Maurin, for if her thinking was correct, and Earl Morcar had Serena, it would bring the Normans to Mercia were they to know.

Cassie had filled a bag of food and changed to a simple brown tunic before leaving for the stables, assured no one had seen her. She was hoping to slip out while Sir Maurin and the other Normans were occupied.

Once inside the stables, she set the small saddle on Elfleda, and tightened the girth. The sound of soft footfalls in the dirt behind her caused her to turn. There, garbed in his green and brown clothing, stood Rhodri.

"You go in search of her, then?" he asked.

She glanced around. At least for the moment they were alone. "How did ye know?" she whispered.

"You are infrequently in the stables, lass. When I saw you slip through the door, I was curious. I have been planning to go myself, as I was certain Serena would not have left without telling me. And I am obligated to see to her welfare. I made my oath to her brother."

"Ye have seen Steinar?"

"Yea, but none know of it, not even Serena."

"Why did ye not tell her? She has been anxious for word of him."

"Steinar asked me to say nothing to her until we were ready to leave to join him. He never considered she would want to stay. Nor did I."

Nodding, Cassie set her will to her task and finished saddling the mare. "I want to go, Rhodri. Serena is not only my lady, but my dearest friend."

"It is not safe for you to travel alone. You are not Serena, adept at the bow and dressed like a lad, whereas I can travel with few knowing I am in the woods. No one suspects a bard has any purpose other than entertaining."

"I must go, Rhodri. I owe it to Serena."

"If you insist on following after her," he said reluctantly, "I would go with you. You can travel as my wife to any who ask. And I am familiar with the Mercian earl's holding, which I have no doubt is your destination."

Surprised at the bard's astute observation, and not unhappy to have the protection of his bow, Cassie agreed. Traveling together would make her feel safe.

"Aye, Rhodri, I welcome yer company."

"Does anyone know you are doing this?"

"I asked Eric to deliver a message to me mother after I have left, saying I have gone to the west manor. I would not want her to worry."

Cassie only hoped that Sir Maurin did not connect her with the missing horse.

* * *

Through their conversations at meals following her arrival at Adlington,

Serena learned much of what had happened to the Mercian brothers after Hastings. It seemed the Norman king had not been constant toward them, and his promises, freely given, had all come to naught.

Edwin was especially bitter about having been promised William's daughter only to have the girl's hand withdrawn at the urging of the king's courtiers. And Morcar had lost Northumbria to a man of the Norman king's choosing. In turn, the Mercian brothers no longer believed William was owed their fealty. While Serena had much sympathy for their plight, and shared their view of the Norman king's deceit, she resisted Morcar's plans for herself. But since he was not aware of her reluctance, she was free to roam at will over the lands that surrounded Edwin's manor in Mercia.

From her conversations with the servant who oversaw her baths and dressing, Serena knew Adlington lay fifty miles south of Talisand. She could be home in a day and a half if she had a good horse. Using the excuse of a ride with Morcar, she intended to find one for her journey north.

The horses Edwin kept were fine palfreys any nobleman would be proud to own. The one Morcar had saddled for her this morning was a chestnut mare. Stroking the palfrey's mane, she realized it was the same color as the Red Wolf's hair and it caused her to wonder. Was he well? Had he returned from Exeter? She did not want to think of the powerful knight as wounded or worse, but she shuddered to think of his reaction if he returned to find her gone.

She and Morcar rode over the green hills speaking of earlier times, of an England free of Normans. When they came to a small rise that looked east over Mercia, Morcar pulled rein and dismounted. As he helped her down, he pulled her into his arms.

"I would show you something of my ardor, my lady." So saying, he bent his head and kissed her. She thought to resist but he was so quick his lips were on hers before she could do so. He was gentle but his kiss stirred no passion nor sent any shivers down her spine like the kiss of the Red Wolf. To Serena it was more like the kiss of a brother.

"On the morrow, the priest comes, my lady," Morcar said, holding her gaze. "And you will be properly wed to a Mercian earl." He smiled as if he could think of no greater honor to bestow upon her.

She smiled back and walked to the edge of the rise, looking into the distance while Morcar secured the horses. At one time, she might have considered wedding Earl Morcar a great honor but unbeknownst to the earl, Serena's feelings had changed. Once she would have gladly married him to escape the fate of a Norman's wife, but that was before she had spent weeks with the knight called the Red Wolf. She had told the

Norman she would be his lady and, though it had taken her some time to realize how sincerely she had meant those words, with Morcar's kiss, her course was firmly set. She would not alter it.

"And what follows after, my lord?" Serena asked. "What will you do when the Norman knight discovers you have stolen his bride?"

The handsome earl took her hand and gave her a confident grin. "Why, my lady, we will not tarry here for William's wolf to find us." He kissed her knuckles. "I intend to take you to York where the loyal Northumbrians are preparing even now to meet Edgar and his men. I imagine your brother will be among them. He will be anxious to see you."

York!

Her brother would be in York. She was eager to be reunited with Steinar, but she could not bring herself to marry this Mercian to see it done. No matter it would please her brother for her to wed Morcar and escape the grasp of the Red Wolf, she knew in her heart she must return to Talisand. From there, she would seek a way to find Steinar herself.

"I would very much like to see my brother."

Early the next morning, Serena slipped from her chamber, silently creeping to the stables. She had donned the green undertunic and gown with the wide skirt that would allow her to ride astride. The mare whinnied softly as Serena lifted the small saddle to the horse's back. Unlike Talisand, where the Normans had posted guards at the gate, there was no guard here, so that she was able to disappear unseen into the gray light of dawn.

* * *

"She's gone, I tell you!" exclaimed Morcar, anxiously staring out the window at the trees in the distance being stirred by the wind. "And today was to be our wedding."

"Calm down, brother," Edwin urged, "mayhap she took a fancy to ride alone. Brides can be nervous."

"'Tis a possibility, but the servant who has been acting her lady's maid told me Serena was gone when she went to attend her this morning. I wonder if she has not run north to York. She rides well, you know. Mayhap, she decided to avoid a wedding and seek her brother directly. She and Steinar were close and she seemed eager to see him."

"I need you this afternoon, Morcar, to help me oversee the plans for the rising in Northumbria. Why not send the Norman mercenary after her and let him bring her back if, indeed, she has fled?"

"Aye, 'tis an idea. Sir Hugue was here this morning asking if we've another task for him, and he speaks English well enough."

Immediately thereafter, Morcar dispatched Sir Hugue, and watched as the mercenary rode away from Adlington. Though he would have preferred to go himself, Morcar had trusted the mercenary once before with good results so he would trust him again. He had told the knight to search to the north and to watch for signs that Serena might veer east toward York.

The Norman seemed happy for a chance to regain the woman Morcar had lost, assuring him that she would soon be back at Adlington.

CHAPTER 16

Hearing the sound of the river, Renaud raised his hand to halt the column of men behind him. "We stop for a brief rest to water the horses," he said to Geoff riding beside him. Dismounting, he added with a grin, "Should all go well, we will arrive at Talisand in time for the midday meal."

"Aye," said Geoff, sliding to the ground, as the men around them also dismounted, "though I would ride on without stopping for Maggie's cooking, the horses will fare better for this respite before our last hours of travel."

Renaud handed Belasco's reins to Jamie and took the dirt path that cut through the trees, anxious to stretch his legs. Their ride north following the siege had been exhausting, particularly since he and his men were tired when they began, and the wound in his arm still pained him. A few of the days brought them rain, which turned the road into a stream of mud, but now the skies were clear and the sunlight pierced woods to light their path.

Briefly he touched his aching left arm, then dismissed the pain. It was a small wound compared to others he had received in battle. And he was comforted by the thought he would soon be home.

Troubled by William's words as they had left Exeter, Renaud wondered to what battle his sire would next summon him. While the good citizens of Exeter had finally seen the wisdom of surrendering to the king, their resistance had come at a great cost. William had lost half his army and, to Renaud's regret, it had changed the king's attitude toward the English. Never again would he trust the people who had held him at bay for so long.

Renaud walked along the path strewn with yellow wild flowers and turned his thoughts from Exeter to Talisand—and to his spirited bride.

149

He was eager to look into her violet eyes and even more eager to take her to his bed. In his mind, he saw her long flaxen hair laid out on the pillow, her beautiful body bared of clothes and her ripe breasts quivering for his touch.

Soon.

Joining Renaud on the path, Geoff rubbed his stomach. "I am anxious for the food of Talisand."

"More important than your stomach, my friend, is that this eve I will have a bride in truth and can be about the business of creating an heir." The prospect of getting Serena with child even now urged him on to their destination.

"'Twill please William and give his court something to gossip about. The warrior priest succumbs to the lovely Lady of Talisand. But beware lest the vixen becomes your weakness," Geoff said with a grin.

Though Renaud knew his friend was jesting, he could not dismiss the truth of his warning. "I am ever wary."

He'd known from the first time he'd touched her that he craved her as no woman before. He had admired her spirit, even her defiance, though at times it angered him greatly. But the maiden's response to his kisses told him much. She may despise her Norman conquerors, but she did not loathe the Red Wolf's touch. He would seduce his bride if he must.

Anxious to be on his way, Renaud turned and strode back to where Jamie waited, holding Belasco's reins, Geoff hurrying behind.

"Do not take offense, Ren. I, too, have a weakness—for the lovely Eawyn."

"Aye, I'd forgotten about the dark-haired beauty you are so fond of. Which appeals more, her cooking or her?"

"If I am fortunate, I will have both," Geoff said with a wink. "These English women are winsome, are they not?"

Renaud just chuckled under his breath. *Winsome, indeed. And difficult, rebellious and stubborn!*

"Yer horse is watered, m'lord," said his page. Renaud thanked the lad and with some pain to his arm, swung into the saddle.

The column resumed its journey north and, after a few hours, Renaud arrived at the top of the familiar ridge looking west toward Talisand. The sun was at its zenith not unlike that first day he had seen his lands. But the sight had changed. Next to the manor, a timber castle was now rising from a great motte.

Behind him, Renaud heard the horses snorting, restless to return to their stalls and their oats.

"It appears that Sir Maurin and the men of Talisand have served me well in my absence."

"Yea, 'tis a great sight," said Geoff. "There is no castle like it in this part of England."

"William should be pleased. Mayhap he'll pay us a visit." Renaud did not have to wonder what Serena would think of William at Talisand. She would not look forward to such an occurrence.

Renaud was first through the gate, followed by Geoff, Alain with the banner, then Mathieu and Jamie and the other squires and men-at-arms. He dismounted and handed Belasco's reins to the waiting Eric. Doffing his mail would come next but for that he would seek his chamber. He glanced at his leggings splattered with mud, hoping a bath awaited him.

"My lord," hailed Sir Maurin, coming through the door of the manor. "I have been eager for your return. You have fared well?"

"Well enough. It took nearly three weeks and many lives, but William has his victory." Renaud doffed his gloves and handed them to the waiting Jamie, then turned his attention back to Sir Maurin. "And Talisand?" Renaud gazed about the yard where his men were greeting those who had stayed behind. He was disappointed not to be rewarded with a glimpse of his bride. Mayhap she was occupied within the manor.

"Talisand fares well, my lord, but there has been an incident."

Renaud was instantly on the alert, seeing the anxiety in Sir Maurin's blue eyes.

"The news is not good." Lines of worry etched Sir Maurin's weathered face as he ran a hand through his hair.

Renaud narrowed his eyes. "What has happened?"

"There is no way to soften the news, my lord. Lady Serena has disappeared."

Renaud shot a glance at Geoff then returned his eyes to Sir Maurin whose fallen countenance spoke of regret. A storm rose in his chest. "Disappeared? When? How?"

"We know not what happened, my lord, only that one morning when her handmaiden went to the lady's room, she was gone. A search revealed she was not within the manor or in the village."

"What of Sir Niel?"

"The knight guarded her continuously. He never left his post. And none at Talisand know anything of it. But I believe he and the guard at the postern gate were given some kind of sleeping draught. They both suffered an aching head the next morn. I sent Sir Niel and another man to search to the north where she had gone before. Since then, he has returned and both the lady's handmaiden and the Welsh bard have disappeared."

Renaud stormed through the door of the manor, Sir Maurin and Geoff trailing behind, his anger rising with every step. So, she had plotted with the Welshman and her handmaiden to leave! *How could she do this after her pretty speech about taking her place as the Lady of Talisand?*

"How long?" he demanded.

"Three days, my lord," said Sir Maurin, "since the Lady Serena disappeared. Only one since Cassie and the bard could not be found."

Renaud's stomach clenched at the thought of his bride being alone on the road that long. "Did you see any signs of Lady Serena's going?"

"It rained after she disappeared, but seeing no sign of her to the north, Sir Niel was just preparing to ride south when you arrived."

"South?" Why would she ride south if her brother is in Scotland? But he did not linger on the question. No, he would track her like an animal and bring her to ground as he had done once before. Only this time, he would show no mercy to his English bride.

No one defied the Red Wolf, least of all a woman who was his by the king's command.

* * *

It was afternoon when Serena pulled reins, her growling stomach reminding her that the bread and cheese were gone long ago. She had no weapon with her and, in any event, would not want to take the time to hunt. Yet, both she and the horse needed water. Leaving the horse tethered by the stream, she walked the short distance to where she had seen red berries growing in a thicket at the side of a clearing. She plucked some and began to eat, tasting the tart juice on her tongue.

Hearing a rustle of something moving in the brush behind her, she jerked her head around.

"At last we have found ye!" exclaimed Cassie, as she stepped from the woods. At her side was Rhodri leading their horses.

"Cassie! Rhodri!" exclaimed Serena. She ran to embrace them. "You came for me?"

"Why else would we be so far from Talisand?" said Rhodri with a sarcastic smile. "This far south is no mere ramble."

Cassie gave her a puzzled look. "Serena, I thought to find ye at Earl Edwin's. But here ye are halfway to Talisand. Why?"

"Until early this morning, I *was* at Edwin's manor in Mercia. He and Morcar stole me from Talisand for a wedding."

"A wedding?" asked Rhodri with drawn brows.

"Yea—my own and Morcar's, if you would believe it." At Cassie's sharp inhalation of breath, Serena explained, "He thought to rescue me from the Normans. In truth, I would have welcomed his plan some time ago, but not now." Observing her handmaiden's obvious confusion, she added, "I escaped."

"I expect he will follow," said Rhodri.

"Or worse," replied Serena, "he will send his new henchman, Sir Hugue."

"The mercenary who rode with the Red Wolf?" asked Cassie with raised brows.

"Aye. Somehow he has come to Mercia and now does the bidding of the earls, though I doubt he has told Morcar that he was sent from Talisand in disgrace."

Rhodri's face bore a look of concern. "He did not hurt you, did he, Serena?"

"Nay. But I was never at peace knowing the Norman was near. You heard the tale of the attempted rape of Eawyn?" At Rhodri's nod, she said, "He was the one."

"So you travel back to Talisand," Rhodri said with a resigned expression.

Serena nodded.

"Are you resigned, then, to wed the Red Wolf, Serena?" he asked.

Serena smiled shyly. "Yea, I believe I am. It is what I want, Rhodri, though I cannot imagine what Steinar will think of it."

"He will like it not," said Rhodri darting a glance at Cassie. "Did you tell Morcar of your decision?"

"Nay. He could not envision it, I am certain. And I was afraid if he knew of my intention he would try to detain me."

"'Tis a wise thing ye do in returning, m'lady. The Red Wolf will be good to ye. Sir Maurin says so."

Serena smiled at Cassie. She would believe anything Sir Maurin told her.

"Are you hungry?" asked Rhodri. "We can rest for a while before setting off for Talisand."

"Yea, I am," said Serena, "did you bring food?"

"Aye," said Cassie, reaching into a bag she carried and handed Serena some dried venison. It was a bit tough but, together with the berries, satisfied Serena's hunger for the moment. As she chewed, Elfleda walked forward and nudged her shoulder. Serena stroked the soft skin of the mare's nose.

"I'm glad you brought my horse, Cassie. I missed her."

Serena and Cassie sat on a fallen log at the edge of the clearing and spoke of the abduction and how it might have occurred. Rhodri went off to water the horses, then returned to listen to their conversation.

"I remember nothing of that night," confided Serena.

"They had to have help within the manor for none to notice," said

Rhodri standing at the edge of the woods. "The next day all at Talisand was the same. There were no signs of struggle."

"I have thought on it some," said Serena looking into the concerned face of her handmaiden. "I believe it was Aethel who altered the ale. She was the last to fill my cup. I wonder if, in her mixed up thinking, she believed it would please me. She knew of my desire to leave. She had offered to help once before."

"Aye, Aethel might have done so," said Cassie.

"Were any hurt?" asked Serena.

"Nay," said Cassie. "The guards were fine, save for their aching heads. I am certain the Normans suspect me of giving them a sleeping draught as I delivered Sir Niel his ale that night. Sir Maurin has said nothing, but he sent Sir Niel to find ye."

"Say nothing of Aethel's involvement until I can speak with her," said Serena.

Serena was looking at Cassie when Rhodri, who had been standing in front of a tree, suddenly slumped to the ground.

"What—" Serena rose and began to walk toward the bard lying supine on the ground when a huge shape loomed from amidst the trees.

Sir Hugue!

"Ah, two little doves ripe for the plucking," said the mercenary as he stepped into the clearing, a wooden cudgel in his hand.

Cassie rose and Serena stepped back, pulling her handmaiden with her as she retreated from the Norman mercenary and his lecherous gaze. She remembered it all too well.

"'Tis a shame one must be returned untouched to the earl," said Sir Hugue. "But the other," he leered at Cassie, "aye, that one is mine to do with as I may."

"No!" protested Serena. "I will not go with you. I do not wish to return." Serena took Cassie's arm and dragged her back still farther until more distance lay between them and the mercenary.

Cassie drew a seax from her waist and held it high, the point aimed at Sir Hugue. "Ye'll not touch me, ye dog," she said.

"Cassie, no!" shouted Serena. Her handmaiden was no match for so burly a knight.

The Norman mercenary slowly stalked toward Cassie, a sickening smile on his face.

Before he reached the handmaiden, the thunder of hoof beats sounded in the woods. Sir Hugue turned his head to see, but the riders were not yet in sight. The moment he looked away, Cassie threw her seax. The blade sank into the Norman's shoulder. Dropping his cudgel, the Norman pulled Cassie's blade from his shoulder and sent the deadly looking knife flying through the air and into Cassie's chest.

The girl dropped to the ground as the Norman mercenary turned and fled.

With a shriek, Serena crouched at Cassie's side. "Cassie!" Moving her hands over the place where the blade had entered the handmaiden's chest, Serena thanked God it was lodged near the girl's shoulder, and not in her heart. The wound poured forth blood as Serena withdrew the blade. Tearing the hem of her undertunic, Serena wadded the cloth and pressed it to the wound.

Cassie opened her eyes, dazed, and looked down at her chest. "He...he hit me." Then lowering her head, she added in stilted words, "I thought he had...something else...in mind."

"Likely he did. The man is evil. But we were lucky. He fled when he heard riders coming." Cassie shut her eyes, moaning in pain. Serena kept the pressure on the wound. "Stay with me, Cassie."

From a few feet away, Rhodri began to stir as mounted knights rode into the clearing in a flurry. Serena was alarmed until she saw the Red Wolf led them. Her heart leapt in her chest.

He came!

Serena experienced both joy and relief at seeing the Red Wolf on his magnificent stallion, but her spirits fell when she saw the anger in his eyes as he looked down upon her.

He dismounted and strode toward her. "What have you done now, my lady?" His words dripped sarcasm.

"I can explain," she offered.

"Indeed you will," he said with a stern look.

Sir Geoffroi and Sir Niel slid from their saddles. Sir Maurin had already dismounted and rushed to Cassie's side where he knelt, taking her hand.

"Cassie, my love," he said in accented English. "*Qu'est-il arrivé?*"

Cassie's green eyes filled with tears at the sight of the knight's anxious face. It was clear to Serena that Sir Maurin was as enamored with Cassie as she was with him.

Rhodri sat up and rubbed the back of his head.

The Red Wolf stood over the small group. His fierce gray eyes held Serena's gaze for a long moment, then glancing at her handmaiden, he said to his knight, "Geoff, get the bandages from my bag before the girl bleeds to death."

"Aye," Sir Geoffroi acknowledged, and strode to their horses.

"Sir Niel," said the Red Wolf to the younger knight, "make yourself useful and find some water to clean the wound."

Without a word, Sir Niel took a skin from his saddle and headed for the stream.

"What has happened here?" the Red Wolf demanded of Serena. There was more than anger in his eyes now. Was it a look of concern? Knowing he was close made her feel safe, no matter he was displeased. Relieved at seeing him returned from Exeter a whole man, she wanted to fly into his arms but his forbidding manner kept her still.

"We were attacked by the mercenary you sent away from Talisand, the one called Sir Hugue."

"Sir Hugue?" asked Sir Geoffroi, incredulous as he handed Serena an oilcloth containing fresh bandages.

"What was the mercenary doing with you in the woods, Serena?" the Red Wolf asked.

Serena felt the cold chill in his voice. "He followed me," said Serena, realizing that told him little.

Rhodri, still rubbing his head, asked, "Who hit me?"

"Sir Hugue, the Norman mercenary," said Serena, shooting a glance at the Red Wolf.

"There will be time later to hear the full tale," said the Red Wolf. "We must get your handmaiden back to Talisand."

"First, let me try and stop the bleeding," pleaded Serena. Asking the men to turn their backs, Serena stripped the top of Cassie's tunic and undertunic from her, and with the water Sir Niel handed her, cleaned the wound.

Cassie moaned.

Rhodri spoke from where he was rising. "Serena, Cassie had some herbs with her. Agrimony was one of them. It will stop the bleeding."

"I'll get it," said Sir Maurin. He rose from Cassie's side and hurried to the horse Rhodri directed him to.

When the knight returned, Serena lifted the cloth she had used to cover Cassie's chest and sprinkled the dried herb over the wound.

Still conscious, Cassie winced.

To Sir Maurin, who stood looking grief-stricken, Serena said, "'Tis not good, Sir Maurin, but hopefully not so grievous as to take her life."

Cassie's eyes fluttered and then closed.

Sir Maurin stared fixedly at the redhead, then dropped to her side to hold her hand once again. The Red Wolf hovered above them like a dark threatening angel.

When the flow of blood slowed, at Serena's signal, Sir Niel and Sir Geoffroi gently lifted Cassie into the arms of Sir Maurin where he sat upon his horse. The knight balanced her on his lap, one arm around her shoulders and the other on the reins, allowing her body to rest against his chest.

Watching Sir Maurin's embrace of the handmaiden, the Red Wolf said, "We'll have to travel more slowly." Then looking at Serena and Rhodri, "There will be time for the tale."

They mounted their horses, Sir Niel leading, followed by Sir Maurin holding Cassie. Next came Serena and the Red Wolf riding abreast. Sir Geoffroi and Rhodri brought up the rear.

Aware of the Red Wolf's anger, she managed to say, "I am glad to see you safely returned, my lord."

"Are you, indeed, my lady?" The tone of his voice told her he was unconvinced. "As you must have discerned, I came from Talisand where I found you missing once again. It seems you have a penchant for stealing away." He did not hide his displeasure.

"I only escaped this morning," she explained.

"Escaped? I was told you left Talisand days ago."

"I was *abducted* days ago. Surely you do not think I left on my own?"

She could plainly see that is just what he thought.

"*Abducted?* Do you expect me to believe such a story when Sir Niel was given a sleeping potion? Surely it was your doing, my lady, or someone aiding you, mayhap the Welshman."

Serena knew he had not trusted her, and with good reason. He could not know her heart had changed. Before the abduction, she had decided to accept her duty and take her place at his side as the Lady of Talisand, but now it was more. It had taken an English earl to show her she wanted only the Norman knight.

His jaw flexed, as if barely suppressing his wrath. She desperately wanted to make him understand. "I, too, must have been given a potion, my lord."

"By Sir Hugue? What was his role in all of this?"

"He was working for my abductor. I thank you for sparing us the mercenary's wrath. Cassie threw her knife into his shoulder, but he pulled it out and sent it into Cassie's flesh. He was very angry when he fled at hearing your horses."

"What about your handmaiden and the bard? Were they a part of this?"

"Nay. They went in search of me and only crossed my path a short while before you did."

"Surely they aided your escape."

"They did not. Ask Rhodri for yourself."

The Red Wolf turned in his saddle to glance back at the Welshman. "She speaks the truth, my lord," said Rhodri. "Cassie was eager to go in search of Lady Serena and I insisted on joining in the hunt."

"Mayhap they do speak the truth," offered Sir Geoffroi from where he rode next to Rhodri.

The Red Wolf huffed, and turned back to Serena. Beneath his anger she saw a weariness she had not observed before. Likely, he had not rested when he returned to Talisand.

"Go on then, out with the rest of your story," he said, appearing resigned to hearing it.

"I will tell you if you promise not to take revenge on the one who took me."

"And why should I make such a promise, my lady? If, indeed, you were taken against your will, and Sir Hugue had a hand in it, such a crime would be deserving of the severest punishment."

She knew he meant death. But Serena could not let him kill Morcar and his brother. "Because the ones who took me were of my own people and believed they acted in accordance with my wishes and my father's."

"I will shelter no traitors at Talisand!" the Red Wolf declared.

"I know of none, my lord." But even as she said the words, Aethel's face came unbidden to her mind. Still she could not think of the herb woman as a traitor. Instead, she was sorry for what the woman's life had become. "Tell me you will not take revenge and I will tell you from whom I escaped only this morning."

"Did he touch you?" the Red Wolf asked, his gray eyes clouded, his voice stern. "That I could never forgive no matter his motive."

"Nay, he did not. He intended to wed me and that is why I left, and why I must ask for your word that you will not seek to harm him. He was a friend of my father."

The Red Wolf stared at her as if weighing her request. Finally, he said, "You have my word. Now tell me, who would dare steal from the Red Wolf? Tell me, and I will decide if you can be believed."

Knowing him to be a man of honor, Serena trusted him not to seek vengeance for her disappearance. "'Twas Earl Morcar."

The Red Wolf's frown deepened. "...the English earl?"

"Aye. When my father still lived, the earl asked for my hand. Morcar believed he was doing what my father wanted. What I wanted."

"It matters little."

"I suppose you are right, and anyway, there was no contract. But Morcar had spoken to my father and had hoped one would follow." She looked into the Red Wolf's gray eyes. The anger she had seen only moments before seemed to soften. "He could not have known that I wished to wed a Norman, that my heart had changed. And I did not tell him. He would not have believed me any more than you do. Instead, I sought to escape and return to Talisand."

"You are practiced at escape, my lady." The Red Wolf's gaze lowered to her lips, still stained, she knew, with the juice of the red berries. "Mayhap I believe you," he said. "Or mayhap I merely want to. How were you taken from Talisand?"

"I know not, though I suspect Sir Hugue played a role. He now serves Morcar. I went to sleep in my chamber and awoke in another, one I came to learn was in Earl Edwin's manor in Mercia."

"Earl Edwin had a part in this treachery?" he asked with a look of surprise.

"You must understand," she said, trying to convince him of the truth. "The earls feel betrayed by your Norman duke who would be England's king. He demanded their fealty and then broke his promises, taking his daughter from Edwin and Northumbria from Morcar. Then, as if that were not enough, he built castles on the Welsh border of Mercia and gave his abbot control over some of Mercia's shires." Looking directly at the Red Wolf, she said, "It seems your king does not keep his word, my lord."

"Enough of this!" he shouted. "I'll not listen to you criticize William and defend the English who defy him. The king has had enough of such treachery." Then looking away, he added, "After Exeter, he will show no mercy."

Ignoring his disparagement of her people, she asked, "Did all those you took with you to Exeter return?" She had to know if any had been lost. She could not bear to see any killed, particularly not Jamie.

"They did."

She breathed a sigh of relief. Despite his anger and mistrust, Serena was comforted by his presence and glad he had found her, especially with Cassie bleeding from a knife wound. She needed the Red Wolf's strength. Although she trusted him, she had purposely not spoken of Morcar's intention to travel to York. It might only draw the Red Wolf into what could become another battle, this time one involving her brother.

Trying to appease his lingering anger, she said, "Thank you, my lord. I was worried about Jamie especially."

From behind her, Sir Geoffroi said, "You have his lordship to thank for the lad's health, my lady. He took an arrow for the boy."

Alarmed, Serena turned to face the Red Wolf. "You are wounded?"

"Yea," he said looking down at his left arm, "but not grievously."

She could see no bandage but she remembered his wince when he mounted his stallion, and he now held the reins in his right hand. "You protected the lad. And you have spared me the wrath of Sir Hugue. For both, I am most grateful."

"What about the mercenary?" he inquired. "You cannot tell me it was

159

chance he encountered you and the others in the woods."

"Nay, it was not. As I said, he has pledged his sword to Morcar and his words to us suggested he was sent to find me."

CHAPTER 17

By the time their cavalcade arrived at Talisand, a host of people had gathered to meet them.

Maggie was one of the first to approach, a worried look on her face. Her eyes scanned the horses crowding the yard. Alighting on her daughter, carried in Sir Maurin's arms, she screamed, "Cassie!"

Sir Maurin gently handed the girl to the waiting Sir Geoffroi and Sir Niel, who had dismounted and come to his aid.

Serena dropped from her horse and watched the knights. Maggie ran to Serena as the men carried the handmaiden into the manor. "I will tend her myself, Maggie. Fetch Aethel and tell her to bring the herbs."

"Cassie was supposed to be at the west manor," Maggie said, her voice desperate. "What happened?"

"She and Rhodri came after me. She was stabbed with a knife."

"Who would do such a thing to me lass?" The cook's green gaze followed the knights as they carried Cassie through the front door of the manor. "Will she recover?"

"'Tis serious, Maggie, but I pray not fatal. I can explain later what happened. Right now I must make sure the bleeding has not begun again."

Serena followed the knights into the manor and directed them to take Cassie to Serena's bedchamber. Sir Maurin followed and now stood by the bed looking down on the unconscious girl. Cassie's skin, usually glowing with health, was nearly colorless, a stark contrast to her flaming red hair.

"Sir Maurin, I ask you to leave us alone for a time. I must undress her and see to the wound. I will call you when I have finished."

He nodded. "I will be waiting downstairs, my lady." He turned to go.

161

Serena had never seen the knight looking so forlorn.

As he reached the door, she said, "I will do my best, Sir Maurin. I know you care for her, as do I."

"Aye, I do," he said and left, closing the door behind him.

Aethel came in after the knight departed, her satchel of medicines and herbs with her. "Maggie is half out of her wits," said Aethel. Then seeing the handmaiden lying as still as death, she asked, "What happened to her?"

Serena looked up from where she was carefully cutting away Cassie's tunic. "You are not the first to ask. We were in the woods, on our way back to Talisand when the mercenary, Sir Hugue, found us."

"The knight who attacked Eawyn did this?"

"Yea. He is now with Morcar, who I doubt is aware of the snake he shelters."

Aethel, Serena noted, did not looked surprised at the tidings.

Since Serena had worked with the herb woman before to tend the sick and wounded, they now quickly fell into their prior routine. Serena prepared the wound and Aethel took from her bag the herbs she would apply. As they worked, they talked.

"Ye came back, m'lady," Aethel said.

"Yea, I did. Did you doubt I would?"

"I thought ye wanted to leave." Serena watched the herb woman's dark eyes carefully, noting the sincerity.

"Once that might have been true, Aethel, but no longer. I meant what I told the people of Talisand. I am their lady and I will wed the Red Wolf. Earl Morcar wanted to marry me but that was not my will. Were you not aware I was resigned to becoming the Norman's wife?"

"Nay, I thought ye would be happy to leave. Happy to wed the English earl."

"I know you were a part of it, Aethel." Then looking down at Cassie, "But you see where Morcar's abduction has led."

"I am deeply sorry," said Aethel. The woman looked contrite.

"If you are, Aethel, then end your traitorous behavior and help me to care for the people of Talisand."

"Aye, m'lady, I will." Her dark eyes filled with tears.

"Then I will protect your secret."

While Serena would keep a careful watch on the woman, she would give her the chance to change. How could she do less when her own heart had changed from wanting to flee the Normans to wanting to wed one?

Before they finished, Maggie rushed in to check on her daughter. Assured Cassie was doing well, she kissed her daughter's forehead and hurried out to see to the returning men.

Serena rose from Cassie's bedside. "I must speak to Sir Maurin."

"I will sit vigil through the night," Aethel volunteered.

* * *

"Can I believe her?" Renaud asked Geoff as they ate the evening meal. He had watched Serena ascend the stairs, knowing she went to tend her handmaiden, and he had wondered then if she was back to stay.

"Only time will tell," said Geoff. "Her tale was plausible. If Morcar and his brother seek vengeance on William, what better way to exact it than to rob one of his knights of his bride, as Edwin claims he was robbed of the king's daughter?"

"A foolish thing for Edwin and Morcar to do if it happened as she says," replied Renaud, still angry at having to track his bride through the woods.

Maugris, who sat with them, leaned in to whisper. "Men behave foolishly when it comes to beautiful women." He sat back, his wizened face crinkling in a smile.

"Indeed they do," said Geoff with a chuckle, "especially if they can cook."

"The both of you too easily excuse a man's folly that nearly deprived me of my bride," said Renaud impatiently. "And now I have the mercenary to contend with again."

"Aye," agreed Maugris. "That one is worthy of your vengeance."

Renaud still seethed at the knowledge the mercenary had been a part of stealing Serena. The bard had posed no obstacle to Sir Hugue's evil intent. Would Serena have been the mercenary's next victim had he not run at the sound of their horses?

He had mixed feelings about Serena's sincerity. She seemed firm in her conviction to wed him yet he knew from William's court that betrayal could come from one who feigned loyalty.

He had been eager to bed her when she was a mere servant with dull brown hair and dressed in an ill-fitting tunic. Stripped of her disguise, she was beautiful beyond compare. Standing in the woods in her green tunic, her violet eyes blazing and her red lips beckoning, he had fought the urge to take her into his arms and crush those lips beneath his. Had his men not been with him, he might have done so. Yet he had also been tempted to shake her for he had been maddened by the possibility she had lied once again.

Mathieu came to his side and whispered a message that brought a smile to his face. Turning from his companions, Renaud said, "If you will forgive me, I've a mind to be alone with my lady."

Leaving Geoff and Maugris with startled faces, his gaze drifted up to his chamber.

* * *

Serena sank into the steaming bath letting the water bring relief to her aching muscles. The fight for Cassie's life, which had only begun, had taken much from her. She loved the girl like a sister and the thought she could lose her weighed heavy on her mind.

Since Cassie was sleeping in Serena's bed, Maggie had arranged for Serena's bath to be placed in the lord's chamber. Seeing his warrior things strewn about she was instantly uncomfortable and wondered if Mathieu's assurance that she would be left alone could be counted upon. There was no guard at the door.

Thoughts of the knight who slept here plagued her. She knew he was angry even after her explanation. During their brief exchange of words on the way back to Talisand, his steel gray eyes, as threatening as the blade secured at his waist, portended ill. Might he still believe she left Talisand of her own accord? She had no desire to fight with him now, not when she had finally accepted the truth of her feelings. She had wanted to explain all that was in her heart, but the presence of his men and the concern for Cassie had kept those thoughts locked within her.

By now, Sir Hugue would have made it back to Mercia, assuming Cassie's blade had not stopped him. If Morcar knew she was again in the hands of the Red Wolf, mayhap he would not pursue her. He had said he would soon leave for York. Was Steinar already there? She remembered the city, southeast of Talisand, only a short distance from Stamford Bridge where Eawyn's husband Ulrich had fallen.

Picking up the rose scented soap, Serena scrubbed her body and hair. Once the soap was rinsed from her hair, she wrung the water from it, reached for the drying cloth and rose from her bath, wiping the water from her wet skin.

The door opened with no warning knock.

Serena gasped and pulled the cloth over her breasts and belly, keenly aware her legs were bare for anyone to see.

The Red Wolf stepped into the chamber, his piercing gray gaze sliding over her body and coming to rest where her breasts strained against the thin cloth. She could feel the heat of her blush as she looked to see the drying cloth clinging to her wet skin.

Without saying a word, he turned to the side and took off his belt. Then, with a grunt, he pulled his mail over his head and struggled out of his tunic. She would have offered to help had she not been so scantily clad. Had she not been so shy of his disrobing before her.

When his tunic slid to the floor, she nervously asked, "What do you intend, my lord?"

"I should think that was obvious, my lady. I am claiming my bride."

"Now?" She gripped the drying cloth more tightly to her still damp body. The long strands of her hair, wet from the bath, clung to her skin. No man had ever seen her in such a state.

"Yes, now." His eyes considered her carefully, and he shook his head. "God knows I've left it overlong."

While still staring at her, he shed his spurs and boots and doffed his linen shirt, leaving his chest bare and his lower body clad in only hosen and braies. He was a beautiful man with his bronze skin and muscled chest. Her eyes were drawn to the white cloth circling his upper arm.

"Your wound," she said, as she focused on the white bandage around his upper arm. The wound from the arrow he took for Jamie. How could she not love such a man?

"Aye." He glanced down at the bandage. "My token from the siege at Exeter."

"Does it pain you?"

His gray eyes narrowed intently. "If you are asking if it will impair my performance in our bed, nay."

Serena could not take her eyes off his body as he peeled off his hosen and unwound his braies, leaving his long lean form exposed and his manhood rising from a thatch of dark chestnut hair at his groin.

She swallowed, her throat suddenly dry and her teeth biting into her lower lip. She had never seen a man fully naked. Or one who was...aroused.

Gingerly stepping out of the water, she thought to delay his purpose. Maggie had told her his first taking would bring her pain. Serena would postpone it if she could.

"Our marriage has yet to be blessed, my lord."

"Maugris tells me the priest will return on the morrow," he said sternly. "There will be a blessing then. But I shall claim my bride now. I'll not risk you disappearing in the dark again while still a virgin another man can claim. Come here, Serena."

Seeing the desire in his eyes, Serena knew the time had come. She would not shy from a fate she had come to accept. One she had chosen.

The pride of a thegn's daughter rose within her as she lifted her chin and slowly stepped toward him, her gaze ever steady. She shivered as if his hands were already touching her.

Closing the distance between them, he pulled the cloth from her, tossing it to the floor. The cool air against her bare skin caused her nipples to pucker. She covered her breasts, crossing her arms over her chest.

"I would see all of you, Serena." He pulled her hands away from her chest. She met his gaze, determined not to cower before him. His eyes raked her body from her breasts to the flaxen hair at the apex of her thighs. "You are more alluring than any woman should be, bride or no."

Serena was suddenly shy in the face of his devouring gaze. She had known this moment would come, but it was all so new.

Pulling her against his powerful chest, their bodies met. The heat from his naked skin was a welcome warmth causing her breasts to tingle. She looked into his eyes, a darker gray than before, and saw his intent. Nothing would stop him now.

He kissed her, a kiss of possession. Deeper than any he'd given her before. Her breasts pressed into his muscled chest and she breathed in his scent of horses, leather and sweat—the scent she recognized from his first kiss. Sliding her hands up his arms, across the bandaged arm, she was sharply reminded this man was a warrior who had known many battles, and mayhap many women.

His tongue claimed her mouth as his hands roamed freely over her buttocks. He gripped them and pulled her into his hardening flesh.

Grasping his shoulders, she steadied herself. Then she was lost in his kiss, in his touch, in the feel of him surrounding her. A part of her wanted to flee, but another, stronger part, wanted to stay.

This must happen. It would be the end of her old life and the beginning of a new one. And somewhere deep inside, Serena knew she had wanted this man for a long while.

His aroused flesh grew more rigid against her belly, his size frightening her at the thought of what she knew was to come. She would soon know this man more intimately than any other. She would be the Red Wolf's wife in truth.

The kiss ended and his lips swept across her neck and to the top of her shoulder, sending ripples of pleasure through her. She knew the man who held her so tightly was one of the dreaded Normans, but all she could think of was the passion his touch was stirring within her. It was a passion she had wanted and only from him. She tilted her head back to allow him better access to her throat and reveled in the enticing feel of his lips nibbling at the skin at the base of her neck.

There was no enemy here, only a man whose every silent question her body answered with "yea."

Bringing his hands to her face, he cupped her cheeks. Her lashes fluttered open. The Red Wolf's eyes were like liquid silver. His breathing came hard, as did hers, her heart racing like a wild doe before a predator.

"It is time, Serena." He took her hand and led her to the bed. Pulling back the cover, he gestured her forward. She lay down, lifting her damp hair onto the pillow, and looked back at him in nervous anticipation.

"I have waited long to have you. But never before have I taken a virgin. Though I do not intend to hurt you, I may."

She did not speak but found comfort in what she saw in his eyes. The anger was gone. He would try to ease her pain if he could.

He joined her on the bed and pulled her against him, his arm stretched possessively across her chest where his hand kneaded her breast, until she moaned with pleasure. She turned into his embrace. A tingling ache arose at the apex of her thighs as he slipped his knee between her legs.

He kissed her again, and rising on one elbow, bent his head to her breast. Her flesh was on fire as he took her nipple into his mouth. Her fingers delved into his thick chestnut hair and she held his head to her breast. The warmth of his tongue and the gentle scraping of his teeth caused her to writhe. The feeling was almost more than she could bear.

"Oh…my lord."

Returning his mouth to hers, he kissed her deeply. Lifting his head, he said, "I am your husband and soon your lover. Call me by my given name."

"Renaud," she breathed, as his mouth sought her other breast. He drew his thigh up between her legs to press against the place that was aching with want.

As he kissed her, his hand moved to her intimate flesh where he parted the folds and touched her. All her senses came alive as he moved his finger, slowly circling the most sensitive place. She grasped his shoulders, seeking more.

He circled the spot again and again, nearly driving her to madness as she writhed against what had become the center of her world. The invasion of his fingers that followed brought a building pleasure.

Before she could think what was coming, he rose over her, settled his body between her thighs, pressed his hard flesh to the entrance of her womb and thrust deep.

Serena cried out in response to the sudden pain, only to be silenced by his mouth covering hers, as he stilled. She tried to calm her clenching muscles, all the while feeling the fullness, the stretching and the pain from his hard shaft invading her virgin's body.

Then he plunged more deeply, until she was nearly rent in two. The pain gradually eased as he began to move within her, forcing her flesh to accommodate his domination of her body.

With his forehead pressed into the pillow next to her head, he slipped his hands under her hips, lifted her and drove deeply. Her muscles clamped around his hard shaft, and her nails bit into his back. She held onto him as he moved within her, feeling her own passion rise with his.

His deep moan resonated through her as he suddenly tensed, then collapsed upon her.

Serena lay there, feeling his weight and listening to his breathing slow while his shaft seemed to shrink where they were joined. Her own breathing calmed and she wondered if this was the lovemaking the servants gossiped about.

He rolled to one side, drawing her with him and kissed her temple. Pressing her head to his shoulder, he spoke in a low voice. "We will do well together, Serena. I have always known it would be so. Had you been honest with me, this would have happened sooner, and I might not have been so quick to reach my release."

"I did not trust you." She spoke truthfully. "You were a Norman conqueror."

"I am still that, but now I am also your husband. Do you trust me now?"

She would not deny him the truth. "Yea, I do."

"To hear that speaks well of our future. I would it would always be so."

They lay together for a while, the Red Wolf idly running his hand over the curve of her waist and down her hip, his fingers gently caressing her still sensitive skin. Her leg was draped over one of his, her breasts pressed into his side.

It felt right to lie next to him. They fit well together.

While there had been no words of love, she had not expected any from the knight who wed her out of duty to his king. And for her part, she had thought to become his wife for the sake of her people. They would never have met, much less married, save for the Bastard duke's conquering of her country. But if she confessed the truth, she wanted no other as husband. For though the Red Wolf had taken her to wife out of duty, she had come to care for him. Mayhap even love him. Was it possible?

She was nearly asleep when he spoke. "This time I will make love to you more slowly. This time you will join me in my release."

"This time?" she whispered. Still feeling a bit sore, she was in no hurry to repeat their joining.

"You did not, per chance, think I would take you only once this day? Nay, I have much to make up for, *wife.* And I would not deny you the pleasure I would have given you had it not been so long since I had a woman."

He pulled her on top of him, so that she faced him with her hands on either side of his head. What was he about? She placed her hands on his shoulders as he spread her knees apart and pulled them up, forcing her to sit up and straddle him. The position left her sensitive flesh atop his shaft that was hardening once again. To her surprise, her own flesh became wet and she had the urge to move against him.

"You will like this position. Serena, since you ride so well."

She stared into his eyes seeing amusement.

He brought his hands to her full breasts and began gently kneading the sensitive flesh, sending ripples of delight through her.

"You have beautiful breasts, my lady. Even a servant's tunic could not hide all your treasures."

She smiled, letting her head fall back at the waves of ecstasy that flowed over her when he shifted his hands to her hips and slid her back and forth over his manhood until it was slick from her own wetness.

"It feels...good," she uttered.

"Move your hips to rock back and forth." She did, and soon wanted more.

He groaned and his eyes closed as he rubbed his warrior's rough palms over her nipples causing them to harden into tight buds.

She continued to rock back and forth, sensing a rising need to be joined with him. He must have shared her need for he opened his eyes, and with his hands on her waist, moved her forward.

"What—" She was about to ask what he wanted her to do when he lifted her onto his shaft and pushed down until he was fully sheathed inside her. "Oh...," she sighed, closing her eyes at the pleasure she felt from the fullness of him inside her.

He pulled her head down to kiss her, then allowed her to sit up. She could see what he wanted and leaned forward, her palms on his chest as she used her legs to move up and down on his hardened flesh until her pleasure increased with the rising tension in her body.

His shaft, buried deep, caused her to throb with need. The tension where they were joined grew more urgent, and she rose to meet it, moving against his upward thrusts. Their coupling became a wild exchange of passion as Serena strained toward the release he had spoken of. He uttered sounds that told her he was nearing his own fulfillment.

Suddenly, he rolled her beneath him and plunged deep.

Her muscles constricted. She soared into a world of blinding sensation. Then she was floating, floating, as ripples of pleasure coursed through her, her muscles throbbing around his hardened flesh.

"Ahhh..." she rasped. Opening her eyes, she looked up at his face, their gazes meeting. Could he see the passion in her eyes? Could he see the love in her heart?

"Serena…," he said, his breathing ragged, "my Serena." Bracing himself above her, he tensed and shut his eyes tightly. A flood of warm liquid flowed into her passage as he fell upon her. But he did not stay there. Rolling to one side, he drew her against his chest and wrapped his arms around her, holding her close. He pressed a light kiss to her forehead, a tender gesture for this hardened knight.

Never could she have imagined the wonder of what they had shared. And with her acceptance of their union, Serena experienced a peace. From the first time he'd kissed her, she had desired him. It was that desire that had frightened her into fleeing, knowing he was a Norman. Now she was his wife and would be for as long as they lived.

Stroking her back, he spoke words of comfort in French, smoothing the damp strands of hair from her face.

She turned and pressed a kiss to his lips, which he returned.

"Serena," he said, "you are mine. After this day, you will sleep only in my chamber."

"It shall be as you wish."

She had fought her own desire to run from him. But with the certain knowledge she was his came the guilt of submitting so fully to her conqueror, not merely her body, but her heart. For in their joining, she had truly bonded with this man in a way she had not expected. She had submitted for her people never fully realizing the pleasure she would find in his arms. Never realizing the truth their coupling would reveal hidden in her heart. Against her will, a fledgling love had been born for the knight called the Red Wolf.

She was now his mate. Maugris had spoken the truth: she would birth his sons. Even this day, his seed might have taken root. Strangely, the picture of small versions of the Red Wolf following after their father brought a smile to her face.

CHAPTER 18

"I'm so glad ye agreed to the blue silk," Cassie weakly uttered from Serena's bed where she watched Serena dress for her wedding the next afternoon. "It brings out the blue in yer eyes."

Eawyn nodded her agreement and carried the gown to Serena.

"I will wear it as a token of our friendship, Cassie," said Serena.

"And mine for ye is woven into every fold," came the soft reply from the bed.

So that Cassie could be a part of the day, Serena had chosen to dress for her wedding in her old chamber. Sir Maurin, who frequently checked on the object of his affection, had to be shooed away to allow the women to prepare. In Cassie's place, Eawyn and Aethel were to help Serena don the gown she and Cassie had sewn in anticipation of this day.

Serena's gaze drifted to Aethel who had remained mostly silent. Now sorry for all the damage she had caused, the woman had not left Cassie's side since they carried her back to Talisand. Serena believed Aethel was trying to atone for her misguided act. Her demeanor had changed, that much was certain. Sir Alain might have had something to do with it for Serena had observed the knight speaking in hushed tones to Aethel more than once last evening.

"How are you feeling?" she asked the handmaiden.

"Better." Fortunately, the knife that had sliced through Cassie's skin entered at an angle and had not gone so deep as to jeopardize her life. Still, she would need care for some time to recover. Aethel's knowledge of herbs would be helpful.

Serena gave Cassie a warm, encouraging smile. "Each day will be better."

She turned to admire the finished gown Eawyn held out to her. The undertunic was of soft linen dyed a pale blue. The fine outer garment Eawyn slipped over Serena's head was a shimmering sapphire silk. Around her waist was a belt of silver links.

A knock at the chamber door sounded and Jamie peeked his head in. "Are ye ready, Serena? I have yer father's sword." The boy, now proudly wearing a midnight blue tunic bearing a snarling red wolf, hefted a sword nearly three feet long. According to their custom, there would be an exchange of the weapons following the priest's blessing. Renaud would give her his longer, ancestral sword, one he told her he held in reserve, and she would give him a weapon to symbolize his protection of her and their children.

She had chosen her father's sword, retrieved by his men after he'd fallen at Hastings. Shorter than a Norman sword and lighter and more flexible, it was the final symbol of her acceptance that she was the willing bride of Sir Renaud de Pierrepont, now Earl of Talisand.

"You can come in, Jamie," said Serena. "We are nearly finished."

Jamie stepped through the door, hefting what for him was a heavy sword. He stood admiring the polished metal. "Did ye know, Serena, that the Red Wolf saved my life at Exeter?"

"Yea, Sir Geoffroi told me. How did it happen?"

"He took an arrow for me." The boy's eyes glowed with adoration as he spoke of his lord. Then with a sheepish look he added, "I was in the wrong place."

"You like him?" she asked, though it was clear from the boy's face that he did.

"I do! And I am happy ye are to be his wife." Jamie carefully set the polished sword on the chest at the foot of the bed and walked to where Cassie lay, obviously happy to see her awake. Taking her hand, he asked, "How are ye, Cassie?"

"Getting better," Cassie said with a weak smile.

"Is not Serena beautiful?" he asked the bedridden woman as he turned to stare at Serena's gown.

"Aye, lad, she is."

Then to Serena, he said proudly, "I'm to lead ye down."

"Ye're dressed for it," said Aethel as she placed the cloak of purple velvet over Serena's shoulders, securing it with the sapphire jeweled brooch Renaud had given her. She would have expected the gift the morning after the wedding night, but Renaud had seen fit to place the gold circle set with sapphires in her hand as he rose from their bed that morning. The gesture had caused her cheeks to burn reminding her, as it did, of all they had shared. But since she'd given him her maidenhead, she supposed it was right that his gift should follow.

Along with the brooch, he'd given her a pouch of gold coins, and told her she would also have title to one of the manors and its surrounding land. As a husband's gift, it was generous, though she could not help but recall that all of Talisand would have been Steinar's save for the coming of the Normans.

At Renaud's request, she had worn her hair unplaited and without covering save for the circlet of silver and gold her father had given her which Eawyn placed on her head.

Dressed in her finery, the women pronounced her ready, and she followed Jamie down the stairs.

* * *

Renaud watched his bride slowly descending the stairs to the manor's entry where he waited surrounded by his senior knights. *She is mine!*

Once again, Serena appeared like a queen, this time in a shimmering gown of blue framed by a purple cloak thrown back over her shoulders, his gift of the gold sapphire-studded brooch secured at her neck. He preferred to imagine her as she was that morning when he'd left their bed: sleepy, naked and tumbled from his lovemaking. Never before had his soul merged with a woman, but he was certain it had happened with Serena when they joined as one flesh.

He could hardly wait for his wedding night.

"My lady," he said, offering her his hand. "You are a vision for this humble knight's eyes to feast upon." Then his mouth twitched up in a grin. "I was half worried you would appear dressed as a lad."

She laughed and placed her hand over his. "And embarrass my husband? Nay, I would not."

He was glad she could accept his teasing on this day that would see her wed to a Norman in the eyes of the church. Mayhap she no longer resented him. He could only hope.

His knights moved aside as he and Serena walked to the door Geoff held open. Jamie, beaming a smile for his lord, took his place next to the senior knight.

"The priest awaits us at the entrance to the chapel," he said to Serena as he led her into the yard.

All of Talisand turned out to celebrate the marriage of their lady to the Red Wolf. The yard was filled with his men and the villagers. He well knew some of them came out of curiosity. But the averted eyes of others told him there were still some who were unhappy their lady had been forced to wed a Norman. They should have drawn comfort in the knowledge that at least one member of the thegn's family remained to

173

see to their needs.

The crowd parted as he and Serena proceeded through the village to the chapel where Father Bernard waited for them in front of the doors. Renaud stopped before the priest, who covered their hands with his and began to speak.

Father Bernard talked of the Master of the Heavens' love for his children and the importance of the gift of marriage. They were simple words but significant in their meaning. Then he blessed their union.

The ceremony concluded, Renaud slipped a gold ring on her finger and whispered, *"Seulement l'amour entre nous."* Only love between us. The words he'd had engraved inside the ring.

She looked up startled. He had never uttered the word "love" to her before. Mayhap he did not give his heart now, but he wanted no strife, no rancor between them. He was not certain there would be love. As Geoff had said, only time would tell if she could be trusted. And for Renaud to love would demand his trust.

He turned and, with his palms outstretched, accepted from Mathieu the long Norman sword of his family, the hilt carved with intricate designs and decorated with rubies, emeralds and sapphires.

Looking into Serena's eyes, more violet because of the cloak she wore, he said, "I give you this sword to hold for our sons."

She solemnly thanked him and accepted the sword onto her own palms and handed it to the tall blond Theodric, who now served Renaud. Since Exeter the English guard had cut his hair in the Norman style and now looked like one of them.

Serena faced Jamie who held in his palms the same sword Renaud had seen him holding earlier, a shorter Saxon weapon.

Laying it carefully across Renaud's welcoming palms, with tear filled eyes, Serena said, "This was the sword of my father. It represents the honor of the thegn and that of the people he loved. With this sword, keep our home safe."

Meeting her gaze, he promised, "I will."

With the words spoken, Renaud handed the sword she had given him to Geoff. Then he took her hand and led her from the church back to the manor. Along the way, they were greeted by the smiles of the people of Talisand who were pleased with the marriage. He snatched glimpses of her smiling at the villagers and his men and rejoiced that his beautiful bride loved the people of Talisand, now his people. If he could only trust her, she would be a worthy helpmate.

The celebration that followed was much lighter in spirit. Both mead and ale flowed freely as all work was set aside for the rest of the day to allow for eating, drinking, music and dancing. His men had hunted the day before enabling them to dine on fresh fowl and venison. Even a lamb had been slaughtered for the feast spread before the people who crowded into the hall.

Renaud looked down the high table to see Geoff on Maugris' other side with the dark-haired Eawyn. The two seemed to be acting good friends, though Renaud knew his fellow knight hoped they would one day wed. On the other side of Serena sat Sir Maurin, who every now and then looked toward the wide opening that led to the manor and to his lady love still abed.

Before them, the Welsh bard entertained all with his lively music, accompanied by the lyre, a reed instrument Serena told him was a shawm, a drum and a pipe whistle. The bard kept darting glances at Serena, as he strolled among the wedding guests singing his Welsh tunes, which caused Renaud to wonder what still lay between them.

At the high table, Maugris kept them entertained with stories of other brides and bridegrooms, including the story of Renaud's parents' wedding. Though he had heard it before the story still held a kind of charm for him. It was, by all accounts, the one time his stern father had allowed himself to appear besotted. The wise one delighted in retelling the story and said Renaud's father would be quite pleased with the turn of events at Talisand.

"I must send your father and brothers an account of your success and your beautiful bride," said the wise one.

Renaud didn't smile. He wondered, instead, if he was yet successful. He had claimed his bride, but there was still Morcar and Sir Hugue to contend with. And what of Serena's brother? Might he show up any day with a band of wild Scots to protest what had happened to his sister and try and retake his lands?

* * *

Aethel heard the lively music drifting up from the wedding celebration to the bedchamber where she kept watch on the handmaiden. She did not mind missing the gaiety. It was meager penance for her part in Morcar's scheme and her failure to see that Serena had changed her mind and was truly resigned to marrying the Red Wolf. With a shudder, Aethel reflected on what might still happen to her if the Red Wolf were to learn of her perfidy.

I pray, in time, all will be forgiven.

A quiet knock drew Aethel's eyes to the door, which opened to reveal the hulking form of Sir Alain.

"If ye're here to see Cassie, she's sleeping."

"Nay, Aethel. I am here to see you."

The big, burly knight stepped into the room making the chamber seem smaller. "Me?"

"Aye." He reached back and closed the door, darting a glance at the sleeping handmaiden before he slowly walked toward Aethel. "When I heard that the guards had been given a potion, I immediately thought of you with your knowledge of herbs. It was you, was it not?"

She rose from the bench. "I meant her no harm. I thought she wanted to leave."

"Does Lady Serena know of your involvement?"

"Yea, she does," Aethel said contritely. "I think she has forgiven me."

"All that to the good, it is time you had a husband to keep you from further mischief, Aethel."

She looked into his hazel eyes and decided with not even a kiss between them that she wanted him to be that husband. "Mayhap ye are right, sir knight."

"Aye, I am." He closed the small distance between them, wrapped his powerful arms around her and, drawing her close, kissed her.

She knew then she would never want another man.

* * *

Serena could not take her eyes off her husband. He had come to their wedding magnificently attired like the Norman lord he now was. He wore a tunic of the darkest blue over a cream undertunic and brown hosen crisscrossed by leather straps. On his feet were short leather boots. At his waist was a belt of silver to which was secured a scramaseax; the handle of the long knife was studded with silver. Around his neck was a wide necklace of gold and silver bejeweled with the same stones that decorated the sword he had given her. On his head was a black velvet cap that gave him a regal appearance with the chestnut waves of his hair curling at his nape. The warrior was cloaked and the earl revealed in all his splendor. Admittedly, he was a magnificent exemplar of a man.

"My lord, you appear as one on his way to your king's court," said Serena, unable to resist a grin.

Setting down his goblet of silver, he smiled. "And would you look forward to a visit to William's court, *wife*?"

Serena stared at their shared trencher. "Nay, I confess I would not."

"William may yet visit Talisand, Serena. You should be prepared. He will want to see his castle. And I've heard rumors of discontent in the north that may draw him to Northumbria before the year is out."

Serena had not forgotten what Morcar had told her about the

anticipated gathering of the Northumbrians and their allies, but she said nothing, only worrying her lower lip between her teeth as she considered what might take place in that city. She preferred to think of Steinar safely in Scotland and her new husband safely at Talisand, not meeting on a battlefield. Yet she feared it might be inevitable.

They finished the meal, and Renaud took her hand leading her from the dais to the area cleared for dancing. The tables had been pushed close to the walls allowing the couples to dance around the central hearth, which did not bear a fire this day. Instead, the wooden shutters were thrown open to allow the sunlight to fill the hall.

The music of the harp, lyre, bone whistle and drum urged them to join the others. The steps involved much turning and gesturing as Renaud led her through the dances he knew. Sir Geoffroi and Eawyn joined them, as did the rest of the knights and many of the villagers. Soon every maiden was partnered with either a Norman or an Englishman. The hall was crowded with bodies moving in time to the music.

Angus pulled Maggie into the twirling couples, causing Serena to smile.

"You are pleased, my lady?" Renaud asked her.

"Aye, my lord. It has been a long while since any at Talisand had cause to dance."

* * *

Sunlight from the windows in the hall shimmered in Serena's flaxen curls drawing Renaud's gaze to her beautiful face and to the swells of her breasts rising above the neckline of the elegant gown, enticing him beyond measure. Content he had finally claimed his English bride, he wanted to be alone with her. To lay her down on their bed and make long, lingering love to her. *Enough eating, dancing and celebration.* He wanted his bride naked in his bed. And he wanted her now.

As their heads passed close with the movement of the dance, he whispered in her ear, "When the music ends, my lady, we are away to our chamber."

Serena blushed as he'd expected she would. Still new to lovemaking, she had much to learn before she would be comfortable with all he wanted to share with her. But her passionate response to his forays the day before told him she would enjoy what was to come.

The song ended and Renaud swept Serena into his arms and carried her from the hall with much cheering and ribald raillery shouted from his men.

"My lord!" Serena gasped as they passed through the doorway

leading from the hall to the manor. "Must you carry me like a sack of grain?"

"Ah, Serena," he replied kissing her on the forehead while striding through the entry, "it is but a small thing to hasten our departure. Besides, my men heartily approve, and your maidens are all bearing smiles. I like having you at my disposal."

Up the stairs he hurried with his bride in his arms. Kicking open the door to his bedchamber, he crossed the room and tossed her playfully upon the bed's cover.

"You have little idea what torture I experienced at being so close to you yet allowing propriety to have its sway. Now you are mine!"

He closed the door and returned to her, unlacing her gown and sliding it from her.

"I see you are in haste to dispense with my clothing, my lord. Would you like me to help divest you of yours?"

"Saucy wench," he said with a grin.

Her arms were outstretched to him, but he was too anxious to wait. Setting aside his blade and belt, he pulled his tunic over his head. Kicking off his boots, he doffed his shirt, leaving him only in his braies and hosen.

Casting her a smile, he fell upon her, raining kisses down her neck and over her face as her arms wound around him. He took her mouth in a gentle assault, his tongue reaching for hers. He pressed his hips to her belly and felt his passion rise. She wrapped one of her legs around his as she returned his kiss.

Raising his head, he looked into her violet eyes, darkening with her pleasure. "You are not in a hurry, are you my love?"

She blushed. "You have made me eager with your kisses."

"Not so eager as I." And with that he made short work of their remaining clothes to leave them both naked.

Her flesh was soft and warm and he wanted to sink his shaft deep within her. His gaze devoured her. She was so lovely, skin as luminous as cream, her rose tipped breasts rising and falling with her rapid breaths. He could wait no longer to sample them. Threading his fingers through hers and raising her hands above her head on the pillow, he pressed his shaft against the juncture of her thighs and she opened to him. Taking a nipple into his mouth to feast upon the hard crested peak, he pressed against her moving his hips in an action designed to drive her wild.

"Oh, Renaud..."

Quickly he let go of her hands and moved his mouth to her nether region where he lapped at her wetness with his tongue, feeling her shiver beneath his hands kneading her breasts.

"So ready, so soon," he said. He could not wait a minute longer to have his bride. Rising above her and positioning his shaft at her entrance, he plunged deep.

Serena inhaled and sighed out her breath.

She was so tight, her muscles gripping his shaft with a vengeance; it took all his control not to spill his seed. But he had no intention of quickly concluding this lovemaking. Slowing his heart from its racing pace, he began to move while bending his head to kiss her deeply. She clung to him raising her hips to accept his thrusts.

He raised his head to look at her face flushed with passion.

"Your leisurely pace inflicts its own pleasant torture," she spoke huskily.

"'Twas my intent, my lovely Serena. I would extend this time beyond our enduring." With his warrior's control, Renaud took his time until she was near the peak only to back off 'til her passion subsided, and then to raise it again 'til she was moaning beneath him, tossing her head on the pillow.

Soaked in the sweat of their lovemaking, he plunged deep, hard and fast, and together shouted their release.

And this was just the beginning of a night Renaud knew he would never forget.

CHAPTER 19

Serena woke to see Renaud's gray eyes staring at her as he leaned on one elbow, his expression serious.

"What is it?" she asked, suddenly wide awake, for he seemed worried.

"Are you, indeed, content to being the wife of a Norman?"

It was too early in the morn for such conversation, but she could see he was determined to have an answer. Wiping the sleep from her eyes, she said softly, "I made my vow to you before the people of Talisand. And we have joined our bodies as one. Surely you cannot doubt me now." It was with eyes of love that she looked at his strong masculine face framed by his tousled chestnut hair. But looking back at her were eyes of disbelief. Hoping to persuade him, she said, "Though you were my enemy, Renaud, now you are my husband and my lover."

"I would that it always be so, my lady wife," he said as he kissed her and rolled to the edge of the bed. "Only love between us. Nay forget."

"I never shall." And she meant it. After their night of lovemaking, how could he doubt her?

Renaud rose from their bed and began to dress. His muscled lean body drew her attention even as she pulled the bed cover over her breasts. Their intimacy was still new.

While donning his clothes, he told her that after they broke their fast, he wanted to see the castle with her. Though tired from their night of lovemaking, Serena would not turn away from an invitation to be with him for the morning, particularly when there were still doubts in his mind. Besides, she was eager to get a glimpse of what would be her new home, even though leaving the manor would be another step in leaving behind all that had gone before—her parents, her brother and the memories of the life they had shared together.

Nearly everyone had left the hall by the time she and Renaud finished breaking their fast. They stepped into a cloud-filled morning.

Renaud looked into the sky. "A good time to see the castle before the rain descends."

"While you were in Exeter, Sir Maurin made the castle his favorite theme at the evening meals. I have heard much about it, but not yet viewed the interior."

"Then come my lady." He held out his hand. "There are stairs we can ascend to view all." She placed her hand in his and together they walked over the new wooden bridge that spanned the moat and up the wooden stairs that led to the top of the motte.

Serena had not realized just how high the mountain of dirt rose above the yard until she stood at its summit. She estimated it was about fifteen feet to the ground below, and from where she stood, the new keep rose another thirty feet into the sky. It was a large square structure with a protrusion on one side. All was surrounded by a wooden palisade like the one below that circled the yard, stable and outbuildings, now a part of the bailey.

They walked into the keep, where servants had lighted the torches set into the walls. On the ground level there was a hall with a large hearth and stairs at the rear leading up to the solar and sleeping chambers. It was larger than the old hall. The smell of new wood surrounded them, as she realized the large space was clean, but as yet unfurnished.

On the second level, the bedchamber for the lord was larger than that of the manor and connected to a solar, a place for her husband to work and meet with small groups of his men. There were other bedchambers as well. Above that, a third level contained a viewing platform with vertical slits set into the wood on each side that provided a grand view of the countryside—and a safe place from which to shoot arrows at an enemy. It was there they viewed the knights sparring just beyond the palisade.

"How far we can see!" she declared. "Much farther than from the manor's roof walk." In her imagination, she could see the west manor miles away.

"Yea, 'tis a better vantage point," he said with a look of satisfaction.

Impressed with the *donjon* and aware of the statement it signified to all who viewed it, her thoughts drifted back to the Norman bastard who would be king. She could not help but ask, "Why did your Norman duke think to conquer England?"

"If you knew William, you would not need to ask," he said smiling. Then in a serious tone, "He believed he had been promised the throne by your King Edward for one thing. And William, unlike Harold Godwinson, had a blood tie to the throne, so he did not think it above him. Too, in Normandy, William was but a duke; in England he is an anointed king."

"But to terrorize the people into submitting? Was his slaughter in the south necessary?"

His frown made her wonder if she had reminded him of his own role in that slaughter.

"Whatever you say about William's methods, Serena, they have been successful. He would not give up a prize like England, one he had come to think of as his by right. I admit he can sometimes be cruel, but have no doubt, he means to rule England."

"His castles are *meant* to intimidate," she muttered to herself. But it was quiet where they stood for there were few hammers pounding at the moment, and she realized he had heard her.

He did not respond at first, but stared into the distance as if pondering. Then with a sigh, he let out his breath. "Yea, they are. William does not want the English to forget he is now their sovereign— that he is here to stay. He builds more of them where the people doubt his intent."

The conversation had soured Serena on the tour of the castle as it reminded her the structure dominating all of Talisand was yet another symbol of her country's invasion.

As they returned to the ground floor of the wooden tower, she saw a door left open to what appeared to be a chapel and remembered the room that jutted out from the keep she had seen from the outside. "Your new church?"

"A chapel for the family and our guests," he said. Then taking her hand and kissing her fingers, he led her into the chapel, adding, "It will be here that our sons will be christened."

She did not speak her thought that it was constructed as penance for the lives he had taken. Had her father's life been one of those? Somehow she had to find a way to let such questions go if she was to give herself completely to this marriage, and to him. Such things were now in the past.

"It is good to have a chapel as a part of the keep," she said. "There will be times a place of prayer will be needed."

"Aye, I have always found it so."

They left the keep and stood at the edge of the motte looking into the yard. Rhodri was walking through the gate with the archers, headed in the direction of a clearing in the woods where Serena knew they oft practiced.

"Why is the bard still here?" Renaud asked. "I thought he wandered from place to place?"

"It is true that Rhodri comes and goes as he wills and oft travels far. In that he is much like the wind. We are fortunate he has lingered so long among us." The look in Renaud's eyes told her he was displeased. "Would you have me bid him go?"

"He watches you with interest," he said with a scowl. "I like it not."

He was jealous of the Welshman? Mayhap he cared more than she had thought. "You need have no worry for Rhodri, my lord. He was trusted by my father and is much loved by Steinar. The bard merely protects me in their absence."

"Even from your husband?"

"Of course not! Why would you ask such a thing?" She turned to look at his face. His eyes that had been the color of rain only moments before had hardened to the steel of his sword as they narrowed on the bard.

Without answering her question, he asked, "Will you be taking up your archery again now that you are no longer acting the servant?"

So he would remind her she had once lived in disguise. It made her restless to think that was still between them. Would it ever be so? "I trust you only tease me my lord, and you are not still angry for my early deception. You know why I did it."

"Aye, but I liked it not."

She could do nothing to change the past, only try and build a future.

"Well, to answer your question, I do sometimes practice with Rhodri, but not oft."

"I would see your skill on display, Serena. Mayhap another shooting match is in order. Now that I think of it, tell me, did you miss that first arrow you aimed at Sir Hugue?"

"Nay."

"You were aiming for—"

"His arm, aye. Sir Geoffroi just assumed I missed the rogue's heart. That would have been my next shot."

"I still remember those rabbits you felled in the forest. Yea, we must have another match at Talisand."

Serena's cheeks burned at the memory of what occurred that morning on the bank of the stream. "If it would bring you pleasure, my lord."

* * *

A few days later, Renaud persuaded Serena to leave Cassie for the time it would take them to visit the west manor where Geoff had ridden earlier that morning to see his lady love, Eawyn, who had offered to prepare a noon repast for them. It would be his first foray to one of the three distant manor houses that were a part of his lands, and this one held a special interest for him since he believed that one day it would be the home of his friend.

They crossed a narrow bend in the river and rode over the rolling hills of the countryside. Renaud was struck by the peaceful nature of the land bathed in summer's colors of green and gold. The sounds of birds chirping in the trees and the occasional bleating of a sheep or the bark of a dog were far different than the harsh sounds of battle or the clamor of London.

For the foreseeable future, he would have to straddle two worlds, heeding his sire's call to battle while becoming a man of the land. He hoped he could do well by both.

He was grateful to Serena for helping him understand the needs of the people. Since their wedding, she had become the dutiful chatelaine, working with the steward Hunstan to see that all was as it should be. Her hands were never idle. Though he'd not seen her embroidering or working on a tapestry as one might expect of the lady of the manor, she worked tirelessly at other duties. She and Maggie made the decisions about what food was to be served and together they planned for adequate stores to be laid up for winter. They set about assuring that a supply of candles and mead was available for the cheerless months.

He vaguely recalled his mother busy with similar tasks at their estate in Normandy, but since he had been made a squire at a young age and then a knight, he was rarely home and gave scant attention to his family's lands tended so well by others. His life had been as a leader of men in battle. Now he must learn to be a different kind of leader, hoping for a day he could set aside his sword.

The king's messengers, and his own, had kept him informed. All was not quiet in the north. William harbored concern over the Welsh, who had supported Eadric the Wild, and were now leaning toward an alliance with the rebellious Earls Morcar and Edwin. Beneath its calm surface, Northumbria seethed with rebellion.

The light filtering through the trees caught Serena's flaxen hair, glistening like the sun. With each passing day, his ardor for his new English bride grew, and the resulting vulnerability he experienced worried him.

Lovemaking consumed their nights as Serena grew ever more adventurous, which pleased him greatly. She was a willing bedmate and seemed content, even happy. Still, he wondered. Would she be loyal if he was forced to face the English in battle again? And if he were killed, would she mourn?

"You are very quiet," his lady wife teased from where she sat on her white palfrey. "Is all well?"

Stirred from his musings, he answered, "Aye, for now. We will move into the castle next week. I trust that pleases you." Seeing her smile, he reminded her, "Some rooms will be bare for a while 'til the needed furniture is finished, but still quite livable, I think. The carpenters are being kept busy. Between the old hall and the new, my men will be able to bring their pallets inside when winter comes, though I'd ask you to reserve a bedchamber for Maugris. His old bones would benefit from a soft cushion.

"Aye, my lord. I had thought of that. He is well loved by all at Talisand, and I would see him comfortable. There is a chamber that looks out on the river I think he will like. At night the stars are reflected in the waters."

"You seem to know the wise one well," he replied, pleased with her insight. "He always seeks a view of the heavens. That is why he sleeps outside while it's warm enough to do so."

"What think you of keeping the lord's chamber in the old manor for Sir Maurin?" she asked. "The other two chambers would serve for guests, at least until Sir Maurin marries and sires children."

Seeing the smile on her face, he realized she was thinking of her handmaiden.

"I would be pleased to reward him," he said. "You know Sir Maurin seeks the hand of Maggie's daughter."

"I do. At least that is what is written on his face. When Cassie took the mercenary's knife in her chest, Sir Maurin hovered over her like a beast protecting its wounded mate. Though she now recovers, he still is reluctant to leave her side."

"Yea, 'tis true. I fear the knight is besotted." Renaud had no doubt Sir Maurin would be speaking with Angus before summer's end.

"Will you keep the old kitchen?" she asked.

"Aye, I would think both kitchens will be needed. If she would have the position, your handmaiden could become housekeeper in the manor, at least until she marries Sir Maurin. Then another can be found to serve as cook. Maggie and Angus can move from their cottage into the castle. There's a large bedchamber on the first floor near the kitchen for them. It will be warm in the winter."

"I believe they would like that. And Maggie would have her husband close."

"William will be sending me more knights and men to add to those already here. Angus and his workers will have much to do."

"More men? Why?" she questioned with furrowed brows.

"Surely you must realize Serena, England is not yet at peace. Talisand's castle is one of only a few this far north. It stands as an outpost against rebellion and to guard against the Scots for he trusts not King Malcolm. William would have a small garrison here for as long as it is needed."

"Oh," she said with a small pout of her perfect lips. "I suppose a conqueror must have his soldiers, but I did not think of a garrison at Talisand."

"Some will have their families with them, but not many."

"It will change our home, my lord."

"Yea, for a while, but I will insist on discipline and adherence to my rules."

She pouted again and all he could think of was laying her back in the grass and making love to her. Reaching for her hand, he said, "When you look at me like that, Serena, it is difficult for me not to pull you from your horse and have my way with you in yon meadow."

Serena gazed at the swath of grass-covered land surrounded by wild flowers. "My lord! You would not!"

He smiled a forewarning. "I cannot say what we might find ourselves doing on the return to Talisand when I am sated with food and ale, but for now you are safe as we are expected, and I would not have you arrive looking like you fell from your horse."

She laughed and he delighted to see it.

Slowing his horse, and pulling her hand towards him, he turned it palm up and kissed the sensitive skin, making a silent vow to have her in the grass ere they arrived back at Talisand.

"Renaud..." she whispered, her cheeks flushed. He released her hand, and she smiled. She enjoyed his attention, of that he was certain. "Forget your schemes and tell me of your family in Normandy. I have long wondered about your origins. Surely it was not a wolf's den in the woods as some of your men suggest when they are full of wine."

"Nay, not so humble as that. I have two older brothers, Robert and Raoul, and a younger sister, Aveline. My father and mother still live, though one day our holdings will pass to Robert."

"And your family's home?"

"Saint Sauveur lies on a peninsula of farms jutting into the waters of the channel between England and Normandy. My father's *demesne* is the largest. He owns much land."

"But not enough for his youngest son?"

"Nay. Younger sons must earn their own lands and titles. I have always known my destiny lay with my sword. That is how I came to serve William. It is the same with Sir Geoffroi and the other knights."

"But can you be happy, Renaud, so far from home?"

He was pleased she was using his given name, more often now as their intimacy in the bedchamber grew. "I am content with what William has given me, but sometimes I think of Normandy. I would like to see my family again."

"I cannot imagine being so far from home surrounded by strangers."

"Talisand is no longer a place of strangers for me, Serena. It is my home, this is my land, and you are my lady. But mayhap one day I will take you to Normandy to meet my family." Seeing a look of worry cross her beautiful face, he added, "You would not find the land strange. It is as green as Talisand, just warmer and wetter. Would you like to travel there with me to meet them?"

"I would like to have our children know their uncles and aunt, and their grandparents since I can offer them none," she said sadly. "Steinar is the only uncle they shall ever know, yet he might not want to return to Talisand. Surely it would be difficult for him seeing his lands in the hands of another."

"As it is for you, wife?"

"Aye, sometimes 'tis awkward, but at least I am still the Lady of Talisand."

Renaud did not doubt the truth of her words, nor the dismal future for any Englishman whose lands had been forfeited. If he were in her brother's place, he would never return. But he was aware that she and Steinar were close and she would miss him. "There is truth in what you say." His gaze shifted to the flaxen strands of her plaits falling beneath her head cloth. "Does he look like you?"

"Aye, he does," she said with a bashful look at her hands holding the reins. "Older, stronger and taller, but with the same hair and eyes, though he has a beard and it's somewhat darker than his hair."

Their conversation was interrupted with their arrival at the manor house nestled amidst a copse of oak trees. It was difficult for Renaud to picture his favorite knight in such a place, but as he dismounted and helped Serena down from her horse, Geoff strode through the door with Eawyn close behind him, as if they were already a couple and this was their home.

Renaud handed the reins to the waiting stable boy.

"Greetings, my lord," Geoff said, stepping aside to allow Eawyn to welcome them with a curtsey and a warm smile.

"I am honored to have you here at the west manor, my lord, and my lady," Eawyn said, her gaze moving from Renaud to Serena.

Renaud had always liked the dark-haired woman with her easy manner and pleasing face. But no woman tempted him, save his own wife. Serena could be difficult at times, but he admired her courage, her devotion to her people and her sense of honor. She was everything he could have wanted.

But could she be loyal?

CHAPTER 20

It had been some time since Serena had visited the west manor. Watching her husband duck his head as he entered to avoid hitting the lintel reminded her of its smaller size. Larger than a cottage, the manor had a main sitting area with an alcove, a hearth, a separate kitchen in the rear and two large bedchambers. Above was a loft reached by outside stairs where travelers or field workers could lay their pallets for the night. Behind the manor was the stable.

Inviting smells from the kitchen wafted through the air as she stepped through the door. A servant girl brought ale for the two knights, who took their tankards to the hearth where they sat and talked.

Serena followed Eawyn into the kitchen. The servant girl took her place beside the hearth and stirred the stew.

"How is Cassie, Serena? I've not heard since your wedding."

"Cassie recovers. Maggie and Aethel tend her and Sir Maurin takes her for short walks. He is finally smiling again. The two are very much in love, I think."

"Sir Maurin is a good man. And a knight. Cassie would do well to wed him. Do you think he will ask for her hand?"

"Yea, and I think it will be soon. I do not believe Sir Maurin intends to sleep alone this winter." Serena chuckled at the thought of the powerful Norman knight smitten with her friend.

Eawyn's laughter echoed Serena's.

"What about you, Eawyn?" And in a lower voice so low only Eawyn could hear, "Sir Geoffroi seeks your company oft and, when he is not here with you, I sometimes see him staring in the direction of the west manor. I am certain 'tis you he thinks of."

"I know he pays court, for he does not hide it," said Eawyn, "but it was not so long ago that Ulrich sat at my table and shared my bed. I still miss him."

"He was a fine man, but it has been a long while since you lost him. Surely you want to marry again, for you must want children."

"Yea, I do."

"The man need not be a Norman if you find the prospect not to your liking. Still, there are few men who would make as good a husband as Sir Geoffroi. He is kind and he laughs much." In spite of his being a Norman, Serena liked the blond knight, who but for his lack of a beard, appeared almost a Saxon. And she thought all the more highly of him because he had protected Eawyn from Sir Hugue.

"When the time comes for me to wed," said Eawyn, "I would look with favor upon Sir Geoffroi's suit. He is a man of honor, I know. Still, I think it may be awhile before I am ready."

"Sir Geoffroi will be dismayed to hear it, but I know he will respect your wishes."

"And you, m'lady," said Eawyn, her blue eyes focused intently upon Serena, "how is it with you?"

"It is well, or as well as it can be, given all that lies between the Red Wolf and me. He still mistrusts me, I think. Sometimes I see him watching me from the corner of his eye as if he expects me to escape into the night."

Eawyn smiled. "Mayhap he fears one of your arrows in his back," she said, her eyes full of mirth.

"I think we are well past that, but it will take time before he trusts me fully." Serena twisted her wedding ring, recalling the words inscribed inside. Why had he used the word love? Could there ever be love between them?

"The stew is ready, m'lady," said the servant girl. "And the bread is just out of the oven. I have only to set the cheese and berries upon the table."

"Then let us see the knights fed as they are no doubt famished," said Eawyn in her usual cheerful manner.

With the help of the servant girl, Eawyn and Serena set the food before the knights and joined them for the repast, settling easily into conversation about the crops and tasks that must be accomplished before winter. It was apparent to Serena that Renaud had much to learn about rural life, for he thought only of hunting for deer and game and had only a vague idea of all that must be done to see the people through the harsh months. But she would help him and, in doing so, she would help the people of Talisand.

* * *

Renaud stood in the hall of the castle carefully folding the parchment the messenger had brought him that morning. He had been receiving word from William's men, so the arrival of the messenger wearing the king's livery did not surprise him. What he had not expected was the message itself, written by the king's companion, William FitzOsbern, Earl of Hereford: The king was coming to Talisand with a part of his army. And he expected Renaud and his men to join him as he rode on to York. It could only mean one thing: the rebels in the north had made clear their intent.

He dreaded telling Serena.

"William is coming to Talisand for a visit, my lady," he told her that afternoon.

Serena looked up from where she was bent over the gray goose feathers she was preparing to fletch into a new set of arrows. In his idle moments there had been times in the past when he had thought of a future with a wife sitting by the fire on an eve. Always the woman he envisioned plied her deft fingers pushing a needle through cloth, taking small straight stiches in the embroidery of some feminine design. Never had he considered his wife might sit worrying over the placement of goose feathers in arrow shafts. Though she was now a countess, Serena was more particular than his archers in the distinctive way she placed the feathers so her arrows would fly straight and true.

Her hands stilled and her violet eyes flashed in alarm. "Your king comes here? Wherefore?"

"I told you he would want to see his castle. And it seems he has business in the north. I do not believe he will be here long, but I thought you would appreciate the notice. It takes much to feed and entertain a king." *I'll not dismay her with my being ordered to follow William to York.* With Serena he was learning to take one hill at a time.

"His men? How many?"

"In addition to his retinue of knights and retainers, William is bringing some of his army. I cannot say how many, but I would plan on filling both the new hall and the old. And if that is not enough, William ever travels with tents. We can give the king our chamber and take one of the keep's guest chambers."

He could see from the frown on her face as she set her feathers aside that she was not happy about the news.

"I suppose I should have seen this day would come. I dread his being here but 'tis not something we can avoid, is it?"

"Nay, wife, it is not."

Serena let out a sigh. "'Tis a good thing the bed cushions are finished. I will talk to Hunstan and Maggie about the rest of what must be done."

* * *

A sennight later, Serena sullenly watched as William and his long column of men dressed in colorful livery rode two abreast into the bailey. A banner with two golden leopards on a red field waved in the wind and the sound of many horses filled the space between palisade and the manor. Thanks to a man standing watch on the top of the keep's tower, they had warning of the king's impending arrival.

Once in the bailey, the king and a few of those with him broke off from the mass of mounted knights and men-at-arms, dismounted and approached Renaud and Serena where they waited in front of the manor.

Not since the blessing of their marriage had her husband donned such fine apparel. He did not wear his mail or helm, nor the pelt of the wolf, but instead, his broad shoulders and lean body were clothed in a fine tunic of dark green Talisand wool embroidered with silver threads. At his waist was a belt of silver studded with gems, and his chestnut hair was tamed in anticipation of meeting his king. For her own clothing, she had decided to wear one of her new gowns and the head cloth, which now marked her as a married woman, was crowned with the circlet of gold and silver.

"Sire," Renaud bowed, "Welcome to Talisand."

The king smiled. "We think you look every bit our royal subject today, and not the wolf we know you to be, Lord Talisand."

Renaud chuckled. "Ah Sire, 'tis merely a disguise for your benefit. Beneath the surface is the same snarling wolf you know well."

"We are counting upon it!" The king gestured to the richly dressed man who stood at his side. "You know Fitz, of course."

"Aye, I do. Welcome to Talisand, Lord Hereford. How goes it in Herefordshire?"

"'Twould be better if I did not have that madman Eadric to contend with. Thank God he has retreated into Wales."

"The one called 'the Wild'?" Renaud inquired.

"Just so," replied Lord Hereford.

Serena's ears perked up at the name of the Saxon who still harassed the Normans in the south. She could not be sad about that unless it drew her husband to another battle.

The king turned his eyes upon her, and Renaud's hand slipped around her shoulders, mayhap to remind her of her promise to show the king no dishonor. She was surprised at the king's height, nearly as great as her husband's, though he was burly where her husband was lean, like the wolf for which he was named. The Norman who was now a king held himself with an air of confidence she could hardly miss—a man who, as the bastard Duke of Normandy, thought naught of conquering an entire country. His piercing blue eyes were framed by short, sun-lightened brown hair beneath his golden crown. A not unattractive man except that she loathed him for what he had done to her family and her people.

"Sire," said Renaud, "I would present to you my lady wife, Serena, Countess of Talisand."

Because she had steeled herself to the encounter, Serena was able to curtsey before the king and Lord Hereford. But she did not utter a sound.

The king seemed not to notice. "Ah, we have given you a bride fair of face and form, Lord Talisand. And from the way you are looking at her, your bed must be ever warm."

Lord Hereford chuckled.

Serena's cheeks burned at the bold statement. Was that all she was to this king? A bed warmer for one of his knights? Anger rose within her at the Norman usurper, but she held her tongue and managed a slight smile for her husband's benefit.

"Yea, Sire, you gave me a great boon," Renaud agreed.

She knew her husband feared she would say something that would embarrass him, and she was sorely tempted to fling the king a bitter retort. But she had too much respect for Renaud to do so. Still, he must have sensed her anger in the tension flowing through her body for he was quick to move on to another subject.

Turning to one side, he gestured to the *donjon* behind them. "What think you of your castle, Sire?"

"We like its position with the river to its back, its waters filling the moat. And the keep looks from here to be large enough to house the men we will give you. We have with us a part of our army as well as Fitz' men. The main group rode on to York."

York? His men rode to York? It was as she feared. There would be a battle in the north.

Shooting her a glance that told her he'd seen her rising panic, Renaud turned toward the king. "Shall we go inside, Sire? I expect some refreshment is in order after your long journey."

"Aye, we covet some of your country mead. The road was long and dust ridden."

Renaud snapped his fingers and the waiting servants hurried to comply with their new lord's unspoken command. The king's party ascended the stairs to the keep at the top of the motte. The doors stood open, and the king and Renaud entered the hall, she and Lord Hereford following.

Within the hall, torches blazed and tables were set with a repast for the king and his retinue.

Renaud gestured to the stairs. "Your chambers are ready, Sire. And your baths will be ready shortly. I assume you will want to rest before the evening meal but we have some food ready now for your pleasure."

Serena knew well it was her place to offer the king his comforts, but she was doing well just to be civil.

Gracious was a step too far.

* * *

The king and his men filled every available chamber in the castle and manor, the rest spilling into tents they erected for their comfort. Serena was relieved when her husband told her his men would hunt to add to Talisand's stores of food. Yet, even with that, there was bread to bake and food to cook that was far above what they would ordinarily have had to provide so that the kitchens were filled with torchlight from before dawn to late at night.

The Norman army, or the part of it the king brought with him, was a constant source of worry. Renaud had to remind them that the female servants were not there for the taking. Sir Maurin nearly got into a fight with one of Lord Hereford's men who thought Cassie fair game. Sir Alain protectively guarded Aethel, too, but no Norman would come near her with the bear-like knight in attendance. And Sir Geoffroi would not even allow Eawyn to leave the west manor. The Red Wolf's knights were taking no chances with the women they had claimed as theirs.

The new hall was a splendid display of the Red Wolf's accomplishments at Talisand. Tapestries, some of which were taken from the old hall and some her father had kept in storage, graced the now white washed walls. New benches, nearly the length of the room, were filled with both Normans and English. At the high table, the king in all his finery took the lord's seat with Renaud on his right and Lord Hereford on his left. Sir Geoffroi seated himself on Lord Hereford's other side. Serena was between her husband and Maugris, who the king reminded all, he had known as long as the Red Wolf.

"We are wondering how you have fared so far from Normandy, wise one," the king mused aloud. "We still remember how you nearly swooned as you left the ship."

"I was fully recovered after a week on firm ground, My Lord," insisted Maugris. "Talisand is now my home and happily so. I do not expect to be at sea again."

The king seemed pleased with that news, as was Serena. She would not like to see the old Norman, of whom she had become so fond, return to Normandy.

William leaned in to speak to Renaud. "Cospatric, you will recall, gave us much gold to secure the Earldom of Northumbria. It seems he has now joined Morcar and Edwin behind the banner of Edgar Ætheling in rebellion against us, dividing our bishops as well."

"I thought Archbishop Ealdred supported you, Sire," said Renaud, seemingly puzzled.

"He does, which is to his credit. But he was unsuccessful in his attempt to discourage the discontent in the north," said the king. "The Bishop of Durham, we are not happy to see, supports the rebels against us."

"They have not yet seen your army, Sire," said Renaud with a wry grin.

Serena could hardly manage to stay in her seat as she thought about the Norman army marching on York.

"Nor our castles," replied the king. "We erected some as we rode north from London. Warwick was the first. But there are more. Talisand's castle will be one of many. And, with God's help, I will see one in York before the month's end."

The talk of war in Northumbria made Serena's restless stomach churn. She wondered if Steinar and the men of York were prepared for the Norman horde that would soon descend upon them.

Toward the end of the meal of roast pork, goose and fresh fish, conversation died as Rhodri stepped in front of the dais to entertain them with his harp. Surprisingly, the Norman king seemed to enjoy the Welsh music.

At Renaud's insistence, Serena reluctantly agreed to sing for the king.

"The countess sings?" William asked as she slowly walked toward Rhodri, who sat in front of the central hearth. Candles and torchlight filled the new hall casting a warm glow on all the faces that now turned toward the two who would sing for the king. While the benches were filled mostly with Normans, there were English among the king's men. Some of the old thegn's men had also been invited to the meal.

"Aye, she does," said Renaud, "as beautifully as a lark."

"A lady of many talents," said William. "What other pursuits does your fair wife enjoy, pray tell us?"

"She is gifted with a bow," Renaud said with a look of amusement. "As fast and true a shot as my best archers." At his words, Serena saw a smile spread across Maugris's face where he sat at the high table.

"A she-wolf, then," remarked the king, rubbing his chin with his fingers. And then with a grin, he slapped the wooden table. "A fitting mate for my wolf!" The king roared with laughter, apparently his own words humorous.

As Serena took her seat next to Rhodri, she glanced at her husband, wondering at his reaction. Then, with all eyes upon her, she began to sing the Welsh songs she loved.

* * *

A few days later, William ordered his men to make ready to leave. Renaud was not unhappy. Notwithstanding Serena's calm demeanor during the days of the king's visit, of which he was quite proud, he sensed ripples of unease flowing through her. That and her labors explained her fatigue.

She had worked hard to act the countess before the king, and was so exhausted in the evening, when he was finally able to take his leave of the king, he found her in their bed fast asleep. But knowing he was riding to battle, last night he'd awakened her to make love. Warm and willing, she had welcomed him into her arms. Their coming together had been brief, but passionate, and afterward, she had curled against him like a contented kitten.

"I am glad your king leaves, my lord," she said as she watched the king's men taking down the tents that lay outside the palisade. They stood together at the top of the motte watching the activity. "It will take Talisand some time to recover from so heavy a burden. Angus has had a hard time keeping up with the demands for his smith services. And Maggie and Cassie are so tired, they nearly fall asleep while pounding dough for the many loaves of bread that must be baked each morning."

"It is an honor to entertain the king, Serena. Many would seek the privilege shown us."

"Well, I am not one of them. I welcome only your company once they are gone."

"Serena," he spoke with a serious tone, dreading what was coming, "William expects me and my men to accompany him to York."

"What?" She looked aghast. "You would go to York?"

"Yea, I must. But hopefully the rebellion there will soon be over." His wife looked crestfallen.

"What is it, Serena? You know I cannot refuse the king."

"Aye, I know. But York...." Her voice trailed off and he saw pain in her beautiful eyes.

"What is it about York that concerns you so?"

A shadow crossed her lovely face and this time he saw fear in her violet eyes. "You will fight my countrymen once again," she said. "Have you and your king not killed enough English? Must there be more dead?"

"As long as the people choose to rebel against their anointed king, William's knights must deal with them. I serve as William dictates."

"And I am ever in the middle," she cried, "torn between my people and my husband. I cannot bear it!"

"You speak of your people, Serena. Is it the rebel Earl Morcar you think of? William tells me he is at York." Could she still harbor feelings for the earl who abducted her to wed her? The prospect stirred jealousy within him. "The earl and his brother are with Edgar Ætheling, nephew to Edward the Confessor. Now they have a cause they did not have before."

"Nay, Renaud," she pleaded. "I do not think of Earl Morcar, or his brother, or of Edgar, though I would not see them harmed. I think of my brother, Steinar."

"What makes you think Steinar is in York?"

"He was in Scotland where Edgar claimed refuge," she said. "Would he not travel south with the rightful heir to the throne?"

"We can only hope he does not," Renaud said with a frown.

CHAPTER 21

No matter her pleading and her tears, Renaud could not be persuaded to remain at Talisand. It was his duty, he said, and as the wife of a knight, she should understand.

Serena had always known Renaud placed duty above all. It was the reason he had wed her. But the idea that he again rode to war tore at her heart. He might be wounded or killed. When her tears had persisted, he had assured her he would return whole and hearty. That brought her some comfort, believing her powerful warrior would be safe, but what of Steinar? Would it be her brother who would face the awesome sword of the mighty Red Wolf?

She had been teary eyed and tired for the last week and had thought it was because of the Bastard king's visit. But she was coming to believe it was not merely that, or her husband's soon departure, but portended more. She had seen enough women with child to believe she carried a babe. Though happy at the possibility, she hated the idea that the father of her unborn child might soon be locked in a battle with the child's uncle and the men who fought with him for England.

"I am leaving Theodric and Sir Niel here with nearly a score of men to guard you and Talisand," he assured her. "You need have no fear." How wrong he was.

He stood before her in the yard, once again the proud Norman knight, the wolf's pelt riding the shoulder of his hauberk. He had told her that knights in both Normandy and England had come to fear the sight of the beast's fur, so he never failed to wear it into battle. At his side he carried his sword and a shorter blade on his opposite hip. He was a vision in dark blue, iron mail and silver, fierce in countenance, a knight any would see as dangerous. It did not surprise her men feared him.

Taking her into his arms he kissed her slowly, passionately and the scent of him so familiar to her now, lingered. Tenderly, he brushed the tears from her cheeks. She reached to his forehead to set aside an errant chestnut curl.

"I will come back to you, Serena. I promise." He brought her fingers to his lips and kissed her knuckles. Then he donned his helm, his eyes the same color as the steel protecting his head, and mounted his gray stallion.

It seemed her fate to always be watching the Red Wolf ride away with his knights and his men, this time following his king, to whom she had bid Godspeed. But unlike before, Serena did not intend to wait for her husband to return to Talisand. No, this time she would follow him to York.

Rhodri must have suspected her plans for as soon as the Normans departed, he approached. "If you are planning to travel to York, Serena, I would go with you. I promised Steinar to see to your welfare, and I shall."

"You have spoken to Steinar?" she asked, surprised, for it was the first she had heard of it.

"Aye. Who do you think sent me to Talisand? But he bid me say nothing until we were ready to leave."

"My brother. Of course. I should have known. But how did you—?"

"Find him?" At her nod, he said, "I knew something of his plans before he left. Then, too, I knew King Malcolm was in Dunfermline and I suspected Edgar Ætheling and his followers would find their way there."

"I would see Steinar, Rhodri. I miss him and I worry for his life."

"Prepare yourself for his anger, then. I came to help you escape, but you were determined to marry the Norman. I do not think Steinar will be pleased with either of us."

"Aye, mayhap you are right. I did intend to flee the fate the Norman king decreed for me, but by the time you would have aided me, it was too late. At first, I stayed for Talisand, but now...."

Rhodri let out a sigh. "You care for him, I know. I have not sent word to Steinar of your marriage. I do not think he would believe it was your choice, much less that you could care for a Norman knight."

* * *

It was the next day before Serena and Rhodri were able to get away without being followed. She had found little sleep in Renaud's bed, missing him and imagining what he would say when he encountered her in York.

The journey took them nearly two days and, because it rained the first day, the trip was a miserable one. Sodden, weary and sick to her stomach each morning, Serena refused to be deterred.

She was determined to see Steinar, even to help him if she could, though she trembled, knowing it meant she defied her husband. She dreaded the thought of Steinar falling victim to a Norman's sword. Ever mindful her husband might wield that sword, she feared all the more. And what if Steinar or one of the Northumbrians killed the Red Wolf? She could not bear to lose the knight who owned her heart, the father of her unborn child.

By the time they drew close to York, Serena could smell the acrid smoke. From what they learned from fleeing villagers, the Normans set fires as they approached York. Like locusts, they had swept across the countryside wreaking havoc in their path, intent on forcing the Northumbrians into submission. All that was left behind were the burned out shells of cottages.

On the morning of the third day, as she and Rhodri reached the outskirts of the city, she heard the sounds of clashing swords and shouts of men. In the distance were the River Ouse and the buildings that comprised York.

Urging Serena into the trees, where she found a thick branch to sit upon, Rhodri followed and readied his bow.

"Take care not to be seen!" he whispered.

Serena flipped her plait over her shoulder and nocked an arrow. Before them lay a great open field where the Northumbrians were engaged in a fierce insurrection, the thegns and their warriors locked in a clash of swords with the Normans, the latter having left their warhorses to fight the English on foot. Serena's ears filled with the sounds of men shouting and metal clanging against metal.

Pressed close together as each side struggled to prevail, it would have been difficult to distinguish the individual warriors, except for the Normans' longer shields and the Northumbrians' round shields, longer hair and beards.

She took in the scene, anxiously searching for a glimpse of her brother and the Norman who wore the wolf's pelt. One Northumbrian fell close to where they hid in the trees as a Norman blade sliced through the flesh of his neck. Blood shot out of the victim, splashing onto his attacker. She could nearly taste it as the metallic odor wafted up to where she hid. Serena clamped down her jaw, refusing to give into the compulsion to spew the contents of her stomach.

"There!" shouted Rhodri. "Do you see him? 'Tis Steinar."

Her gaze followed Rhodri's extended finger, straining to see through the cloud of men moving and shifting as their swords locked as they attempted to block each other's deadly blows. At last, she sighted his flaxen hair extending beneath his helm. Her heart seized in her chest.

Steinar stood on a slight rise, his sword already covered with blood, as he valiantly tried to fight off three Normans. He was so brave, this brother she loved. And yet so young.

Oh, Steinar, I pray you stay safe. I could not bear to lose you, too.

Quickly, she moved her bow into position. At least she could even the odds.

With a sudden whooshing sound, her arrow flew with lightning speed to strike the shoulder of the man closest to Steinar. The arrow sunk deep into his flesh and the Norman fell to the ground. With her second arrow, she slayed the largest of the two remaining. Her heart soared as Steinar quickly dispatched the last one.

She fixed her gaze on her brother as he turned to face another Norman's sword. Faster on his feet than larger men, her brother slashed again and again at his enemy while adroitly dodging the blows meant for him.

Out of the corner of her eye, she caught a glimpse of a tall Norman wearing the pelt of the wolf on his shoulder.

Renaud!

He was magnificent in his mail and helm, his shield blocking blows as his strong sword cut a swath through the line of men who attacked him. The set of his jaw told her the undefeated warrior she had heard so much about was here in all his glory.

A superb swordsman, he was ruthless and fast with his blade, powerful and lithe in his movements. As she had witnessed in the practice yard, he fought with panther-like grace slicing through the flesh of the men who opposed him. For a moment she forgot it was Northumbrians he was slaying. She thought only of her husband who wielded the sword.

At Renaud's back was the bear-like knight Sir Alain, fighting with sword and shield. Men fell away from them at a terrible rate. It was no wonder some warriors avoided the Red Wolf, for his reputation was well earned.

Nearby, Steinar slayed the knight he fought and, without warning, turned and lashed out at Renaud. Seemingly stunned for a moment, the Red Wolf fought back, defending himself.

Serena swallowed, her teeth closing on her knuckles in suspense as fear gripped her, fear for the lives of the two men she loved most in the world now locked in viscous combat. It could not be!

"Rhodri, do you see? Steinar and the Red Wolf!"

"Aye I see them, Serena. What would you have me do?"

Serena's arrow was nocked and ready, but she was frozen, unable to move. Steinar's blade sliced through the air, blocked by Renaud's sword. Her brother...her Norman husband, she could not choose between them! If her love for Renaud had not been sure before, it was now.

"Naught, Rhodri. Do naught." Serena's heart shattered as she watched the two men she loved lock swords again and again, Steinar attacking, Renaud defending. Was Renaud holding back? His thrusts seemed less vigorous than before.

She lowered her bow. "I cannot shoot, Rhodri. I must not. I love them both!"

Rhodri sat back against the trunk of the tree, resting his bow on his leg. "Then pray, my lady, and let God decide."

And pray she did. Her gaze fixed on the battle raging between them, she asked God to save them both.

Suddenly Steinar was drawn away by another Norman's challenge. Renaud turned as a blow from a Norman knight struck his shield. The Red Wolf stumbled and turned to confront the challenger, pausing as if surprised to see a fellow Norman wielding a blade against him.

Confused, Serena studied the Norman knight who was slashing at her husband. The swarthy complexion, dark beard and swaggering stance were familiar to her as the Norman shouted taunts at Renaud.

Sir Hugue! He fights with Morcar.

The weight of his evil presence settled upon her. His hatred was strong for the Red Wolf. Serena had her own hatred for the mercenary who had tried to rape Eawyn and had sunk a knife in Cassie's flesh.

The battle raged between the two Norman warriors, the clash of steel rising again and again. Renaud twisted to deflect a blow from Sir Hugue and stumbled over the body of one of the slain. Falling to one knee, he fought to regain his balance, his sword still clutched in his hand.

"Rhodri! The Red Wolf is in peril!"

Taking advantage of Renaud's vulnerable position, Sir Hugue swept in, raising his sword to inflict a deadly blow. In a flash of speed, Serena focused on the mercenary's neck and let her arrow fly. Before Sir Hugue's blow could find its target, her arrow pierced the flesh of his neck. Blood spurted from the wound. A second arrow, shot by Rhodri, hit the mercenary's chest, the bodkin arrow piercing his mail.

Sir Hugue paused as if suspended in time, the arrows seeming to hold him up. Then with a crash, he fell to his knees and to the ground. Renaud stood looking down at the body.

Serena's heart raced as she held her hand to her chest and breathed a sigh of relief. She could feel no sorrow for the man guilty of so much treachery.

"Aye, 'tis done," said Rhodri.

Serena tried to find Steinar in what remained of the battle, but she had lost sight of him. The battle was waning. As she scanned the field, a Northumbrian warrior darted across the field toward the trees where she was hidden. As he neared, he stripped off his helm.

Morcar!

He ran through the trees, passing beneath her, followed by several other Northumbrians.

* * *

Renaud stared down at the body of Sir Hugue and his neck pierced with an arrow.

That arrow fletching.

The fletching bore the same feathers his wife had so carefully fit into her arrows that night by the hearth, distinctive in their style. He looked up to follow the path the arrow had taken, the arrow that had spared him Hugue's sword. His eyes caught a flicker of flaxen hair amidst the green leaves of the trees. He had known the moment the first arrow hit the mercenary that no ordinary archer had shot it.

Serena!

How was it possible she was here?

Squinting into the distance, he saw Rhodri on another branch, mostly hidden by the color of his clothes, but visible to the discerning eye. Had they come to join the Northumbrian rebels? Surely she would fight for her brother. He had seen his wife's same violet eyes and flaxen hair on an English warrior who'd attacked him earlier. Somehow he knew it was Steinar whose thrusts he had parried, and so he had not slain the young warrior. And then he had lost him among the other Northumbrians when Sir Hugue attacked him.

"It's nearly over, Ren," said Geoff approaching with his sword dripping blood. Looking over Renaud's blood splattered body, he asked, "Are you wounded?"

"Nay," he said, still staring into the trees, "an arrow from a friend spared me the insult."

"An arrow?" Geoff asked incredulous as he spotted the mercenary lying at Renaud's feet. "'Tis Hugue!"

"Aye, killed by arrows."

"From where? There are no archers here."

"The trees, Geoff. Look to the trees. Me thinks they hold a fair English archer and a Welsh bowman."

Renaud might have laughed had he not been so angry with his wife for putting herself in danger. The thought of Serena being exposed to the sights and sounds of battle, of seeing him slaying her fellow English, covered in their blood, made him clench his teeth. But a worse fear confronted him. He could have lost her, his English wife who had so bewitched him. He did not question the truth that came to him then. Panic took hold of his heart at the thought he might have to live without her. Whether he trusted her or no, one thing was clear: he loved her.

In his frustration, he expelled his next thought. "The damn woman will nay stay put."

"Aye, but mayhap this time you are glad she did not." Geoff's eyes twinkled with mirth.

Shaking his head, Renaud stalked toward the trees as his other knights joined Geoff to take stock of their wounds and count the dead. The battle was over.

At the base of the tree, Renaud shouted into the branches above him, "Come down *wife!*"

The Welsh bard, Rhodri dropped to the ground. Renaud threw the Welshman a scowl for his part in Serena's perfidy. Looking sheepish, the bard bowed his head and slinked off toward the battlefield, now a sea of bodies splayed across the ground. Some of his men slogged through the blood of the slain to reach those who would live. Others rounded up the Northumbrian prisoners.

He turned his attention back to the thick branches above him, watching as his wife slowly climbed down. He was unsurprised to see her wearing a lad's clothing in the colors of the forest. When she arrived at the lowest branch where he could reach her, he looked into her violet eyes, set his hands on her waist and snatched her off the limb. He had intended to scold her, but without thinking, he wrapped his arms around her and gave her a fierce hug and a deep, searing kiss.

Thank God you are safe.

CHAPTER 22

Serena met her husband's harsh glare as he loosened his embrace. The blood that splattered his hauberk was now smeared across her clothes. His eyes were like shards of steel and his anger a tangible thing. But still she had to know. "You are well, my lord?"

Ignoring her question, he demanded instead, "What were you thinking coming to York, a place you knew would see battle? A place you might have been *killed*?"

She spoke the truth for she had no other reason to give him. "I thought only of you and Steinar. I would see neither of you harmed."

"I am a man of war, Serena, and Steinar chose to be here with the rebels, knowing what he would face. But you, a woman, might have been wounded, raped or worse!" His chestnut brows drew together in a frown so severe she shrank back. He grabbed her upper arms and shook her. "Did you not consider my wish that you remain at Talisand where you would be safe?"

She could see fear in his eyes and knew it was for her. At that moment, she was glad she'd not told him of the child she carried. His anger would then know no bounds. "I'm not sorry I disobeyed you, my lord. I could not stand idly by while you and my brother were in danger. I had to be here."

"Did you not trust me?" he pleaded. "Did you not believe I could defeat the mercenary?"

"I was worried." Was it the face of a caring husband she looked into?

"Aye, well, if 'twas worry for your brother, the English rebel I encountered earlier with your same eyes and hair was still standing when I left him. But William is not yet through with York, Serena. Of that, I am certain. He has ordered the torching of the city, and he intends to build a castle here where he will garrison hundreds of his knights."

"Your Norman castles are becoming as numerous as the stars," she said, unable to resist the sarcasm. "And just as cold." She did not want to fight him. She wanted him to take her in his arms again and hold her again. For all her bravado, the sight of the battle had taken its toll. Feeling wobbly, she needed his strength. And she wanted his love.

"You fight what you cannot change, Serena."

"I know you are right," she said casting her gaze to the field of bodies lying in the sun, "but I cannot do otherwise." She looked up to study his face and saw the anger that still lingered. "I loathe the burning, Renaud. Must it always be? The English cause is lost. You have won. Why destroy all that remains of this city? On our way here, Rhodri and I saw many cottars' homes laid waste. It was horrible."

"The fires were set on William's order."

"Must he be so cruel?"

"William intends to put his stamp on York so the Northumbrians will not soon forget. Come," he took her arm, "I will see you back to my tent where Jamie waits."

"Nay" she wrenched her arm free. "I must find Steinar first. I must see him!"

From the midst of the body-strewn battlefield, she heard Rhodri's shout, "Serena, over here!"

Without thinking and fearing the worst, Serena ran toward the sound of the bard's voice.

Renaud shouted, "Serena wait!"

She did not turn back, but as she ran, she heard his heavy steps following.

They reached Rhodri together. The Welshman was kneeling beside the still form of a wounded Northumbrian. She knew even before she looked upon his face that it was her brother. His helm had been removed and the ends of his long blond hair were matted with blood, as was his tunic.

"Steinar!" Falling to her knees, Serena took his limp hand between hers. His skin was cold. His eyes fluttered open, the same blue violet eyes that were her own.

"Ser...Serena," he breathed haltingly. "How—"

She smoothed the blood-spattered hair from his face. "Steinar, do not talk. I am here and I will get help."

"What wounds has he?" Renaud asked Rhodri from where he stood above her.

"His right leg, my lord. A nasty gash, and the bone is badly broken. We must get him to a healer, and soon. He has already lost much blood."

Serena's eyes shifted to her brother's bloody leg. "I'll need help with the bone," she explained, "but for the rest, I'll tend him myself."

"Serena, there are others—" Renaud urged.

"Nay! I'll not leave Steinar in the hands of others, but I would be grateful if you could ask your Norman healer to set the leg. We must move him where we can clean the wound."

"I will carry him," said Renaud. His words brought her comfort.

"Let me first try and staunch the bleeding," she said. "Fetch my satchel, Rhodri, and two sticks."

Rhodri returned with two sticks and her satchel containing the herbs and bandages she had brought with her. She did what she could with Rhodri's help, and then stood wiping her hands on her tunic.

"I can do no more here."

Renaud lifted Steinar and began to stride away. She and Rhodri trailed behind the tall knight whose strength never wavered as he plodded through the muck of the field to where the Norman tents were clustered some distance away.

"Serena!" Jamie exclaimed as she followed his master into the tent. She gave the boy a quick hug. Jamie's face looked stricken when he recognized the one Renaud carried. "Is Steinar—?"

"I do not know, Jamie," she said, setting to work.

"Mathieu," the Red Wolf addressed his squire, "fetch some water from the stream and see that one of the king's healers is summoned. 'Tis my lady's brother who lies wounded."

"Yea, my lord," said the squire, darting a glance at the wounded English warrior laying on the pallet before hurrying off to do his lord's bidding.

Serena lifted Steinar's tunic off his leg and, as carefully as she could, peeled down his hose. With a sharp knife, she cut the braies from his thigh. Tears rolled down her cheeks and blurred her vision as she took in the terrible wound he had suffered. A sword had cut him to the bone below the knee and the blow had left the bone sticking out of the wound. The damage was such she could not be certain it would heal, or that he would even survive.

Rhodri and Jamie dropped to her side offering their help.

As she worked on Steinar, Renaud's knights returned, one by one, to report to their lord. Sir Alain was wounded with a slash to his face. There was so much blood on the men it was difficult to tell whose blood it was.

Her husband expressed his thanks to God his knights were still on their feet, though he had lost a few men-at-arms.

Sir Geoffroi entered the overcrowded space. She barely noticed him as she gave her attention to Steinar. But she heard the knight say, "I have news, Ren."

Renaud and Sir Geoffroi stepped out of the tent to confer in hushed tones.

Serena was weary when her husband returned to the tent, vaguely aware that he donned a clean tunic as she finished her work.

Coming to where she knelt, Renaud looked down. "I go to see William, but I will not be long. The healer should be here shortly. When I return, we have much to discuss, my lady."

Seeing his stern countenance, Serena could only imagine what he wanted to say.

Chapter 23

Renaud headed toward William's tent, Geoff silently walking beside him. He was relieved the battle was over and Serena was safe. There was a chance her brother might live, and because he knew what Steinar meant to her, he prayed it would be so. He could not bear to look into those tear-filled violet eyes if her brother were to die from wounds inflicted by a Norman sword.

"What of Sir Maurin's condition?" he inquired of Geoff, not sure he wanted to hear the answer. The news Geoff had brought him earlier—that his knight lay gravely wounded—had chilled him to the bone.

"He took a blade in his side near the end of the battle. My squire tells me Sir Maurin still bleeds."

"Where is he now?"

"In his tent. One of the healers is seeing to him."

"Will he live?" Next to Geoff, Maurin de Caen was his most senior knight, with him since Normandy. While he would not want to lose any of his men, this knight was also a friend.

"It is not known."

"As soon as I've seen William, I will go to him."

Renaud acknowledged the guard posted in front of the tent flying the royal banner, then entered. William's tent was larger than the others and set apart. Inside, the king sat upon a chair, his retinue standing around him discussing the day's events while they studied a map of the city of York spread on top of a small table.

The king raised his eyes in recognition.

Renaud bowed. "Sire."

"You are late, sir wolf, leaving us to wonder if you lay among the dead." The king scrutinized Renaud, seemingly satisfied he had all his parts. "We are glad you and Sir Geoffroi stand whole before us. Come, see our map and hear our good news."

Renaud and Geoff joined the knights gathered around the table.

The king slapped his leg. "We have won! The thegns of York have surrendered in terror of our army and presented us with keys to the city and hostages. Better still, Archil, the leading thegn, has offered us his son as hostage." The king straightened his shoulders. "What think you of that?"

"A victory, My King," said Renaud. He exchanged a glance with Geoff. Renaud's only emotion was relief the rebellion in Northumbria was over.

"We have told the thegns if they swear fealty to us, they will retain their holdings," said William "but we are loathe to keep that promise." The king shrugged as if dismissing the thought of something so mundane as breaking his word. "Just now, we are choosing a site for our castle."

Acknowledging the knights with a nod of his head, Renaud leaned over the map.

"We would have your opinion, Lord Talisand," said William.

Renaud studied the drawing. York was an important city, the second in all of England after London, prosperous since Roman times. He looked at the two rivers running through it. The "V" shaped area formed by the confluence of the larger River Ouse and the smaller River Foss drew his attention. "If you put it here," he said, pointing to the area, you will have all the water you need for a large moat as well as a good defensive position."

"A worthy idea," said William. "One that occurred to us only moments ago."

Renaud smiled at his king. He had served William long enough to know he never asked a question to which he did not already have an answer. "I am not surprised your judgment precedes mine, Sire." The returning smile on his king's face told him William was content, both with the outcome at York and his plans to leave his imprint on the city.

"My Lord," said Richard FitzRichard, standing to the king's right, "the creation of such a moat will require us to flood the whole of the Coppergate area. Over a hundred acres would be lost."

"A necessary loss, for it will accomplish our purpose," said William. "See to it, Fitz. We will leave you in charge with five hundred of our knights as a garrison. We name Malet here," he gestured to the stout man standing on his other side, "Sheriff of Yorkshire to see to the peace."

Renaud knew William Malet because both had been with William at Hastings. FitzRichard was another the king trusted. The decision to leave them in charge of a place as significant as York did not surprise him.

"Any news of the leaders?" Renaud asked Malet.

"Edgar, the Saxon who would be king, and Cospatric have escaped to Scotland, my lord. Morcar and Edwin, with their usual distaste for battle, have sought the king's pardon."

Renaud turned his eyes on his king.

"And we have granted the brother earls their request," said William, "though they will be closely watched since they are currently in our disfavor. Any sign of disloyalty and, by the splendor of God, we will have our revenge!"

Renaud said nothing, only nodded. What could he say? William would suffer no rebellion without assuring it ended in a crushing defeat. As Serena had reminded him, William had allowed his men to harry wherever they would on their way to York and Renaud deeply regretted it.

A strange thing had happened once he claimed Talisand as his own. No longer was he merely a knight following the orders of his sire. This was now *his* country and the north was *his* home. He would not see it ravaged if he could help it, not even to please his king.

As for Morcar, Renaud would have liked to deal with the earl himself for his bold attempt to claim Serena, but that would have to await another day.

He knew the English defeat at York would leave a bitter taste in the mouths of the Northumbrians. As at Exeter, there had been English among the soldiers in William's army, but that would matter little to the Northumbrians who thought of Wessex as another land.

Renaud had a sense of foreboding as he thought of the brief battle, followed by the Northumbrians' quick capitulation. Many of them lived to fight another day, and Edgar was safely ensconced in Scotland should they be of a mind to engage in further rebellion on his behalf. But he did not remind his sovereign of those facts. William would not have appreciated them.

Once the castle's location had been agreed upon, and Renaud had spoken with a few of his fellow knights, the king gave him leave to depart.

His last words to Renaud made him sigh. "We have a mind to visit you and your lovely English bride before we return to London."

"As you wish, Sire. We would welcome you at Talisand." He bowed and with Geoff at his side, departed, hastening to Sir Maurin's tent. He was worried about Serena but first he had to see to the welfare of his knight.

The large man lay on a table in the middle of his tent, pale and unconscious. His black hair was still coated with blood from the battle and his mail and tunic had been stripped from him. A blanket, thrown over his body, was pulled up to his chest.

Renaud raised a brow in question to the aged healer who looked up from where he stood washing blood from his hands.

"If the fever does not claim him, my lord," the old man advised, "he will recover. The wound is not deep but it is long and required many stitches. Now he needs rest. He should not try to walk for a sennight or more. Can you take him home on a litter?"

"We've done it before," Geoff said to the healer. And then to Renaud, "With your permission, I'll have the squires prepare one."

"Yea, see it is done. And one for Steinar, should he live."

"Aye," Geoff said, and departed on his errand, leaving Renaud to stand vigil over his knight, whose deathlike visage caused him to pray for Sir Maurin's life.

"He sleeps?" Renaud asked the healer who was drying his hands on a cloth.

"Aye, I've given him a potion of hemlock, wormwood and henbane mixed with ale. He will sleep like the dead until tomorrow. It will help him endure the pain."

Renaud was familiar with the combination of herbs used to induce sleep in those who would suffer much pain. *Mayhap 'twas the same potion given to Serena by Morcar.*

"I may need more of your potion for our travel tomorrow," he told the healer. "He will have a litter but he will certainly be jostled about."

"Here is the rest of what I made," the man said handing him a leather flask of liquid. "Take it; I have more. But try and feed him, broth at least, before you give him another drink of it."

Renaud accepted the flask and handed it to Sir Maurin's squire who stood at the end of the table. "Guard this and your master well. I will send someone to relieve you in two hours."

Anxious to return to his bride, Renaud stepped into the sun and rapidly covered the ground to the trees that sheltered his own tent.

* * *

Serena knelt at Steinar's side, tears streaking down her cheeks. She could not stop them. He slept now, but for a time he had suffered so much his shouts of agony had cut through her heart.

She had cleaned his leg as best she could while he grimaced and bit on a strip of leather, as sweat rolled off his face. Before the Norman healer had begun his work, he gave Steinar a potion. But it did not take effect soon enough. He set the bone and stitched the wound, all the while

Steinar moaned, valiantly bearing the pain. The leg now lay between wooden boards secured tightly with wrappings of cloth.

Steinar had finally succumbed to the effects of the herb potion, allowing Serena to relax a bit. The pain he bravely endured was more than she could bear.

As he slept, she looked down at his face and thoughts of the young boy, her valiant protector, filled her mind. He had oft played with her at the river's edge, teasing her with his friends. Yet if any boy harassed her overmuch, Steinar would rush to her defense. Steinar had always been her staunch defender.

I cannot imagine life without you. You are the only one who shares with me memories of being a child. You are all that is left of my family. The brother of my soul. Unable to quell her sobs, Serena pleaded with God. *I beg of you, spare his life.*

Rhodri and Jamie shared the small space in Renaud's tent, standing vigil over the man they both loved. Through her tears, she glanced up to see them. Jamie's face still reflected despair. Rhodri was more stoical, his emotions hidden beneath his calm exterior.

Once the healer left, she sat back, wiping her eyes. "There is no more to be done," she told them. Weariness overcame her. She wiped her hair from her forehead with the back of her hand. "He is in God's hands now."

Jamie nodded, hope evident in his blue eyes. Rhodri said nothing.

A shadow fell across the interior of the tent as the light from the open flap at its entrance was blocked. She turned to see her husband stepping across the threshold.

"How does he fare?" asked Renaud, coming to hover over her.

"The wound has been tended and the bone set. He sleeps now but he was in much pain for a while."

"He'll have a litter so he can travel with us on the morrow," he assured her. Then kneeling by her side, he took her face in his hands. His gray eyes were filled with emotion and with something she'd not seen before. "I will do all I can to see that your brother is well again, Serena."

"Thank you," she said. Fresh tears rolled down her cheeks.

With his thumbs he wiped away her tears and kissed her forehead.

She drew upon his strength and allowed him to hold her. Then she sat back and looked at him. "When Sir Geoffroi came to get Mathieu to help build the litter, he told us of Sir Maurin. How is he? Cassie will be distraught to learn he was hurt."

"He's been seen by a healer and the bleeding has been staunched. Now he sleeps. The healer gave him a potion, probably the same one given your brother."

"Yea, the healer left some for Steinar," she said. "It must be their remedy for all those gravely wounded."

"So it would seem." Turning to Rhodri and Jamie, he said, "Leave us."

Without a word they departed.

Alone with only the sleeping Steinar between them, Renaud stood and helped her to rise. She looked long on his face. Though the blood of battle was gone, he appeared tired, the few lines in his face now etched deeper. Yet his strength had not failed her.

His gray eyes studied her, concern showing in their depths. "I would you had not come, Serena. Battle is no place for a woman, much less my wife."

She was unsurprised by his declaration. "I could not do otherwise, you know that."

"Aye, so I have realized."

"What news from your king?" she asked. "Has William had his fill of vengeance on the Northumbrians?"

He let out a breath. "Fortunately, the short battle and the torching of a part of the town have resulted in a surrender of the city's keys. Now William turns his attention to a new castle."

"Aye, that would be his next move," she said averting her gaze.

"Serena," he whispered as he pulled her into his arms and looked into her eyes. "I told you on the day the priest blessed our marriage that I wanted only love between us. Would it be so hard to forget the rancor you have for William and look to the future? Should Steinar recover, I will provide a home for him. Your brother will always be welcome at Talisand."

She let out a deep sigh, knowing his words were wise. "Aye, I know I must. But it is hard, my husband." Then looking into his eyes, she said, "For the sake of our son, I will try to forget."

"Our son? You speak of a son as if he had already been born."

She let him see the smile that came to her lips as she thought of the babe growing within her. "'Twill nay be long, my lord, for I am with child."

Elation, then anger flitted across her husband's face as if the two emotions warred within him. "You came to York knowing you carried my child?"

So it was to be anger. "Aye. I could do no less knowing the two men I love most in the world would be here."

He stared at her for a moment. She hoped he could see the love in her eyes.

Recognition dawned. "You love me?"

"Yea, I do." She smiled, thinking of the ring on her finger, remembering the words inscribed inside. "I suppose I should have mentioned it afore this."

"You might have." He drew her more tightly to his powerful chest and she crossed her hands at his nape. He gently pressed a kiss to her lips. "I love you, Serena."

A feeling of great happiness welled up inside her. She had never thought to hear those words from the Norman who wed her out of duty to his king. But she had hoped.

He drew back and put his hand on her still flat belly, looking amazed. "A son for Talisand," he said smiling. He kissed her again. "My wayward English wife," he said as his lips lifted from hers. "I should be scolding you, but I would rather carry you to yon meadow and make love to you. But the babe...."

She smiled, feeling his rising passion pressing into her belly. "I am certain the babe is not so large we must worry about your lovemaking. And, I think we can find a better place than a meadow, my lord. I trust not your knights to leave us be."

CHAPTER 24

Several days later, Renaud led his entourage through the gates of Talisand, as he shouted orders for help with the litters. Their slower pace had lengthened the trip, but it was necessary for the sake of the wounded and his determination to assure his unborn child was not jostled overmuch.

From where he dismounted, Renaud saw Sir Geoffroi near the back of the column helping Serena down from her white palfrey. She had insisted on riding next to her brother's litter, though Steinar slept most of the time, as did Sir Maurin.

Waiting in front of the manor with anxious faces were Maggie, her daughter Cassie, the dark-haired Aethel and Sir Niel. Renaud handed Belasco's reins to Eric, then turned to the small group.

"We have wounded, but no deaths," he said, answering their unspoken question. "Sir Maurin and Serena's brother, Steinar, are carried upon litters." Gasps sounded from Cassie and her mother as they covered their mouths.

"Sir Alain?" Aethel asked her brows drawn together.

"The bear has a new scar not unlike Sir Niel's," he said glancing at the young knight, "but otherwise he is well. Look for him near the rear of the column; he guards Sir Maurin."

The dark-haired Aethel and the redheaded Cassie took off running.

"How bad is Steinar, my lord?" asked Maggie. "I raised him as if he were me own son."

"He took a sword in the leg. The wound is serious. It will be some time before we know whether he or Sir Maurin will heal. At least they are home now."

"Aye, my lord. They be home." He knew the woman's words were spoken in recognition that Talisand was home to both Norman and English and he was grateful. Briefly, he watched as she walked in the direction that her daughter had run, leaving him alone with Sir Niel.

"All is well at Talisand?" he asked the young knight.

"Aye, my lord. Hunstan saw to the manor and lands and Theodric and I managed the remaining work at the castle and the men-at-arms you left as guard. We've food ready should you want a meal and beds for the wounded."

Renaud shed his gloves and waited for Serena who was coming toward him with two men carrying Steinar's litter. Behind them Sir Alain and Leppe carried Sir Maurin's stretcher. Cassie held the sleeping knight's hand and Aethel followed her.

Much had changed since he'd come to Talisand. In their grief for the wounded, they were forging a new people, neither Norman nor English, but with the strength of both.

* * *

"The king comes!" shouted the watchman from the top of the keep, telling Serena that William had returned to Talisand. Renaud had given her warning, but still her nerves were on end and her stomach was unsettled as her mind rebelled. The king would once again sleep under her roof. They had only been back for a sennight and now they must again entertain him! For Renaud's sake, she would try to be gracious.

From the top of the motte, she watched the line of Norman knights and retainers in their bright colored livery and waving banners flow through the gates to fill the bailey.

"It would be best if we greeted him below, Serena," said Renaud as he took her elbow. They descended the steps together and crossed the bridge.

"I like it not, husband. Steinar is only now able to smile. Can you imagine what he will say when I tell him the Norman who calls himself king is sheltered in his home?"

"'Tis *our* home, Serena. And I worry more about what William would say were he to know I harbor one of the York rebels."

"Then do not tell him. Surely he will not tarry long."

By the time the king approached the bridge leading over the moat, Serena and Renaud were waiting for him.

"Sire," Renaud bowed before the king, "welcome back to Talisand."

William, wearing mail and a scarlet cloak fastened with a gold brooch, dismounted with ease, his blue eyes shining. Was it with pride at his recent victory over her countrymen?

She had to admit he was a vigorous man. He had the look about him of one whose orders were never questioned, a man who did not just come to rule England, as others had, but to change it forever.

"We have wine to refresh you, Sire," Renaud said, "and tonight the meal you will be served in the castle's hall will provide the best of Talisand's food."

The king's gaze bore into her eyes. She raised her chin, determined not to cower before the Bastard who had claimed England.

"We look forward to enjoying your hospitality, my lord," said the king. "And that of your lady." He looked at her. "We still remember your lovely voice, my lady, on the occasion of our last visit."

Serena dipped a modest curtsey to the king but resented that she had been required to sing for him. Would she again?

* * *

Renaud knew none of his English villeins were happy about William's return, and certainly not his English wife. But he could not very well deny his sire the tribute that must be paid to one's king.

Glancing to his right where Serena sat with him at the high table, he was pleased she had accepted her role as chatelaine, assuring the dinner set before the king was a rich bounty of Maggie's best dishes. He would have to bestow a special gift on the cook for all her labors.

Of the king's trusted men, Turstin FitzRolf, who had fought with them at Hastings, had joined the king on the dais. Renaud sat on the king's right with Serena and Maugris. Sir Geoffroi and Eawyn sat on the other side of FitzRolf. Since Renaud knew William enjoyed Maugris' musings, he made certain the wise one was present. Sir Maurin, who might otherwise have been included, was still abed recovering.

The meal began with a broth of carrot and ginger accompanied by rich brown bread, butter and honey. Wooden platters laden with roast lamb spiced with cumin and mint, and fish baked with coriander and bay leaf, soon followed. The spices, Serena had told him, were ones her father brought to the manor. Venison was served, as well, bathed in a dark sauce that rendered the deer meat succulent. Peas boiled in water and wine, sweet to the taste, joined the other dishes. Renaud knew William was pleased for he loved to eat as much as Sir Geoffroi.

"'Tis a welcome feast you have set before us," said the king. "We thank you, Lord Talisand, for our travels here did not see such grand fare."

"We could do no less for you, Sire."

As the meal wore on, Renaud noticed the king studying Serena.

Leaning across Renaud, he asked her, "Have you heard, my lady, of our great victory in York?"

"Aye, I have heard." Serena said in a flat voice.

The king obviously had something in mind as he rubbed the fingers of one hand over his chin and his blue eyes narrowed on Serena. His brown hair, golden in places from the sun, showed beneath his crown making him look regal, every bit the king he had become.

William's eyes shifted to Renaud. "We have heard tale of a woman felling one of our Norman knights at York with an arrow. What say you to that strange story, lord wolf?"

Renaud hesitated in answering the king's question. Did William know Serena had been at the battle?

From beside him, Serena spoke. "If the king would know the truth of it, I slayed Sir Hugue. He was a man without honor. Men like him are a blight on our lives."

"My lady speaks the truth," Renaud interjected. "The mercenary was dismissed from my service but apparently harbored a grudge. He attacked me on the battlefield, and when I stumbled over a body, my wife, hidden in the trees, came to my rescue."

"*You*, my lady?" said the king, incredulous. "It was *your* arrow my knights speak of?"

"Aye, one of them. I shot him in the neck, and would do it again. He did much to harm the women of Talisand."

"Sire," Renaud interjected, "you should know that Sir Hugue fought with Morcar, not your army."

The king looked puzzled. "How did a Norman come to fight with the Mercian earl?"

"I know not. But I suspect it was for revenge."

"Mayhap we are glad the mercenary is dead," declared the king, "especially since your lady spared our wolf the rogue's blade. Still, we find your wife unusually blood thirsty for a woman." The king's eyes bored into Serena.

Renaud was worried when she sat up and returned the king's stare. "It was not the only arrow I shot that day, My Lord," said Serena proudly. "I slayed other Normans at York to save my brother." Renaud was shocked Serena would reveal such information to the king after she had cautioned him not to reveal Steinar's identity. But then he saw the glimmer in Serena's eyes and noted the honey that coated her words. She was enjoying her recitation of the Normans she had killed at York.

"You would be proud to slay my knights, my lady?" William asked indignantly.

"Aye, My Lord, to save my brother, I would slay your whole army!"

"We demand to know what happened to this brother who fought against us!" insisted the king.

"He lives but lies gravely wounded in a chamber above us," she said matter-of-factly as a shadow of pain crossed her beautiful face.

Renaud opened his mouth to defend her lest his king seek retribution for all she had done, but William's outstretched hand stilled his voice.

The king's gaze narrowed on Serena. "You harbor a rebel in this very *demesne*—the castle we gave to *our* knight?"

Serena stood, raising her chin. "This is my brother's home as well as mine, My Lord. He is welcome here."

Renaud could see William's temper had been roused and dreaded what was coming.

The king stood and pounded the table. "We demand you turn over this enemy of ours!"

"I will not!" Serena shouted back. "Nor do I regret the Norman lives I have taken to protect those I love."

Renaud had heard enough. Rising from the table, he faced his sovereign. "Sire, my wife has served you well for I would not be standing here had she not felled Sir Hugue. Could I do otherwise than to give her and her brother my protection?"

The king huffed and sat down, taking a long draw from his goblet. Then he let out a loud, belly laugh. "Ha! The Norman wolf defends his English she wolf! You see what we have accomplished, FitzRolf?" he remarked to the silent Norman at his side, "our wolf's mate slays his enemies and those of her brother!"

FitzRolf smiled, nodding.

Addressing Renaud, the king said, "Your fellow knights will be teasing you in London, lord wolf. First the warrior priest, now the knight whose lady's arrows slay his enemies. You have given them much fodder for talk." The king laughed heartily. "'Tis just what this England needs, we think—a bonding of our knights with the fair maids of the land. Aye, and we would have more of it!"

"A good result from your wise command, My Lord," said Maugris.

The king smiled at the old man. "We are pleased you agree." Then to Serena, "Be seated fair lady. We are not currently displeased with you, because you defended your Norman husband. Instead, we have decided you may keep your rebel brother. But your husband must assure us this brother of yours will not fight against us in future, and that *you* will henceforth take up no arms against our army."

Renaud bowed his head to William, relieved his sire's anger had been turned. Taking Serena's hand, he pulled her into her seat. "You have my assurance, Sire, and my gratitude."

"And the lady's?" asked William looking at Serena.

"Aye," said Serena and she turned to Renaud and bestowed upon him a glorious smile. "To please my husband who has honored me, I agree to all your demands."

Renaud's heart soared.

William winked at Maugris. The wise one smiled back his approval. "She will bear strong sons to serve you, O King."

"We trust you see the future correctly, Maugris," said the king, "but as a token of the lady's gratitude for our mercy, we would have her sing!"

* * *

Serena stood in the bailey as the king mounted his Spanish stallion and waved good-bye to her and Renaud. She was glad to see him leave.

"He will not soon visit us again, I think," said her husband, putting his arm around her shoulder and drawing her close. "That should please you, wife."

Serena wrapped her arms around his waist and smiled into his gray eyes as his chestnut hair blew about his face in the rising wind. Remembering the way he had defended her to his king the night before, she said, "*You* please me, my lord."

He bent to kiss her and she breathed in his earthy, masculine scent. "And you please me, Serena. *Mon Dieu*, how I love you!"

EPILOGUE

Christmastide 1068

Serena stood at the top of the motte, surveying the bailey that had seen so much rain in the weeks leading up to Christmastide. At least it had not snowed last night, though frost had covered the ground that morning. The pale sun that had risen this day did not bring much warmth.

She drew her woolen cloak tightly around her against the chill and rubbed her growing belly feeling the child move again. Her thoughts drifted idly toward spring when the flowers would return.

It would be her time to give birth.

In the bailey below, the harsh sound of wood clashing against wood disturbed the winter quiet as Mathieu and Jamie sparred with practice swords. A short distance away Steinar sat on a cask watching the lesson. His leg had healed but he limped and often used a walking stick, especially when treading rough ground. Her brow wrinkled in worry for him. He was bitter and discouraged. Who could blame him?

Rhodri sauntered through the gate with his bow and arrows slung over his shoulder and joined Steinar to watch the swordplay. "When you finish training him to the blade, Mathieu," he yelled over the sounds of mock battle, "I will train him to the bow."

Jamie's face lit up as he blocked a blow from Mathieu's wooden sword. "Aye, the bow next!"

Serena heard her husband approach behind her. Wrapping his arms around her middle between her breasts and swollen belly, he said, "In a year's time, Mathieu will be ready to be a knight and Jamie can become my squire."

"He would like that," she said, laying her hands over his. The feeling of warmth between them had not dimmed in the months since York. Their love had only grown stronger. Renaud had been most gracious to Steinar and the two men had found a semblance of rapport between them, avoiding the difficult subjects that would have brought on an argument. For that Serena was grateful.

Seeing Cassie stride through the yard to the stable where Sir Maurin had gone a short while ago, Serena smiled at the memory of the weddings that had taken place. As she now reflected upon them, she should not have been surprised. Maugris had grinned in reply to her wondering at so many, telling her he had seen them in his visions.

First there was Sir Alain and Aethel, to the surprise of many. In the weeks following York, the herb woman had tended the knight's wounded face, and they had become inseparable. When they wed, Serena allowed them to make their home in the manor Renaud had given her. After weeks abed, Sir Maurin had recovered, and Cassie and he had claimed the priest's blessing. They now lived in the main manor. Both women had recently declared they were carrying their husbands' babes. With the coming of summer, Talisand would be full of new life. Mayhap in time, even Sir Geoffroi and Eawyn would wed.

It was her brother who gave her sleepless nights.

"I worry about Steinar," she said aloud. "Now that he is healed in body, he still appears troubled in soul. He grows restless. I know he wonders what future he has in England. I fear he will seek Edgar again in Scotland."

"I see the bard sits by his side," said Renaud. "Why does the Welshman linger?"

"He stays, I think, for my brother. He worries, as do I. We both fear Steinar will leave. Rhodri but waits to see what direction he will take so that he may follow. The two are like brothers."

Drawing her closer into his chest, he whispered in her ear. "Steinar must make his own life, Serena."

She let out a sigh. "I know you are right and that he will go. But I will miss him."

"You will be busy with our child. By the bye, what shall we name him? Shall it be an English name or Norman?" Renaud teased.

"I have been considering our choices, husband. What say you if we name the babe after our fathers?"

"I like it, and it would please my father."

"I just realized I do not know your father's name. What is it?"

"Alexander."

"So our son would be Alexander Sigmund of Talisand." Serena thought on the name. "Aye, 'tis a good choice. But what if the child is a girl?"

He tightened his embrace as he spoke. "Maugris is certain the babe will be a son, the first of several he tells me. But if the wise one is wrong, let us name the girl child after a saint and pray she is not like her mother."

Serena laughed and batted his hand. "You jest!"

"Mayhap I do," he chuckled. "In truth, my lady wife, I would love a violet-eyed girl child to hold on my knee. For I love her mother more than life." He nuzzled her neck.

Serena twisted her wedding band, remembering again the words inscribed inside and turned in his arms to look into his face. The face of the knight she loved. "Your lands do not hold your heart, my lord? The prize your Norman king gave you?"

"Nay, my lady. The lands would be only a place to dwell were you not here to share them with me. Maugris was right when he said it was here I would find my prize. *You* are that prize, Serena, not the lands. You are my peace, my love."

Sliding her hands to his nape, Serena pulled him toward her and kissed the Norman she loved, content to be the Red Wolf's prize.

AUTHOR'S NOTE

I hope you enjoyed my foray into the medieval world of 11th century England. (If you did, please write a review!) I set my story in the north west of England, in the area known today as Lancashire where the River Lune winds its way through the countryside. It was a place of quiet in the storm that we refer to today as the Conquest.

In 1066, William did not reach as far north as Northumbria, but eventually the north drew his attention because the English there refused to accept his claim to the throne and because York was too important to ignore.

I wanted to explore how a spirited daughter of an English thegn would feel about being one of the conquered, given against her will to a Norman knight who had fought the English at Hastings and might have slain her father. How would she handle her hatred for a man to whom she was also attracted? When I thought of Serena I thought of a courageous young woman who tried to hold back a tidal wave, but found herself swept away by the passion for a bold Norman knight whose sons would one day be a part of the country he now claimed as his.

Why a map? You may ask. When one of my writing friends, who had read the early manuscript, asked me to show her where Talisand was on a map of England (not realizing it was fictional), I knew a map was in order. So, I included one that shows the locations mentioned in the story. I do love maps. Now you know just where to find the lands of Lady Serena that William the Conqueror gave to the Red Wolf.

A plaque in the church at Dives-sur-Mer in Normandy lists the knights who accompanied William, Duke of Normandy in September of 1066 when he set sail for England. Among the knights whose names are recorded there are Renaud de Pierrepont and Geoffroi de Tournai, Normans who held land in England in 1086 when the *Doomsday Book* was written. Whether those two real life Normans bore any resemblance to the knights in my story is the subject of conjecture. I like to think they might have. We do know that many younger sons of noble Norman families became knights and risked all to fight with William and, as a result, gained lands in England. We also know that many English women fled from their path, some taking the veil. My fictional heroine, Serena of Talisand, would likewise flee, but not to take the veil.

You might ask what language they spoke in England, particularly in the north. While the Saxons in the south would have spoken a form of English, and William did make an attempt to learn it, in the north, the area known as the Danelaw, the language would have been Danish and the dialect would be Scandinavian. The commoners probably did not speak English. However, for the sake of my story, I kept to English, though it is possible Renaud could have spoken Danish as William did.

The manor houses of the thegns, such as the one built by Sigmund, Serena's father, varied in size depending on the wealth of the thegn. Most were only one story and, if they had a second story, stairs to the second floor might have been on the outside or more rudimentary than you might picture from my novel. It is also unlikely the bedchambers, save for the thegn's, were enclosed. (They might have had alcoves off the main hall used as sleeping chambers.) But there would have been no upstairs corridor. Those came later. As I needed bedchambers for some of my scenes, they are included. I hope you allow me the deviation from the English manor houses of that time. Perhaps some smart thegn even thought of inside stairs and bedchambers. We will never know.

Having learned their lessons from the Viking raids where wooden churches were burned, the English did build stone churches before the Conquest, and some survive to this day. I have based the church Serena's father built at Talisand on the ones I have researched, so I believe it is true to the period. They did not have pews as the faithful stood, but the English painted their churches with vivid pictures and stories from the Bible as in my story. You can see one such church on my Pinterest board for The Red Wolf's Prize.

You might wonder what kind of a bow the Welshman Rhodri brought to Talisand. There is evidence that the Welsh made use of the longbow against the English prior to William's invasion in 1066. There is also evidence to suggest the longbow was introduced into England during the Danish invasions prior to the Conquest. However, the Bayeux Tapestry shows only one Saxon bowman and he has a short bow. (The rest of King Harold's forces used the shield and battle-axe.) The Norman archers, who, according to tradition, won William's victory for him, also used the short wooden bow. In my story, Rhodri made shorter bows for the women as the longbows, if he used them, would require too much arm strength for a woman to use.

Why, you might ask, didn't Renaud and Geoffroi ride their destriers around the countryside? The simple reason is that destriers, like coursers, were warhorses trained for the battlefield and not easily handled. Destriers (a type of horse, not a breed) were reserved for battle. The knights would have other horses, such as palfreys and rounceys, which they rode off the battlefield. In Renaud's case, he rides a Spanish stallion gifted to him by Duke William. William shipped hundreds of horses across the English Channel when he invaded England in 1066, and he also had a Spanish stallion that was given to him. While the Saxons rode horses to war, they fought on foot, which proved to be a mistake.

Did you wonder about the timber castle Renaud built? For the most part, the early castles were not the stone edifices we think of today, the monuments that remain. The castles the Normans first constructed, the ones built in mere days, weeks or months, were timbered structures erected upon a "motte", or a mound of earth with a flat top, and surrounded by a deep ditch sometimes filled with water (a moat). These would be enclosed with a timbered palisade, wooden poles sharpened to a point at the top. The land around the castle would be the "bailey". We call them "motte and bailey" castles today. By 1100, it is believed 400 such castles had been erected in England. You can see one on my Pinterest storyboard.

Initially, William allowed some Saxons to keep their holdings and made an effort to learn English and work with the nobles, but as I have said, not all in England accepted the Conqueror as their king, particularly in the north. They had more ties to the Vikings than they did to the south of England. They were not Saxons, but Mercians or Northumbrians. In 1068, William changed his strategy and took back all the land in order to give it to his own loyal men. Most of the English noble and military class was slain, exiled or mutilated. William conquered not only by might, dealing brutally with his enemies, but also by ensconcing his Norman barons and knights in various places and ordering them to construct castles, then leaving them to keep the peace.

Just as I have portrayed them, Earls Edwin and Morcar were handsome young men, well loved by the people of Mercia and Northumbria. When King Edward reigned, he used them as a counterpoint to the power of the house of Godwin, and that may be the reason the brothers did not fight with Harold at Hastings. Instead, they aligned themselves with William, perhaps thinking he would leave them to run their own lands, but alas, the Norman king was untrustworthy.

Through William's actions, Englishmen who once had status were reduced to no more than slaves, and their property confiscated. It must have been humiliating for the English to be conscripted by the Normans into building the castles that symbolized their dominance. Most Norman barons were not like the Red Wolf in his mercy shown to the people of Talisand. (If I were writing a 1980s bodice ripper, this would have been a very different tale, but likely more accurate for the time.)

I like to think the English have had their revenge upon the Normans, for today English is the language spoken in England, not French (though many English words have their origin in French), and English as well as Norman blood, flows through the people. That is what I had in mind when I thought of Renaud and Serena, the Lord and Lady of Talisand and their children—the Red Wolf's cubs who, according to Maugris, would advise kings for generations—all because one fair English maiden gave her heart to a bold Norman knight.

If you'd like to see the pictures that go with **The Red Wolf's Prize**, take a look at my Pinterest story board:

http://www.pinterest.com/reganwalker123/the-red-wolfs-prize-by-regan-walker

I expect I'll be writing more stories following the further loves and adventures of those at Talisand: Sir Geoffroi's story (**Rogue Knight**), Steinar's story (**Rebel Warrior**), and perhaps Alexander's (**The Red Wolf's Cub**). I've titled the series **Medieval Warriors**, as each hero is a warrior in his own right. But those books will have to wait until 2015, as my next novel will see me in the 18th century with the prequel for the **Agents of the Crown**.

To Tame the Wind is my next project. It will be a tale of adventure and love set in France and England in 1783—with Captain Simon Powell, an English privateer, and the wild Claire Donet, a French pirate's daughter! If you read **Wind Raven**, you will have a hint as to where the story begins.

For more of my historical novels, and to sign up for my newsletter so you can get word of my new releases, visit my website, www.reganwalkerauthor.com. I'd love to hear from you. You can also write me at Regan.Walker123@gmail.com. I love to hear from readers! Let me know whose story you want to see next!

AUTHOR BIO

As a child Regan Walker loved to write stories, particularly about adventure-loving girls, but by the time she got to college more serious pursuits took priority. One of her professors encouraged her to pursue the profession of law, which she did. Years of serving clients in private practice and several stints in high levels of government gave her a love of international travel and a feel for the demands of the "Crown" on its subjects. Hence her romance novels often involve a demanding sovereign who thinks of his subjects as his private talent pool.

Regan lives in San Diego with her golden retriever, Link, whom she says inspires her every day to relax and smell the roses.

www.ReganWalkerAuthor.com

SYNOPSIS

HE WOULD NOT BE DENIED HIS PRIZE

Sir Renaud de Pierrepont, the Norman knight known as the Red Wolf for the beast he slayed with his bare hands, hoped to gain lands with his sword. A year after the Conquest, King William rewards his favored knight with Talisand, the lands of an English thegn slain at Hastings, and orders him to wed Lady Serena, the heiress that goes with them

SHE WOULD LOVE HIM AGAINST HER WILL

Serena wants nothing to do with the fierce warrior to whom she has been unwillingly given, the knight who may have killed her father. When she learns the Red Wolf is coming to claim her, she dyes her flaxen hair brown and flees, disguised as a servant, determined to one day regain her lands. But her escape goes awry and she is brought back to live among her people, though not unnoticed by the new Norman lord.

Deprived of his promised bride, the Red Wolf turns his attention to the comely servant girl hoping to woo her to his bed. But the wench resists, claiming she hates all Normans.

As the passion between them rises, Serena wonders, can she deny the Norman her body? Or her heart?

OTHER BOOKS BY REGAN WALKER

The Agents of the Crown trilogy:
RACING WITH THE WIND
AGAINST THE WIND
WIND RAVEN
and
THE TWELFTH NIGHT WAGER (Novella)
THE HOLLY & THE THISTLE (Short Story)
THE SHAMROCK & THE ROSE (Short Story)

Coming soon:
TO TAME THE WIND, prequel to the Agents of the Crown

11388678R00136

Printed in Great Britain
by Amazon.co.uk, Ltd.,
Marston Gate.